Snake Eyes

An Amber Farrell Novel
Book 8 of the Bite Back series

by
Mark Henwick

Published by *Marque*

Series schedule, reviews & news on
www.facebook.com/TheBiteBackSeries
www.athanate.com

Bite Back 8: Snake Eyes
ISBN: 978-1-912499-58-8

Published in September 2024 by Marque

Author's Notes

Asian names:
Throughout this series, I use the Western sequence (First, Middle, Last Name) to depict names, so as to match with the majority of characters in the books. Most Asian societies would use Last, First, Middle Name.

Continuity:
The Bite Back series is a continuous story rather than a string of episodes. It's not advised to start anywhere but at the beginning, with Book 1, Sleight of Hand, and read through in order.

There is a prequel novel, Raw Deal, dealing with Amber's brief time in the Denver police, and has background on a character in book 3, Wild Card.

There are three novellas between Bite Back 5 (Angel Stakes) and Bite Back 6 (Inside Straight). Two are set in Michigan and explain the background to House Lloyd (The Biting Cold & Winter's Kiss), and one is set in New York (Change of Regime) and provides the background to Skylur's decision to choose Livia as his new Diakon. It's not essential to read them before Inside Straight, but they do provide much more information on the side stories that feed into Bite Back at this point.

Acknowledgments

My readers, who had to wait far too long for this one.

AMZ251027

DEDICATION

Bite Back 8 took far longer than expected, and longer than I promised several times.

There were many reasons for the delays, but the worst of them happened in 2024.

At the start of January my lovely sister, Gail, was fit, happy and apparently healthy.
At the start of February, she collapsed and was taken into Intensive Care.

She passed away on the 14th.

She was always the first to read my work: before editing, before other beta readers, before I was happy with it, she got my stories, section by section, sometimes chapter by chapter, she even got the text with my 'come back and fix this' comments still included.
She would call me every week to discuss.

This book is dedicated to her.

Gail Vanessa Henwick 16.4.1954 - 14.2.2024

New York
Chapter 1

We etched a pale line, high in the vastness of the night sky. A metal arrow aimed at New York.

Someone awake below might look up, but the jet and its condensation trail would be invisible to them, hidden by the urban light pollution.

People clustered into cities like the one below, seeking money and opportunity, pleasure and power, never worrying that, in exchange, they lost their sense of community, lost their horizons, lost their perspective, lost their night sky with its great, wheeling stars.

Lost their bearings.

Lost their way.

The relentless rush of *now*, of *urgent* masked the understanding of *important*.

It was vital I didn't lose my way in the rush of what was happening to me. I needed to deal with the crap and remain focused on the important.

Tall order.

That city below us was full of distracted people being pushed and pulled and polarized. It was a warning to the paranormal community. Human politics seemed to be becoming the art of making everyone *us* and *them*. Politics seemed to need that tension to work. But to achieve that division, perceptions had to matter more than reality. People were becoming blind to truth.

Maybe that was the only way human politics could be, but paranormal politics had taken that shape too, when it was essential to be united, because humanity was about to find out all about us. Repairing paranormal politics was *important* and *urgent*.

This was the last chance. It had to be fixed. Enemy action, bad luck and worse timing made me the only one available to do it, so the real arrow in the night sky was me, and I was aimed at the rotten heart of the Assembly.

If it goes wrong…

Suddenly I wasn't sitting in the jet. I was soaring, like some abstract angel, looking down on the world. A different world. One torn apart by civil war. One where the countryside had been plunged into darkness and the city was a horrific mosaic of red and black. Red where whole blocks were burning. Black where bombs had left nothing to burn.

Not real!

As if the vision was reacting to my disbelief, I was on the ground, down there, right in the fighting.

They're coming out of the darkness. They know we can see them from the heat of their bodies. They know and they're still coming. They're coming because they know we can see them. Because they know we're different and they've been made to fear that. Because they're humans, and they believe we're not.

No!

The attack is a feint. The sky seems to tear apart with noise. Missile strike! Big one.

I know it's the end. Thermobaric explosion. Double tap. First to spread the vapor. Then to ignite it. This whole block will be torn apart, and every person here will die, human or not.

I finally blinked the mirage away and pulled in a shaky breath.

I was back in House Ellicott's ritzy private jet, in an area laid out in a horseshoe of sinfully comfortable sofas, covered in leather that was soft as a mother's goodnight kiss. I had four people with me in this section. Flint was wide awake, sitting on my left. Xavier was to my right, lying asleep with his head in my lap. Kane and Jo were sleeping a little further away.

Luckily, only Flint would have noticed I'd had another of those damned spirit visions.

He cleared his throat. "*Not* a prophesy, Boss."

"Yeah. Not real. At least not yet," I answered.

"And maybe never."

"Hmm."

Our auras were connected because I was helping keep the spirit shield running while Kane slept. A shield I needed because I couldn't afford to have Tezcatlipoca slithering into my head right now.

But sharing our auras had made the vision a shared experience. He'd seen what I'd seen, just as he and Kane had both seen the first one yesterday.

We'd been at Talleyrand, Marguerite Labastide's plantation house, where I'd been recovering from the strange poison which the Queen of Diamonds had infected me with. The three of us were having a video conference with Gwen and Alice to learn how to create a kind of mobile spirit shield to keep Tezcatlipoca, 'my' Lost God, out of my head.

Gwen - Gwendolyn Enkeliekki, former Hecate of the Northern League of Adepts, now the leader of my Denver coven. *Wendy Witch* as my outlaw shamans, Flint and Kane, referred to her, which had led to them being called the *Lost Boys* in return.

And Alice – Adept Alice Emerson, Skylur's kin, who had been outcast by the Adepts because of her relationships with Athanate. Alice, who'd arrived with the *Mayflower* and continued to outlive those Adepts who continued to declare she was cast out.

Between them, we could have had no better tutors in the secrets of the spirit world. It would have been much better for us to be together in one room, but I knew there was no time for us to divert through Denver, and Gwen was worried that Kaothos wasn't strong enough to be left on her own yet, so she couldn't come down to Louisiana.

Not ideal.

What the Lost Boys had managed to do was going to have to be good enough. It was a spinning, tumbling hoop of spirit energy that surrounded our immediate area. Invisible to anyone who couldn't peer into the spirit world. It created just enough of a barrier that Tezcatlipoca couldn't reach in and influence me.

I was no Adept, but even I got a feeling that the working was somehow untidy and inefficient. Gwen and Alice seemed happier with it than I was, but maybe that was their way of supporting Flint and Kane.

It *was* inefficient; it needed a couple of us to keep trickling energy into it to keep it going.

All fine, but the shield was a thing of the spirit world. While we used it, we were skimming the spirit world. Not enough to attract the attention of predatory substantiations like the City of Lost Gods, but just enough to engage the powers of the spirit world. That was how it worked, after all.

And the shield working couldn't discriminate on which of those powers it activated.

So, the first time they tested the shield, one moment I was standing there in the airy living room at Talleyrand, listening to Gwen guiding the Lost Boys, the next I was stumbling through a vision of the smoking ruins of the building, stunned, bewildered, finding my way outside… to where the mutilated corpses of the entire household lay scattered.

It was gone within a couple of seconds, but Flint and Kane had witnessed it too.

I'd thought it was something of Tezcatlipoca seeping through the shield.

The four Adepts disagreed, but they'd argued about what exactly it was. Flint and Kane said it was a spirit vision, something that shaman Adepts got, which warned of the future.

Gwen and Alice said true spirit visions were only possible for a senior Adept, and only after long training. Spirit visions were part of the toolkit that Adepts had to develop to become Truth Sensors. Spirit visions revealed the truth of the present and hinted at the truth of the future.

I was a complete rookie as an Adept. I'd had practically no training in any substantial magic skill. What I could do, I'd stumbled into or copied from others. I should certainly not be able to have semi-prophetic visions.

Gwen and Alice said the poison had to have caused the fever-dream, as they called it, and I wouldn't get any more once it was finally flushed from my Blood.

Which raised the question about what the hell the Queen of Diamond's poison actually was.

Normal poisons wouldn't affect an Athanate. This one had nearly killed me, and only Diana's considerable skill had saved me. She was on her way to Denver with the intention of researching the Dark Library to find out any hints about what it was and how to protect against it in future.

Well, if the visions were just an after-effect of poison, that was a small price to pay for surviving. They would be irritating and useless, but at least they'd go away.

They were useless because, as Gwen and Alice explained, without considerable training even 'true' spirit visions wouldn't show what *would* happen, only what *could* happen, based on a kind of subconscious extrapolation of the situation, and without any information as to what anyone could do to cause or prevent it happening.

The second part, yes, it didn't give any clues as to what I could do to avoid it happening.

The first part, however, I wasn't so sure. These visions, both the one at Talleyrand and this one now, had shown me things I really believed could happen if Emergence went wrong.

But whether going to the Assembly was the *cause* or possible *prevention* of the disasters I'd seen? No clue. None at all. They could be warning me to keep the hell away from the Assembly in New York, or they could be an insight into what would happen if I didn't go there.

Or what would happen if I went there and failed.

Worse than 'useless', the visions were *dangerous* if one could sneak up on me when I needed to focus. But I got no clues from the Adepts how to stop them while the poison was being eliminated from my body.

"Are we nearly there yet?" Kane sat up, rubbing his face. Despite the joke, he looked unsettled. The vision must have seeped into his dreams.

"That's DC down there," I said. "Means we're about half an hour out of New York."

He twisted around to look out the window, probably to convince himself there was no sign of the destruction we'd imagined.

"So, we're flying right over where Skylur is," he said.

"Presumably."

Skylur had said he was heading to DC, with Naryn, but he'd cut off all communications while he was working his way through a set of secret meetings with the hierarchy of government.

This was *it*. Emergence was beginning down there, right now.

"Still think he should be the one going to the Assembly."

"Yeah."

We'd argued it to a standstill. Skylur was the one with enough authority and connections in the Assembly to be sure of bringing everyone together. But he was also the person who had to take point on Emergence, and he couldn't be in two places at the same time.

Which was exactly why Correia, current president of the Assembly and leader of the Hidden Path party, had called this Assembly now. And why Jacob Tosun had sent a team on House Ellicott's jet down to New Orleans to collect me in a hurry.

If not Skylur, then Diana was the next best choice to attend. But if she turned up at the Assembly and revealed that we'd duped the Empire of Heaven about her death, then we'd lose Diakon Huang's support, and we couldn't afford that. His weight of vote was what was holding Correia in check.

I sighed.

"Skylur can't. Diana can't. That leaves me," I said.

"There are lots of Skylur's allies who are more senior," Flint said.

"But not more qualified. They don't have the experience in Athanate politics, or the connections to factions."

Kane snorted. "As far as I can see, your experience of the Assembly consists of being hauled up and threatened with execution a couple of times."

"And as for 'connections'," Flint took up the argument seamlessly, "half of the Assembly members still regard you as an abomination."

"Which is mild in comparison to what the Confederation Were think."

"Or that bitch Hinton. Now, I reckon she's *really* got it in for you."

They were arguing with my safety in mind, not to score points off me. They were genuinely worried for me, and I loved them for it. I also loved that they would argue with me.

And the fact they were gorgeous didn't hurt one bit. Not to mention their habit of wandering around shirtless.

Regardless of all that, they were making good points.

I could argue with Athanate and Were, maybe persuade them, but Hinton? Not so easy. I imagined the more Faith Hinton found out about me, the less opportunity there would be to find any common ground. Hinton suspected I had contact with a Lost God. If she confirmed my spirit connection with Tezcatlipoca, there probably wasn't anything she wouldn't do to have me killed. That's probably what I would do, if our situations were reversed.

But whatever Flint and Kane said, and however right they were that I was heading into a den of enemies, I had to do this. I had to confront the Assembly. The alternative... I could feel that spirit vision pressing at my mind. There was no way I could logically explain my gut feeling to them, but I was convinced the war we'd seen in those visions was the outcome if I didn't halt the slide of Athanate politics now.

I didn't get into that with them. Instead, I just said: "Diana has taught me how to work the Assembly."

They knew this. Diana had taught me, using the same eukori-enhanced technique which had transformed my House and pack these last couple of months, and which had taught me Athanate in a few weeks instead of years of study.

I knew it was a thin argument. Apples and pears. Being able to speak Athanate, or to know the rules of the Assembly, didn't make me a great orator or a canny politician.

Kane thought so too. "Learning isn't experience. Not even if the eukori link makes you think it is. You learned it up here..." He tapped his head, then his chest, "but not here, yet."

"Like expecting a professor of politics to be able to give a speech good enough to turn the senate around," Flint said.

"Yes, I understand, but my enemies won't expect it," I replied. "They'll think I'm helpless and ignorant of Assembly law. They'll make mistakes based on that. Here's a bit of Sun Tzu for you: *mystify, mislead, and surprise the enemy*. He also said *surprise would lead to victory*."

Flint snorted. "Yeah, I bet Sitting Bull and Crazy Horse were surprised when Custer attacked a camp four times larger than his cavalry company."

It was a fair point. They were right, again, and they were wrong.

"I've fought people bigger and stronger than me," I said. "Over-confidence and surprise are major weaknesses."

Flint: "If there were only one or two of them."

Kane: "Diana agreed you have too many enemies in the Assembly. Like Hinton."

Diana had said exactly that. We'd argued. I felt a pain in my chest that we'd parted with the argument unresolved. She had to be in Denver. I had to be in New York. It hurt.

"Hinton and the Northern Adepts aren't full members of the Assembly," I pointed out. "Neither are the Were."

"But they're *there*. And if they do get in, they'll be major parties. The Assembly is going to be aware of that. They're going to take their opinions into account."

We continued to argue. They said I should get one of the other major groups, like the Midnight Empire or Theokos to halt proceedings, but there was no time to persuade them.

They also thought they should have fed Hinton to the alligators when they'd had her down in Louisiana. I couldn't agree, but I had to admit, it would have made things easier for this Assembly.

Our arguing woke Xavier.

"Coffee all around?" he asked as he sat up.

"Please."

I was dying for coffee.

He walked to the next section which had cooking facilities and a fancy coffee machine. He started the hunt for pods, mugs and spoons.

Beyond the little galley, there were two rows of business-class seats facing each other. The Labastide security team had commandeered them, meaning that the Eastern Seaboard Association team that had come to fetch me were relegated to another cabin at the front of the jet, after the restrooms, in a sort of business suite.

While Xavier was up, Kane came over and took his place next to me.

My fever had ramped up during the flight. He couldn't help but notice the effect on my body temperature.

"Damn, you're hot!" he said, and Flint snorted.

I laughed and dropped my hands onto their thighs. "You say the nicest..."

An odd tingling sensation ran up my arms and then we weren't sitting in the back of House Ellicott's jet. We were in a bedroom, the three of us. Naked. I was pressed between them, and there was nowhere to put my hands that wasn't hot and hard and downright eager for me to put my hands there.

Okay. So, spirit visions didn't come in bleak all the time. And they could be *influenced*.

I blinked it away, my face getting even hotter.

"*Not* a prophesy, boys."

They were both grinning, fit to split their faces.

"Yeah, but…" Kane began.

"It's a maybe. A definitely possible future event," Flint finished.

"Can it. That was you two—"

"We recognized ourselves," said Kane.

"As I was saying, you two, leaking your overactive imaginations into our shared aura. That isn't any kind of predictive vision."

That didn't stop them grinning, and I couldn't be too angry at them. *Some* of that sexual heat had to have come from my overactive imagination as well.

I shook my head. I was House Farrell, and they were in my House. As far as Athanate rules went, I was entitled to enjoy them for more than just Blood. And although they were Amanda Lloyd's kin, she was a mature and confident Athanate, who was happy for me to enjoy them, knowing they'd return to her.

But I already had a husband, a wife, and a surprisingly patient fiancée.

Not to mention far too much going on to be distracted, however pleasantly.

As Xavier returned with our coffees, the door to the business section opened. A guy called Watson, the leader of the Eastern Seaboard Association's team, emerged. Two of his team followed behind, trying to look tough, but ending up looking awkward instead.

"Showtime," Kane muttered.

"Stay out of it," I muttered back.

Chapter 2

This was the kind of fight that the Lost Boys didn't have a feel for. This was my kind of fight, even if I wasn't going to use fists and feet. This was a fight of surprises, and maneuvering for advantage, and leading an opponent into making a fatal mistake. And above all, timing.

Jacob Tosun, the person who'd summoned me to the Assembly, had already started to cede advantage when he had to notify me that a jet was coming down to collect me. His first note had been rude, simply saying the Assembly *urgently required* my presence. Then he'd shown his hand in the second message with a change of tone: that a private jet had been provided *for my convenience*.

All he'd really done was confirm that I had to be at the Assembly when he wanted me to be. That gave me a timeframe to put my own plans into action and an insight into what he was trying to do.

That was his first mistake. His second was his choice of team leader to come down and collect me: this guy Watson. Tosun had probably chosen Watson because he knew he'd obey orders without question. He'd have been better off with someone more flexible. Someone less desperate to prove himself.

Watson had been on the back foot from the start.

He'd wanted me alone and isolated. Wasn't ever going to happen.

When I told him Flint and Kane were coming with me, he'd assumed the Lost Boys were my kin, and he couldn't stop them accompanying me. Athanate law.

Then he'd blinked when it turned out I would also be accompanied by a House Labastide security detail, and they were *very sorry, but those are our orders*, and *House Farrell goes nowhere unless we do too*.

I could see him justifying it to himself. Marguerite Molayo Labastide, House Labastide, was known to be hardcore, old-style, ultra-traditional Panethus. She was highly regarded in the Eastern Seaboard Association, which still functioned, despite being formally disbanded. Watson 'knew' it wasn't remotely possible that she'd be on my side. And so it made sense to him, looking at it that way, that Labastide security regarded me as their prisoner. He'd had to concede they were coming too.

What he didn't know was that Marguerite had given me the freedom of her House, and, far from being arrested, that security detail was for my protection.

I imagined he'd started to feel uneasy when the Labastide team insisted that I would be in the back of the jet and they would take the next section, relegating Watson and his team to the business suite at the front, with a closed door between us.

That uneasiness was growing, and it was affecting him. I sensed he was starting to second guess himself and was about to try and assert his authority.

And now he could see that two of the Labastide security team, Jo and Xavier, were with me in the back lounge area. And he'd be able to sense that I'd bitten them during the flight.

My fever had made me thirsty.

I could see the wheels turning in his head.

His full team still outnumbered us, but they were just ordinary Athanate members of House Tosun. The Labastide team was Marguerite's elite security detail. They knew their business and they looked the part.

Both sides were armed, but firing automatics in Ellicott's fancy jet at 30,000 feet wasn't a great idea for either side.

How was Watson going to handle it?

He squared his shoulders.

"House Farrell, I am required to—"

"Cut the crap, Watson," I interrupted. "You have no requirements to tell me anything. No authority to do anything but sit on the same plane. Don't try and dress it up as if you're for my protection either. I have my own security team with me."

Goad him.

Watson turned back to look at Saul, the Labastide team leader, who nodded in confirmation of what I'd said. In fact, the whole team stood up, half to face the door to the business suite, where the rest of Watson's team were waiting, the others to press into the back with us. Luxury section or not, it got full very quickly. I was the only one still seated.

The pressure was too much, with the Labastide team crowding him. Now, Watson was nervous *and* angry. Angry people make mistakes, but I wanted him to make the right mistake.

Watson's tongue touched his lip, and he reached abruptly into his jacket. His hand didn't make it. Saul captured his wrist in an iron grip, and the other security team members stepped between Watson and his two colleagues.

For a moment, no one so much as breathed.

I held up my hand to stop them from doing any more.

"Let him retrieve whatever he was reaching for… very carefully," I said.

Watson was smart enough to move his hand slowly. He extracted a piece of folded paper, which he handed to me.

"This isn't going to look good for you," Watson ground out, and there was a gleam of triumph in his eye. He thought this was his trump card.

I shrugged, reading the paper.

It was the same as the one David had hacked off the New York servers as soon as we'd realized that Correia was calling an Assembly. It had been intended that the official version would be handed to me on arrival in New York.

This was a copy rather than the original, and *that* was a significant misstep, but only if I used it at the right time.

The notification was designed to both anger and scare me, but being forewarned by David's hacking and Diana's analysis eliminated the shock Watson expected.

It informed me that Jacob Tosun, Skylur's temporary head of security, declared a *nomicane* against me—an Assembly trial essentially—and authorized my detention and forcible transfer to the Assembly, where I would face execution for actions against the interest of the Assembly, allies of the Assembly *and* House Altau, and for being an abomination etc. etc...

The original had been timed, dated and extravagantly signed by Jacob Tosun himself, presumably in his own Blood, all as laid down in the strict rules of the Agiagraphos.

"I'm not accepting this," I said. I folded the paper and slipped it into a pocket.

Watson couldn't believe it. His assumption had been that a notice of nomicane would have had me cowering. He went back to being angry again.

"Refusing a legitimate order from the Assembly won't do you any good," he blustered.

"I don't imagine anything I do would count higher than the charges being laid against me. Falsely, incidentally. I'm going to the Assembly anyway, Watson. I'll deal with it there."

I nodded to Saul, and the Labastide team shepherded a complaining Watson and his colleagues back into the business suite.

Our cellphones weren't working, but obviously Watson had communications capabilities in the business suite. The issue was how he used them. Would he contact his boss or try and deal with it himself?

I didn't want him to contact Tosun, because Tosun would probably give him calm-headed, good advice.

No, I wanted Watson to call ahead for reinforcements and try to arrest me by force at the airport so he could tell Tosun later that he'd handled it.

Back in my Ops 4-10 training days, Ben-Haim had drilled it into me as we sparred. *Don't always rush to capitalize on a small mistake. Let it develop. Wait until it becomes a big mistake. Timing, Farrell. Timing.*

Yeah. *Timing.*

Diana wouldn't agree. She was for the subtlest approach—to disguise your strength. That would work for her. She could make the Assembly stand on its head simply by turning up. I couldn't. My strategy here was more in line with Ben-Haim's advice; to wait until revealing the mistake would have most impact. And then, I'd follow Top's advice. *Get inside their reach and strike hard, and keep striking, faster than the opponent can respond. Give everything. No holding back. No pain. No fear. No rules. No prisoners. Go berserk.*

That's how you win when everyone says you can't possibly win.

One thing that Diana and I had agreed on was what our enemies' strategy was: once they'd condemned and executed me, the next step would be a nomicane against Skylur himself.

That was the last point we agreed on. Diana said this was Skylur's fight, and he would have made plans against this eventuality. It was Skylur's chosen arena. I should just make myself scarce until Skylur returned.

I argued that Skylur had shattered tradition by making me a House as well as syndesmon to the Were, and I needed the Assembly to respect my powers and abilities. If I didn't turn up to defend myself in the Assembly, and instead hid behind Skylur, it would prove to the traditionalists that I'd been elevated beyond my worth and weaken his position with them. I didn't care what they thought of me, but it would be taken as evidence that Skylur's long leadership of Panethus was beginning to fail. There would be challenges, at the very point that we needed unity.

Also, if I didn't turn up, the Assembly could issue a kill-on-sight order. If I was hiding out in Denver, Bian wouldn't execute me, but my hiding and her refusal would become Skylur's responsibility. The Assembly would demand he execute both of us. Even if he did, it wouldn't fully restore his reputation, and again, there would be challenges, just when he needed to be able to concentrate on Emergence.

Diana said Skylur knew all of this, and he would have plans to handle it. She also pointed out that if I did turn up, and the nomicane went against me, it would be as bad for Skylur as if I hadn't turned up. Skylur had bound me that closely into his strategy, even against the advice of his Diakon.

All of which just proved to me that the only acceptable outcome was for me to attend the Assembly *and* defeat the nomicane.

I was Athanate, Were and Adept. And Carpathian.

And I had actual, recent success in fighting Matlal's allies which had yet to be reported to the Assembly. I sensed it was in my power to not only defeat the nomicane, but to shift the Assembly onto the right path. Part of that 'right path' included opening the Assembly's eyes to how much Matlal was doing to undermine them. It shouldn't have been my job. It was a diversion from what I should be doing, which was physically attacking Matlal, but righting the Assembly was more urgent and more important, and Mirela Tucek was a key to doing that. I couldn't wait for the next Assembly meeting. I had to convince them to work together. I had to get Mirela in front of them. *Today*.

But first, I had to defeat the nomicane.

I wasn't much of a politician, but if I attended the Assembly, they would have to let me speak. That would be the equivalent, in hand-to-hand fighting, of letting me get inside their reach. I had a history of defeated enemies who'd made that mistake.

There would be Blood on the floor of the Assembly today. Whether it was mine or not was another matter.

Chapter 3

We landed as the eastern sky became light enough to show the first hesitant blush on the long banners of cloud streaming in from the Atlantic. Airfield hangars were just becoming solid in the gloom.

Morgengrauen, as my Ops 4-10 instructor Ben-Haim used to call it—the time to talk to ghosts and spirits. The spirit world was closer now than he ever knew back then. But I couldn't afford to talk to the spirit world right now. I was doing everything *not* to open a channel for Tezcatlipoca.

In desperate need, while I'd fought the Queen of Diamonds, I'd bargained with the Lost God for the use of his powers, and he'd given them. In return, he'd claimed me as his priestess. He'd sunk his claws into my soul. But those claws were only so deep. I'd refused to sacrifice the Queen of Diamonds to him. Smart move. That sacrifice would have passed all her powers to him and doubled his grip on me.

Any use of Tezcatlipoca's powers was going to make me less able to refuse him, until I was nothing more than a channel for him to return to the physical world.

Not gonna happen.

The aircraft taxied down the ranks of hangars, turning into the space between the last two. Out the window, I could see there was a group waiting for us. Watson had called up reinforcements.

Good.

He and his team emerged from the business suite as the jet came to a halt.

"Come with us, Farrell. Now."

I yawned, just to irritate him again.

"It's House Farrell to you, Watson," I said. "And you'll want to get out there first, and make sure you have all your ducks in a row. Wouldn't want to have to report any incidents to Tosun, would you?"

Up to that point, I wasn't sure that he *hadn't* called Tosun, but I saw confirmation in his eyes. He wanted to deliver me with a 'no problems I couldn't overcome' type of report. Now he was stuck with his choice.

He glared at me, but the movement of Labastide security behind him convinced him to do what I wanted him to do and make the arrest outside.

I watched him leave, along with the flight crew and the rest of his team.

My team hurriedly finished a whispered conversation as I turned around.

"We should go out first," Jo said. "They won't try anything with us. We can send videos of them to Diakon Flavia—"

"No." I cut across her. "Thank you, Jo, but I want all of you to stay inside until I call you."

"Amber, you can't go out there alone," Xavier said. "They could just shoot. They'd call it an accident…"

"They won't have the chance." I raised my voice and spoke to them all. "As much as I value you being here for me, that outside…" I nodded at the group waiting for me, "that's my type of fight. The kind of fight I've been fighting for a long time. You're not ready for it, and neither are they."

I looked through the windows and smiled. "Trust me. They obviously think they're ready. They've made a plan, but like the famous quote goes, everyone has a plan until they get punched in the mouth."

My team knew I'd planned for this, but they all looked worried. Especially the Labastide security team, because they knew that Marguerite Labastide would expect them to protect me the way they'd protect her.

But I wasn't Marguerite.

I should have taken more time to reassure them, but it was getting lighter outside. It was time.

"On your oaths, stay here until I say."

"But what if the arrangements don't go as planned?" Xavier said.

"Then we'll be there," Flint replied. "Right behind her."

"Inside the plane," I said and stepped out onto the top step of the stairs.

Flint and Kane were too close behind – only technically 'in' the plane.

Disobedient pups. I loved them anyway.

Watson and his team had been reinforced by a Tosun security team. There were now sixteen of them, to discourage any attempt at resistance on our part. The jet was parked between two looming hangars, out of sight of the rest of the airport, and the Tosun security team had automatics in hand already. Not pointing yet. Relaxed, alert. Ready for anything.

No pushovers.

Next to one of the hangars was a helicopter. I hadn't counted on that, but it made sense. Tosun would want me at the Assembly as quickly as possible.

Should have thought of that.

I turned my attention back to the waiting group.

Watson was standing slightly in front.

He wanted this done quickly. Every second increased the chance of an outsider seeing what was going on. There was no point delaying it any longer. I wanted to keep this out of sight as much as he did.

"Put your hands up and walk down slowly," Watson called out.

I raised my hands. Watson started forward.

"Stop right there," I told him, and I put all my Athanate dominance into the command.

There was a ripple of shock. They all knew I was an upstart House, promoted to that position too quickly. I was not supposed to have such a weight of command.

Watson paused, which was all I needed. Weight of dominance aside, I wasn't old enough or powerful enough as an Athanate to compel him for any length of time without resorting to other weapons at my disposal, but I shouldn't need to.

My priestess doesn't need to compel them.

Flint and Kane had been distracted. The voice of Tezcatlipoca hissed in my ears. I did *not* need this.

I felt a pulse of his power and it grew dark in my eyes, as if night had stolen back the gray of the coming dawn. Transfixed where they stood, every person in the semicircle facing me just *melted*, screaming in agony.

No!

One or two of them who were more sensitive to the spirit world looked around them in confusion at the feeling of the unseen threat hanging over them.

No!

It was dawn. Not night. I pushed the temptation away. I would not channel Tezcatlipoca's appalling magical powers. These people didn't deserve that for obeying their House's orders. And I wasn't going to give the Lost God any more hold over me.

The Lost Boys refocused. Tezcatlipoca and his visions faded.

I had this. *If* everything went to plan.

I spoke again, loudly, so they could all hear. "I'm not surrendering. My arms are raised to save your lives. If I drop them too soon, you will all die."

With my hands raised well above my head, I finger-talked.

Time seemed to slow right down, and I stopped breathing.

What if my team weren't there? However cleverly I made plans, there were a million things that could have gone wrong.

But they were there.

My House Farrell team, hidden on the neighboring hangar roofs, switched from invisible to visible infrared scopes. Every member of Watson's security team on the apron lit up with laser targeting spots.

My breath rushed back, loud in my ears.

Watson and his team froze.

I called out. "All of you, one at a time, starting with the one on my right, place your weapons and any comms devices on the ground very, very carefully."

The woman at the end I was pointing to hesitated.

"You have three seconds to comply," I said, staring at her. "Given the way you're all bunched together, I can't guarantee any of you will survive if one of you tries to do anything other than obey my commands."

She knelt and placed her automatic on the tarmac in front of her. Her cell joined it.

"Next," I called out.

I left Watson to last. He was furious, and he would have tried something if he'd had any support. Luckily for him, he didn't.

A couple of black-suited ghosts emerged from the twilight, swooping down in front of the semicircle to gather all the discarded weapons and cellphones into bags.

That was a dangerous point, with our own people in the line of fire, but the speed and completeness of their defeat had taken the fight out of the Eastern Seaboard team.

Mostly.

Watson couldn't help but look behind him to where the helicopter sat. I assumed the pilot was also part of their team, and I'd bet Watson was wondering if he'd been able to make a call to alert their allies about what had happened.

No such luck for him. The pilot was being escorted at gunpoint to join his colleagues.

A large panel van came around the side of the hangars. I'd been wondering what Rita had planned for our prisoners. I didn't intend to harm them, but I wasn't going to let them find a way to alert Jacob Tosun.

Some of my team loaded the prisoners in the van while the rest came to greet me and meet the members of our new associate House, who were exiting the plane.

I hugged Rita, Keith and Julie. The comfort of my own marque, blended with Yelena's, folded itself around me, and I sighed.

"Where's Yelena?" I asked.

Julie frowned. "Off grid. Something must have come up. No explanation. We thought she must have been called to join Skylur, or we were wondering if you'd sent a message for her to do something else?"

"No, I didn't. I'd have told you if I had."

I didn't like it, but there had to be a hundred different reasons to explain it. Yelena was still Skylur's *pelea*, his personal bodyguard. Skylur *could* have sent orders for Yelena to go down to DC, for instance.

"Problem?" Rita asked.

Why hadn't I been informed?

"No." I tried to push the worry aside. I trusted Yelena with my life. I'd find out later what had happened, but meanwhile, time was short.

"What now?" Keith asked.

"I still have to attend the Assembly," I said. "And I'd rather get there before Jacob Tosun and his Eastern Seaboard allies realize what's happened here."

Watson's reinforcements came from House Tosun's security. They were much more clued in than Watson's team. They'd have set up a schedule and someone would notice when they didn't report in. Shortly after that, Tosun would know, which would give him time to prepare.

Not going to let that happen.

I looked over at the helicopter. They'd obviously planned to take me to Manhattan in it anyway, so I might as well use it. The Assembly was being called in Skylur's HQ building, and that had a landing pad on top.

"Can't fit much backup in there," Keith said, seeing where I was looking. "Your plan was for a full team supporting you."

"I know. But surprise is the key here."

Despite my confident reply, I didn't like the way the plan was gathering changes quicker than I could think them through.

Kane had taken the hint and he was already running to the helicopter to prepare for the flight across to Manhattan.

Besides Kane and me, we could fit another six people in. Flint, Rita, Keith and Julie from my House. Xavier and Jo from House Labastide.

It felt unbalanced. They were all good, but none of them had the fingertip feeling for Athanate politics that Yelena had.

It wasn't a matter of getting into the Assembly without being arrested; Skylur's security ran the whole building, and although they were currently answering to Tosun, he wouldn't know I was coming until I was there.

No, it wasn't getting *in* that was the problem.

It was getting out alive.

Chapter 4

More things started going wrong the minute we landed on the roof of Skylur's HQ in Manhattan.

We were met by one of House Altau's admin assistants, tasked with coordinating helicopter traffic for the Assembly. He told us there was no room to leave the helicopter here, because more were scheduled to come in later. Kane was going to have to fly it down to a heliport where parking had been arranged. It could take him an hour to make his way back.

I'd changed plans to use the helicopter to keep ahead of the news, and I hadn't had time to think it through. Little changes make bigger changes happen. Kane was part of my team to keep the shield up against Tezcatlipoca while I could concentrate on the Assembly. More than just that, he and Flint were powerful together, if Hecate Faith Hinton tried something.

Diana had made me promise to keep them close. Gwen and Alice had made me promise to keep them close.

No choice.

Everything was a risk, with Tosun, Hinton and Tezcatlipoca waiting to pounce on me the minute I was distracted or let my guard down.

First Yelena's unexplained absence, and now this. The bad feeling I'd had of losing control intensified, but there wasn't any way back now.

Kane took off again, and the rest of us crowded onto the elevator waiting to take us down.

I took the moment to force myself back into the right attitude. The fever was making focus difficult, and I couldn't afford that now.

Hinton wouldn't try anything magical in the Assembly. There were Adepts there who'd notice. Even as an outsider, she'd know she'd be breaking Assembly laws. And from what little I knew of her, it wasn't her style. I'd lay good odds that she'd cultivated Correia and Tosun well away from the notice of other Adepts and she'd influenced them into working together against me.

If that was right, Flint wouldn't need to worry about Hinton. Instead, he'd have to take the bulk of the work to ensure the shield against Tezcatlipoca continued to function while I was involved in the politics of Assembly, starting with defeating the nomicane.

If Tezcatlipoca broke through…

I shuddered. *That* would put the politics into perspective. Flint and Kane had orders if it seemed to them that Tezcatlipoca was going to force his way through me into the physical world. But would they know it was happening? Probably. Whether they would or could carry out their orders was another matter.

I shook my head, forcing my fears down.

Trust my team. Concentrate on my task.

The elevator took us directly to where the Assembly was being held. No chance to rest, freshen up, or recover from almost being arrested.

The doors opened on an area similar to a theater lobby—elegantly and tastefully decorated, with places where visitors could leave their coats, and order refreshments in the intermission. But instead of several sets of doors like in a theater, there was one—with a squad of armed guards flanking it.

Altau security.

I felt slight easing in the knots of tension in my stomach. I'd been half-expecting a team on loan from the Eastern Seaboard. Having Skylur's people here made me feel safer, especially because I recognized their leader.

"House Farrell." He greeted me with a head bow. "Welcome."

I returned the bow.

"House Demetriades. You're a welcome face."

He snorted and looked more closely at me, frowning.

"Are you all right? Is there anything I can get you? You look…" His remark faded away.

"You're trying to tell me I look like shit."

Athanate Blood is aniatropic. It heals. It dismisses the infections and viruses that plague humanity. Athanate are supposed to look good all the time. I knew I didn't at the moment; the effects of my lingering fever and unhealed wounds from the fight with the Queen of Diamonds were plain to see on my face. It didn't help that I was back to avoiding sleep. I felt I couldn't, because in that sleep, what dreams might come. Or in my case, what Lost God.

I didn't doubt that some in the Assembly would use my feverish appearance to prove I was unworthy of the elevated role that Skylur had given me. Or worse, that I was about to go rogue.

Demetriades and I didn't have time to discuss it. His eyes flicked past me; there were other parties emerging from the bank of elevators. He spoke quietly and quickly.

"A suite on the 15th floor has been put aside for you and your House," he said. "I recommend you go there and delay your arrival into the Assembly by a couple of hours."

My turn to snort.

"It's not your appearance," he said, continuing to look over my shoulder at the new groups behind us. "Something's not right. The timings seem to have changed. And the members arriving so far—"

"Are mainly supporters of the traditionalist factions," I interrupted him.

I wasn't having a spirit vision exactly. Maybe it was the clarity that you sometimes get between bouts of fever, but I could almost see the traps laid out for me in the Assembly room.

All the more reason to get inside. In addition to catching Tosun off balance, I might be able to rally some support.

Demetriades grunted in surprise, confirming my hunch, but he didn't leave it there.

"Not just that," he said, and lowered his voice. "Look, you know the Assembly has to be *seen* to be powerful to keep its authority. And you know that the way it is at the moment, with Altau and the Empire of Heaven preventing Correia moving forward... that makes the Assembly look weak. The members want a show of power, and there's one easy way to deliver. There's death in that room, House Farrell."

"Thank you, I understand," I touched his arm. "But I need to go straight in."

He nodded unhappily and cleared his throat before speaking louder, for the benefit of the people behind us as well. "No firearms, recording or communication devices are allowed in the meeting."

"No cellphones?" I asked. "That's new."

Demetriades shrugged. "President Correia's decision."

We were directed to place our weapons and cells on the table. "Each House has a designated locker in a secure, guarded room," Demetriades said. "Your belongings will be perfectly safe and may be retrieved at any time."

The bag Jo was carrying contained all my bladed weapons that I'd been using in Louisiana. The matching Japanese swords that had been a gift from Bian. And the two Chinese swords: the straight-bladed jian and curved dao; mine by right of my victory over the Queen of Diamonds.

I raised a hand to stop Jo's bag being whisked off and opened it.

Strangely, I felt I wanted the jian, but that would have been foolish. Almost all of my training from Bian had been on the katana, and that's the one I pulled out.

It looked gorgeous in its silky black sheath. It was a named sword, this katana: *Onibi*, spirit fire. It was about five hundred years old, and a spell had been hammered into it when it was made. I didn't know what the spell actually did, but Onibi's blade had glowed when I fought the Queen of Diamonds. She'd told me the sword would turn against me, but then again, she was screwing with my mind at the time.

Demetriades blinked. Assembly laws were quite specific. Firearms weren't permitted in the meeting. But by the far older laws of the Agiagraphos, a House was entitled to carry bladed weapons when meeting with others. I hated the Agiagraphos, but I'd use it for my own purposes in a heartbeat.

"You won't need that," he said. "No one has issued a formal challenge to a duel in an Assembly meeting for over fifty years."

"Really? Then again, no one ever does anything since the last time, until the next time. And Bian was on the point of challenging some of the Warders at the last Denver Assembly."

He bowed his head and conceded the point.

I was carrying my cell and took it out to hand it over.

Missed calls ending with two of the briefest messages, one from Yelena and one from Diana.

Yelena: *Carpathians. Will call and explain shortly. Hold back.*

Carpathians? What would Yelena be doing with them that would be so important? The visiting delegation had sat in their ship down in the dock for ages now, barely communicating and taking no visitors. That was one of the reasons for this Assembly being called, and for choosing to meet in New York. Yelena knew I believed that part of 'fixing the Assembly' included getting the Carpathians to participate, but was that what she was trying to do?

Was she down there in the port? Or had they come off the ship?

Again, it felt as if things were starting to slide out of control.

And Diana. One word: *Call.*

Shit! I should have checked my cell earlier. Now, it was too late. I couldn't delay, I couldn't call. There was no time. I'd have to put off speaking to Diana and Yelena or lose the element of surprise over Tosun. Any moment now, he'd be alerted that the security team had gone off-line.

I switched the cell off and left it on the table.

We moved on into the passage that led to the chamber while the next group was being processed by Demetriades' team. I paused at the top of the steps, while we were still mainly out of sight from the inside. I intended to read the room in the way that Diana had taught me.

Assess the opposition. Identify the supporters.

Instead, the reality of what Demetriades had been talking about shocked me.

The Assembly chamber filled most of the two lowest basement floors of the building. This had been the Warder's chamber, and unlike other Assembly rooms, it was built like a huge amphitheater, divided into sections. With this design, it was impossible for your eyes not to be drawn to the stage.

Shit!

Demetriades had warned me there was death in this place, and it had taken a very literal form. A tall figure stood on one side of the stage. He was masked and robed in crimson cloth. His hands rested on the pommel of a longsword that had to be five foot tall.

His title was the Blade of the Assembly. If the Assembly decided you'd broken their laws, or the laws of the Agiagraphos, the president could call on the Blade for an immediate execution. It was an *old* tradition, pre-Assembly even. The Assembly didn't need the Blade to execute someone, and the Blade hadn't been present at an Assembly in fifty years. It was very deliberate to have him here now.

I tore my eyes away, but there was nothing less threatening in the remainder of the room.

So far, the voting members of the Assembly who were present were almost all traditionalists. Most of them were Hidden Path party, and none of those would be friendly to me. Even the Panethus delegates were heavily biased towards the traditionalists, like the former Eastern Seaboard. No close allies of Skylur like House Passau. No Midnight Empire. No Empire of Heaven. No Theokos.

None of my powerful allies were here.

If Correia had been willing to manipulate the Assembly invitations and timings as Demetriades had warned me, then she would also be prepared to start proceedings early and take advantage of the skewed representation. She was going to go all out.

This wasn't just a threat to me. It was a threat to the Assembly as a whole. And to Emergence.

I kept looking around. There were the honorary delegates from the Were and Adept communities. I spotted Faith Hinton, head down and talking intently with others. I had *no* support coming from there. My coven and the Adept associations beginning to form around Denver hadn't been going long enough to be recognized and invited to the Assembly.

As to the Were community, Felix and Cameron's pack had a sole representative. It was the LA alpha who had relocated to New York to undertake politics for the League. He still called himself The Heights, from his LA days. He was a strange werewolf, but I knew I could count on him for support.

Great. One friendly voice.

The other shifters in the room were probably from the Central Mountain Confederation. If it hadn't been so serious, it would have been funny. They hated the Athanate, but they had to be here. They couldn't afford to *not* know what was going on. Regardless, since I'd been responsible for the death of one of their ruling alphas, and the defeat of their attempt to invade New Mexico, they would hate me. Like the rest of the honorary delegates, they had no votes, but they could speak, and the sheer numbers would add weight to their words.

Were *all* my enemies acting together?

Still partly hidden from sight in the doorway, I closed my eyes and *reached*.

My eukori had grown more powerful since I last attended an Assembly. I could feel the gathering Athanate like bees in a hive. A background murmur, lit by clusters of conversation. Emotions rippling through them.

I expected it to be difficult to see what was going on, but I could visualize it. Not something concrete, but more like a mist stretching between groups.

Could I believe it? Could I really be sensing Correia, the Hidden Path and the Eastern Seaboard conspiring? Were there different agendas here? Tosun, focused on a nomicane against me and failing to see how he'd bent the Assembly into the form that Correia wanted? Correia, betting everything on getting rules changed that would allow her to herd the Assembly in the direction she wanted?

Was this like the spirit visions?

Just my subconscious feeding me confirmation of my fears?

Of course, opening out like that made me more accessible to Tezcatlipoca, despite Flint's efforts. This time the Lost God spared me visions of every person in the room melting and screaming. There was no more than a feeling of the vast darkness in the Temple of Night, a hint of movement like a jaguar in the jungle at night, a subtle sense of the power he could make available to me if I called on it.

And a whisper. *Blood calls to Blood.*

I shivered.

The call of that power was so seductive. It would be so easy…

The group behind us was pushing to get through. Assembly officials were saying they had orders to close the doors.

Of course they had orders. This was a trap.

"Keith. Julie. Back outside, now! Go up to our suite. It'll have full comms capability. Call everybody. Tell them Correia's going to start proceedings right now with a quorum that has been deliberately skewed. Tell them to force their way in if they have to. This is an attempted coup."

They wanted to argue, but there was no time.

"Go."

They went. It reduced my team, but this wasn't their kind of fight.

Wasn't really mine, either, but I had to do it.

A memory from my Ops4-10 training. Looking at an apparently deserted building we had to get in. Ben-Haim whispering in my ear. *Knowing it's a trap is the first step to defeating it.*

The next step…

I walked tall, slowly and deliberately moving down the steps, staring at the group on the podium. President Correia and Diakon Flavia were arguing. Tosun was trying to interrupt.

Like ripples in a pool, the silence spread as people in the amphitheater noticed me. Alerted by the change in noise levels, Tosun glanced over his shoulder and froze in shock at the sight of me, flanked by my team, clearly not under arrest, and carrying a katana.

Correia looked up and immediately turned to Tosun and hissed something at him.

Not going to plan. She doesn't like it either.

Livia, Diakon Flavia, also turned and saw me. Her face betrayed nothing, but I saw her give a tiny nod. I guessed it wasn't a nod of approval so much as *well, okay, you've decided to fight it.*

She was on my side, I guessed.

An aide scurried up to Tosun with a message the old-fashioned way, scribbled on a slip of paper. He read it and his jaw clenched.

Bad news from the airfield?

I forced myself to smile at him as my team and I took places down at the front.

Every Assembly had a sense of anticipation that grew as the session approached, but this was different. There was a hunger. An eagerness that seemed sharpened as delegates knew something unusual was happening, with the Blade waiting, and Diakon Flavia and House Tosun still clearly arguing.

I'd been right about the timings.

"We're about to start," Correia said. "Take your seat, Diakon Flavia,".

I swiveled my head and guesstimated the numbers. It was quorate. Just. It was blatant what she was doing, but if she was careful, she might get away with it; the Assembly was hesitant about repealing new rules. As Demetriades had said, its authority depended on the appearance of strength. Overruling a president's initiatives would look like weakness, even if those decisions didn't reflect the full Assembly.

But to get it all to work and leave her in power afterwards, she'd need to maintain innocence of rigging the balance of delegates. She'd need someone to blame.

I wondered when Tosun would realize he was the designated fall guy.

Another aide trotted in and whispered urgently in Correia's ear.

Her eyes narrowed and she looked directly at me.

Maybe she'd found out that I'd sent Julia and Keith back. If that was it, she'd know she had a time limit for what she wanted to do.

Livia sat down beside me, face blank but every muscle in her body tense with anger.

"You realize this is a trap," she muttered.

I nodded, also keeping my face blank.

"Your confidence borders on arrogance," she went on. "I trust you can back it up."

Confidence? Arrogance? No, I was terrified. The visions of what might happen flickered at the edge of my sight. The jarring feel that longsword would make as it struck my neck. The world burning. A darkness falling.

Correia gestured impatiently and one of her aides made the customary announcement: "We are now in session."

A large display screen above the podium lit up with a welcome sign.

Behind us, at the top of the stairs, the door slammed shut.

Chapter 5

As president of the Assembly, House Correia started, speaking in Athanate.

"Delegates, my apologies for a brief and informal greeting. There appear to have been some miscommunications on timings. This session was not scheduled to start until later today. However, by precedent, it is permissible to raise and debate urgent matters any time we are quorate. We happen to be quorate, and we have some such issues."

I assumed that by speaking Athanate, Correia was trying to make me feel isolated and unsure of the procedures the Assembly used.

Mistake.

Diana had spent the weeks when we were quarantined in Denver teaching me Athanate. As subjects for discussion, she'd used the Agiagraphos, the Assembly and the other assorted rules and etiquette of Athanate society. Bian had also helped to teach me Athanate, although her choice of study material had been very different from Diana's.

Regardless, I was an expert in the language *and* the rules.

Time to start the fight back.

I stood up, ignoring the feeling of fear in my stomach.

Correia glared at me. Tosun leaped to his feet to try and speak before me.

I could see Correia think about letting him speak first, but she needed to appear impartial, so she backed down.

"House Farrell," she said, in English. "You have something to say?"

I answered in formal Athanate. "This Assembly is at a pivotal point. Although there seem to be endless delays in formally admitting the full range of paranormals into the Assembly, I'm pleased to see that at least some of them have been invited as observers."

I switched to English, but kept it as formal as I could. "When our new members are included as full delegates in the future, all laws and procedures are going to have to be in a common language. Until that time, inviting them as observers to this meeting is meaningless unless it is also conducted in a language that they all understand. I reference previous decisions on communications at the last Denver and Los Angeles Assembly meeting, which have created precedence. I move to continue in English."

I sat down again.

I didn't care whether the observers knew what was going on, but I needed to rattle Correia and Tosun. They'd probably assumed I would be passive while they conducted proceedings in Athanate. Now they needed to re-think.

And they couldn't halt the session to coordinate a change of plan with each other.

I could feel the Assembly in the ranks of seats behind me. They might hate me, but my point was valid. Correia could see it, too.

"Very well." She stopped and frowned at her notes.

I hadn't had time to think the effect of my interruption through. I assumed Correia and Tosun were working together, but with different agendas, but I hadn't anticipated the effect that would have.

"In light of this change," Correia said, "I believe we should re-arrange the provisional agenda to focus on the most important of the early issues."

She tapped a pad on the table and the display behind her flicked past two screens headlined *Nomicane* and settled on the third.

Two nomicanes? What the hell?

"Thank the gods," whispered Livia beside me.

The agenda item she'd landed on was all Correia. It gave bullet points for *streamlining* and *efficiency* and *rationalizing* and *subcommittees*. Hiding changes that meant more executive power to the president and less debate and decision-making in the Assembly, as Diana had explained to me. *This* was Correia's agenda, and the delegates here would probably give her the powers she wanted just to not have to sit through the discussion.

"No!" That was Faith Hinton, on her feet.

Tosun got into it as well. "I urgently request to approach," he called out.

They'd stalled themselves, so I took the opportunity to question Livia.

"Why thank the gods? Who was that second nomicane?" I asked.

"A nomicane against the entire Athanate community of New York, for revealing our existence."

I understood. The case would be solid. Pia monitored developments across the whole of America for my House, and she'd told me that there were clubs throughout New York where it seemed everyone knew 'vampires' existed and how to spot them. We were an open secret. New York had just grown that way under the blind direction of the Warders, before Skylur's tenure, so not really a nomicane matter for him. It didn't directly affect anyone outside of New York either, but it was against the highest law of the Agiagraphos. It *was* a matter for a nomicane to discover which Houses were in breach, and potentially execute any of them that were.

Skylur had chosen Livia as his Diakon partly for the strength of her commitment to this strange Athanate community in New York. I knew instinctively she'd offer her own life as korheny to save the lives of her community.

And Correia would accept. Livia would face the justice of the Blade because the execution of Skylur's own Diakon would shatter Skylur's credibility much more than the execution of defaulting Houses in his domain.

But if that nomicane was delayed, and Skylur returned to declare that Emergence had begun, then the case against the New York community failed because the Agiagraphos no longer applied.

Livia and I had been reprieved by my delaying tactic.

But I couldn't let that happen: Correia getting her package of Assembly measures through would be just as bad for the paranormal community as the effect of losing me and Livia to the Blade.

I couldn't prove it, but as I thought it through, the edges of my vision seemed crowded again with the apocalypse of humanity at war with the paranormal.

I had a chance to derail Correia or delay her with my nomicane until help arrived. I didn't with the procedures item. I had no acknowledged expertise in the functioning of the Assembly's behind-the-scenes committees— Correia could steamroller me.

"Trust me," I said to Livia and ran up to interrupt the heated, whispered discussion on the podium.

"House Farrell?" Correia said. "What do you want?"

She was a political Athanate, and her expression was well controlled, but it didn't matter. I could see her aura. She'd have me executed without trial right at that moment if she thought she could get away with it.

As this was a private discussion and I wanted to rattle her cage again, I spoke in formal Athanate. Because I didn't want it to be completely private, I spoke louder than I needed to.

"I cite the requirement that a nomicane must not be unnecessarily delayed. Furthermore, putting aside correct procedure, it's also highly disrespectful to the office of the Blade."

"I judge it's a necessary delay," she snapped back.

"Then you must justify that delay to the meeting and explain why it's so urgent, *for the Assembly*, to debate your bureaucratic measures ahead of a nomicane."

She couldn't, and she knew it. A nomicane was about Blood and oaths and the Agiagraphos; it looked at the heart of what it meant to be Athanate. The Assembly loved nomicanes, or at least had a sick fascination for them. Her proposed measures were dust and dull talk in comparison. And the more attention she focused on why her organizational changes were supposed to be more important than a nomicane, the more she risked the Assembly seeing that they were really designed to shift the balance of power in her favor. Even the traditionalists might baulk.

Her eyes narrowed as she tried to see my reasoning. "You are aware it's *your* nomicane that is first?"

"Of course I am. And I'm ready to counter any charges. As for the second nomicane, House Altau is in talks with the government as we speak. Emergence is here, and the Agiagraphos has already been put aside to enable that to happen. There are no grounds for the charges against Houses in New York."

Correia was trapped. She could argue my dismissal of the second nomicane, but she couldn't refuse my demand for my nomicane to be heard before other business. By the time the Assembly got around to looking at her agenda items, the balance of delegates might have changed enough to sink her proposals. That would force her to delay her plans for another time, and she wouldn't be able to skew the vote by pulling this timing trick twice.

She had to be furious, but she kept her face calm and her voice level.

"Very well, we'll see whether the Assembly agrees with your defense. As they say in English, it's your funeral."

I'd prevented Correia's agenda, but I'd also made the presiding officer at my trial hate me even more. She had the power to halt a nomicane and call for a vote at any time. I'd have to keep ahead right from the start. Her change in power structures might be her real target, but even if all she got for her maneuvering was my death, it would still be a significant blow against Skylur, and would achieve part of the same aim.

I could see her reaching that conclusion and changing her focus to target me.

And with a sinking, slipping feeling, I got the sense that she believed she might get me executed swiftly enough to get back to her agenda before others arrived, as long as she dropped the second nomicane against the New York community.

Too late to back out now.

My heart rate and temperature were way up. Fear and fever combined to make me lightheaded, but there was only the way forward now. I was thirsty as well, and I wished I'd taken time to drink some water before we rushed in here.

It wasn't good. At all. I'd need to speak convincingly in front of the Assembly. They'd put some of my condition down to fear, but too much…

too much would lead to someone claiming my Athanate powers were breaking down and I must be going rogue.

We returned to our seats, and the delegates leaned forward, eager to find out what was happening.

Correia switched off the display behind her and cleared her throat before resuming in English.

"It has been argued we should return to the original first item before proceeding to the important items on the Assembly's structure and procedures. I am allowing it. House Tosun, currently operating as Head of Security for House Altau, has an issue about a member of that House which I judge serious enough to be examined in a nomicane. In the absence of House Altau himself, he has my permission to introduce it."

Livia stood up.

"Diakon Flavia?" Correia's tone managed to imply Livia was wasting everyone's time.

"House Tosun does not represent House Altau. In the absence of Skylur, I am the representative of House Altau."

"No question," Correia replied. "However, House Tosun is not claiming the Altau vote. He's currently Head of Security for Altau, and since we're in New York, Altau is hosting the Assembly, all of which makes him Head of Security for the Assembly, and therefore a temporary official of the Assembly. It's in this role he's raising an issue, even though he cannot vote on it."

Correia had anticipated that challenge. She'd done her background work, and her response was completely in accordance with the rules.

Livia had to sit down again.

"Thank you," I whispered to her. She'd tried.

Tosun was on his feet. He couldn't help but glance at us as if he expected to be interrupted again.

Good. Anything to put him off his stride.

It was important. The Assembly always claimed that decisions were taken purely on the strength of the evidence rather than the way it was presented. That was horse shit, of course. I'd seen Diakon Huang hold an entire room of delegates on the edge of their seats by the simple power of his voice. I'd been included that time. I couldn't do that the way Huang could, but neither could Tosun, and the more he got rattled, the less convincing he'd be.

Tosun also realized now that he had a fight rather than a railroad, and his 'ally' had tried to bail on him at the first hurdle. That wouldn't do his style much good either.

But all of that wasn't enough, yet, to change the outcome.

The Hidden Path delegates didn't need convincing about my charges. They'd vote to have me executed unless they could be challenged for ignoring evidence. The Panethus traditionalists were mixed. They might all regard me as an abomination, but many of them might grudgingly acknowledge I was a useful abomination, and I'd caught the attention of some by pointing out Correia's disrespectful attitude towards the Blade. That sort of thing counted with traditionalists.

My best strategy at the moment seemed to be to slow it down and hold out for some supporters to arrive. I'd keep Tosun's procedural mistakes in reserve.

The trouble was, Correia knew that. She'd also know that I would anger the delegates if I slowed things down too obviously. And if she thought they'd gotten angry enough, she'd call the vote.

It was going to be a deadly dance. I swallowed hard. My lips had dried out. I needed that drink of water, but there was no way to delay this.

Tosun started.

"As President Correia has stated, matters have come to my attention, and they are serious breaches of the Agiagraphos and Assembly directives. They involve House Farrell. You are all aware that House Farrell was very recently received into this community and was elevated with alarming swiftness to her current position. There is an argument that such a swift elevation was a mistake and her lack of awareness of her responsibilities might be argued as a mitigating factor. Regardless, in my position as Head of Security for the Assembly, I am required to report these matters for the deliberation of the Assembly, and I therefore declare a formal nomicane against House Farrell."

He paused. I wanted to interrupt straight away, put him off some more, but it was a delicate balance between arguing everything and angering the delegates by delaying the revelation of what these charges were.

As it was, I didn't need to.

The Heights stood up. "I am here as the observer representing the largest Were association, which is the League. Thank you for speaking in English, but to make any sense of this, you're going to have to explain Athanate words like nomicane, and the rules you're claiming that one of the League's primary alphas has broken."

Oh, good wolfy! Smart, smart wolfy.

Beside me, Livia quietly let out a relieved breath. Without either of us needing to do anything else, The Heights had just sunk Tosun in a mire of explanation that would take the whole day.

Tosun looked at Correia.

They both knew it was a delaying tactic, but he didn't know if their alliance still held.

It did.

"Please sit, Alpha Heights," she said, mangling his title. "As honorary delegates, you may only speak if you're asked to by a delegate. To answer your question, a *nomicane* is a legal trial by the Assembly. It's not practical for you to be briefed on the full detail of Athanate laws as we go, but I will ensure English translations of the relevant Agiagraphos and Assembly regulations are made available afterwards. Please continue, House Tosun, with due care about clarity, but with speed. We have a full agenda."

Damn!

She'd completely dismissed The Heights' delaying tactic.

She'd also pissed off the Were and Adepts by telling them they had no right to speak. Unfortunately, they couldn't vote either.

But… The Heights had reminded the Assembly I was also an alpha of the largest Were pack. I could feel the hint of a stirring behind me.

I'd take that for the moment. I'd have to.

Tosun restarted.

"To address the first of the issues regarding House Farrell," Tosun stepped forward and faced the auditorium. "Assembly law is a manifestation of Agiagraphos law, and the highest law of the Agiagraphos is for the Athanate community to remain hidden from humanity. We're receiving reports of actions taken by House Farrell in Texas, Mexico and Louisiana that break this law and show utter disregard for the directives of the Assembly."

Hinton was frowning. I guessed this wasn't what she was expecting to be raised first. That made two of us; I was expecting to be charged straight away with consorting with dangerous elements of the spirit world.

"During the course of a mere two days, militants associated with House Farrell slaughtered members of the packs in neighboring states of Mexico, including the destruction of a Were-owned business in Ciudad Juárez and culminating in a bombing of a ranch at Villa Ahumada, over two hours' drive from the border. There were massacres at both locations."

The Confederation Were stirred and passed comments among themselves, but Tosun hadn't got the attention of the Athanate delegates with that news.

He did with his next statement.

"These attacks were apparently launched from El Paso, the domain of House de Socorro, and it appears that, in circumstances yet to be clarified, both House de Socorro and Isabel Cuarón, Diakon de Socorro, died violently, at or around that time."

That got their attention.

Shit!

Now I understood. I didn't know how he'd found out what happened, but this was a masterful move by Tosun. If I defended myself and he asked the right questions, the truth would come out. The Truth Sensors would force it. I'd have to admit that I'd tried to help House de Socorro, at Isabel's insistence. He'd gone rogue and we should have killed him, according to the Agiagraphos. *Not* killing a rogue Athanate was an executable offence.

I wished I *had* killed de Socorro. The fact I hadn't was a wound on my heart, because Isabel would be alive if I had.

I couldn't say any of that without getting trapped.

"All of this: the violent, overt attacks in El Paso, and in Mexico, which is outside of your jurisdiction; and the questions over what happened with House de Socorro, demand explanation, House Farrell."

Correia looked at me.

If I spoke, Tosun would be able to question me. If I didn't, the Assembly would assume I was guilty. Correia would call a vote.

Shit, again.

Chapter 6

There *might be* a way out. Not one I'd planned. Not one I'd talked about. A risk. It could backfire completely.

I stood and forced a cold smile in response to the look of eagerness in Tosun's eyes. I felt anything but confident, but I couldn't let that show. The delegates would zero in on that like sharks sensing blood in the sea.

"As the president of the Assembly has pointed out, you're *acting* Head of Security for House Altau, only appointed in the last week, so there is an argument that your ignorance of House Altau operations is a mitigating factor."

Correia interrupted me. "House Tosun is not facing a nomicane, House Farrell."

"No, but by raising a nomicane against me, he exposes himself to retaliatory justice. Section 5 of the nomicane regulations. The Blade may yet have business today."

Tosun flinched, and there was a satisfying, shocked silence in the auditorium.

I went on: "I have made my Blood oath to House Altau, and my actions in El Paso and Mexico were approved by him."

Not a lie. Approved after the event, but still. The Truth Sensors watching me didn't blink.

"If Altau were here to brief you, you'd be congratulating me." I let that sink in a moment, but Tosun was starting to speak, so I rushed on. "I get it; this meeting wants to hear that report from someone else."

Outside of my House there were two people who knew what had gone on. Livia was one. The trouble was, she knew too much, and the Truth Sensors were listening. Tosun could ask her questions which would end up incriminating me if she answered them.

But there was someone else who knew what had happened. Someone I *hoped* didn't know everything and therefore couldn't be caught lying.

"I call on The Heights to provide a summary of my actions—"

Tosun tried to stop me, claiming it wasn't appropriate, and I turned on him.

"I remind you, House Tosun, *acting* Head of Security for the Assembly, that I am the syndesmon to the Were, a *permanently* appointed official of the Assembly. And my actions may represent the Assembly *or* the Were community."

"Not representing us," someone from the Confederation called out.

I appealed to the president, and she had to remind them that they could only speak when asked. She didn't enjoy it, and neither did they. I did.

She took her revenge by reminding me that she was the person to decide if retaliatory justice was applicable, and in this case, she judged it wasn't. But then she had to hand over to The Heights, since she couldn't deny I was allowed to call him.

I sat down. This was a *huge* risk. The Heights wasn't a veteran of Athanate meetings. He didn't understand the convoluted details of Assembly law. I had to go to him. He *was* a smooth operator, and he was aware that there were Truth Sensors listening.

I was out of other options anyway.

I felt lightheaded. Visions of failure seemed to press in on me, and my hands began to shake. I hid them under my thighs and bit my tongue.

The Heights stepped down to face the delegates. He didn't pad it out. "House Farrell was acting in her capacities as co-alpha of the Denver pack, co-alpha of the El Paso pack, agent of the League with respect to the amalgamation of Colorado and New Mexico packs, *and* syndesmon between the League and the Assembly. She has the complete support of Felix Larimer and Cameron Zerenegus, the co-alphas of the League, a union of packs which covers the majority of Were in North America."

The Confederation *hated* that, but it was the truth.

The Heights had made a damn good start, and as he built on it, my heart rate slowly eased.

"As well as endorsing Amber Farrell's actions, I also need to correct the implications made by House Tosun, out of his lack of knowledge. Firstly, the precipitating action was an attack *by* the Ciudad Juárez pack *on* the El Paso pack, *in* El Paso, which was intended to assassinate League alphas Alex Deauville, Amber Farrell and Zane Quivira. That would have left the packs from New Mexico and Colorado leaderless. The League suspects that the raid was a preliminary move prior to a widespread invasion of Were packs into the southern states. The retaliatory attacks by the El Paso pack, supported by House Farrell, and by the Colorado and New Mexico packs, were essential. The Mexico packs which were hit were not only actively hostile to the League, but also allied with Matlal and Basilikos, and therefore hostile to the Assembly. I believe this Assembly approves of action against Matlal and Basilikos."

The Heights didn't wait for a response. "I'm also going to emphasize the fact that the packs in Mexico had no regard for your laws regarding secrecy. In Mexico, they bribed and intimidated everyone into avoiding them. That solution wouldn't have worked in this country if they'd been successful in crossing the border. Eliminating them was completely in keeping with the Assembly directives, as I understand them."

Tosun was looking at the Truth Sensors, who hadn't moved. The Heights stared at Tosun until he turned back. Only then did he continue.

"I don't know whether the Assembly will accept 'clarification' from me of the Athanate side of what happened in Texas, but the El Paso pack was informed that Isabel Cuarón died by her own hand in korheny to try and prevent House de Socorro from killing all his House members, and that House de Socorro himself was eliminated on Altau's orders because he had clearly gone crazy and was unfit to manage the Athanate domain of El Paso."

That rippled through the Assembly, but The Heights carried straight on.

"As for Louisiana, I can't tell you much, because my alphas are still considering the impact of what was discovered and what we need to do about it. I can confirm that there was a pack leadership challenge which was intended to kill Felix Larimer and Cameron Zerenegus. As there were three challengers, Amber Farrell took part with them, at risk to her own life. When that challenge was defeated, the rival pack then attempted to kill our alphas outside of the rules of challenge. With the help of House Farrell, that was also defeated. Given that those attacking packs were, like the Mexican packs, allies of Matlal, this Assembly should be in no doubt that House Farrell was operating in your interests. As you can imagine, the League completely endorses all of Amber Farrell's actions in Louisiana."

And right *there*, he skated close to the edge of truth. Felix and Cameron couldn't endorse anything that didn't relate specifically to the Were.

I saw delegates looking at the Truth Sensors, but neither of them gave any indication that The Height's speech had been anything but truthful. He hadn't *lied*, but he'd omitted all the details which were legally dangerous to me.

Clever, clever wolfy.

I could feel the mood of the delegates behind me. There was nothing in what had been said that the Assembly would convict me on, and the delegates were becoming impatient with Tosun. They'd be interested to hear more about what happened, of course, but not from someone like Tosun who clearly didn't know the details.

It wasn't a matter for a nomicane. Correia and Tosun would have to move on without further questions on this one, and I could see they knew it.

I let out a long-held breath and sat back in my seat.

Round one to me.

Correia wrapped the first section up and didn't call a vote. Not a surprise, but she didn't let me off completely.

"This item appears to be insufficient to warrant further investigation at this time," she said. "I would note that, although House Farrell's opening remarks criticized the Assembly for failing to progress the acceptance of the Were into the Assembly, *she* is the reason the Central Mountain Confederation is hesitating to join the Assembly. Despite her position as the Assembly's intermediary to all Were, she has openly allied herself with the group opposing the Confederation, the League, even accepting positions within the League hierarchy, and so created insurmountable obstacles to the Assembly's stated aims of *all* paranormal inclusion."

There were sub-vocal growls from the Confederation wolves.

True, and potentially damaging to me as syndesmon, but the Assembly weren't going to execute me for that. It was time for round two. The round that Hinton was impatiently waiting for.

Correia segued into it. "In a similar way, House Farrell is to blame for the difficulty in coming to an arrangement to include the Adepts. With her interactions with the Were community, House Farrell has an excuse that she has chosen the largest grouping of packs to become involved with. In her position of syndesmon, she can claim Assembly authority for what she does. That's not the case elsewhere, and she has intentionally broken the rules of the only acknowledged Adapt community, the Northern League of Adepts. She has taken dangerous and unregulated outlaw shamans into her own House. In fact, I see one of these shamans present, which is a calculated insult to Hecate Hinton, the representative of the Northern League."

Flint smiled brightly as heads turned to look at him.

He was putting on a brave face. I could feel him tiring and I had no attention to spare to help him maintain the shield against Tezcatlipoca.

"That insult is barely the start of her transgressions against the interests of the Assembly and the Adept community."

Correia had breached the rule for the presiding officer in a nomicane to remain unbiased, but I didn't think it was worth interrupting yet. If I called her on it, she'd issue a retraction and we'd proceed in under a couple of minutes. Better to wait.

She gestured for House Tosun to take the floor again.

Tosun first attempt to pin a breach of the Agiagraphos on me been a reach. A *cunning* reach, if he'd managed to get me answering questions about El Paso and de Socorro, but it'd been too complicated and nuanced. There wasn't any nuance in the next issue. Tosun was going to talk about the spirit world now, and there was no dodging this. I was Tezcatlipoca's priestess, and I had used his powers, and I had no authority to do anything like that from the Assembly or any Adept organization. *And* it was a horrendous risk.

"I'm not going to go into the complex theories of whether the Athanate and Were are magical creatures or users of magic…" Tosun began.

"Thank heavens for small mercies," muttered someone behind, and there were some smirks in the audience. Maybe I had a few more friends after round one. Not enough yet.

"…but I will distinguish between the Adepts and the rest of us. The Adepts deal with the essential force that makes us all possible. Given this, the regulation of the Adepts is even stricter than the regulation of Were and Athanate, and rightly so. For untrained or unregulated users of magic to dabble is extremely dangerous. The Athanate and Were communities, across all political divides, do not allow rogues to live. The Adept community take this responsibility as well, and yet feel themselves constrained now, when those they must regulate shelter under the protection of other communities."

"My colleagues, we all know the Assembly is the very heart of the Athanate community, and I realize that many of you resist the integration of others. But integrate we must. The concerns of the Adept community must be our concerns. Their regulations must become ours. For details, I call on Hecate Hinton."

Theoretically, there could have been a possible objection to allowing Hinton to speak in this unrestricted way, given she was an observer and only an honorary delegate, but I'd called on The Heights. I couldn't play technicalities to dig my way out of this confrontation.

Round 2.

Chapter 7

Hinton walked down to stand at the center of the floor, in front of the podium. Whether it was deliberate or not, she and Correia had chosen similar styles today. Dark, professional business suits. Gold jewelry. Minimal makeup. Black hair, shoulder length, cut and expensively styled to frame their faces like raven wings.

Unlike Correia, Hinton's jewelry had workings woven into it. I was obviously becoming an experienced observer of spells because they felt untidy, inefficient. They were mild, *trust-me* kinds of spell, much like an Athanate might put out pheromones in a meeting.

Interesting, but not important.

Now she was on show, Hinton was as self-controlled as Correia was.

"Thank you for allowing me to speak at this important point," she said quietly, standing with her hands clasped together in front of her.

My skin prickled and the hair on the back of my neck rose. She was forming a working. She was powerful, even if it seemed tightly controlled.

Flint and I tensed, but the magic wasn't directed at us.

She parted her hands; soft lights floated upwards throughout the auditorium.

"My blessing on this meeting," she murmured. "My apologies for the demonstration, but I need to emphasize the point that House Tosun was making. Magic is what makes the paranormal different from humanity. Magic is what binds us together. Magic means that this Assembly must work, and it must work for all of us, together, or it won't work at all. And magic... practiced, conscious, deliberate, *controlled* use of the raw form of magic... that's the domain of the Adepts."

She'd set the scene and pulled them all in. There was a quality to the watchfulness I felt all around. *All* around: even the Confederation were hanging on her words.

Good for the Assembly, I guessed. Bad for me.

Something about what she'd said didn't quite ring true, but I had no time to think about it as she continued.

"The Heights made House Farrell sound quite the heroine, and with some justification. Yes, she *did* beat back those packs, and they *were* allied with Matlal. She has immense skills in that area, and she achieved remarkable victories."

I had a feeling calling me a heroine was just preparation for tripping me up.

"But it didn't end with the packs, because behind those packs was a completely different type of enemy, also an ally of Matlal. An Adept. Possibly the most powerful Adept in the world. One who calls herself the Queen of Diamonds. Bravery is admirable, but for a woman lacking any formal magical training, to challenge the Queen of Diamonds was foolish.

"I knew nothing of it until I heard that an Adept, Gabrielle Desmarais, visiting Louisiana for the purposes of the Northern League, was kidnapped by the Queen of Diamonds. House Farrell entered the spirit world to rescue Gabrielle. As I say, brave but foolish. I had to work swiftly with the local coven to extract House Farrell and Gabrielle from the clutches of the Queen of Diamonds."

Flint snorted loudly.

No, not the way it happened at all. But the Assembly won't care.

"Did I extract them swiftly enough? I hoped so, at the time."

She gestured, raising her hands, palm up, and everyone watching knew she meant she hadn't been in time.

"The spirit world is the most dangerous place," she said. "A place where the raw power of magic comes from. A place of uncontrolled forces and malevolent entities. I know that, as we progress in our future partnership, we will need to reveal what we know about the spirit world and how magic works to the whole of the paranormal community. For this meeting, I'll simply say that we refer to those malevolent entities as Lost Gods, and it's sufficient to regard them as the god-like beings their name suggests. The only thing that protects us from the Lost Gods is that they can only enter the physical world through us, and only through some of us. Any visitor to the spirit world is in danger for themselves, but *we* are in danger from those individuals who have the potential to channel the power necessary to allow a Lost God to enter the physical world."

She paused, and I could feel the slow heartbeat of the auditorium and the intensity of their focus on her words.

"The Northern League allows only the most senior Adepts to venture into the spirit world," she said, "and then, only with backup. House Farrell went alone."

She was wrong again, but I wasn't going to tell the Assembly that Mirela was with me and open that can of worms. Not yet.

"Exceptional Adepts, such as the Queen of Diamonds may carve out a sanctuary within the spirit world, but it is their sanctuary and every bit as dangerous to others as the rest of the spirit world. I wouldn't go there alone. I think Farrell stood no chance. I'm not relying only on my knowledge of the spirit world for that assessment, but on what she said when we got her and Gabrielle back. Two things, in fact. Firstly, she admitted that Gabrielle had been placed under a compulsion by the Queen of Diamonds. I believe the Assembly has seen that sort of abominable mind control before."

I felt the revulsion sweep down through the delegates. Hinton let it gather and waited for the right moment before she spoke again.

"What about Farrell herself? She presented herself as having escaped and said she was seeking help for Gabrielle. She *seemed* to be acting on her own initiative, but these things can be subtle. As you know, it's not always obvious that a person is under compulsion, as the Assembly found with Judicator Remy.

"But it was the second comment she made that truly raised my suspicions. She claimed she had 'damaged' the Queen of Diamonds and needed to put an end to her. The way she said she would do this was to channel the power of the massed ranks of Were which she had gathered in Louisiana through the League. An untrained Adept conducting an unregulated working with the least governable of the paranormal community."

Some of the Were growled quietly, but Hinton ignored it and shook her head.

"And as I started to question Farrell about this, her House attacked us."

She took a couple of paces, head down, seemingly in thought, and then stopped.

"I am the Hecate of the Northern League," she said, frowning. "I am strong. And I was knocked out," she snapped her fingers, "like that."

"There are questions House Farrell must answer, under the conditions we have here," she indicated the Truth Sensors, and started to count items off on her fingers. "Why am I not allowed to see Gabrielle to check she is indeed 'recovered' from this compulsion? Why has Hecate Gwendolyn Enkeliekki split from the Northern League and why does she refuse to meet with me? Who knocked me out in Louisiana and how? Where did the strength to do that come from? What has happened to the Queen of Diamonds and how was that achieved?"

She stopped, right in front of me and turned to face me. I felt the gathering of her powers. Not hers alone, but the coven she'd brought with her as well.

"What these questions come down to, at the end is this: is Amber Farrell under the control of the Queen of Diamonds? Or worse, in seeking to eliminate one threat, has she enabled a far more dangerous one? Did she make a deal with entities in the spirit world to defeat an Adept who was far stronger than her? This Assembly cannot allow either of those possibilities.

And if neither is the case, it remains that she is a dangerous, untrained, unregulated user of magic. The Adepts cannot allow unregulated users of magic to exist, in the same way the Athanate cannot allow unregulated Athanate to exist, and even the Were regulate their communities. If this Assembly is to include the Adept community, then to be blunt, our regulations must be part of the Assembly regulations, and the Assembly must deal with Farrell. Or the Northern League will."

A tingling in my hand warned me I was gripping the sheath of my katana so tightly the blood had stopped circulating.

Hinton's wall of power loomed behind her, visible to my spirit senses. She was formidably strong, almost as strong as Gwen. The masking spell we were using against Tezcatlipoca wouldn't keep her out. Not that my shield wasn't strong, but it was tuned to Tezcatlipoca. If she attacked, I'd be overwhelmed.

Unless I call on Tezcatlipoca.

Then nothing she could do would touch me ever again.

But her display of power remained just that—a display for those with spirit senses. Maybe half the Athanate and Were shuffled in their seats, aware of *something* in the chamber.

She turned away.

She'd made an effective call for my execution. She'd made it eloquently, with well-judged drama. And she'd taken the Assembly with her.

I was staring down the gun-barrel.

Correia sensed it. She had to allow me to speak, but unless I defused Hinton's claims, Correia would call the vote immediately after, and it would go against me.

I had arguments against Tosun's procedures and Correia's management of the nomicane, but I couldn't use them now. The Assembly would ignore them in favor of the greater issue.

Even as I thought it through, my heart sank. Hinton had a case. The threat from the Lost Gods was worse than the appalling war that a badly managed Emergence would cause.

Not your focus, Tara whispered in my mind. *Executing you might protect the world from Tezcatlipoca, but you're the only one that can prevent Matlal bringing Quetzalcoatl through.*

I had to defeat Hinton, but I couldn't do it in a way that caused the Adepts to withdraw from the Assembly. The result of that was there would be a war between humanity and the paranormals. *That* pressed on the edges of my vision again.

In the ringing silence after she returned to her seat, I had to say *something*. Silence would be an admission of guilt.

I'd anticipated being asked about my connection with the spirit world, of course. I hadn't anticipated that it would come directly from Hinton, who wasn't even a delegate. It only confirmed my guess that Hinton had put a compulsion on Tosun to hand over a major part of his nomicane to her. But because she had, she'd tangled Adept matters with Athanate matters.

I couldn't let that pass. I had to separate Adept issues from Assembly issues without breaking the connection altogether. I had to save myself *and* Emergence, and I was going to have to make it up as I went.

Think! Think!

I stood up. "I can answer all the questions that have been raised, in an appropriate manner, and I'm certainly not under any compulsion, or even an influence."

I looked at the Truth Sensors, and… they shifted in their seats.

"As mentioned by the Hecate, previous experience with Judicator Remy shows we are unable to be certain with that type of compulsion." They looked at each other. "We can say you do not *appear* to be under compulsion, nor any unusual degree of influence."

Shit.

Of course they had to say that. But all the nomicane procedure needed was a seed of suspicion. The Assembly laws didn't require delegates to be convinced beyond doubt. At the moment, if Correia called a vote now, I would lose.

I moved, walking slowly in front of the podium, trying to shake off the feeling of falling behind. If this were a physical fight, maybe I'd throw a couple of punches as a test, give myself some breathing space, gauge how my opponent was reacting. But this wasn't one opponent, it was the whole room, and all I had to monitor how I was doing was my gut feel and the amount that the poison-triggered, apocalyptic spirit vision seemed to press in on me.

My body felt so weak, and that vision was like darkness gathered in the sides of my eyes.

Have to try something. Anything.

On the far side of the podium, a clerk sat. Originally, the role had been to record events and provide access to the official copies of the Agiagraphos and Assembly rules. Recording and access was done electronically these days, but tradition demanded the clerk write notes and keep reference copies of the books on his desk.

Ahh. Cogs started connecting in my head. Tradition. Rules. I had to disentangle the web of connections Hinton had made and address them separately, using *rules*.

I pulled the weighty book of Assembly rules to the front of the desk and flipped the leather-bound cover open.

"House Farrell?" Correia's icy tone rang out. "What are you doing?"

"Just looking for the sections of the Assembly rules that deal with the use of magic and visiting the spirit world. Because we work *literally* by the book in the Assembly, don't we?"

I turned back to face the auditorium. I was a lousy Adept, but I could channel a little power from Flint. Enough power to run a working which kept the book's pages flipping over, one by one, as I walked away.

"Yes, I am an Adept, in addition to all the other complications I present to this Assembly." I forced a smile and got a scattering of thin-lipped responses. "A hybrid Athanate-Were-Adept. And do you know, there's nothing in the Assembly rules that says you can't be a hybrid. The Agiagraphos calls me an abomination, but that's not because it has anything against the idea of being hybrid, but because the challenges of being part of two paranormal communities can cause the hybrid to go rogue.

"But I've dealt with that before, haven't I? I've had to prove my stability as an Athanate in front of the Assembly and as a Were in front of the shifter community. Now Hecate Hinton is saying I have to do it for the Adept community."

"That is not the entirety of the Hecate's position," Tosun said. "And this is a procedure of the Assembly."

"No, you're right, House Tosun. I have a lot to answer, including the assertions and insinuations made by President Correia, you and Hecate Hinton. I'll deal with them in the way that makes most sense for the Assembly and addresses your nomicane."

He sat back down and went quiet.

"The Queen of Diamonds was a threat to the Assembly, and she was the source of the undetectable compulsions which Matlal used against us. She is no longer a threat. I dealt with her. It was my duty to the Assembly and to the paranormal community."

I gestured to the Truth Sensors. There was a stirring in the auditorium, delegates leaning forward to see the slightest twitch by the Adepts indicating there was anything false in what I said.

Nothing.

Of course, some of them would rationalize it, whispering to their companions that I could be compelled to believe what I said was the truth. I had a long way to go.

"The kidnapped Adept, Gabrielle Desmarais, *was* under a compulsion, but is now safe and recovering under the care of Gwendolyn Enkeliekki, who is the new Hecate of the Denver coven. Gabrielle has left the Northern League and joined the Denver coven. She is no longer any responsibility of Hecate Hinton. And if Hecate Hinton needs to meet Hecate Enkeliekki, they should speak and arrange it between them. I am only a member of the Denver coven, and my Hecate does not defer to me on Adept protocols, so I can't answer questions as to why they haven't spoken. While I'm dealing with the matters raised about Adepts; there is no single, universally acknowledged Adept community, certainly not from within the Adept community itself. For President Correia to state that any one Adept community is unfit because another says so, or that the rules of inclusion in the Denver coven are an insult to any other community, is misleading. And potentially biasing, if those matters were included in the nomicane, which they should not be."

Correia looked daggers at me, but there were some nods of confirmation in the auditorium. I turned to look at the pages still flicking over behind me.

"I'm not having any luck finding anything in the reference book that says it's against Assembly rules for Athanate to visit the spirit world."

It was theater, of course. I wasn't reading the book magically, but I knew there was nothing in the rules. I was carving the case against me into slices. The nomicane had to be about Assembly rules and the interests of the Athanate, as defined in the Agiagraphos. The Adept rules had to be settled separately. Splitting those without damaging the potential of a full Assembly of all paranormals was a problem I was rushing towards without the benefit of planning.

"As for anything magical to do with the Assembly being regulated by the Northern League," I said, and frowned as I walked slowly toward the section where the Adepts sat. "The Assembly has always had Truth Sensors in attendance. At the last one in Denver, for instance, the team included Adept Alice Emerson."

I stopped in front of Hinton as if something had just occurred to me.

I turned to her. "Was Adept Emerson regulated by the Northern League when she attended the Denver Assembly?"

"No, but—"

"No. The answer is 'no', Hecate. Adept Emerson, and the other Adepts that the Assembly have used for Truth Sensors have *not* been associates of the Northern League, even if those attending today are. In fact, Adept Emerson's status with the Northern League is similar to mine with some members of this Assembly—she's an 'abomination' in your eyes. She has extended her life through being kin to the Athanate and she regularly changes her appearance, both of which break your rules. She is an outcast; in the same way my shaman and I are."

Hinton tried to break in, but I rode over her.

"Flint over there, and his friend Kane, Alice, Gabrielle, me... we're all members of the Denver coven, and we're governed and regulated by Gwendolyn Enkeliekki, former Hecate of the Northern League. One Hecate's leadership and regulation might be better than another's, but it's not something this Assembly can decide on. Whether I'm regulated and whether that regulation is sufficient isn't part of this nomicane."

Tosun was looking as if he'd argue, but he'd have to wait.

At the other end of the podium, the book of Assembly rules slammed shut.

"There is *nothing* in the rules that says the Assembly governs the way Adepts handle their business, and that means, *by the book*, there is *nothing* about my status in the Adept community that is relevant to this nomicane."

I'd got through to some of the delegates. It wasn't a strong defense, casting reasonable doubt on some of what Hinton had said, and implying that doubt made the other things she'd said less convincing.

A vote would be too close to call, at the moment.

I had to push back on Correia as well, and as I thought about it, I realized that strengthened the point I was trying to reach.

"President Correia has made allegations about my duty as syndesmon. She says I'm the reason the Confederation might not join the Assembly. She claims I'm biased against them. She's either ignoring the facts of what has happened, or she's showing her ignorance of Were community politics."

Tosun stood up again. "You're avoiding the questions the Hecate has asked."

"The nomicane rules say that I'm entitled to answer all issues raised against me. There is nothing in those rules which say which order I need to address them. It *does* say that unjustified and unnecessary interruptions should count against the person making the interruptions."

Tosun sat back down, scowling.

"The facts of the matter are that the Confederation chose to attempt to invade the territory of my pack and got beaten back. For the Athanate

Houses here; imagine a Were alpha telling you that it's your fault you're not getting on with a neighboring House that had invaded your domain, and you'll have my perspective on President Correia's comments."

"Despite that, I have continued to offer access to my halfy ritual to individual Were within the Confederation territory. And despite what the Hecate implied, that ritual requires only the magical power of the Were present. It does not require more power from the spirit world as she suggested."

I paused to let Hinton look at the Truth Sensors, and for everyone else to see that I wasn't lying.

"On a last point regarding my attitude to the Confederation, one which is relevant to the Assembly; would one of the Confederation's delegates stand up and declare that their invasion of New Mexico and Colorado was *not* planned in cooperation with an Athanate House they knew were Basilikos?"

The Confederation delegates glared, but they knew enough to realize they wouldn't be able to lie about that in front of the Truth Sensors.

Everyone saw they didn't take my offer.

I spared a moment's attention for Flint. He had to be tired, running the shield against Tezcatlipoca by himself. But he wasn't. He'd somehow managed to reach out to Ash. I could feel the Irish soultree's cool power flowing into us, supporting us.

Which gave me another option. Another *unplanned, dangerous* option.

"By definition, this nomicane is restricted to Assembly rules and Agiagraphos laws. There is nothing in the issues raised that is against those rules. There is a general exclusion; for matters which threaten the Athanate community as a whole. If I were to provide a channel for a Lost God to enter the physical world, that would count. But the competence to assess that isn't one the current Assembly has."

As I said it, I realized I'd argued myself into a corner. I'd followed the logic, and I'd arrived at this point: I had to convince Hinton that I was trustworthy. She was giving every indication that she'd developed a serious distrust for me, and I could *feel* the balance of the delegates behind me. It was against me. Without her withdrawing her opposition, the vote would definitely be to execute me.

I wasn't in the best shape to do anything, but at least the Athanate elethesine and human adrenaline coursing through my Blood seemed to be holding off the fever; so much so that I felt cold. My focus was painfully bright and clear.

No other help was coming in time to change the balance of the vote that Correia was itching to call as soon as I finished speaking.

And there was no option for a delay in a nomicane.

Which left me the one, very dangerous path forward.

I spoke directly to Hinton.

"I believe we actually want the same thing—an Assembly of all the paranormal people, with three different processes for internal resolution: one for Athanate, one for Were and one for Adepts, each using their own regulations. We've got to convince this Assembly. Together. Right now. I've got to persuade you to trust me in a hurry."

And then I opened a substantiation around us, pulling on Ash's power.

Chapter 8

It was a shallow substantiation. Barely skimming the spirit world. Keeping well away from Tezcatlipoca and anything else from the City of Lost Gods.

It was so shallow, we'd still be visible to the Assembly, but the time differential would make it impossible for them to hear what we said, if Ash's power had let me set that up.

It seems it had.

I could see the room around us, not quite frozen in the moment, but time passing so slowly there it seemed like it.

Hinton was glaring at me.

"What do you think you're doing?" she hissed at me.

But behind the portrayal of outrage, there was a calm, ordered mind. I had to put aside my unconscious evaluation of her, thinking that she was the same woman as the image she projected. She appeared to be a rich, shallow New Yorker, and a petty, vindictive woman who hated me because she'd been made to look weak in front of the Lafayette coven last time we'd met.

I had gambled she wasn't, based on what Gwen had said about her, based on whatever I could read of her beneath the surface.

And here, in my substantiation, I could read her much better.

She was *strong*.

She was an extremely clever and powerful Adept, and since she was that clever, I didn't need to answer her question. Instead, I watched her carefully, noting the changes in her aura as she examined my trap.

Ash had produced a substantiation just big enough for the two of us, and shaped like an egg. The edges were visible as a pale shadow, a weave of leaves and branches, but we could see the auditorium beyond the barrier.

It didn't feel like something that one of the Lost Gods would have created, and I could see that awareness rising in Hinton's aura, displacing the fear. Because she *had* been afraid. I'd caught her off guard, separated her from her coven and she was in my substantiation.

She *could* have been at my mercy. She could have been in the damned Temple of Night as an offering to Tezcatlipoca.

But I hadn't done that. This was a neutral substantiation, and she was a stronger Adept than I was. I wasn't entirely at her mercy either, but only because I could close the substantiation and return to the physical world.

I saw her awareness of all these facts flicker across her aura and reflect on her face.

On top of that, I might not be as powerful as her, but I was stronger than she'd thought, and I had powerful friends like Ash. Friends who were clearly *not* Lost Gods. And without the fever in my Blood, I would have been even stronger.

I saw those thoughts in her aura and expression as well, just before she saw me watching and she abruptly took on an unnatural calmness. Her eyes became dark and hooded as deep wells. Her aura seemed to sink back into her skin and become much less readable. All I was left with was my standard sense with wolfy add-ons, which told me she was recovered from her shock and becoming confident again.

She was a *lot* scarier like this.

"This is cozy," she said. "Since it's just the two of us, and we've been underestimating each other, we should probably get on first name terms."

Trap. That was Tara.

Just psychology 101, making the opponent realize you're a person, I thought back.

Yeah, but don't let your guard down because she seems nicer all of a sudden.

Tara talking to me was somehow visible to the Hecate. I caught a flicker of surprise as she saw a glimpse of what my spirit guide was. Not a full reading, just enough to tell Tara and Hana weren't from any of the usual set. Her aura recovered quickly, too quickly for me to get a look at what her spirit guide was.

"I'm fine with that, Faith," I said.

Psychology 101 worked for me as well. I wasn't here to fight her. I wouldn't have said I wanted us to be friends, but to get her to see my position and withdraw her claims, I was going to have to get her to trust me. Without letting her too far inside my defenses.

Oh Lord, give me an opponent with guns or swords, every time.

"So... Amber. We need a sidebar, apparently," she said. "Let's talk."

"A sidebar involves the judge," I replied. "And nothing I can say will move this judge from her position, which is to find me guilty, regardless of the facts."

She huffed, without indicating she agreed or not. Then frowned.

"You're running a fever," she said. "Surely Athanate..."

"Normally, yes. This is the result of an Athanate-specific poison the Queen of Diamonds infected me with when I fought her. It'll pass. We don't have time to discuss it."

She gestured for me to go on.

"We're walking a tightrope between two apocalyptic threats," I said. "On the one hand, Emergence needs a body that represents as many of the paranormals as we can rope together, because if we don't have that, factions will divide us and it'll end in a war between everybody, including the humans. The Assembly is the only body that could possibly hold us together. If it doesn't, Emergence will be a disaster for the whole world."

A tiny tilt of her head. Maybe agreement.

"And on the other hand?" she said.

"A worse scenario. The Lost Gods return to the physical world."

"Forcing the various paranormal factions into the Assembly is beyond anything I can influence," she said. "However, I might be able to prevent a Lost God from returning by eliminating the channel he needs to use."

I snorted. *Yeah, by killing me. Psychology 101 needs more work.*

"That's an example of half the truth being more dangerous than the whole."

"So give me the whole, Amber."

Her aura swelled back out. I met it with my own, but I wasn't inviting her to merge auras. I kept mine as impenetrable as I could while still sensing hers. Not easy. I couldn't have managed it without Tara, but it meant that we both got a good look at the other's spirit guides.

Faith Hinton's was a bear. Not a cuddly bear, a damned Kodiak.

Her aura wasn't attacking me, but it wasn't friendly either. She wanted to read me, all the way down. Which would mean she found out about everything, my Blood magic, Kaothos, Tezcatlipoca—*everything*. I wasn't prepared to let her. An invasion that deep would leave me vulnerable to a compulsion. Hinton didn't seem as bad as I had thought, but I did *not* trust her with that much power over me.

Her eyes glittered. She hadn't expected me to be strong enough to prevent her digging into my aura. And sure as hell, she hadn't imagined I'd have a fire-wolf spirit guide.

While she was processing that, I tried words again.

"If I really had a Lost God on tap," I said, "do you think I'd be here, trying to fix the Assembly?"

"There I was, thinking you were here trying to dismiss your nomicane."

I smiled. *Psychology 102, use humor.*

"It's all part of one strategy," I replied. "If the nomicane goes against me, then Altau is damaged. He's the only person who can gets this Assembly into shape, and he can't if he's fighting Panethus leadership challenges because the person who he has favored is executed."

"Altau isn't even president," she said. "What's more, I'll tell you something for free: Correia is trying to snatch him back from the negotiations, on the basis that she hasn't authorized it."

"Too late."

"Maybe. Don't trust her."

There wasn't any chance of that, and offering me advice like that was just another trick to see if I weakened my defenses at all.

Nope.

Our auras weren't really fighting. It was more like sumo practice. Posturing and pushing, looking for a weakness. Bouncing off each other. But I had no doubt if she saw a weakness, it wouldn't be a practice session any more.

She was smart enough to realize that my defense to an all-out attack would be to close the substantiation. We'd be back in the auditorium. That meant she saw a benefit to staying here and coming to some kind of compromise.

Either that or trick me when my defenses weakened.

"Okay, so no whole truths the easy way," she said. "Let's take this one little truth at a time then. Why do we have to hide what you might say to me from the Assembly?"

It was a fair question. I didn't want to talk about Tezcatlipoca, but maybe I could reveal other information that the Assembly shouldn't know.

"Both Diana and Kaothos are alive. The deaths at the end of the LA Assembly were faked." I crossed my fingers and hoped Kaothos would be okay with this. "It was Kaothos' power that overwhelmed you in Louisiana, but only in my defense. You'll have access to Kaothos if you help me here."

She snorted. "You're going to have to break the news about Kaothos at some stage anyway."

"Yeah. That's for Skylur and Diana to manage. Drop it on the Assembly now, and we risk the Empire of Heaven pulling out. That's just another way that the Assembly falls apart."

"I can see that, but it's not enough. As I've said, the Assembly isn't my primary concern." She pulled back her aura a little. "You're dodging what *is* my concern. You implied you don't have a Lost God on tap, but what about, let's see... what about a *connection* to a Lost God?"

Clever bitch. Her aura had snapped back as she spoke, trying to dig beneath the shield of my aura and gauge my response. But I was expecting these questions, I was expecting her attack, and my aura held. Just.

"Your concern is barking up the wrong tree," I said. "All the shit going down with the City of Lost Gods? That's not me. That's because Matlal is channeling Quetzalcoatl."

She flinched as if I'd poked her with a stick.

Oh, yes. She knows all about Quetzalcoatl and Tezcatlipoca.

Now my aura pushed at hers, and felt it give, but only so far.

Still, I learned something about her technique.

"Matlal's good at this," I said, while I used what I'd learned to improve my shield, "but there'll come a point where he slips up and Quetzalcoatl will just burst through. *Then* we'll have a Lost God back in the physical world."

"*If* what you're saying is true, and I can't tell that with your aura keeping me out. Come on, you're a solutions sort of person, what's your solution to this?"

"You're the Hecate, the leader of the largest group of Adepts. You're more powerful than I am. More knowledgeable, too. What's *your* solution, Faith, if it's Matlal you're after and not me?"

A small smile slipped across her face. "Flattery won't lower my aura defenses."

Neither will your display of a sense of humor lower mine. I didn't say that aloud. I was finding I liked her a lot more, now I saw past the image she projected, but I wasn't going to lower my guard.

"If it's Matlal, then clearly I have to go after him," she said. "It's my duty and he would be the vulnerable point."

"Yeah, right up until he thinks he's got nothing more to lose and calls Quetzalcoatl through. But you'd never get near him anyway," I said. "He's based down in Yucatán, and he's surrounded by defenses in the physical world. It's not your style to fight through those, but if you try and sneak through in the spirit world, you can bet you'll run into Quetzalcoatl's defenses. You'll never make it through that way either."

More things fell into place.

"Now I think of it," I said, "that's why the Lost City has become bound to the physical world. It's so Quetzalcoatl can protect Matlal."

"And be ready to come across in an instant," she added.

But my jibe that she wouldn't have enough power in the spirit world had gotten under her skin. Her aura felt a bit looser. Just a little less concentration being spent to keep it impenetrable.

"The force of the coven combined—"

She stopped when I smiled.

"What are you smiling at?"

"So it's okay for *you* to wield power that would be equivalent to Quetzalcoatl," I said, "but not me. Don't you agree, it's not the power, it's the responsibility and restraint shown by whoever's using it?"

"No." I could feel her barriers slam back down. "It's both the source and the safeguards," she said. "But even though you've avoided telling me your 'solution', you've revealed it with your questions. You *do* have a connection to a Lost God. Question is, which one?"

Shit.

There wasn't much point in hiding that anymore. One Lost God was as bad as the other, and I was sure Faith would come to the conclusion about who it had to be from my conviction that he had sufficient power to combat Quetzalcoatl.

"Tezcatlipoca."

She shuddered. "Two questions. Why *him*? And who chose *you* to do this?"

"One answer," I said. "He chose me."

She took a deep breath, and I sensed changes in her aura. We'd been getting along better than I thought, but it seemed that was about to change.

I didn't have time for this.

I wondered how she'd react to a direct threat.

"I'm at a literal dead end here. If I don't beat this nomicane, I'm dead. That means the Assembly fails, which means…" I let my spirit vision surface.

She frowned. She'd know that I shouldn't be getting spirit visions, but bound together in this substantiation, maybe she'd also know that was a real spirit vision.

She recovered quickly. "Remarkable you get them, but trusting in a neophyte Adept's spirit vision isn't a way I can go forward. They aren't accurate predictions."

"I have to believe them, and I have to believe the feeling they give me that my death is as much a trigger for this all-out war than failing to integrate the Adepts into the Assembly. So, unless you agree to withdraw your claims about me in the nomicane, I'm going back there and I'll ask you, in front of the Truth Sensors, whether you've used compulsion or magical influence on either Tosun or Correia."

She blinked.

"I know you have, and that's the end of any chance of including the Northern League in the Assembly. You probably wouldn't even make it out of the auditorium. It's the nuclear option, the second worst case, but I've nowhere else to go."

Her eyes grew wide, and I thought for a moment I'd got her.

But no.

"My survival, and the survival of the Assembly are not as important as preventing a Lost God from entering the physical world. You must see that."

My defenses had softened as it seemed we were getting somewhere. Now I hurriedly strengthened the shield again, expecting an attack.

Which didn't come.

Back to stalemate and I'd run out of time. The Assembly would be noticing the substantiation in the auditorium. Any longer and there was a chance someone would do something about it. My spirit vision was pressing in on me.

Shit! Shit! Shit!

One last possibility. *Trust her.*

Gwen had told me she was a good person at heart. Committed to her vision of the way forward. But as long as she thought I was a threat to her plans, she'd want to eliminate me.

Much the same way Skylur would, if he thought I threatened Emergence.

I had to persuade her that what I was doing was the only way forward. She had to see everything from my point of view. She had to know everything I said was true.

Shit again.

I felt sick with fear.

I opened my aura and cringed, expecting her to explode into my head.

Didn't happen.

A single, cold, shining thread seemed to strike my chest and disappeared inside.

What had she done? Would I know it if she'd sunk a compulsion into me?

"I haven't done anything to you," she said after a moment that seemed to stretch for eternity. "You win."

Being a chronic paranoid, my first reaction to that was *trap!* But she didn't need to trap me any more.

"We should return now," she said. "I will withdraw my claims and state that Adept issues, even for hybrids, require to be settled by Adepts."

Relief flooded through me, but I had to ask: "You saw everything? You balanced it all, just like that?"

She was silent for a few seconds. I thought she wasn't going to answer, but she did eventually.

"In truth, the largest factor wasn't your plans, such as they are, or aren't, but the lie you told me, and the reason why it was a lie."

"Huh?"

"You said you'd bring the whole Assembly down by telling them I'd used a compulsion on Tosun and Correia. You lied. You wouldn't. You'd sacrifice yourself rather than damage the Assembly, because what you actually believe is that the risk for the paranormal community is greater with the Assembly gone than it would be with you dead and the Assembly still functioning, despite what the spirit vision seems to be saying."

There wasn't anything I could say to that, so I kept quiet.

"I can read all that in your aura," Faith went on, "just as I can read that you'd risk your soul to have the power to fight Matlal and Quetzalcoatl. And that you desperately need training, help and monitoring in this fight, whether you think you do or not. I will incorporate you into a plan involving all of us who are working for the right solution."

We'll see about that.

But I liked the 'us'.

As I began to undo the substantiation, she said one more thing, quietly.

"I'll give you two other bits of information for free: firstly, the Assembly is about to get a shakeup regardless of what we do, and will be much less likely to break afterwards. Secondly, I admit I did think of compelling Tosun and Correia, but I found I didn't need to anyway. Beware of both of them. They are utter snakes."

What?

No time.

With the substantiation gone, we were back in the auditorium, facing each other across a few rows of seats.

Faith turned to Correia and spoke. "House Farrell and I have had a discussion, Adept-style. I withdraw my complaints against her. I will repair any breach with Hecate Enkeliekki, and after that, the Denver coven, including House Farrell, will be working together with the Northern League with the same aims. I will ensure any necessary safeguards are in place. In light of this, the issues I raised earlier are not suitable charges for an Athanate nomicane, which should therefore be dismissed. The new Assembly, with all paranormal races included, will have a more suitable process for resolution of these matters, including any issues regarding hybrids."

A double ripple went through the auditorium at her words. Firstly, Faith was getting very close to telling the Assembly what to do. Secondly, this was a very abrupt change for the delegates. As far as they were concerned, we'd been arguing, then there was a blur where we'd been standing, and suddenly we were allies. Yeah. Disconcerting.

Correia's face was now very still, but I could see her aura seething.

"This isn't a human court, Hecate Hinton, and in any event you're not a direct participant," she said. "As House Farrel has said, we run the Assembly by the book. It is up to the Assembly to decide what is in its interests, and the scope of its nomicanes. And it is up to me to decide when this nomicane should be concluded."

Chapter 9

The expectant silence after Correia's words was interrupted by the sounds of argument as the door to the auditorium was forced open.

Marguerite Molayo Labastide, House Labastide, made a measured and dramatic descent of the steps down to the front of the auditorium. Behind her came her security team, and Kane. They'd obviously converged outside at the same time. Behind them came her sub-Houses, Broussard and Leandre, from Lafayette and Baton Rouge respectively.

House Tosun smiled a welcome, but it looked as if he wasn't completely sure about it.

He knew Marguerite had been brought back to New York by Livia for him to question, though I'd heard that he'd been too busy to start that. He'd assumed being brought to New York meant she was under suspicion. That she would be angry at Altau and probably wouldn't be supporting me. But I guessed he was also party to the skewing of invitations, and she was here before time. So now he was realizing that the news was getting out that the session had started. He'd be wondering how many others would get here. How quickly? And would there be enough of my supporters to swing the vote in my favor?

Marguerite's expression remained so completely unreadable that I started to doubt whether she was on my side.

Would she turn against me? She had granted me freedom of her House and I'd exercised that. I'd fed from her kin; I'd brought her security team to New York and I'd involved her whole House in the inter-faction struggles against her former association. What if I'd gone too far?

She paused at the foot of the stairs while she looked around the room.

"What a strange and troubling day," she said thoughtfully. "I was alerted that the session was in process despite my invitation stating a far later start time. Then I arrive and House Tosun security attempt to prevent my entering the Assembly."

A ripple of shock went through the auditorium, like wind through a field of wheat.

Marguerite went on: "A House, arriving at the Assembly, under the absolute protection of the Assembly has their entrance refused! Refused to the point of violence being offered by the security team of the Head of Security."

Offered. Actual violence would have been a fatal mistake, and there was a swelling of anger behind me. One of the inviolable rules of the Assembly was that the truce was absolute. No one should attack or hinder a House on the way to or from an Assembly. Except of course, a prisoner being brought to a properly conducted nomicane.

"House Tosun," Marguerite's eyes were like lasers, "you owe a tremendous debt to House Altau, because it was Altau security outside that prevented your team physically preventing me from entering."

"It was a mistake," Tosun had to say. "A regrettable misinterpretation of my instructions."

"A mistake? Really. And the different start times? Also a mistake? A strange mistake that results in such a marked political asymmetry, to all the delegates arriving before the start time that was originally given."

Another stirring in the auditorium: heads turning, mutters.

Tosun stuttered a reply that he was responsible for the security rather than the administration. He looked at Correia, but she did not call the meeting to order. He was suddenly realizing exactly how exposed he was.

The delegates' attention was captured by the drama, but from the corner of my eye, I saw the Truth Sensors were shaking their heads.

I was still standing in front of the auditorium.

Marguerite walked up to me and took hold of my hands in hers.

"*Garheem, dokaria,*" she said clearly and loudly.

The shock went right through me and the rest of the Athanate in the room.

Garheem was an everyday Athanate greeting. *Dokaria* was one of those Athanate words that didn't translate well. I knew, from Diana's teaching, that the word originally came from the name given to old style columns used to support the roof of a large building. Used like this, it meant Marguerite was announcing that we were effectively one House. She was rejecting the Eastern Seaboard and making an association with me instead.

We moved together into the lamia, the formal Athanate greeting embrace.

"Thank you," I said quietly into her ear. "But association with me is a dangerous venture at the moment."

She replied, barely audible even to me: "Maybe. My choice. Look, Tosun's not the danger. There's something else going on here. Something that happened last night. Something big. It involves your Diakon, Yelena Vylkove. I have no details, but I think Correia intends to use it. Her security team is scurrying around preparing some evidence. Watch out."

Yelena?

What could that be about? Where was she? What was she doing?

That message on my cell?

Carpathians?

There were so many things that could go wrong with a sensitive issue like the Carpathians, but I trusted Yelena with my life.

With a worried look at my face, Marguerite touched my arm and we parted. Rita moved seats to accommodate her and to emphasize that she would be sitting next to me.

Tosun was clearly having trouble getting his head around what was happening.

The room was buzzing, but eventually Correia tapped on her desk, and it quietened.

I was still standing, and this was still my show, but the auditorium felt different now. Marguerite's arrival, the effect of what she'd said and where she'd chosen to sit had lingered beyond the initial shock. I wasn't confident about a vote yet, but I had them listening to me.

And given Marguerite had opened the issue of Tosun's handling of the Assembly, it had to be time for me to hit the delegates with the truth and demand a vote. I sensed it was too early. I needed to be more certain of the vote, but delay would only let Correia take control and raise issues about Yelena, whatever they were.

I glanced at the president.

A few minutes in the substantiation seemed to have sharpened my ability to see auras. Her aura was roiling. But it wasn't anger that I'd upset everything. She was angry alright, but mixed in with it was excitement and anticipation.

"Have you concluded your response, House Farrell?" Correia asked.

She was all too eager.

"No," I said.

I was dizzy with the fever. I needed water. I needed Blood. I needed rest. *No time for that.*

The cogs that had been connecting in my head started to work together. I could see a solution. A *possible* solution. It would need some careful work to pull it off. Tosun and Correia had to make a misstep or two.

Tosun was stuck unless he'd got more charges to bring. I answered everything—The Heights's testimony had blunted all the charges down from the fighting in Texas, Mexico and Louisiana. Faith had withdrawn her Adept issues. None of that was a slam dunk, but it wasn't the basis of a vote against me as it stood.

Correia was the problem. As president, she could dig deeper. And she still had the power to stop the process and get a vote. I'd kept just ahead of her so far, or at least, just where she couldn't be sure of the vote. I'd need to keep doing that. I'd need to put aside the dizziness from the poison and the pressure from the spirit vision and turn the tables on them.

Starting with Tosun.

Round 3.

Chapter 10

I picked up the sheathed katana I'd left propped against the armrest of my seat and felt a collective hitch in breath throughout the Assembly.

Good.

During one of her training sessions, Bian had told me *every blade sings*. I'd dismissed it as one of her Zen techniques, but now I could feel the blade of the katana, hidden in its ornate sheath, and there was something there. Not so much a song, but a spiraling sequence of notes, tricking the ear into thinking it climbed forever.

"House Farrell—" Correia started.

"I am accorded a right of reply," I interrupted her with the phrase from the Assembly laws covering the nomicane. *"Perathia e ithesia.* Defense and attack."

If Correia was neutral, I could take my time. But she wasn't. She'd been getting messages passed to her, and I suspected she already knew my allies were being called to the session. She'd want to stop me and call the vote before the delegates reached a balanced representation. But she couldn't stop me right away because the laws said I had a reasonable length of time to reply.

A delicate balance over a tightrope.

And yet her aura… I sensed she wasn't waiting for the right moment to stop me. She was waiting for something new, outside of the charges Tosun had brought. *Something big. Something to do with Yelena.*

I'd have to deal with that when it happened.

First, catch Tosun out. Then use that to catch Correia.

I began to walk slowly toward where he sat.

"The Assembly exists only because it rests on an old Agiagraphos law which allows for Athanate enemies to put aside feuds," I said to the Were and Adept attendees. "There is a sacred right of free passage to and from the Assembly. It was one of the tasks of the Warders, before they were corrupted by Basilikos, and removed from their office. Now, the duty to enforce the safety of delegates falls to the House hosting the meeting.

"This is House Altau's mantle, so it's House Altau's duty. As he is not present, responsibility falls to his Head of Security, House Tosun."

Tosun shifted in his chair, eyes darting toward Correia. She didn't stop me.

"House Tosun is not a direct part of House Altau. In keeping with House Altau's determination to strengthen bonds between all Athanate factions,

Skylur chose a sub-House from House Ellicott to be his temporary Head of Security, even though House Ellicott was part of a conspiracy to unseat Altau as head of Panethus at the Assembly in Los Angeles."

Movement caught my eye, and yes, there was House Ellicott, sitting in the middle of his associates.

"Objection," he called out.

"Matter of record," I turned and pointed at the Clerk of the Assembly, who had to confirm.

"It is so recorded," he said.

Ellicott subsided, glaring.

"That conspiracy was headed by House Ibarre of the former Eastern Seaboard association, and when he failed, it was shown that the conspirators had acted against the interests of the Assembly and the Athanate *and* were traitors to Panethus. Altau could have had the entire association put to death. He restricted himself to House Ibarre, who, for all his faults, had a profound sense of honor and committed korheny, along with his entire Assembly delegation, to plead for the lives of the rest of his House. Altau granted that. The Eastern Seaboard association was disbanded and had to give their Blood oaths to House Altau. They are now bound to Altau, with all the weight and responsibility of Blood oaths. For all intents and purposes, they are sub-Houses of Altau, so it's sensible that Skylur should appoint one of them as his temporary Head of Security. After all, who can you trust, if not those Blood-sworn to you?"

The entire association were shifting uncomfortably in their seats. The association had been disbanded, and here they were, sitting together and clearly associating and supporting Tosun's actions. Everyone in the room could see it, and, despite everything, I had the attention of the rest of the delegates. This was the sort of Athanate politics that caught them. Blood oaths and bonds and the possible stench of betrayal.

As I arrived in front of Tosun, I held Onibi out, pointing at him. He shrank back.

"*This* is the person who has the sacred duty of ensuring safe and unrestricted passage for everyone coming to the Assembly. The person whose team were about to physically prevent entry for House Labastide, due to a 'misunderstanding'."

Tosun thought about replying, but his eyes slid to the Truth Sensors. With the focus on him, he didn't dare repeat the lie.

"*This* is the person whose security team attempted to arrest me with force this morning, on the way to this Assembly, in violation of Assembly rules."

"It was an escort—" Tosun began.

"An escort? The House Tosun security team, fully armed, with weapons drawn, demanding I raise my hands as I stepped out of the jet?"

There were murmurs from the delegates. Tosun risked losing his supporters, traditionalist or not. I had him cornered, with one route left. The route I wanted him to take.

"I sent a team to escort you, and they collected you without threats or force from Louisiana. If your subsequent actions escalated the situation, then an arrest was sanctioned by the laws. I had declared the nomicane."

He had silenced the murmurs, but he'd fallen into my trap, and he suspected it as soon as he'd spoken. I could see the sweat starting to glisten on his forehead. There were clauses in the Assembly laws that allowed use of force to ensure the target of a nomicane could be arrested, but they were oh-so-detailed. Tosun knew them. He knew that failure to follow the rules precisely would rebound on him. That sweat on his brow showed he was worrying about Watson's ability to follow those rules.

He was right to worry.

"Yes, you had declared a nomicane, though you failed to inform me when you did."

"That's not a requirement—"

"You're correct," I admitted. "It's allowed for the target of the nomicane to arrive at the Assembly, ignorant of the charges. Or be 'escorted' there without being told."

Onibi was singing in my grip. It *wanted* to be unsheathed. I had to lower the katana, resting it on the floor.

Tosun sucked in a breath, but it was still my show.

"But…" I said, and let it hang for a couple of seconds. "When the target is informed, there is a very specific method requiring a very specific document. I'm sure you have an example in your brief, House Tosun."

He didn't move, so I flicked open the file in front of him, and sure enough, there was the notice. I picked it up and held it so others could see.

"A declaration, with the charges, the date, the time and signed by the person responsible for bringing the nomicane. All done correctly in every aspect, and signed in Blood, as required by the Assembly laws."

"What is your point, House Farrell?" House Karamazin said. "You've admitted the requirements of the nomicane have been met."

House Karamazin was Hidden Path, and as traditional as they come. He made no effort to hide his hatred of me. He knew what was going on today, and he'd taken a front seat to watch me die.

"In House Tosun's copy, yes."

I could see Tosun frown as he realized where this was heading. I tossed the notification back to him.

"But *this*," I pulled out my version, "this is the one your House gave to me."

Watson had given me a printout copy, not the original.

House Bancroft, from Wilmington, one of the former Eastern Seaboard Association members leaned forward and peered at it.

"It's a copy. So what?"

"The Assembly rules say the notification document produced at an arrest must be signed in Blood."

"Really, House Farrell?" Correia spoke. She sounded exasperated, and the mood of the delegates was probably swinging that way too. "You're going to try and defend yourself with technicalities?"

She shook her head.

My argument about detail was correct, but it wasn't what the Assembly wanted, especially today. They'd come into the room under the unnerving gaze of the Blade. They'd know something profoundly *Athanate* was happening. Something about Blood and oaths and betrayals. Something deadly. Not whether a piece of paper had been signed in the approved way.

Correia was banking on it. The Assembly wanted a resolution, and she wanted my head. Literally.

She was about to stop me and call the vote. But she'd gotten over-eager again, and she'd had fallen right into my trap.

"Assembly laws on nomicanes are 'technicalities', House Correia? Which can we ignore? Where is the list that tells us? Which Assembly voted on that?"

She jerked as she realized her mistake.

"House Correia?" I pressed her. "Which laws can be ignored, please?"

There was nothing else she could say: "None."

"Good. Then we agree: there is a law which House Tosun has broken in pursuit of this nomicane. What other Assembly laws have been broken this morning? Preventing Houses entering the chamber... that was a 'misunderstanding'? The bias in the delegates given an earlier start time... that was an 'administrative error'?"

I turned to point at the Clerk. "You are recording proceedings *and* broadcasting?"

He looked uncomfortable. "I am recording. I understand there's a minor technical hitch, but broadcasting will commence shortly."

"Ah, a technical hitch. And once corrected, there will no doubt be a collective meltdown of cellphones with messages on the lines of 'what the hell is going on?'." I paused. "But, of course, President Correia decided we wouldn't be allowed cells in the chamber today. So, no possibility of voting remotely either."

I'd poked her and she had to respond.

"The organization of the Assembly isn't the subject of the nomicane," she said. "You are, House Farrell."

"I am, still, even though each of the charges has been answered. I did not initiate the werewolf battles in Texas and Mexico and Louisiana, and my response was completely within my rights as an alpha of the League and my duties as syndesmon to the Assembly. Those actions were appropriate and proportionate to the threat, and they were approved by House Altau. I did not kill House de Socorro or Isabel Cuarón. Hecate Hinton and I have an understanding on Adept issues, which are anyway outside the scope of the nomicane."

A clerk handed Correia a message, distracting her for a moment. Something was happening, or about to happen.

"I repeat; you are the subject of the nomicane, House Farrell, and I determine when it is to be concluded. If there were errors in the process, that is separate from the charges and determination of your nomicane, and the prosecutor is ultimately responsible for them."

Another hitch of indrawn breath in the room and a gasp from Tosun. She'd cut him adrift. She'd isolated the nomicane vote and the sentence from any mistakes by Tosun and his team.

Not so quick.

I lifted the katana and swung back toward Tosun, making her quick to call out. "I also remind you that I've also adjudicated that retaliatory justice is not applicable."

"I'm not proposing retaliation for the failed charges against me," I said. "This goes far deeper and wider than that."

Onibi, still sheathed, was back in his face. The sword still sang to me. Still urged me to draw the blade and cut him down.

Was this what the queen had meant? That the curse would make the sword turn against me?

"Oaths define us," I said, and the room got that *focused* feel again. "They define Athanate actions. They bind us. They bind House Tosun to House Ellicott. They bind House Ellicott to House Altau. They bind every one of the former Eastern Seaboard Association..." I lifted the katana and pointed at them. "All of them present. Houses Carr and Talassio of Brunswick. Thorpe from Savannah. Abell and Lemaire from Providence. Pettygrove and Winthrop. Ceretti, Bancroft and Calvert. All of you and all your sub-Houses are bound by your Blood oaths to Altau."

Tosun leaped up and interrupted. "This is nothing to do with House Ellicott or the Eastern Seaboard. If I made mistakes, they were mine alone."

I was surprised at the backbone he'd decided to show, but it didn't suit my purposes.

"Sit down, Tosun," I said. "That's not how it works in the Agiagraphos."

He subsided, looking anxiously over his shoulder at the others. Oh, yes; they were all in it together, and he'd been carrying out their orders.

"Any one of the Houses I've named wants to stand up now, in front of the Truth Sensors, and state clearly that this nomicane against me was not intended to weaken House Altau? That you've been acting loyally according to your Blood oaths? Faith for faith, as the oath says? That your intended vote on my nomicane was to be solely dependent on the facts? Anyone?"

Silence. The closer delegates leaned away, as if the Eastern Seaboard Houses had something contagious. The rest of the room leaned forward to witness. This was the heart of the Athanate, the bloody outcomes of the Agiagraphos.

I had them again.

"What about something simple," I continued, "like your association has been dissolved as ordered by House Altau?"

Still nothing. I couldn't make them speak and condemn themselves out of their own mouths, but I didn't need to. They were screwed, the whole room knew it, and as soon as that broadcast began working, the whole Athanate world would know it.

The scale of their treason overrode even the rules of the Assembly. I held their lives in my hand. I could challenge Tosun to a duel. I could demand the Blade to execute them. But Correia could prevent me from doing that in an Assembly. What she couldn't stop me doing, and what every single Athanate in the room expected me to do, was to declare House feud on the whole Eastern Seaboard Association. Even if I was executed, House Altau and all Houses bound to Altau would take up the feud. If I made it so, none of them would survive, not even kin or Aspirants, and not a single Athanate would raise a protest, given the depth of their betrayal. That was the power of the Agiagraphos that I held over them.

I hated the Agiagraphos, but I had to use it. The trick was not to overdo it. I needed to get my nomicane proceedings dropped, but that was just the beginning. Emergence required the Assembly to include every sane paranormal group, and to be strong. It wouldn't be strong if I tore it apart in revenge for what Tosun had been trying to do to me.

I had to use the delegates' expectations of the bloodbath to make my damned point, and once I'd done that, to salvage something from the mess.

In the oldest Athanate traditions, you declared feud over a bare blade with your own Blood, and this meeting was full of people who held to their traditions.

With a snap I drew Onibi to reveal a hand width of the sharp blade.

I hadn't really thought about what effect it would have on the sword to open it in front of a large crowd of paranormals.

Blue-white light, vivid as a welder's flame, sprang out and crackled in the air, hissing and spitting. Tosun froze. Delegates fell back in shock. There were shouts. Curses.

I slammed the sword back into its sheath and the eerie light was gone. The hairs on the back of my neck were going to take a while to settle back down.

Damn! I guess I *had* wanted to catch everyone's attention.

An utter and absolute silence had fallen. Every eye was on me.

"I do *not* declare feud," I said loudly. "I cast aside the recourse offered in the Agiagraphos. Until the paranormal community has survived Emergence, any such distraction weakens us at a time when we cannot afford it. Stop the senseless politicking and start integrating the other paranormal races."

Chapter 11

The auditorium was stirring uneasily as I returned to my seat.

They were like a beast woken in the darkness. Surprised, unsettled. Some of them angry.

I hadn't made new friends with my defense speech, but I felt I'd made the greater point, what the Assembly *should* be working on, while I'd still answered the charges against me.

I had to have improved the outcome of a nomicane vote, even if Correia pressed for one.

The Eastern Seaboard *wouldn't* be voting against me. The fact that I hadn't called feud didn't mean that Skylur wouldn't when he saw what had happened here. They couldn't afford to give him any further reason to come down on them.

The other Panethus, whether they thought me an abomination or not, had something to think about. And there was a threat over their heads as well—if they voted against me knowing how this nomicane had been rigged, there was little reason Skylur couldn't call feud on them too. Apart from drastically weakening the Panethus group.

The Hidden Path Houses? Well, I'd never had much chance with them anyway.

"Very well done," Livia said as I sat down. "You're a natural lawyer and politician."

"Since I seem to be in a forgiving mood, I'll overlook those insults as well," I replied, and even Marguerite laughed.

Rita handed me a bottle of water and I drank it greedily. I was still dizzy from the poison, and I still needed Blood. Not going to happen right now! But at least Kane and Flint had resumed working together, along with Ash, so I should be safe from Tezcatlipoca. Even my nightmare spirit vision seemed to have stepped back, though I could sense it lurking, like the threat of a migraine.

Two Panethus Houses from Canada had entered the auditorium quietly as I'd been speaking: d'Orléans from Québec, and Petaccia from Toronto. Canada was more traditionalist than the States, but they both bowed to Livia and me on the way past. Then they sat together, away from others. They were aware of the groupings and tensions in the room, but unsure where exactly their interests fitted in best. A bit like some others: the noise level was rising and a few Houses very deliberately moved seats. There was a buzz of conversation from the Were and Adept sections, as the Athanate sitting next to them attempted to describe the workings of the Agiagraphos and the strength of oaths in Athanate society.

It was surreal: Assemblies never paused, but this one had.

Tosun wasn't about to get back on his feet and Correia herself was distracted by more urgent messages being brought in by her staff. She hadn't stopped the nomicane, and her aura didn't seem defeated in any way.

Quite the opposite.

The latest message appeared to be what she'd been waiting for. Her staffer leaned across and set up a connection on her laptop. There was a complex flare in her aura that I was sure wasn't good news for me, one way or another.

Time to put her off her stride.

I stood and walked toward the podium. The noise from the delegates lowered a notch or two.

"President Correia."

Her eyes snapped up from examining whatever was displayed on her laptop and narrowed as they focused on me.

Aware of the recording and broadcasting, I found myself still speaking formally: "The urgent business of this Assembly is to proceed with the inclusion of all paranormal factions. I've answered the charges put to me in the nomicane and a vote should be held immediately so that the matter can be dismissed, and more important business dealt with." I paused and looked over to where Tosun and the Eastern Seaboard Houses clustered. "It is also clear that House Altau will need to initiate a nomicane on the administration of this Assembly. All parties need to see that the Assembly organization is run fairly. It obviously hasn't been today. A review of who ordered what, when and why, in the presence of Truth Sensors, is needed."

Ultimately, the president was responsible for the administration. If different opening times had been sent to different Houses, she *should* have known about it. If she didn't, someone in her staff was taking decisions that were against the interests of the Assembly.

"If you think that qualifies as urgent," she replied, "it's your right to append it to the existing discussions, though you might not be involved, because I have something more important and immediate regarding you, House Farrell. The nomicane has not been concluded, but a matter like this would have interrupted *any* proceedings, but it conveniently fits in the existing nomicane."

Silence spread through the room at the sense of threat in her words.

I saw her plans then. She was a meticulous politician. I'd managed to throw enough spanners in the works today to make it look as if she wasn't, but that impression wasn't right.

Her primary aim at the beginning had been to give herself more power by changing the Assembly rules. Her support for the nomicane against me had been mostly a way to get Tosun to skew the voting, so her reform went through. Then something had happened overnight, and now she thought weakening Skylur by having me executed would achieve the same end.

She was getting into her stride, her hands flexing with pleasure.

"House Farrell been placed in a position of enormous trust, not just within Altau, but within Panethus, the Assembly and the whole paranormal community. House Farrell members seem to be everywhere. For example, Jennifer Kingslund kin-Farrell is assessing the finances of long-established Houses of North America. Then there's Yelena Vylkove, Diakon Farrell, who's temporarily Skylur Altau's personal pelea, right at the heart of Panethus."

She'd lingered on Yelena's name, and her aura flared. This had to be what Marguerite had warned me about, but I couldn't think what Yelena could have done that Correia felt was such a slam dunk.

Correia made a show of stopping and frowning. "An odd choice of pelea, Yelena Vylkove. I understand you're allowed to be… *eccentric* in your choice of members for House Farrell, even in your choice of Diakon, but House Altau is different. He has greater responsibilities. I had to ask myself at the time, why would House Altau choose a Carpathian spy as his pelea, even on a temporary basis?"

I couldn't let that ride. I stood. "A *former* Carpathian spy, and a spy against Basilikos, not Panethus. Now bound to House Farrell, and through me, to House Altau. A skilled and efficient bodyguard."

"So you claim. Of course, part of Altau's reasoning might simply have been to ensure his easy access to a former leader of the US Army's most covert forces, Colonel Laine kin-Vylkove."

"It's possible that was part of his reasoning," I said. "Colonel Laine has proved how valuable he can be."

"Oh, I agree. Extremely valuable." There was an eagerness to Correia's response that unsettled me. She went on: "House Altau has appointed Colonel Laine to be the person responsible for the fallback position of Panethus here in the US, if Emergence goes wrong. Despite being human, despite being kin to someone you believe is a 'former' Carpathian spy, Colonel Laine has been given access to every single Panethus House's personnel lists, security status, capabilities… even their computer networks. On top of that, I understand Colonel Laine has been instrumental in recruiting from his former military unit. Some of those highly skilled military men and women, probably still loyal to Colonel Laine, have been distributed to almost every House in the US, especially those that are most vulnerable. This has made the Colonel one of the most important assets, not just for Altau, but for all Athanate, because Altau's plan is to lead Emergence from North America and the rest of us must all depend on a good result here. I'm not exaggerating by saying the hopes of our entire society rest on the shoulder of this one man, who isn't even Athanate, let alone bound to our society, as opposed to bound to one person; a 'former' Carpathian spy."

I seethed at what she was implying, but there was nothing factually wrong with what she was saying. Correia could only have learned those details by spying on Panethus, but the North American Panethus delegates weren't thinking of that, they were thinking how exposed they were. And the delegates from the rest of the world were realizing how exposed *they* were to what was happening in the US. Correia was doing a clever job; not saying anything that was untrue but making every delegate here suddenly concerned about something that, really, was being done for their benefit.

The way she said it would have made the most stable House paranoid.

I couldn't let her continue unchallenged. "Are you suggesting that Colonel Laine is a traitor?"

"I don't know. But Colonel Laine *is* kin to Diakon Vylkove. Colonel Laine will do what Vylkove tells him to."

I wasn't sure he would, if she told him to betray Panethus or the wider Athanate society, but I had no way to persuade the room of that.

"You're insinuating my Diakon is a traitor. Or given she's bound to me, that *I* am."

"It's certainly an interpretation that any sensible person would have to consider."

Pulling that substantiation earlier had sharpened my ability to read aura, but it came at a price. Every power does. Everything can have a dark side to it. To read Correia's aura was to sample it. To know the strangely obscene pleasure she was experiencing now, because she thought she had me.

When she continued, Correia spoke slowly, making an effort to sound reasonable, and to hide that fevered pleasure. Trying to sound concerned and startled, as if she hadn't been planning this, as if she wasn't practically squirming on her chair at the thought of having me executed.

"Tell me, House Farrell, why has your 'former' spy, your Diakon, Yelena Vylkove, taken Colonel Laine to the Carpathian ship in the port without clearing it with anyone?"

She clicked on her laptop and the display behind her showed Yelena, followed by the Colonel and Vera, walking onto the deck of the Carpathian's ship.

Shit!

Yeah, the traditionalists wanted the Carpathians to join, because Carpathians were supposed to be ultra-traditionalist, but no-one actually *knew*, because they were ultra-secretive. And they maintained that secrecy by being ultra-powerful.

Now everyone was thinking about what reasons this secretive, powerful group would have to bypass the Assembly and invite someone like the Colonel aboard.

"Unless she cleared it with you?" Correia said. "In which case, please tell me what the purpose of this secretive visit is, and why it's been necessary to hide it from me?"

I glanced behind me, to see the evidence of how much effect Correia was having on the room.

A lot. Even Marguerite had gotten to her feet to stare at me, eyes wide at what she thought was my betrayal. Beside her, Livia's face was like stone.

"No," I said loudly, turning back to glare at Correia.

"What exactly do you mean 'no'?" Correia was all sweet reasonableness.

"No, this isn't the way you're making it seem," I said in a rush. "No, I haven't betrayed anyone, neither has anyone in my House. I don't know why they went there, and nothing was said to me before."

My fault. I'd decided to ignore Yelena's message on my cell: *Carpathians. Will call and explain shortly. Hold back.*

If I'd taken the time to call Yelena, I'd know what was going on.

But, whatever it was, she *wouldn't* have betrayed me, or the Assembly. And on the other hand, without my being here for the start of the Assembly, Correia might have redesigned the executive powers, and condemned us all the hell I saw in my spirit vision.

Focus.

The auditorium was beginning to seethe behind me. I'd previously witnessed Diakon Huang's elegant and emotional speech make the room fall into sync with each other. Now I was witnessing Correia do it, with shock and perceived threat. The Assembly was a beast on the brink of lashing out.

I couldn't stop my eyes from flicking toward the Blade, still standing silently behind Correia. I could see the glint in his eyes, and they were fixed on me.

Yelena taking the Colonel down to the ship might have a dozen different explanations, but the Athanate creature in the room wasn't going to listen to anything other than a clear answer with an acceptable reason, which I didn't have to give them.

I had to try, even if they weren't listening.

"I understand that you're trying to make a case that this is a Carpathian plot, without any idea of what is happening or why."

Correia snapped back: "What other reason could there be, other than espionage? Every House in this country is compromised."

"I could call her. Or we should wait till she comes back."

"She has been called. There was no response, though I have to say I would hardly have given any credence to a protestation of innocence."

"Why are you assuming the Carpathians would want to attack? They're members of this Assembly."

Both the Empire of Heaven and the Carpathians had been included in the Assembly when Skylur had created it. Every Assembly meeting since then had had a communications line open to them, even if they'd never taken it.

"They've never taken the Assembly oaths," Correia pointed out. "And even if they don't attack, their knowledge of the weaknesses in North American Houses could be used for political pressure."

"You're building on speculation as if it were established fact."

"The established facts are these: Members of your House on a Carpathian ship. You have no idea what is happening. The Agiagraphos says you are responsible, and the laws don't distinguish between actual damage to the community and the threat of it. I make this assessment as president: your negligence amounts to treason."

I was standing right in front of her now. I lowered my voice.

"You don't have that power in a nomicane."

"Very well. I'll call a vote now, as you demanded a few minutes ago. Do you think they will support you?" She gestured at the room behind me. "However you justify it, that swathe of death you've cut through the south makes you a dangerous psychopath. A borderline rogue."

I didn't need to look around. The delegates wouldn't support me, because Correia had hit their buttons at the right time.

She went on: "If you make it easy and admit to treason, I'll restrict the scope of the judgement to you personally. If you don't, then my judgement will include your House and associates."

She gestured again, and despite my anger, I glanced behind. Marguerite and Livia had gotten over their shock and decided that I was being railroaded. Faith and The Heights were talking urgently to them, and it looked as if they were going to come up and protest.

Correia was doing this to goad me. She was enjoying it.

If I admitted to treason, the Blade would execute me immediately and no Agiagraphos law would force her to honor any promises she'd made to me.

Skylur would stop her, but he wasn't here now, and it'd be too late for me. And Jen was in DC, in House Ellicott's mantle. With the judgement of the Assembly behind him, Ellicott could order her immediate execution. Maia Kiriani couldn't protect Jen against the whole House. Again, Skylur would order Ellicott's death for it, but the whole Eastern Seaboard group might take the risk and run afterwards.

I held up my hand to stop my friends from approaching.

"You're insane," I said to Correia. "Your manipulation of this Assembly will come out. You'll destroy it. Skylur will declare war on you."

"*Skylur*," she spat the name out, "has already destroyed the Assembly. He and Huang have schemed to prevent me from doing anything."

And she was right. They had, for the best of reasons. But by backing the Hidden Path party into a corner, they'd gotten us here, where there seemed no way out that didn't lead to the apocalyptic spirit vision that was pressing in on me again.

What was the least bad way out?

My execution?

I was shaking, as much anger as fear.

"Show of hands," Correia called out. As president, she was allowed to choose the style of vote. I knew she'd go this way. Weight of vote wouldn't condemn me, because Livia could take the entire Panethus vote. But show of hands from those present? Correia had timed it right. I'd lost.

Yelena! What have you done?

I *knew* she hadn't betrayed me or the Assembly, not Yelena, but no one would listen unless she came back right now.

Yelena!

In my feverish daze, I reached with eukori, without even thinking about it. Boosted by an entire room full of Athanate, I reached…

And I got a response.

Not Yelena. Or not *only* Yelena. I got a kaleidoscope of impressions flooding back. Different people. Rushing. Yelena worried. Shoving someone out of the way.

They were close.

But too late.

I shouldn't have reached like this. It broke through the shield and opened me to the spirit world. I could feel magic swirling and growing like a storm breaking.

A pulse of raw power flared up from Tezcatlipoca. It was as violent as the spell in my katana, but invisible to everyone else. It forced open a connection with me and my hands burned with the power of life and death over every person in the room.

I had to clamp down and try to shut everything else out.

Flint, Kane and Faith were there in a moment, lending me strength to close the connection.

And we were losing. Tezcatlipoca was going to burst through because I'd let my guard down. Because Correia had ambushed me in a political dispute.

The air itself seemed suddenly charged with electricity, so much that everyone was on their feet. Correia was shouting.

Then the connection with Tezcatlipoca faded abruptly. In its place was a mounting pressure of something that was of the spirit world, but completely different in feel to the old Aztec god.

The doors at the top of the stairs opened.

Yelena came through.

There were strangers behind her. Everyday people—the kind you'd see on the streets of New York any day of the week. Unremarkable to many, but for me, they were lit up like bonfires with arcane workings.

Behind them, Colonel Laine and Vera.

Thank goodness.

"What is this?" Correia yelled. Furious that her moment of judgement had turned in her hands. She seemed unaware of what I saw so clearly in the newcomers. "Who are these people? How dare you bring them in here?"

Yelena stood to one side and bowed in great respect to the older woman just behind her, who moved to the front.

She *rippled,* this woman, like an image beneath water, and then she was taller, standing proudly, robed, the upper half of her face covered in a gilded mask.

She raised her hands and lowered the mask. In turn, it rippled, and became an antique necklace of gold and rubies.

Then she spoke with a strong voice, in Athanate, in a dialect I'd only ever heard when Diana read from the older books of the library in Haven. "I am here seen. I am named House Selsys, Elder of the Domain of Carpathia. Now is the Domain come to the new Assembly of the Paranormal. Our Blood is yours. May our gathering be in peace, and all that kept us apart be put aside."

Chapter 12

"You have no right—" Correia started as Selsys turned toward the podium.

Selsys simply raised her hand and let a trickle of that Athanate dominance seep out. I could sense much, *much* more behind it. She was *old*. Old like Skylur. And like Skylur she used her power sparingly.

It was enough. Correia's mouth closed with a snap.

"The Domain has every right to be here," Selsys said, speaking now in unaccented English, "and it is our *duty* to be here, to sweep away the old Assembly and bear witness to the dawn of the new Assembly of the Paranormal, which will represent all paranormals."

Correia's mouth worked. "This Assembly—"

"Is finished," Selsys said. "The Assembly of the Athanate must be superseded. It is the true purpose of this meeting to achieve that, not the petty political maneuvering you have seeded into this agenda. The paranormal races must come together as Emergence breaks over us."

She gestured back to the door. "Diakon Huang will arrive in a matter of minutes. House Altau by midday. I have spoken to both of them. They are with me on this matter."

She pointed at the Assembly book of rules I had used. It snapped open. "I remind you that the founding of this body acknowledged the membership of both the Empire of Heaven and the Domain of Carpathia. We were allocated a weight of vote that has not been rescinded, and the weight of our three votes combined are sufficient to halt proceedings and demand a re-constitution of this body."

Correia had recovered, and, like me, found strength in anger. She leaped to her feet and leaned over the podium table.

"They are not here. I am the president of the Assembly. I do not take orders from you. Until such time as they are present, I have matters—"

"Cease this nomicane. Cease attempting to change the executive function."

"My running the meeting is not a matter for a vote until your allies arrive." Her anger had made her strong, but it was also making her stupidly stubborn, and it was stopping her thinking clearly.

Still, she was right about the rules. She had held a vote according to the laws, and nothing anyone could say or do, by the rules, could stop her passing judgement on me.

Others gathered at the podium. The Blade, the Truth Sensors and the clerk stood behind Correia, though all but the Blade seemed uncertain.

"You will not survive Altau's anger if you proceed," Selsys said.

Correia laughed. "Altau's own Blood oaths guarantee the right of safe passage to and from the Assembly. Once I'm back in Brazil, he's welcome to do his worst."

"For the oaths to be binding, the Assembly must exist. You're destroying the Assembly, House Correia. It may not survive your next action, and the oaths will not protect you then."

We'd been joined on the podium by more from both sides. Yelena on my left. The Heights on my right. He was angry too. "The League is not signatory to any agreements," he growled at Correia. "No oaths bind us. You wouldn't make it back to the airport, let alone Brazil."

I could see Correia's response forming, and she wasn't about to back down. My supporters were outnumbered by Hidden Path delegates. There weren't enough Carpathians and League werewolves in New York to fight all of Correia's supporters and their delegations.

And fighting openly in the streets? Insanity.

Stalemate. None of it of any use to anyone.

My spirit vision crowded my head until I could barely see. Every route seemed to end in disaster. There was no solution where everyone won, and that meant everyone would lose. Every path seemed to end in an apocalyptic war.

I was dizzy and disoriented by the vision. As I leaned forward to rest my hands on the table, I misjudged, so that I banged on it instead. That jarred a word out of me may have been a little louder and sharper than it should have been.

"No!"

All heads swiveled around to me. Gazes, sharp as lasers, focused on me. I felt like an insect on a lab bench.

The Blade's sword came up, over the table, moving slowly and hypnotically. It came to rest with the point against my chest.

I had to spread my arms to prevent Yelena and The Heights from responding.

"No," I repeated, a little less forcefully, my eyes locked on Correia's. "We have to stop this. It's not a matter of Assembly rules, or the Agiagraphos, or the incompatibility between creeds. We're beyond all that. Whether Skylur precipitated it or not, Emergence was inevitable, and the one way to ensure it goes wrongly is for us to splinter into warring factions. If we fight now, we all lose. The only group we can't take with us is Matlal and his Basilikos allies. Everyone else has to come together in one Assembly. In peace. We've got to find some compromise."

"Even if it means your death?" someone called out. "That's one of the issues here."

I sighed, trying to see a way that that might work in my spirit vision. I couldn't. All I could feel was a chill coming off that blade and spreading through me.

"If it meant peace," I said and shook my head to try and clear it. "Because without peace, we're all dead anyway, me included."

A murmur or two, then a moment's complete silence.

"This is your 'dangerous psychopath'?" Selsys asked Correia.

Correia's jaw twitched, but she didn't answer, and her eyes remained furious.

"Amber is right about compromise," said Livia, pushing her way through to the front of the growing circle around the podium. "Skylur has been talking about concessions to bind the Hidden Path better into the Assembly. To reduce the points of conflict between the two creeds across the world. That's part of the reason why he chose me as his Diakon."

The beast that was the Athanate group hesitated, but it was like watching the ball in a roulette wheel. It still felt like it could end up anywhere.

The shocks hadn't passed: the treason of the Eastern Seaboard, the rigging of the nomicane, Correia willing to break the Assembly to have me executed, and then on top of all that, finding out that the Carpathians, the supposedly ultra-orthodox, ultra-traditionalist Carpathians, were in fact hybrids. Abominations.

Tosun had picked these Assembly members from the most traditionalist side, those that didn't much like the idea of expanding the Assembly's demographics and unsurprisingly, they *really* didn't like abominations turning up and declaring the Assembly needed radical reform.

It was still a tinderbox.

Another voice was added: Faith Hinton.

"There's a key point we're overlooking on the nomicane," she said. "House Correia suggested that Diakon Vylkove took Colonel Laine to the Carpathian ship for purposes of espionage. You have the relevant people here, and Truth Sensors. Find out why they asked for Colonel Laine."

"We didn't," Selsys replied immediately to stop Correia pointing out the nomicane was over. "We asked for a meeting with her kin, Vera Laine kin-Vylkove. Her husband insisted on accompanying them. We had no questions of him, or any desire to know security details of your individual Houses in North America."

Heads turned to the Truth Sensors, which was a reasonable reaction, since few people here knew who Vera was. The more interesting point for me was that the Carpathians had asked for a meeting with her.

Then I had to fight to keep from bursting out with inappropriate, hysterical laughter, because suddenly I knew. "This was all about 'God is good, good is God', isn't it?"

The Blade's sword scratched my skin, raising Blood. My words earned me a few glares from Carpathians and blank incomprehension from others.

Selsys' brow creased with a slight frown. "Frivolity aside, she is correct. Our presence in New York has multiple purposes. Clearly, we are here to rejoin the Athanate community, and to take part in the formation of a new Assembly. But we are also here on..." her frowned deepened and then she shrugged, "on what you would probably call a spiritual quest."

Now attention came back to Vera, who'd slipped through the circle of delegates and came to my side.

She smiled at me, and at the Blade, before reaching out to gently push his sword up, away from my chest.

"This is no longer the path," she said.

Much as I appreciated the gesture, I sensed anger return to the traditionalists. The Blade's person, and his sword, were sacred. That roulette wheel was still spinning.

And at that precise point, Diakon Huang entered the auditorium.

He wasn't a large or imposing man. Like Skylur, you might pass him in a crowd without pausing, unless your eyes met. It seemed that the effect was amplified when he was angry.

He could be an eloquent man, but he could also be sparing with words.

"Stamatios," he said, in Athanate.

It was the call, defined in the Assembly rules, which allowed a quorum of faction leaders to halt proceedings.

Elder Selsys echoed his call.

Livia joined her, casting Altau's vote for Panethus.

Quorum reached.

Correia had no choice. Yet when she finally spoke, she was clearly still in fighting mode: "I suspend all current processes of the Assembly, pending planning for reconstitution of the body to include all paranormals, and an improved executive structure. The leaders will approach."

"Perakri korasmai," intoned the man in red, the standard Athanate phrase, *the Blade rests,* and the sword swung up and away from me.

Chapter 13

We had to clear away from the podium, but not before I'd caught a glimpse of an acknowledgment between Faith and Elder Selsys.

And Faith had told me the Assembly was about to get a shakeup. She'd obviously talked to the Carpathians and knew all about their Adept capabilities and their plans for the Assembly.

Gift horse and *mouth*; but there were questions I would have for the Carpathians once the dust settled.

I didn't have time to think about it before Yelena swept me up in a hug.

"Sorry," we said at the same time, and laughed.

"I should have answered your call," I said.

"I should have called earlier, but I wanted to let you have more recovery time." She looked closely at me. "The poison hasn't dissipated yet."

It wasn't a question. I shrugged it off. I was feeling slightly better than I had standing there with the sword resting on my chest. *Surprise.*

"Taking its own sweet time. It's fine." I changed the topic. "Watson made sure there was no comms capability on the jet coming up here. When I got here, we were in a hurry."

"Yeah, I gathered that. Got through to Dupuis earlier." She mimicked her voice: "House Farrell has allowed herself to be arrested by a team from House Tosun."

I snorted. Diakon Dupuis, who'd been left in command of House Labastide while Marguerite was here in New York, wasn't my fan.

It wasn't important. Not like what had just happened here.

I stabbed Yelena's with my finger. "You could at least have told me that Carpathians are hybrids."

"She couldn't, Kyria Chrysos."

One of the Carpathians had joined us. He'd just called me *Lady Chrysos* and that earned him a glare from me.

"I can't deny being Chrysos' ehvasi," I said, keeping my voice even. "But I don't have to be happy about it. The late House Chrysos was a monster. Becoming his ehvasi was an accident while he was trying to kill me. Which he would have succeeded at, if I hadn't killed him first. I go by House Farrell. And you are?"

I was being impolite, especially by the old Athanate etiquette, but he'd pissed me off.

He bowed his head. "I apologize, House Farrell. My point was that Yelena Vylkove, as with all Carpathians on duties outside our domain, was under compulsion not to disclose details about us."

"Was voluntary," Yelena said, waving it away. "I agreed to be compelled. It doesn't matter now."

It was her duty to introduce this Carpathian, and she went on to do it. "I present to you Theris Zalissia, House Zalissia, Kyrios Kryfokratos, Elder-elect of the Domain of Carpathia."

Shit.

One of the senior Houses of the Domain, Lord of something, on the point of becoming one of their ruling Elders, and we'd gotten off on the wrong foot. *I'd* gotten off on the wrong foot.

Yelena cleared her throat, which warned me there was more to come.

"By order of the Elders of the Domain, House Zalissia is appointed to House..." she stuttered. She'd been about to say Chrysos. "... House Farrell, in the office of Pelea to the person of Amber Farrell, House Farrell."

My mouth moved.

The Carpathians had just given me a close protection bodyguard. Who was also one of their most senior Houses.

"I don't suppose I could..." I started.

"Please, Boss." Yelena gave me one of her looks. "There's more."

"More?"

Yelena and Zalissia exchanged glances, and I took the opportunity for a better look at him.

Tall. Dark. Black eyes and shoulder-length black hair. A good, modern-day Dracula out of central casting. Physically, he was impressive as well; his body seemed coiled like a powerful spring. Paranormally? I wasn't expert at reading Athanate age, but he was *old*. And even now that he'd dropped the illusion disguise, there was still a sense of magic coming off him like an evening breeze. Made the hairs on the back of my neck stand up.

I didn't like the idea, but I had to admit I understood perfectly well this was an honor that the Carpathians had offered. And, despite being uneasy about their whole arrival today, it had potentially saved my life. That apocalyptic vision wasn't pressing in on me with the same intensity. Had to mean things had gotten better. On top of that, their agenda for a new, full Assembly was exactly the direction I was pushing for.

All of that meant it would be stupid to sour my relationship with them, despite my unease.

I tried the throat clearing thing.

Can we just reset? Erase the last couple of minutes?

"Welcome, Kyrios Zalissia."

I realized as I spoke, I'd gotten his titles mixed up. I dropped the old Athanate, all the complex etiquette, and tried speaking in English.

"We're informal here. Please just call me Amber."

He dipped his head a fraction, a small smile playing on his lips. "Then I must be Theris."

"Okay, Theris. What's this 'more'?"

"While the leaders are talking about talks..." his mouth twitched upwards, and my impression of him went up with it, "we would be best employed in preparing the next step, which requires Mirela Tucek to be brought here. We must brief her on what we need her to say."

"Hold it right there," I said. "I had planned on asking Mirela to attend, once I'd prepared the delegates, so she could warn about the threat from Matlal. But this meeting is still in shock from learning that Carpathians are Athanate-Adept hybrids, and they have to concentrate on the structure of the new Assembly before they start thinking about how the next steps. And you're making it sound as if she's my prisoner. She's not. She's more like part of my House."

He blinked, and then dipped his head. "My apologies, Amber. I've been hasty because the matter is urgent."

He leaned forward to speak quietly and slipped back into the old dialect, which most eavesdroppers wouldn't understand. "Those there are amongst this body who are holden to Matlal. Of all that might know them, Tucek is foremost. The new Assembly must begin afresh, clear of Matlal's spies."

"Tucek is Vega Martine's head of espionage," Yelena muttered in my other ear. "She knows every Assembly member who is actually Basilikos, and all those not actually Basilikos, but recruited into plots against Altau."

Shit. Head of espionage! A gold mine of information.

"*Was* Vega Martine's head of espionage. Not anymore." My correction was automatic, but my head was spinning.

No wonder Theris was keen to get hold of Mirela, but that made me uncomfortable.

Theris continued relentlessly. "We have a short time. Vega Martine doesn't know you've turned House Tucek yet. When she finds out, the Basilikos members who could be exposed will be called away from the Assembly. Everything comes together to our benefit if we do this right now."

"And you trust Mirela to do this?" I asked. His comment about having to brief her seemed odd.

I trusted one of the two Mirelas in my head. The one I'd had to trust because there was no other option when we'd been imprisoned by the Queen of Diamonds on her steamboat. We'd shared auras, and I'd betrayed her, because I'd sworn I wouldn't use my aura to compel her. My mind wasn't clear about the moment I'd accepted Tezcatlipoca's gift of a substantiation where Mirela and her House could hide from the Queen of Diamonds and Vega Martine. Magic and auras are tricky. Had I subconsciously wanted to compel Mirela and her House? Had Tezcatlipoca assumed I had? Was I sure that the substantiation worked like that, just because I later thought I subconsciously noticed a change in Mirela's aura? I'd been poisoned at the time, feverish. Maybe all this was another fever symptom, and Mirela would laugh at me.

Yelena's mouth had drawn into a thin line at my question of trusting Mirela.

It was Theris who eventually answered my question: "I trust Yelena. She trusts you. She believes you trust House Tucek would do this for us. And House Tucek has no other viable options than to ally with us and beg forgiveness of past deeds."

There was something he wasn't telling me, but what he had said, was right.

Those past deeds were the other Mirela I knew. That Mirela, I would struggle to forgive.

But the two Mirelas who seemed so distinct in my mind were the same person. The reason I'd hidden Mirela and her House in my substantiation was that I owed her for her help, and now I owed her for betraying her trust in me. Vega Martine would have ordered House Tucek to be eliminated anyway, just for cooperating with me, but now I understood what Mirela's role had been…

Mirela's analysis of her own position would force her to be as helpful to us as possible.

"I'll ask her," I said. "I won't order her. I won't use the advantage I have of compulsion. It'll have to be the logic of her position and any sense she has of an alliance to me. That should be enough."

"It should," Yelena said.

Theris didn't agree, and wanted more help from Yelena, but my Diakon's jaw was set, and I knew she wasn't going to push any harder.

Instead, she turned to practical matters: "Now we must go. You can spirit walk to your substantiation from here and bring her back?"

"Not a good idea from here in the chamber," I said, "but we could use the suite they've put aside for us."

Yelena guided me toward the exit, picking up the rest of the team as we went, and collecting our belongings.

"There's something you're not saying," I said to Theris as we waited.

"It's not my place to reveal all the... complexities about House Tucek," he said. "I am sure these are matters that will be more painful for the Elders than for you. They aren't important at the moment."

I snorted.

Our bags were returned, and we all got in the elevator.

"You're running a fever," Theris said. "This is the Queen of Diamond's poison still?"

I nodded and he looked concerned.

"Will it affect your ability to spirit walk us into the substantiation? And back out?"

"Us?"

"You have to take Rita and me," Yelena said. "We're not letting you out of our sight at the moment."

Rita nodded approval.

"As your pelea, I must also go with you," Theris said. "I may also help to shield against the Lost God."

Flint and Kane gave me tiny nods. They'd made some kind of assessment of him, and he measured up on the Adept side.

"So five of you, and Mirela to bring back as well. It's not like I have an operating manual or training in this. I don't think it's a problem, but I don't know." I grimaced. "I had a motto back in Ops 4-10: Trust and Jump. I guess that applies to this."

Theris smiled.

Pia, Jo and Xavier wanted to come too.

"No." I said. "It's not like I'm going to need help in my own substantiation. And besides, I need an anchor here. A sort of beacon that guides me back from the spirit world."

We reached the fifteenth floor and came out of the elevator into a reception area.

Skylur had made a statement and given me one of the best suites in the building. *Huge.* It took up half the floor and must have taken an acre of marble quarry to decorate. It had a gym, three bedrooms, luxurious cocktail bar and lounge with chandeliers, patio, business room, dining room, and a kitchen, much of which looked as if it'd never been used.

There was no time to enjoy any of it.

Julie and Keith came out of the business room, where they'd set up the comms equipment.

"We've contacted everyone we can get through to," Julie said. "Most of them are on their way and can't get here any quicker. Those who stayed overnight in the area are already arriving."

"Thank you and well done."

I turned to Theris. "What about Elder Selsys and the Assembly?" I asked. "I was nearly executed because they thought my Diakon had shared sensitive information with you. Now I am actually working with you. I hope I'm not going to be arrested when we get back."

"I could say I think you'll be safe, but I would anyway, wouldn't I? I think you'll just have to trust and jump."

He said it deadpan. I couldn't say I liked him yet, but he was growing on me.

"Weapons?" Yelena broke in.

I shook my head. "Firearms won't work in my substantiation. It has 'rules'." I laughed. "You're probably going to be buck naked and don't be surprised if I shift to being a guy."

Yelena snorted.

Jo held open the bag with the swords. I was still carrying the katana from my confrontation with Tosun in the Assembly. Yelena took the jian and Theris the saber-like dao, leaving the wakizashi. Rita picked it up and laughed.

"We won't need them," I said, but Yelena was wearing that stubborn look. I shrugged. "Nothing's going to attack us."

I wasn't going to win that argument, so I turned my mind to the task of getting us into the spirit world.

Theris was arguing we needed to bring only Mirela back. We could leave the rest behind. Yelena was arguing that, urgent as it was, we had time for a few trips if I couldn't manage all of them at once.

I tuned them out, feeling for that strange compass in my aura. The sensation that something which was part of me lay in *that* direction. *There.* I slid the katana under my belt and grabbed Theris' and Yelena's wrists, one on each side. Kane, Flint and Rita stood behind me and put their hands on my shoulders.

It all felt strange. I felt the pulse of poison still in my veins. The thread in my aura leading to the substantiation that had seemed so defined before had a glow around it. Not in a good way; a sickly way.

"Feels wrong," Flint murmured.

"This is odd," Theris agreed.

Odd or not, that was the path. I *reached* and we fell forwards into it.

Chapter 14

There was something wrong. Not 'odd'. Really wrong.

It was the first thing I knew as we arrived.

Wrong like it was written in fire across the sky. Like a physical force pushing me so hard I stumbled. I let the others go and had Onibi halfway out of the scabbard, spitting blue fire, but I knew I was too late.

Something horribly misshapen, one of those barely glimpsed terrors from a nightmare, lunged at me.

Theris wasn't so slow. His slashing movement was an unsheathing of the dao and a cut all in one flowing motion, unhurried, and yet with the speed of a striking snake.

I thought he'd missed, because the creature struck me.

But it struck me in two dead halves.

It looked like nothing on earth. Roughly wolf-shaped, but with massive forequarters and six limbs, four at the front and two at the back. The 'paws' doubled as callused gripping hands, missing only the thumb. Having six limbs wasn't the worst of it. It had no fur. Its muscles and tendons, veins and organs were half-visible, wrapped in an obscene, translucent, glistening skin. The stench of sickness made me gag.

Flint and I had seen things like this before, lurking in the shadows and creeping through the streets, when we'd spirit walked in the City of Lost Gods. Flayed wolves, we'd called them.

Yelena swore in Ukrainian, and we whirled in place to make sure no more of them were about to spring at us.

"The City's attacking this substantiation," Flint said.

The spirit world was not a gentle place, at least not where it came to the intrusions made by humanity. Every substantiation needed power to keep going, and it got that by consuming smaller substantiations. The City of Lost Gods was the top of the food chain.

But Tezcatlipoca's own power came from the City of Lost Gods. Surely that was strong enough to keep this substantiation safe. Unless he'd decided to punish me for denying him. And if he couldn't get to me directly…

"Mirela!" I shouted, as the more important realization shoved my mind away from wool gathering. "She has no weapons."

We were on the hillside above the little resort. The place where I'd first arrived, but we were in a dip, so I couldn't see…

I raced to the crest of the dip. There were a couple of flayed wolves near, but they ran away, maybe sensing the fate of their companion from its blood spatter on me.

My heart lurched as I came over the top.

The sea was steaming, and the beach was empty. There was no one in the pool area. The cabins lay below me, shut tight and boarded up. The buildings were crawling with flayed wolves, like ants over food that had been dropped on the floor.

"No!"

I ran down the hill.

Cursing, the others followed.

I couldn't reach with my aura in case Tezcatlipoca was waiting. This might even be a trap to make me do just that. But without reaching, I should still have been able to feel something of Mirela and her House. There was nothing.

The horror of the thought I might be too late seeped into me.

The flayed wolves retreated from our charge and the spitting blue light of Onibi. But they circled around behind us, snarling and screaming. The foam that fell from their lathered jaws smoked where it touched the ground.

As we neared the buildings, one leaped at me and I swung the katana. I didn't trust that I had the strength to slice it in half, so I cut through two forelimbs on one side. It made a sound like a soul in damnation and crashed into the ground. I left it to the others to finish off.

Another few strides and I was in front of the main building's doors. This was the largest of them. The only one big enough to shelter them all. The windows had been boarded. The glass from some of them was broken.

"Mirela!" I screamed and hammered on the door. "Open up. It's me."

Which is exactly the sort of ruse some forsaken creature from the City might try.

With the others forming a ring around me to keep the flayed wolves at bay, I rested my head against the door and tried reaching with my aura.

Nothing.

Nothing to my paranormal senses, but my nose smelled death and decay inside.

No!

My aura recoiled, lashing out across this substantiation which I had wanted to be a haven, a place of safety. That lashing out distracted Theris. A group of the wolves leaped at him, and Yelena had to turn to support him. That left Flint exposed. Rita was slashing wildly at the press of snarling jaws and reaching limbs with the short wakizashi. It was working, but more were joining the fray. They were flowing off other buildings like water and even more were surging up from the beach. The sheer weight of numbers would overwhelm us, and there were already too many to fight our way through.

We couldn't go back. We couldn't stay here.

A little working? A tiny thing? Open the locks? Would that be safe? Something I could do without Tezcatlipoca's power or notice?

Flint joined me to place his hand against the lock.

Rita protected us, but the short sword wasn't enough of a threat. Yelena had to split her attention between Theris and Rita. Then her blade got stuck and the wolves forced her back.

I felt Flint's working shift the lock.

"Go," he said.

The door opened outwards. I pulled. I had to reach around and drag Flint and Rita inside after me. Theris and Yelena stumbled through. I slammed the door closed and immediately it was battered by wolves' bodies crashing against the outside.

It shook. It wouldn't hold for long.

I spun around.

The place was empty. The smell of decay came from food in wrapping that sat unopened on a counter at the back.

"They're not here. We have to go," Yelena said, dragging a table to stack it against the door.

"Yes." I said but couldn't think straight.

Where were they? How had they left? How long would that door last?

Flint and Theris moved more tables to use as barricades, but we had nothing to brace them against.

I tried to clear my mind and feel the path back. It was trickier in this direction, and the fabric of the substantiation was breaking down. I could feel it, like sinking sand undermining my feet. Distracting. Then the whole building started to tremble. The ceiling rained dust down on us and one of the barricaded windows exploded as the walls twisted. I could feel the City of Lost Gods dragging my substantiation into its maw. The longer we stayed, the harder the City tried. If it completed… we'd never get back from *there* now, even if the wolves didn't get us first.

I had to find our way back *now*, at the same time as pushing down my fear of what happened to Mirela and her House. There was only one way out of the substantiation. Had Tezcatlipoca kidnapped them? Hostages?

Something bigger arrived outside, and the whole building shook with its assault.

Focus.

I couldn't do anything for Mirela now. I needed to get out of here.

Pia.

I'd known her longest. She was the mentor of my ehvasi. My connection to her should be strong. I grasped for things we'd shared. A quiet moment here and there. Cooking at Manassah. Braiding each other's hair in the light of the setting sun. The sound of her voice. Her scent.

Pia?

There was a cracking noise from the door. It bulged and forced the stacked tables back. The wolves' battering increased. Others started to squirm through the broken window, writhing, cutting themselves, screaming, calling others, redoubling their efforts. Kane hurled a table at the nightmare shapes.

Pia!

There!

I grabbed Flint and Yelena. Kane, Theris and Rita grabbed me. And I *reached* for the clear, distant beacon of Pia's mind.

Falling.

The sensation of falling was so great, we stumbled as we arrived back in New York gripping each other for support, wide-eyed, holding unsheathed swords and covered in blood and dust. Where the saliva of the flayed wolves had touched our clothing, it smoked. Luckily the old rules for the substantiation had failed, otherwise we'd have been naked, and that saliva would be on our skin.

"Shit!" I couldn't remember hearing Jo swear before. She and Xavier looked on in complete shock. "What happened?"

"The substantiation," I gasped. "Under attack. No sign of Mirela."

"She's here!" Jo said, her words tumbling over each other. "In New York, I mean. We got messages. Elder Selsys has the Assembly ready to hear her."

"What? How long have we been?" Theris asked.

"Nearly three hours."

I'd forgotten how much time could slip between my substantiation and the physical world, but that wasn't important.

My heart squeezed and the breath caught in my throat. *How had Mirela got here?*

There were only two ways out of the substantiation. With me. Or with Tezcatlipoca.

Maybe four ways: death, or through the City of Lost Gods, which were much the same.

If Tezcatlipoca had brought her here, what was his reason?

Pia had been listening to something on her earbud, and she cut in. "You need to get cleaned up and down to the Assembly *now*. And we have to find some way to call Mirela. Correia's getting impatient."

"No time for cleaning up," I said, and ran for the elevator.

Pia joined us with some towels to wipe the worst of the mess off.

"The Assembly is nearly full," she said. "Skylur's on his way back. He'll be here soon."

"Any idea where Mirela is?" I asked.

"No. She sent a message to the Carpathian delegation, and they asked us the same question. Is there a problem? I mean, you wanted her to talk to the Assembly."

I was reluctant to let my paranoia out, especially with Theris listening, but he'd probably have thought of everything I had.

"I'm afraid Tezcatlipoca may be using her." I shook my head. "Or even that she thinks she's using him. She and I fought the Queen of Diamonds together, but we didn't agree to be allies beyond that. What if she's here to attack the Assembly?"

"House security won't let her in with weapons," Yelena said.

Theris and I were looking at each other, and I knew what he was thinking. In exactly the same way I'd used Pia as a sort of homing beacon to move from the spirit world into the physical world, getting Mirela into the Assembly room would allow Tezcatlipoca to send the rest of Mirela's House to join her. Fully armed.

The Mirela that had fought alongside me against the queen—she wouldn't do that. But what if she'd reverted to Vega Martine's spymaster?

Chapter 15

We burst out of the elevator, still carrying our blades, and we startled security. Bad move.

Luckily, House Demetriades was right there, so they didn't shoot us.

"House Farrell! What happened to you? Is there a security threat upstairs?"

Damn. It would look to him like we'd been attacked inside the building, which would make him responsible.

"No. I'm sorry, I can't give you any details now, but the building's security wasn't breached, and there's no threat outside this area that I know of."

He gave me a hard look, but finally accepted my lack of explanation with a curt nod. "You're allowed to enter the chamber, but you should know anyone attempting to leave is to be held until Skylur lifts the order himself. That ban extends to the entire building, not just the Assembly rooms."

He was uneasy with an order that broke Assembly rules, but he was going to enforce it.

"Do you know where House Tucek is?" I asked.

He looked surprised by the question. "Your sub-House has just gone in. Not a moment too soon, President Correia is getting impatient."

Theris beat me to it. "Tucek's claiming she's part of House Farrell?"

Demetriades blinked, and looked even more puzzled. "I based that on her marque. Is there an issue?"

"No time to explain." I pushed ahead and the others followed me.

Demetriades didn't know. Carpathians could mimic other Houses marques. Not enough to fool a careful check, but enough to pass most Athanate scrutiny.

Security the world over would need updating.

If I let that nugget of information out now, the Assembly might vote to keep the Carpathians out. More infighting. I could feel Theris' anxiety.

We entered the auditorium as quickly as we could without running. I was hoping to avoid any further attention, but heads turned.

I focused on Mirela. She stood at the front, cloaked and cowled, hidden from view. To the nearest Athanate, her marque would tell them she was House Farrell, and nothing more. No one, apart from the Carpathians, knew who she was. Elder Selsys was in front of her, asking questions. Whatever she was saying, Mirela wasn't really focused on it, because she turned as soon as I came in, and I knew beneath the darkness of her cowl, her eyes found mine immediately.

Demetriades would have checked she wasn't armed, but she looked dangerous.

I trotted down the stairs.

"House Farrell! What on earth has happened?" Correia called out. Wiping stuff off in the elevator didn't fix our appearance.

Theris replied to her, telling her there had been a minor problem, but there was nothing to affect the Assembly.

In response, Correia demanded that we get on with the testimony she'd agreed to.

I tuned the conversation out and ignored Selsys. Ignored everyone but Mirela as I approached. I stretched out with my eukori and aura but wasn't surprised to find she was completely clamped down.

"Amber," she said, her voice pitched low.

"How did you get out? Why are you here?" My questions stumbled over each other.

She saw the state of us, and spoke at the same time: "What happened to you?"

It was like the opening exchange of a sword fight. Neither of us replied, but we'd communicated more than we'd intended. Mirela knew I was suspicious. I knew she'd left the substantiation before the City had begun its attack.

How and why she'd escaped the substantiation wasn't as immediately important. "Why are you here?" I repeated and tried to reach again with my aura. I had been stronger than her last time.

Not this time.

She took a deep breath. I got the feeling she knew exactly what was in my mind. She could sense my turmoil and my fear that Tezcatlipoca was somehow acting through her.

"I'm here to make an end to it," she said, her voice barely more than a whisper.

My heart missed a beat.

Correia banged the table. "House Farrell! We've had enough of this mummery. We've had to interrupt important discussions. Proceed or this session will close, and we'll return to discussing the new structure."

"And end to what?" I asked Mirela.

She was *angry*. She let that escape the wall she'd built around her aura. There was violence in that anger.

Toward me? Maybe.

Toward the Assembly? Another maybe.

I pushed with my aura and got another glimpse that showed me a mirror of myself. Mirela had a mental strongbox like I did. A place where she hid all the pain and anger that had built up in her for so long.

"House Farrell!" Correia was approaching the end of her patience.

I had to ignore her. I couldn't risk Mirela doing something to destroy the new Assembly. But what should I do? My hand unconsciously found the hilt of the katana I still carried.

Mirela's eyes, deep in the gloom of her cowl noted my movement, and she stiffened.

"You can't say things like that and expect me to ignore it," I said.

She looked back up, her face harder. "Trust me, as I trusted you."

That hit me like a punch to the jaw.

Correia shouted again.

Mirela turned to the president in one smooth motion, shedding the cowl and cloak. She stood there dressed in the dramatic style I'd seen down in New Orleans: all black, pants tight as a paint job, loose silk shirt and jacket, tall, slim boots. Dusty pink lipstick and dangling gold earrings. There was a subtle change. Her dark hair was loosely braided and lay on her shoulder; more my style than hers.

But unmistakably Mirela, for those who'd met her. And some had, in the ranks of the auditorium. I could hear gasps. I could feel the blaze of fear in the aura of those who'd had dealings with Mirela in her position as an agent of Vega Martine and Matlal.

Correia was just puzzled. "House Tucek? What's the meaning of this? I was told an associate of House Farrell was coming to provide important information and *you* turn up."

"That was not a lie, President Correia."

There was a baffled murmuring in the auditorium as a few of the guilty delegates hurried to the exit, not realizing there would be no escape.

House Mostar for example. No surprise there, nor in most of the others leaving. Highly traditionalist and from the boundaries of Panethus territories.

But also, House Cortona. Traditionalist, yes, but a House at the very heart of Panethus Italy. An old House. A face that looked as if it had come from a two-thousand-year-old mosaic, with vivid eyes and a haughty expression.

And House Belford as well? Part of the Midnight Empire. *Damn.*

Correia frowned to see supporters leaving, and they *were* her supporters, but she didn't understand why it was happening. That reaction told me she wasn't a Matlal spy. Not a good person, but not a spy either.

Mirela ignored the movement behind her, apart from allowing the slightest smile to pass across her face.

Correia huffed. "The last the Assembly knew of you, House Tucek, you were sent to Louisiana to become a balancing syndesmon to prevent Panethus, through Farrell, from disproportionately influencing the growing Were League. Now you're here, as an associate of Farrell? What about your mission? Explain."

"The mission to Louisiana was a cover, and a ridiculous one at that," Mirela said. "There was never any chance that the League would accept another syndesmon. It wasn't worth even meeting the alphas. They'd have known it was fake, and their reputation for violence isn't exaggerated."

Correia's face paled. The orders sending Mirela to Louisiana had been from one of the dozens of Assembly subcommittees rather than Correia herself, but it was still her authority being challenged.

"So why did you go?"

"It was a ruse to get me there. Not as a member of the Hidden Path, but in my role as an agent for Basilikos."

That got a predictable response. The traditionalists and non-conformists might fight like rats in a sack, but they knew a real enemy. Matlal had tried to assassinate the entire Assembly when it had met in Denver.

"To be clear, you're stating you're an agent for Matlal?"

"I'm saying I *was*," Mirela replied.

"You understand that's still a sentence of death?" Correia raised her eyebrows.

Mirela didn't back down. Her voice was as polite, the anger beneath hidden deeply. "Do you want my testimony first?"

"Hardly a time for flippancy—"

"I don't want her talking at all." That was House Karamazin behind us. One of the ones whose aura had flared when Mirela revealed herself. But he had stayed.

"You wouldn't," Mirela said loudly. "You have more balls than the rest of them put together, Karamazin, but it won't do you any good."

Karamazin was standing now, and I could feel the weight of support he was getting from the Houses of the Hidden Path.

"She's admitted being an agent for Matlal in front of all of us, Truth Sensors included," he said, gesturing widely to include everyone around him. "This Assembly has had enough of Matlal. She's come to sow division in our ranks. I say no. I say silence her. In fact, make that permanent: execute her. There's an Assembly blanket directive covering all Matlal's allies which authorizes execution. The same goes for her sponsors who are guilty by association of working with Matlal. Now that would send out a message of unity that we can all get behind. I call on the Blade!"

There were a lot of Houses who agreed that was a good argument and just outcome. I could feel them gathering behind him. This was a dangerous point that needed careful rebuttal.

Mirela laughed.

There was a disturbing air of fatalism about her, as if she knew there was no way out for her, and she had resigned herself to it. Certainly, even if she survived the Assembly, she'd be hunted by Vega Martine and Matlal. The Blade would be a blessing in comparison to what those two would do to her.

Make an end to it, she'd said, and I felt a chill in my heart again.

There was more than anger hidden under that aura shield. Something corrosive. Such a tide of despair, she couldn't hide it all from me. I sensed bone-deep grief. Shame.

For all her brave front, it crippled her.

The Carpathians believed Mirela's testimony had to be given, but the Assembly was not going to be an easy audience. Mirela had to do it well for it to be a foundation for the new Assembly that the Carpathians wanted.

She was here to do a duty, and it put her in such an internal turmoil, she couldn't see what she was doing. Worse, it wouldn't work if she acted on that anger alone. She'd be like blinded Samson in the temple. The only thing she could do would be to pull the whole structure down around her.

Make an end to it.

I could feel the pressing of my spirit vision returning. Without the Assembly, there would be nothing but a war to end the whole world.

Suddenly, everything clicked into stark, heart-jamming focus.

And then I knew what I had to do. I had to give her back her sight. I had to let her see what we could achieve. I had to do what she'd asked me to, without knowing it: *Trust me, as I trusted you.*

That shame in her had an echo in me. I'd betrayed her. Even unknowingly. Like the Agiagraphos, the laws of shame were irrational and unforgiving.

That shame made me want to shrivel up. I couldn't betray her twice.

All in. All in or nothing.

My breath seemed short and my throat tight as I moved to face her.

Mirela's eyes seemed to take up everything I could see. Beneath the controlled expression I could feel her mania. It was like that point looking out from an Ops4-10 airplane at a dark world beneath you, with nothing but a bundle of silk strapped on your back.

TaJ. Trust and Jump.

I swallowed.

"I offer oath for oath. I offer faith for faith," I said, even though I had been faithless. "I offer Blood for Blood. I offer life for life."

Stunned silence in the auditorium. Panethus and Basilikos did not make association with each other.

Except Skylur had. He'd made this possible by taking Livia, House Flavia, as his Diakon.

Mirela blinked. Her aura shield loosened, and I felt her emotions churning beneath the surface; a wildness, a storm of thoughts and feelings, spiraling up, entwined with threads of anger and hate and shame. She felt uncontrolled. As if she was bordering on rogue.

This was *not* a safe person; my oath was not a safe option. This idea that I could protect her was stupid. She'd as likely pull me down with her. Our linked auras had made this madness contagious. I'd rescued House de Socorro from the brink in El Paso, much good it had done him. And meddling with my best intentions had cost Isabel Cuarón's life.

Too late.

I knew I was being reckless, and it wasn't going to stop me. *That* was scary. That confirmed to me the madness was in my head as well.

My voice was barely a whisper now. "I will not abandon you. I will not betray you again."

"Naïve boy scout," she murmured back. The insult she'd thrown at me on the steamboat. But her eyes had changed. Her aura was different; still wild, still angry, but more focused.

Moving as swiftly as a snake, she gripped my arm and called out so all could hear. "Faith for faith. My Blood, life, loyalty and obedience to House Farrell. I will honor the obligations and responsibilities of the House. I submit to the absolute rule of the House. I offer House Tucek into the mantle of House Farrell entirely. Oath for oath."

The shock of it went through me like lightning. Not an alliance, not an association, a complete submission of her entire House into mine. Binding them to me through her. And me to them.

And on top of all that, binding us all into what was happening here, on the floor of the Assembly, and which would now depend on Mirela to get us out.

"Oath for oath," I repeated the binding phrase. The words seemed to fall from my lips before I could catch them. "I grant the protection, rights and privileges within my gift."

"My Blood is yours. It is done," we spoke together.

Shit.

I felt as if I'd been struck with a hammer.

Chapter 16

People crowded me. My House. Others.

"So witnessed!" rang out. Yelena, in loyalty, whatever her misgivings. Pia, too. Maybe Livia and Marguerite in solidarity? But Theris and Elder Selsys joined in. My earlier worries about their agenda resurfaced.

"That was well done, Kyria Chrysos," Selsys said loudly.

I was going to refuse the name again, but Yelena was hissing in my ear.

"Is protection," Yelena whispered under cover of a hug. "House Chrysos is part of the Domain's association. Means we're all under the Carpathian mantle. All of us. Even Mirela. Remember, Skylur's not here yet."

Mirela scowled.

She was Carpathian, but she had issues with them. I doubted they anticipated how it turned out, but I had the suspicion they'd maneuvered both of us into meeting their requirement. I had so many questions, and no time to ask them.

The Heights joined us. "I will inform the League of your inclusion in the pack of Colorado and New Mexico. Welcome."

And Hinton, saying little other than a greeting for Mirela, but her eyes sharp and clearly very interested in my new sub-House's aura shields.

The Domain, the Leagues of Were and Adepts. Correia couldn't go against that level of support. Mirela was safe for now. And given the way the Agiagraphos worked, I was too.

Whether that held when Mirela completed her talk was another matter.

I still felt the wildness in her, the anger. Things could still go crazy.

What had I done?

Karamazin took the opportunity to storm out, still unaware that arrest waited for him. House Demetriades had been keeping it very quiet, no doubt arranging for the arrests to be made in the elevator or on the ground floor out of sight and hearing from the meeting.

The Assembly Clerk wanted to record the new information in the log of associations, but Correia curtly told him to keep it for later and banged the desk for silence. But as it fell, Mirela decided to answer the Clerk's question on creed and associations.

Her voice seemed both familiar and strange to me. Satin whispering over steel. Controlled, for the moment.

"I am Panethus."

Sneers and disbelief from the delegates.

"Really?" Correia mocked. "A Carpathian rogue, claiming to be Hidden Path while working for Matlal, and therefore Basilikos by creed, dragged back here by Carpathians, where you snatch the opportunity to hide behind an Altau sub-House? Now instantly, magically Panethus?"

Mirela didn't back down. She raised her arm slowly to direct attention to the Truth Sensors sitting to the side of the stage.

The Adepts remained silent; what she'd said was true. The shock of that subdued the room for a moment.

"My associations are now governed by House Farrell," Mirela said. "Which makes me Panethus politically, but my creed has also been changed by her, from Basilikos to Panethus, and whereas you're wrong about the path I followed to get here, such a dramatic change of creed is perfectly possible." Mirela turned and paced to where the Carpathians sat. "Isn't it, Elder Selsys?"

House Selsys didn't move, didn't respond, her face unreadable.

Mirela's body seemed to quiver with controlled rage as she swung around again. "My *first* association and affiliation were Carpathian. I was raised and trained by the Domain of Carpathia and sent to strengthen their spy network among Basilikos. The network headed by House Vega Martine, Diakon to House Matlal. Yes, delegates, Vega Martine was the pinnacle of the Domain's espionage."

A shock in my head as pieces of the puzzle came together.

Mirela and Vega Martine were both Carpathian spies.

Vega Martine had gone rogue, and the Carpathians had sent Mirela in there to see what could be salvaged of their operation.

But right here and now, Mirela was doing her best to piss off everyone. The Carpathians didn't want the Assembly to know about their spying. The Assembly had already had their conception of what the Carpathians were jolted once, and now twice. And Mirela had been involved in Matlal's actions against them. The delegates knew most of them would have died at the Denver Assembly if Vega Martine's plans had worked.

But, as I'd witnessed before, the Assembly was a beast that could be led.

"Such deception, delegates. Layers upon layers of deception," Mirela continued, shaking her head. "The Domain, Matlal and Vega Martine all thought they were deceiving each other. Each one believed themselves to be the only ones with a clear understanding of what was happening. The only ones who had it right. The only ones in control." She paused and lowered her voice. "It was a madhouse... and into this madhouse of smoke and mirrors and paranoia, I was sent, with orders to be Vega Martine's loyal follower."

She'd caught her audience now. The lure had been to glimpse into the hidden worlds that were Basilikos and Carpathia, at the expense of both, but the snare itself was the horror of the orders she'd been given.

Mirela's words now fell like pebbles into a deep lake.

"To be a follower of Matlal's own Diakon meant I had to declare my allegiance to Basilikos. To take Basilikos as my creed." She clenched her fist and held it over her heart, then she began to pace in front of the steeped ranks of the auditorium like a caged leopard. Everyone focused on her, focused on the energy pouring out of her, and she lifted her shields a little and allowed some of the emotion that fueled her to leak.

Softly, she said: "You'll hear people call espionage a game."

Silence, but for her steps and the heartbeat of the whole room. A *listening* silence.

"It's not a *game*," she hissed, and her anger lit the words like fire. "It's not a *masquerade*. You do not *play* at being Basilikos."

She was back in front of the Carpathians, and she knelt, not in supplication, but so she looked straight into Elder Selsys' face.

"To perform my mission, to obey my orders, to *survive...*" her words lashed out, "I had to *be* Basilikos."

A flicker on the Carpathian's faces? Utter silence. Breaths stilled, hearts stalled.

"Just as the Elders of Carpathia knew I would have to be, when they gave me their orders."

An unending moment, caught in the furnace of emotion that passed between them.

Elder Selsys's head dipped the tiniest fraction, as if her spine was incapable of more, and then Mirela was up and pacing again, so swiftly, I wasn't sure I'd seen Selsys' acknowledgment.

"And so I was," she said and threw her arms outward. "I obeyed my orders, and here I stand, obeying for the last time. I not only survived in Matlal's madhouse, I prospered. I formed my House, and we were very good at what we did, so the House prospered too."

I shivered as if the air in the auditorium had cooled, and I felt Yelena stir beside me. She'd been in a similar position. A Carpathian spy placed by her masters into Basilikos Houses. The only difference was where she'd been placed. Yelena had been assigned outside of Matlal's inner clique. Mirela had been thrown into the eye of the storm.

Yelena reached a point where she refused, Tara said quietly. *And she came to us.*

The auditorium stayed quiet, even while they shifted uncomfortably. This was a heart-twisting point in Agiagraphos law—obedience to those to whom you'd given an oath, even if their orders were to give your allegiance to another. To leave the Panethus creed and embrace Basilikos, and not the generic Basilikos creed of most of the Hidden Path party, but the bloody, violent extremism of Matlal's faction.

"I did so very well," Mirela went on, "I was put in charge of Matlal's planning for attacks on Altau, here in the United States. Then for his plans against Panethus in other countries. And given how well I achieved those preparations, my House was the obvious choice to rescue Matlal from imprisonment last year."

"That success cemented my position in Matlal's estimation. But as happens in the madhouse, to rise in one place is to fall in another. I was slow to see that. Vega Martine no longer trusted me. She arranged, by suborning the Assembly's own subcommittees, for me to be sent down to Louisiana with the right to call on the Athanate Houses there. But it was all a plan within a plan. Vega Martine betrayed me. I was abandoned to the mercies of a powerful witch so secretive, most of you don't even know her name. The Queen of Diamonds, as she was known. A witch so powerful, she rivalled Matlal in the potential of damage she could do to the whole world.

"And to survive *her*, I had to make a deal with House Farrell."

Murmurs of disbelief about the Queen of Diamonds. Delegates found it hard to understand how there could be someone so powerful that they'd never heard of. Mirela simply pointed to the Truth Sensors again.

"I made that deal, and so now I'm here, a sub-House of Farrell, associated with both Altau and the Domain, and I am *Panethus* with full knowledge of what I did, what I was ordered to do, while I was Basilikos."

She stopped, her eyes burning, and swiveled back to Elder Selsys.

"And now, I am ready to obey the last command from my former masters, after which there will be an end to it."

A long moment ended with the hint of a reluctant dipping of the head from the Carpathian leader.

Chapter 17

"Part of my role for Matlal was as controller of his spies in the Assembly," Mirela said.

The delegates stirred and some looked to either side.

"Lies," called out one of the delegates. House Haldimann. She was a staunch Hidden Path traditionalist. "We can't trust her. As Karamazin said, she's here to cripple the functioning of this body by making us turn on each other."

"More than you do already?"

Haldimann seethed, but Mirela went straight on. "Did you notice when I revealed myself, a group of Houses left the meeting immediately? Did you wonder why?"

She paced again.

"Those were traitors. They left not because of some minor dispute about overriding the rules of the Assembly to let me in, but because they knew I could identify them."

She'd had the room under her spell, but now enough of them were angry that the cohesion had been lost.

Haldimann took it up as the spokesperson. "You're the traitor. You've just admitted it. You worked for Matlal, and we all were your targets. You can't then throw accusations like that around and expect to be believed. Turning coat doesn't buy you support."

"I'm not here to apologize for what I've done, to defend my decision to obey orders and join Basilikos, or to rationalize my oath to Matlal. I'm not going to justify what cannot be justified. I'm not here for validation. There is nothing I can say that will do me any good in your eyes anyway, so I'm not here to dwell in the past, because the past is peopled with unprofitable ghosts of what might have been.

"I'll talk instead about what will happen, and happen soon, if you continue your current course. I have nothing comforting to say, and it will hurt. That's how you'll know it's the truth: it will hurt.

"I look at this Assembly and see the unprofitable ghosts of the future. Emergence is not 'going to happen'—it's happening as you sit here. *Matlal* has a plan; *Altau* has a plan; *you* have arguments about who gets to plan."

It was the truth, and it did hurt. Delegates leaped to their feet and shouted at Mirela.

We must abide by the rules was their main message.

She ignored them and waited until Correia's gavel restored some semblance of order before going straight back into the attack.

"Get over your precious rules," Mirela said. "You have two objectives you must achieve. You must survive Matlal's plan, and you must survive discovery by humanity."

The noise of reaction rose again, but she spoke over it.

"The two objectives are bound together, because Matlal planted traitors inside this Assembly who have worked to frustrate any progress on how to deal with humanity. You have to deal with them before this Assembly can function."

"These are just allegations. Why should we believe you? You have no proof!" Haldimann again. "I say you've been compelled to come here and give this speech."

Mirela stopped her pacing in front of Livia and took a thumb drive out of her pocket.

"Diakon Altau," she addressed her formally as she handed over the drive. "Here is the proof of what I've said—a list of traitors with details of hidden servers, secure communications, protocols, safe houses, messages, bank accounts. Those are all I've had dealings with. It's not comprehensive: there are even more known only to Matlal. But as for Vega Martine's plans, this drive lists her strategy against the Assembly and specifically against Panethus in this country."

Correia stormed down from the dais.

"As president of the Assembly, I demand you give me that drive," Correia said.

"I'll copy it in front of you," Livia replied, closing her hand. "In fact, I'll copy it to everyone in the Assembly."

"No! I need to evaluate it first."

Mirela held up her hand. "By all means, copy it for everyone to evaluate, but as soon as it's released, everything will disappear. Not because there are more traitors, but because most of your Houses have piss-poor security. I *know*, because that was part of my job too."

Angry words grew to an angry roar.

We were about to lose control of this situation.

Say what you like about Skylur, but you had to admire his sense of timing, bursting in at exactly the right moment. He had Naryn and Demetriades right behind him.

He lacked the magic aura that had made the Carpathian entrance so spectacular, and as ever, his physical appearance was unremarkable. But the sheer weight of his presence rocked the delegates back. That was magic of a different order.

He spoke, and people listened.

"While I have not inspected that file, the evidence of House Tucek's truthfulness fills the foyer outside."

"What do you mean?" Correia said.

"On my orders, my security have held all the delegates and entourages that left the auditorium."

"You're breaking Assembly laws?" Correia said. "You come in here and bare-facedly admit to it?"

"My actions are justified, President Correia, because the delegates outside have broken their Assembly oaths. If they were ever members of the Assembly, they aren't now. The guarantee of safe passage no longer applies."

"You want to see proof?" he said and gestured to some of his security team standing in the entranceway.

Two of the delegates who'd left in such a hurry were brought back in. Houses Karamazin and Cortona. One Hidden Path, one Panethus. They weren't struggling, or even speaking. Their faces were still. Their eyes passed unconcerned and uncomprehending over the room.

Skylur didn't need to explain. Almost everyone in the auditorium had been present when this had happened before their eyes to Judicator Philippe Remy at the Denver Assembly. Matlal didn't trust his spies and traitors. All of them had this horrific, mind-destroying compulsion that would activate if they were caught.

Unconsciously, I reached with eukori. There was nothing there. I shuddered, and many others in the auditorium did too.

"I think we must accept House Tucek has been truthful and listen carefully to anything further she might have to say," Skylur said as he continued down the steps. "And then we need to press ahead swiftly to incorporate all paranormals into the Assembly."

"This is outrageous!" Correia said. "I am the president, and we will not progress until I have reviewed the supposed evidence on that drive—"

Diakon Huang interrupted. "We do not have time to further investigate the veracity of something that is patently true. If you persist in delay, I will move a vote of no confidence and a return of House Altau to president."

Elder Selsys stood. "Seconded."

Correia was tight-lipped with fury, but there was nothing she could do if the leaders of three major factions voted her out, and there was no doubt which way Skylur would vote. She returned to her dais.

"The leaders of factions approach," she said, glaring at them. "The rest, move away."

The fight hadn't gone out of her yet. The Hidden Path needed to be bound into the new Assembly, and they weren't going to be happy if they lost the presidency. However urgent it was to proceed, there would need to be serious horse-trading first.

But it wasn't going to go exactly to her plan either. Faith Hinton decided she qualified as a faction leader. Seeing her move toward the dais, The Heights joined her. And seeing *him* go, the alphas of the Rocky Mountain packs hurried forward.

They had some cookie cutter machine churning out those alphas. All over six foot. Solid. Bull-necked and surly eyed. Hard-wearing work clothes in styles all the way from lumberjack to ranch hand. Shit-kicking boots. I'd have to resort to hair color to tell them apart.

I bit my lip to see them nodding to something Faith was saying, tapping the desk for emphasis while Correia was trying to usher them away.

Skylur didn't immediately go to the table. He took Mirela aside for a brief but intense discussion, while I found myself standing next to Naryn, watching them.

Naryn and I didn't get along well. He was Skylur's former Diakon and had been awarded Ibarre's territory after the Los Angeles Assembly, so now, as House Bazir, he held Boston and Portland. There were no explicit ranks, but he and House Tarez in Los Angeles were probably equal second-in-command of Panethus. I got on fine with Tarez, but not with Naryn. We had uncomplimentary opinions about each other's decisions. It was entirely possible we were both right.

He was looking hard at Mirela, and he spoke quietly.

"Are you entirely sure about this?"

I knew what he meant. He'd obviously been listening to the broadcast, and there was no point in lying to him.

"No." I turned to look him in the eye. "No, I'm not entirely sure."

Our gazes remained locked for several seconds.

"Good," he said finally. "You know, she reminds me of you. Conflicted. Raw. Unpredictable. Eminently capable, but prone to impetuous decisions."

"I'll give you she seems to work on instinct sometimes."

"Toh-may-to, toh-mar-to."

Naryn making jokes?

He nodded toward Skylur, who was now joining the group around Correia. "He's going to close the doors in a minute, and force everyone to stay here until the structure of an agreement covering all paranormals is reached."

That was going to last too long for me. Naryn was giving me a warning to get out while the going was good.

"Thank you, House Bazir."

He nodded, an almost-smile playing on his lips.

Mirela had left while my attention was distracted. I gathered my House and followed. I had questions. So many questions.

Like how she'd escaped the substantiation. I'd start with that.

Chapter 18

Mirela had gone to my suite, up on the 15th floor.

Our suite. Security had given her a key because she was my sub-House and carried my marque.

Mirela wasn't in sight in the reception area, but one of her House was, near the closed door to the gym. I remembered her, the face and the vivid red hair. I had a suspicion she was the one who'd knocked me out when I'd snuck into their 'convent' in Taos.

No sign of that in her expression. In fact, her face was carefully blank.

She recognized me, of course.

"Mistress." She bowed her head the minimum amount demanded by etiquette for greeting the new head of your House, and despite the acknowledgment, her voice was cool.

"Amber," I corrected her, and she nodded.

"I'm Dosia." She indicated the door behind her. "Mirela is in the dojo. She's expecting you."

I could feel Yelena bristle at the disrespectful attitude, but it wasn't important. Dosia, like all House Tucek, had been subject to a compulsion in my substantiation. A compulsion that forced a change on them, and I knew I had work to do to overcome the resentment from that.

I headed into the dojo, Theris and Yelena right on my shoulder.

Dosia let me pass and then put out an arm to stop the others.

I stopped them before anyone could get into the *lose that arm* threats. "I'd like to talk to Mirela alone first," I said. "How about you guys fix some coffees and get to know each other."

Yelena and Theris exchanged calculating glances. They were obviously in agreement about picking their battles, and this was one they decided to skip. I didn't imagine that would apply to many other situations, but a room in the middle of Skylur's HQ, with no other entrance and a woman who'd just sworn an oath to me?

They stood back and I went on alone.

Mirela had found some sweats and boxing gloves. She was pummeling the hell out of a punching bag. Still very, very angry and working it out on the bag.

She pulled off the right-hand glove and tossed it to me.

"Queensbury rules. One handed," she said.

"I don't want to fight you. I want to talk."

"Well, better put the glove on and protect your mouth then."

I sighed and slipped on the glove. Wearing only her left-hand glove made her take a southpaw stance. One-handed, opposite stances? I'd done boxing, but never this. It felt clumsy.

Whatever.

She swooped in and probed at me with jabs, hard enough to tell me she was serious.

I ducked and weaved. Jabbed back.

I *really* didn't feel like fighting. Felt slow. Lightheaded. Slightly nauseous. This goddamn poison was still proving hard to shift.

Mirela swung at me. Too hard. Her left-handed glove whizzed past me. She'd opened herself up.

There was one good way to stop this. I put all my effort behind a straight to her jaw…

I knew that had gone wrong when her jaw suddenly wasn't there.

Something exploded in my face. Everything went black and then I was blinking up at the ceiling.

"You hit me with your right," I said, or tried to say. My jaw felt disconnected.

Her knees slammed on either side of my chest, her body weight pinning me down. She bent down and got in my face.

"How does it feel?" she screamed.

I knew I should get up and fight. *Never lie down. Never. Get up!*

"So heavy," I said.

She grabbed my shirt and shook me. "How does it feel when you trust someone, and they break the rules?"

I'd understood her the first time, but I felt too tired to answer. Too dazed by the blow and too tired to care. My eyes closed. The cuts from the Queen of Diamonds swords had reopened when I fell, and blood now trickled down onto my neck.

I couldn't just lie here, but I couldn't get up. I had to do something, so I might as well explain. I frowned and concentrated hard to speak clearly. "I didn't know about the compulsion. Tezcatlipoca made the substantiation. He put it in. I only worked out what must have happened yesterday. I came to bring you out today and the whole place was falling apart. I'm sorry. I didn't mean to compel you. I just wanted you and your House somewhere safe."

The effort exhausted me. She didn't answer. I could feel her fingers tearing opening my shirt.

"What the hell is this?"

"It's nothing," I said. "The queen poisoned her swords. It's just taking a long time to heal—"

"Shit! *Shit!* Why the fuck didn't you say?"

Her reaction got me to open my eyes. The anger had evaporated.

"Shit," she said again.

"You said that already."

She bent over my neck. "Trust me, Amber."

I snorted. "Says the woman who just cheated and hit me."

Her fangs sank into my neck. No preliminaries. Straight in.

You *have* to trust someone with their fangs in your jugular. All it would take would be one violent twist of the head, one rip. Not even Athanate bio-agents could close a wound like that.

Biting and getting bitten is one of the many bonuses of being Athanate, especially as it's accompanied by such profound pleasure. Except when it wasn't. Mirela's eukori was locked as tight as it had been all day, but we'd shared auras, and that's harder to close off. She wasn't denying me the pleasure of her sensations. She was frantic.

Adepts sometimes recite meaningless formulas that they've associated with the mental construction required in creating a working. I'd heard that some Athanate use the same trick for complex healings.

That was essentially what Mirela was doing—a healing that wasn't one of the standard, almost instinctive healings that Athanate can perform.

Weird and getting weirder was all I could think.

My heart tried to race as I realized she was feeding me pacifics as well— effectively tranquilizing me.

Too slow. They'd already taken effect and there was nothing I could do other than lie there and focus on what was happening.

Too difficult for her to do all that *and* keep me out of her aura. Or to keep our auras from binding tighter. Even though she was angry at me, that was minor. There was anger at the Carpathians, at the Assembly and lots more anger about herself.

I'd taken anger from the Threefold Spiral Coven; I'd taken the fuel for their curse on the first-born of the Farrells. I'd taken it and stored it in my strongbox because my strange brand of aura powers could use that fuel. And so I took some of Mirela's anger and tried to replace it with something less corrosive.

I couldn't really tell if it worked. There weren't any manuals for this.

Long minutes passed before her fangs eased out and her bio-agents flooded the wound, sealing it.

There was no elation. No sense of achievement. I sensed nothing more than a wry acknowledgement of the strengthened bond between us.

She rested her head on my chest briefly.

"Damn you, Amber," she sighed. "Damn you and damn the Queen of Diamonds and damn me and damn everything."

I felt her eukori reach for Dosia, who opened the door quickly.

"Get the others," Mirela said.

It wasn't necessary to get them. They pushed their way in, demanding to know what the hell was going on.

I rolled up into a sitting position. Still a bit dizzy, but better than I had been.

"Relax. I'm fine, guys. Mirela's done some kind of healing on me. Got rid of some poison that the queen used on her blades."

"Oh, shit!" That was Dosia.

I turned to look at her. She'd gone white—the sort of white that's meant in clichés like *as a sheet*.

I frowned.

"What's going on? Why is this such a big thing?"

"I haven't healed you," Mirela said. "I've repaired some damage. No one can heal you of the Queen of Diamonds' poison, except her. Or her antidotes, I guess. Meanwhile, you're dying, and now, I probably am too. Along with anyone else who's tried healing you."

She said it so casually, filled with such fatalism, I almost disbelieved her. Almost.

I could *feel* the cell in my pocket, still switched off, returned to me when I'd left the Assembly.

The last message on it. *Call.* From Diana. Who'd tried healing me down in Louisiana.

Chapter 19

As I'd have expected, the comms in my suite had full video call functionality.

We had Diana, Bian, Tullah and Gwen logged in from Denver.

We had Mirela's Diakon, Salar Lazarescu, on audio. She was hiding out down in Louisiana with the remainder of Tucek's House. She was online with Donatienne Gaudreau, the Rougarou alpha and former captain of the *Queen of Diamonds* steamboat.

We had Livia come out of the Assembly and join us, with Skylur's instruction to *do anything necessary*. Except there wasn't anything obvious we could do.

There was an air of tension as we crowded around the conference system.

"The queen's poisons aren't ordinary poisons," Mirela explained again for the benefit of those who hadn't caught the first rundown. "They don't affect humans. Some of them affect Adepts, some of them affect shifters. What she used on Amber is one of the ones specific to Athanate. It attacks Athanate Blood, and the older the Athanate, the quicker and more powerful the effect. It can pass from Athanate to Athanate in Blood if healing is attempted. It is fatal."

We looked at Diana, who nodded. "I have been poisoned from trying to heal Amber," she said calmly, despite what she'd been hearing. "Possibly Bian, from trying to heal me. But you've done something for Amber?"

"When Vega Martine made a deal with the Queen of Diamonds, we learned about the poisons, but the queen didn't give House Tucek any antidotes. Instead, she gave us a way of delaying the poison's effect and told us we would have to return to her to be cured."

"How much delaying can you do?" Bian asked.

Mirela snorted. "The queen's little joke. I can keep delaying the progress of the poison in Amber right up until the poison takes its toll of me. Then someone else would need to take over, but with the burden of having two people to attend to. They'd become poisoned too, and so on."

"Does anything else help?"

"For Athanate, Blood from humans. It dilutes your Athanate Blood and reduces the speed of progress. It won't harm the human, but no other Athanate should feed from them for some time after, or they risk having the poison transferred to them."

"Oh." I'd fed from Jo and Xavier. "Anyone else bitten you?" I asked them.

They shook their heads, both of them shocked into silence. I got it. This kind of thing didn't happen to Athanate. We could be killed, yes, but not by a *poison*.

"What about a complete transfusion?" Livia asked.

Mirela shrugged. "We hadn't got to testing that. I suspect an Athanate trying it would die anyway. Still, it's an idea. Donatienne was part of the queen's hierarchy. She might know."

"I don't know for sure," Donatienne said. "I doubt it. The queen didn't allow for escapes like that."

There were some long moments of absolute silence, broken eventually by Mirela, who sat with her head bowed.

"Salar..." she said and stopped.

"I understand," The voice on the audio was even. "I'll go to Haven immediately."

"What?" Bian frowned.

"The kumemnon is older than us all," Mirela said. "The poison works faster for older Athanate. We don't have time to argue this."

"I will not have someone offer to kill themselves for a few more days of my life," Diana said. "I forbid it."

"You can, of course, refuse me, kumemnon," Salar said. "But the choice to risk my life is mine alone, and I make it, for both you and House Trang."

"To what end, if we all die?"

Mirela interrupted. "The purpose is to keep you alive while we find a solution."

"Is there a solution?" Diana said.

"We don't know." Exasperation tinged Mirela's voice. "But it would be tragic to find one after you died."

There was background noise on the audio, urgent voices speaking.

"Just confirmed. We've managed to hire a private jet that'll be ready as soon as it's fueled," Salar said. "I'm leaving for the airport now."

More noises.

"Wait—" Bian said.

Donatienne cleared her throat. "She's gone, House Trang."

Bian slammed hands down on the table. "I don't trust this."

"Don't trust what?" Mirela said.

"You! Your House. This 'noble' gesture."

"They are part of my House now, Bian," I said. "Um... our Houses."

"What? Since when?"

"This morning, in the Assembly."

Bian's mouth hardened. I'd taken the oath, but the way Bian and I were, our Houses interwoven, that made them part of *her* House as well.

"Faith for faith, life for life," Mirela said. "We are now within the mantle of House Farrell, with all rights and obligations to House Trang, and to the kumemnon. Salar and I understand this is what House Farrell wants us to do."

"No!" Bian yelled. "You're Basilikos. You're Vega Martine's agent—"

"She *was* Basilikos," I interrupted Bian. "She was also Vega Martine's head of espionage. And now, she's not. She's mine. Ours."

It hurt to argue with Bian when I understood exactly how this must look to her. But I was here, with Mirela. I trusted her and she was part of my House. *Mine.*

No, *ours.*

Unless Bian withdrew.

"You believe her," Bian said. "What do you really know? Did she escape from your sanctuary in the spirit world, or was she taken out? Who by? You travelled out of the spirit world using your connection to Diana. What connection had she got that could be greater than Vega Martine?"

Mirela tried to answer, but Bian kept going. "I mean, think about it. What do we know about her? By her own admission, she was involved in creating those compulsions."

I knew what she was thinking, behind that. Her own House had been affected. Marlon Pruitt had been compelled to betray her, and had suffered the same fate on discovery as the delegates downstairs—his mind had been destroyed. What if Mirela had been the person responsible?

Bian was relentless. "Those compulsions can mask a person from Truth Sensors. What if she's under one? What if this poison isn't as bad as they're claiming, and this is just an excuse to get an assassin in here?"

Mirela held her hands up to stop her.

"Look, I can't prove it to you, House Trang. There are techniques I could teach you and the Adepts which might allow you to see the compulsions. I suspect Hecate Enkeliekki is already capable of seeing them, but she's not here with me and we have no time."

She sighed and shook her head. "The ability to create the type of compulsion you're talking about was something only the Queen of Diamonds had. Your real problem is that if she'd compelled me, I wouldn't be able to tell you about it, so you can't believe me."

"Hold it," I cut in. "Gwen, Mirela's just said you might be able to see whether a person's under a compulsion. What do you say?"

"Probably," Gwen said. "If we spirit walk, Bryn will be able to tell."

"Then, when Salar arrives, you take her on a spirit walk. If you're quick, the City won't notice."

"I can help," Tullah said, and she meant she and Kaothos could help.

"That solves that," I said.

Mirela's mouth twisted without humor. "Not completely. You see, Salar *is* under a compulsion. Not Vega Martine's. Amber's. Or strictly speaking, Tezcatlipoca's."

I'd told Diana that the substantiation Tezcatlipoca had set up had included a compulsion to become more like me. The reason it had the most effect on Mirela was because we'd merged auras while we had been trapped in the Queen of Diamonds' substantiation. But Salar would have been subject to a subtle compulsion for the length of time she'd spent in my substantiation.

Diana waved it away. "Not the same thing as one of Vega Martine's or the Queen of Diamond's."

Gwen agreed. "Bryn would be able see the difference between something compelling Salar to lie and being capable of destroying her mind on one hand, and an imposition or an influence of Amber's aura, with everything she believes in, on the other." Gwen tilted her head to one side, and I could sense Bryn looking through her eyes. "That must be uncomfortable for you."

"You have no idea," Mirela said.

"I am still fascinated to find out how you got out of Amber's substantiation, if Tezcatlipoca didn't do it for you in exchange for something. Normally, I'd expect Amber to be the only other person who would be able to come and go."

Mirela snorted. "She is."

"Explain, please."

"Amber and I shared auras when we had to escape from the queen's steamboat. She has some of me in her, and I have some of her in me, at a whole heap of levels." She wiped a tired hand over her face. "When she had Tezcatlipoca set up a refuge, it wasn't just for me, it was for my whole House. Tezcatlipoca had to use me as a guide to find them. He can't manifest in the physical world. I spirit-walked with him so he could use my connection to reach them. My House was dispersed, so we had to do that exercise nine times. As you've found with your aura-enhanced training, even something very complex can be learned when your auras are meshed. The Amber part of me learned to travel out of the spirit world. After Amber's last visit, when

I realized there was a compulsion built into the substantiation, I moved my House out to secret locations we'd set up in Louisiana."

Giving her enough time to hear about the planned Assembly and receive instructions to attend from Elder Selsys. Thinking it through, it also made sense that Tezcatlipoca had stopped defending the site after Mirela and her House had left.

Not what Bian focused on, though.

"You 'meshed' auras with Tezcatlipoca?" she said.

"Sure. Same as Amber did. You trust her?" Mirela replied. "Look, there's a point where I can't persuade you I'm on your side whatever I say. I've revealed the Matlal spy networks in North America. I've offered my House to Altau to take out the Atrax nests of assassins—"

"The what?" Bian interrupted.

"Remember the ranch on the high plains outside of Denver that you raided last year? The one with the children? That was a project Atrax site. There are similar places outside a dozen of the largest cities in the US and Canada, waiting for Matlal's green light to go kill every Panethus Athanate they can find in those cities."

"Skylur mentioned you'd volunteered to stop them, but there's not enough of you to do it all in the time we have," Livia said.

Mirela dipped her head. "You're right. It'd take us days or even weeks to do it alone. There are reporting protocols for all those Atrax teams, just as there are for his spies in the Assembly. As soon as someone misses their report and Matlal realizes what's happened today, he'll order them to go ahead regardless."

"But *we* can do it. You don't need to do it alone," I said. "We've been training former Ops 4-10 troops and sending them out to Houses that are short of numbers. They may not be in the right places at this moment, but they could be very quickly. You could split your House up and lead them."

"We'd go with that, as a House, except for Salar, who stays with the kumemnon, and me... I'm with you," Mirela said. "Remember, poison, death and so on?"

I snorted. No, I hadn't forgotten, but she'd managed to make me laugh about it.

Bian still looked unconvinced.

"I know you're not going to trust me, certainly not until you've met me," Mirela said. "But promise not to harm Salar and I'll tell you something you'll find worth your restraint."

On the screen I saw Diana put her hand over Bian's.

"I promise," Bian ground out.

"Okay. You took an oath many years ago, House Trang. An oath made in French-era Saigon. All these many years, that oath has remained unredeemed."

Bian's eyes turned pure black, and she went still with fury.

"What do you know of it?" she demanded.

"I am—or I *was* the head of espionage for Vega Martine. We had files on people like you. We had ears in many places, over many years, and no nugget of information was thrown away if verified." She waved it away. "You are the ehvasi of one of the most powerful of Athanate of the time. The man who was your tutor and mentor, who you knew as Yi Song. The Athanate ruler of the free city of Saigon. An ancient Athanate, wise in the ways of death, including by poison."

A twitch in Bian's face acknowledged the information was correct.

"Yet he was killed," Mirela said, "with a poison that he knew only from its effect on him. You took an oath, a solemn Blood oath, that you would kill the person responsible for that poison. Yet you couldn't find them. The nearest you got was to gather rumors and legends of the magical Stone Serpents and the shadowy Maid of Serpents."

Diana gasped. *She* knew what this was coming to, but Bian and the rest of us didn't.

"We've been calling it a poison that's killing us," Mirela went on. "In fact, it's venom. It's the venom of one of the Stone Serpents."

Bian stared from the screen as if she would jump through it.

"Your oath is redeemed," Mirela said softly. "The Maid of the Serpents was also the Queen of Diamonds, and Amber killed her."

Chapter 20

That wasn't what had happened, but I didn't get the chance to speak.

Dosia spoke quietly. "There may be another way to healing, Kiria."

"No!"

Mirela's single, angry word was intended to end the conversation, but there were too many listening for that. Clearly, Mirela and her House knew what Dosia meant, but we didn't.

"Tell us what this is, please," Diana asked.

Mirela's face settled into stubborn lines, but she explained anyway.

"We don't have any antidotes, but Vega Martine *may* have been given an antidote by the Queen of Diamonds."

"That helps us how, exactly?" Bian said.

"In a previous incident with another House that betrayed their oaths, Vega Martine accepted them back on her own terms. Those terms were that the mistress was made to kill one in five of her House in front of everybody."

Mirela lifted her head. "The terms would be worse for my betrayal. Two in five? Three? I can't do it. I couldn't do it the way I was before, and I certainly can't do it now. Besides, whatever she boasted, I'm not sure that Vega Martine actually has the antidote, or, if she does have one, whether it's the right one. And if it's the right one, that she'd let us use it on the kumemnon."

"I can't accept this whether she has an antidote or not," I said to Dosia. "We find another way."

"Agreed," Diana said, and that was the end of that option.

Bian watched us. She'd gone quiet for now.

"This antidote… what is it?" Yelena asked. "A bottle of something hidden in her possessions? A magic working someone else can use? Instructions?"

Mirela shook her head. "I don't know. Donatienne? You were closest to her."

"I'm not sure either," she said. "I can tell you that the queen never kept anything valuable in the physical world. She once said something about keeping her soul in the spirit world, but she often made jokes like that. But whatever this antidote is, it wouldn't be easy to get to. It might be something that was only in her head, but if it's a potion or instructions of some kind, it would be in one of her substantiations."

"The main substantiation, the one that contained the steamboat and the rivers of Louisiana—that was destroyed, wasn't it?" Diana asked.

"Yes," I said. "The substantiation was huge and required the powers of some ancient African gods she captured. I freed them, and I imagine the whole substantiation fell apart and was consumed by the City of Lost Gods quickly after that."

"That boat wasn't the place she'd have kept something like an antidote," Donatienne said.

"How many other substantiations did she have?"

"Several. A modern hotel, a primitive hunting lodge, a nineteenth-century plantation, a sort of Tibetan monastery. Those are the ones I know."

"Did you go to any of them?"

"Yes. The hotel and the lodge."

"Either of them likely candidates?"

"The hotel maybe. It was large, and she kept the top floor for herself. Definitely not the lodge—that was just a shack."

I thought about it while others questioned her. A hotel, even with a floor sealed off, didn't seem a likely place. As Donatienne expanded on what she knew, the hotel dropped in my evaluation. Too many people passing through. The monastery sounded more like it. Isolated. Probably peopled by devotees who would never question her, or look through her belongings.

What would happen to them now? Were the substantiations already collapsing without her power feeding them? Were we too late?

Yelena asked if she'd been to the plantation.

"No," Donatienne answered. She shuddered. "The Sherwood Plantation wasn't for casual visitors. People who went there were being punished or warned. A lot didn't come back. I didn't want to *go to Sherwoo*." She made air quotes to emphasize the phrase.

She'd also changed the pronunciation of the name, dropping the 'd' at the end of Sherwood.

Bian came back into the conversation abruptly. "Why did you say it like that?"

"Ah... we all used that phrase out of her hearing. Dark humor, I guess," Donatienne said. "When the queen went there, she was always in her Chinese persona. That's how she pronounced it. We weren't exactly going to bring it up with her."

"She didn't speak with an accent when she was talking to me," I said.

"No." Bian leaned forward on the Denver screen, animated again. "She didn't. *That's* where the antidote will be. The plantation. The name isn't Sherwood. It's 'shé wū'. It's old Mandarin for the House of the Serpents."

"Well, great," Mirela said slowly, "but even if it still exists, how do we get there?"

"This is probably the time to tell you that I didn't actually kill her," I said.

I could hear Donatienne gasp over the audio connection.

"She's not in any position to harm you," I said quickly.

Everyone waited.

"I can't quite explain it with words," I said. "I'll try. At the end, down in the swamps, the queen got me to fight her with swords, but it was just a distraction while she connected, through me, with Tezcatlipoca. One moment we were fighting in the bayou, and the next we were *there*, in his Temple of Night, in the City of Lost Gods, and she offered to be his priestess instead of me. She would sacrifice me to him, and become his connection into the physical world. His path back."

Theris stirred behind me, shifting his weight, but everyone else was still, and my fever-bright recollection remained as sharp as if it were happening all over again.

"I don't know why he didn't take the offer. I don't know why he let me reach out to others for help. I connected with Ash, the soultree of the Threefold Spiral coven in Ireland, and she spoke to me. She warned me I shouldn't kill the queen. *Threefold thy acts return to thee*, she said."

I took a deep breath, tried to let all the remembered terror of those moments pass out of me with the expelled air.

"Ash brought us all out of the Temple, to the hidden place of the gods I freed from the steamboat. They have a sacred grove now, down by the Atchafalaya. They took the queen and bound her to them, as she'd bound them to her. She's there now, part of them, slow and full of the rhythms of seasons, in an eternity of the moment."

"Well, we go there and demand an antidote," Yelena said. "Or the way to fetch one from this plantation."

"We go there and *ask*," I said. "She's part of them now, and the old gods probably think the score is even between us."

Chapter 21

My House immediately started making arrangements for the spirit walk to the plantation. I was not allowed to help. Apparently, I was all right to possibly fight my way through an evil substantiation, but making a few phone calls might cause me to drop dead at any moment.

I didn't mind. I needed some time to think.

Since Mirela had done her venom-delaying trick, my mind felt clearer than it had done for days. Extra clear. The sort of shocking clarity you sometimes got in a lucid period of a fever. Or maybe, the clarity you got from being told you were dying. I needed to make use of that because I knew that fever-fog was going to come back.

I sat and thought about everything that had happened since the Queen of Diamonds lured me into the swamps for a showdown. I thought about it, and I didn't like the way it came together.

All around me, the suite buzzed like a disturbed hive.

Pia called Diakon Dupuis, currently standing in for House Labastide as mistress of the territory of southern Louisiana, and requested permission to visit, which was granted. She also got a note taken into the auditorium for Marguerite herself, to keep her in the loop. Trust Pia to get the etiquette right.

Yelena organized transport. A helicopter would pick us up from the roof within an hour to take us to the airport, where a private jet was being prepared to take us down to New Orleans. Once we were in Louisiana, another helicopter would be made available to take us into the Atchafalaya basin. Many of the roads were still out from the storm.

Rita called the local Were alpha we'd worked with before, Bill Patout of the Alexandria pack. He agreed to organize airboats to get us along the river from wherever we could safely land the helicopter.

While all that was going on, Naryn came up from the Assembly to explain that Skylur could not leave the room at this moment.

The delegates had been shaken to the core, but that didn't mean we were getting our own way about everything. Getting Were and Adepts formally included was going to be tricky. Before Skylur could even start on that, he had to get the Panethus traditionalists back on side, *and* for them to accept the hybrid Carpathians, *and* persuade the Hidden Path to take him back as president, *and* all of them to retrospectively agree his plan for Emergence.

I was amazed at what he'd achieved already.

Naryn put his head in his hands. "Skylur has had to concede territory to the Hidden Path and the Carpathians."

"What territory?" Yelena wanted to know.

Naryn mumbled something in a language none of us knew before raising his head. "Carpathia takes the Caucasus, Georgia and Armenia, Azerbaijan, Ossetia, the whole west and south of the Caspian, down to Mazandaran. The Caspian is gone," he whispered. "All those Panethus mantles, all that territory with our roots so deep in the soil, that weight of history. All gone, as far west as the south of the Black Sea. The Hidden Path take all the disputed territories east of that."

Yelena's jaw had dropped.

"Georgia? The land of his birth?" she said in Athanate, and Naryn nodded.

"I understand the Hidden Path concessions; Diana told me they were never worth the struggle. But the Caucasus? To the Carpathians?"

Theris turned away in discomfort.

Naryn snorted. "Everyone has their own agendas. Elder Selsys came with a demand not just to sweep away the old Assembly, but to remove the Agiagraphos foundation as well. The Domain expected to lead a council running a new Assembly." He shook his head. "I know what you think of the Agiagraphos, but the traditionalists wouldn't allow that, and Skylur believes we can't afford the slowness of running the new Assembly by committee."

Diana was still on the video conferencing system, thinking ahead about practical concerns. "What's happening to the Houses and the kin from the conceded territories?"

"They're coming here," Naryn said. "The remaining Houses of the Eastern Seaboard will be displaced and demoted. The territories across the whole North American continent are being recalculated. We'll be more evenly distributed."

"Ah!" Diana nodded. "That is the inner play. This will be much better for Emergence. Speaking of which, where did you get to on that with the government departments?"

Naryn raked his eyes over the people in the room before deciding to answer. We made the grade, just, I guessed, because he replied: "Here, in the US, we'll get to meet the president this month. Panethus in Europe have moved approximately in parallel. Theokos, the Carpathians and the Empire say they're on top of things in their areas. Elsewhere, Panethus or Hidden Path, it's less clear."

Prompted by Diana's reaction, I mentally traced the political structure that Naryn had drawn, and suddenly saw the brilliance of Skylur's moves. They weren't just smart, they were masterstrokes. He'd done more than soothed the Hidden Path's anger at losing the presidency. He'd made peace by taking away a lot of the reasons for conflict. Each group was much stronger in its territories now, less likely to be attacked by its neighbors. That strength was going to be necessary in Emergence, because if it went wrong in one region, there was a risk of that failure spreading to other regions.

Skylur had lots more to do. He'd have to juggle creating a new Assembly with actually heading up Emergence. He'd have to work out how to incorporate Were and Adepts into the voting structure, how to settle the huge, disputed territories remaining, like the whole of Africa, how to reconcile Panethus and Basilikos creeds.

What it meant to me was that he wouldn't be able to spare time for my tasks. Skylur had to fight his battles so I could fight Vega Martine and Matlal.

Part one of any plan involving me had to include me staying alive.

Okay. *If* we could enter the sacred grove, and *if* the gods allowed me to question the queen, and *if* she responded, and *if* there was an antidote, and *if* I could use it *and* save Diana, Bian, Mirela and Salar as well...

There was a lot to consider, because up to now, I hadn't thought clearly about what had happened between me and the queen.

I'd fought Bian with blades in training, so I knew an expert swordswoman when I saw one. But the queen had not just been expert enough to beat me, she'd been expert enough to keep me thinking there was a chance of beating her. She'd distracted me with that hope. And she'd pretended she couldn't use magic while she fought physically, which I'd fallen for as well. As we fought, she'd opened a channel into the Temple of Night, Tezcatlipoca's stronghold in the spirit world.

I'd completely underestimated her.

I couldn't afford to do that again.

"Helicopter inbound," Yelena said. "Five minutes."

I let myself be carried along with the rush up to the roof, noting there were too many of us.

I'd have left Theris behind for one, even as skilled as he undoubtedly was. My opinion on the Carpathians had soured a little. Yes, they were badass, and they were on our side, but that territory grab when Skylur had to deal... that didn't sit right. That spoke to the way powerful groups achieved power and the way they did business.

Yet they'd given me one of their Elder-elects to be my bodyguard.

Really?

What strings are attached that we don't see yet? Tara said.

Exactly.

Maybe my mind wasn't working as well as it felt it was, because there *was* something there, something about the Carpathians, which remained just out of reach, infuriating, like a forgotten word.

But it was what it was. Maybe it would come to me when I stopped reaching for it.

Besides, I might need a bodyguard as I headed back into the swamps for another bout with the Queen of Diamonds. Assuming the African gods didn't mind.

All the while, comments from that last fight with the queen kept slipping into my thoughts.

Ash: *Threefold thy acts return to thee.*

And, more sinister, the queen: *Even if you were to kill me, you would simply replace me with you.*

Louisiana
Chapter 22

The flight back down to Louisiana was more comfortable than the one coming up.

Some of that was because I wasn't under arrest and some was because Livia had taken Mirela at her word: while the venom was still active, it was important we had a supply of fresh Blood. There was a group of a dozen kin from various New York Houses who joined us on the jet.

"A vacation in New Orleans, all expenses paid, in exchange for a bite or two? Deal!" said one cheerful youngster. "Get your fangs in my neck already."

I couldn't help but feel better, and I didn't ruin the mood by talking about why I was going to Louisiana. Plenty of time to get worried about that later.

Donatienne *and* Bian were waiting at the regional airport when we landed.

I'd asked for Donatienne to come with us; she might be able to help me figure out the kind of places that the Queen of Diamonds would have hidden her secrets, *if* we managed to get to the plantation. The rest of House Tucek was heading for Denver, then being scattered across the country to lead the attacks against Matlal's Atrax assassin groups scheduled for tonight.

Bian was supposed to be in Denver, but explanations were the last things on my mind.

I swept her into a hug, and we kissed, to teasing cheers from the others.

"Not that I'm complaining…" I started.

"As if I wouldn't be here. I would have been in New York too—"

"But you were out of contact. I know. They told me. They said it was something to do with a couple of packs up near Vernal? Huh?"

Bian chuckled. "Apparently when the real alphas are away, I'm the next best thing for a minor territory dispute. It's nothing. You stirred them up when you had to extract Weaver from the mines."

I rolled my eyes. That was some shifter logic there. Zane, Alex and I weren't available, so my Athanate fiancée got to knock Were heads together.

"Clearly, it worked out."

"Yeah. Then I got flown down in Jen's Pilatus," she said. "Gwen will come as soon as she can. Meanwhile, I brought a couple of weapons. Just in case." She had three large bags.

"I thought you were coordinating the attacks on the Atrax groups tonight," I said.

Bian gave me a lop-sided smile. "I persuaded Naryn that he'd rather do that than spend another few days locked in the Assembly. Wasn't difficult. The only hurdle he raised was that advance parties from the displaced Caucasus Houses will be arriving by tomorrow, and he didn't want to organize that as well."

"How did you answer that?"

She snorted. "Amber, Haven has been operating as a processing center for the El Paso pack to migrate up to Colorado. There's an entire department handling it. I don't need to be there to make those wheels turn." Her eyes dropped and raised again to hold mine. "And I wanted to be here."

We hugged again, but I felt her stiffen as she looked over my shoulder.

"And partly because you need protection from yourself." Her voice had cooled about one hundred degrees.

Ah. Time for polite, face to face introductions between Bian and Mirela.

It took a minute more, because Mirela and Donatienne were greeting each other with the same enthusiasm Bian and I had. Enough time for me to think their relationship through: they'd had plenty of opportunity to form an attachment in my substantiation, where time flowed slowly compared to the physical world.

I cleared my throat nervously and made the introductions in Athanate, because the subtleties of announcing my fiancée to my new sub-House worked better in that language. It emphasized the connections and obligations I had with both of them. And it was perfectly natural to slip in that Mirela was Panethus now.

After hesitating, Bian and Mirela opted to go with the formal etiquette and exchanged the Athanate lamia greeting, but it was stiff and tense as a pair of Were alphas meeting for the first time.

Keeping it very formal kept it polite. Temporarily.

Bian had a massive issue with Mirela. Which of course, I'd known she had, even before I accepted Mirela's offer to be a sub-House. And of course, I could have refused, but the floor of the Assembly hadn't been an easy place to take such profound decisions.

I'd done what seemed right at the time.

Act in haste, regret at leisure.

For all the passion of Bian's greeting me, I knew this decision of mine had hurt her, and damaged our relationship. I'd taken a huge liberty by accepting House Tucek into House Farrell, because that imposed the association on

House Trang as well, and I'd done it without hearing Bian's views on the matter.

I bit my lip. As if I'd had time for any of that in the Assembly.

Mirela tried to help. She stood back and dipped her head respectfully. "House Trang, I can sense the venom is active in your Blood. I offer the same assistance I provided to Amber."

Bian didn't argue the diagnosis, but she wasn't ready for Mirela's fangs in her neck. "Thank you," she said, with stoney-faced politeness. "I'm okay at the moment. I'll defer until it's needed."

We were in a hurry, but I pulled Bian aside. "I'm sorry. I did what I felt I had to in the situation."

Bian didn't say anything, which felt way worse than if she'd shouted at me.

I went on. "It's going to get worse, because we need to work with whatever remnant there is of the Queen of Diamonds. We need that antidote."

"I know," she snapped. "I understand that I have no choice but to go with you and your instincts on this mission, but we have to talk about this afterwards. *Really* talk. Do *you* understand?"

Ouch.

I nodded. That was as good as I could expect from where we were.

The group split, with Jo taking the overexcited kin into the Big Easy. The rest of us climbed into a helicopter and Kane flew us down to a field next to the Atchafalaya, where Bill Patout and another Were waited with a couple of airboats.

We were way upstream of where we wanted to be, because all the closer places a helicopter might have landed were flooded and we hadn't been able to get one equipped with floats.

The time could be put to use anyway; Theris wanted to talk with me. I'd been able to put him off during the flight, as I'd had my teeth into something else, but there was nowhere to go on the airboat. I was jammed in between him and Yelena.

"I am your pelea," he said formally, after a pause. "I am a defense against attacks, whether they're physical or magical."

I waited.

"But I'm not omnipotent. You're rushing into a confrontation with someone who you're making out to be the most powerful witch who ever lived."

"*Was*, Kyrios Pelea. She's kinda dead."

He smiled at my mangling of his title and current assignment. 'Lord Bodyguard' wasn't a very respectful form of address, and he rose another point or two in my estimation by enjoying the joke.

"*Kinda* is one of those wonderful words the English language finds to convey subtle meanings," he said. "That would mean she's kinda alive too, and that's worrying me. I have Adept skills, but I'm not sure I'm at the level where I can protect you against her. Maybe we should wait for your Valkyrie associate to arrive."

"The clock is ticking, Theris. I don't want to try this at the last minute."

He dipped his head to acknowledge the point. Mirela's temporary fix on the effects of the poison was fading already, and she'd told me every subsequent fix would burn out quicker.

"What... form is the queen in, according to Carpathian philosophy?" I asked. "Spirit? Soul? I mean, I don't even know if there was a body left behind in the Temple when I planted her in the grove."

"Go through what happened again, please."

I took him through the whole sequence of events.

I didn't mention my new concerns that I hadn't appreciated the details of what really went on at that point. I wanted to see what he thought.

I spoke instead of how it seemed as if Ash, the soultree of the Irish coven, had channeled the power into me to overcome the queen with a working that lifted her out of the Temple of Night and delivered her to the sacred grove of the African gods.

Theris pulled on his lip.

"So this sacred grove is a substantiation anchored *here* in the physical world, powered by ancient African soultrees who were strong enough to maintain the queen's vast steamboat and river substantiation in the spirit world, even against the City of Lost Gods. Those soultrees were her slaves at the time, now she's their prisoner, and the power to achieve this victory over her came solely from an Irish soultree, while Tezcatlipoca, essentially an Aztec soultree, who has become ever more powerful in the spirit world, stood aside and watched." He shook his head. "I like this less and less."

It seemed that Theris shared some of my concerns that this didn't add up.

"As to what she is, now? We use words like goddess, demon, soultree and spirit, which aren't exactly well defined or particularly accurate, but she doesn't seem to fit easily into any of those categories anyway. Regardless, she's still powerful."

"But she's being held by the African gods, and I freed them from her."

"Gratitude has a short half-life; I believe you would say. Especially among spirits and soultrees. That goes double for a group of soultrees without any obvious source of power to sustain them in the physical world." He took out his cell. "I'm going to call a couple of Elders who will be able to advise me better."

He started talking on the cell and Mirela leaned over my shoulder.

"I'm not expert in this spirit stuff, but let's say we get as far as finding the grove and talking to the queen. If she's still a captive *and* she's willing to talk to you, then it's because she wants something, so that's not where it gets easier, it's where it gets more dangerous."

"If she wants something, that's our ace in the hole. Depending on what it is."

"Yes. But she'll know we want something, too."

"I know. I underestimated her before. I won't again."

"Good. She'll look for weakness. She has a nose for fear. Show no fear."

Mirela sat back as Theris returned.

"The Elders' advice is to wait while they come here," he said. "I agree."

Yelena spoke across me. "That would take even longer than waiting for Gwen."

Theris opened his mouth to argue, and Yelena overrode him. "You're Amber's pelea, not her Diakon. I've learned to trust Amber's instincts. You need to learn to accept them. She says we go, we go."

Theris scowled, but he didn't respond.

My Diakon drew a hard line in the sand, and it didn't matter who she was talking to, or how high they were in the Carpathian hierarchy.

Luckily, we were nearing the place where the queen's steamboat had run aground.

"This looks like the bend," I called back to Bill.

He nodded confirmation and eased off the throttle. We began a long, curving approach to the shoreline.

He was the expert on the river, and theoretically, it wasn't going to be difficult for him to find the exact spot where the African gods' sacred grove was—it had to be close to where the steamboat had run aground. But I wasn't surprised he was looking puzzled as we came closer. For a start, the rise in the river made everything look different. Add to that, the battle here had been fought at night, and half of it had taken place in the queen's substantiation, which was similar, but not the same.

Like a good scout, Bill had worked out the area on maps beforehand and he was checking the view against the display from his GPS.

He was frowning.

A half hour later, he shook his head, and we doubled back. And again.

"Just not right," he said.

He was still unsure as late afternoon began to give way to evening and the GPS quit.

Sullen clouds started to swell up from the horizon to eat the sky.

"It's gotta be in spitting distance," Bill said. "This is the bend where it all went down, but I can't see the exact spot, and it's going to get dark soon. Maybe we come back tomorrow. We can bring drones, or your flying friend."

He meant Bryn. 'Flying friend' was a bit more tactful than what he'd called her when he first saw her—'that winged nightmare'.

I snorted at the memory and opened my aura a fraction, sensing Flint and Kane still shielding me from T-cat. I kept it tight anyway. Felt the river rolling beneath us. Felt the wind coming up from the sea. Felt the brooding shoreline.

But old rivers had secrets, and the Atchafalaya kept hers jealously.

It wasn't working, so I got Yelena to swap with a wary-looking Donatienne.

"I need your help," I said.

"Got that." Her lips went tight.

"I'm looking with aura. That works best when I work with someone who has a connection to whatever I'm looking for."

"I know." She shivered. "I'm scared. I was scared when she was alive, and it hasn't gotten any less."

"I'm sorry."

She nodded silently and edged closer to me. I wrapped her in a hug. Physical contact helped the aura connection, but really, I did it to comfort her. From where she was sitting behind us, Mirela reached over and joined in.

My aura floated out, boosted by theirs.

Yes, the old river kept a lot of secrets, but the one I wanted was given to me.

"Got it!" Holding on to the connection, I clambered back over the seats. "Move over, Bill."

It wasn't difficult to steer, and the brave man assumed I wasn't going to floor the throttle, so he shrugged and got out of the pilot's seat. He probably immediately regretted it because I closed my eyes and aimed the airboat toward the shore, relying on my aura to guide me.

It would seem unwise, especially to Theris, but I felt we didn't have until tomorrow. Now that I was watching for the signs, I could tell that Bian was starting to feel the effects of the venom, and Mirela wasn't far behind. Our ready supply of fresh Blood was partying downtown, and even if they had been here, the poison was accelerating quicker than we could delay it.

There was a flicker of lightning to the south, promising more rain and maybe a storm tomorrow, which would make it even more difficult to find our way.

It was past time to find the sacred grove.

"Amber, you can't go up that creek, it's too narrow and it's looking to be clogged good." A long, low rumble of thunder punctuated Bill's words.

I knew that was what it *looked* like, but it wasn't what I was *seeing* in my mind's eye.

I reached out more with my aura and my vision suddenly became crowded with glimpses of what everyone else was seeing.

"Close your eyes," I told them. "Close them now."

The guy in the boat behind was yelling at Bill.

"Ignore him. Close your eyes. Crouch down. Tell him to do the same."

He didn't so much crouch as cringe, expecting us to hit something.

I slowed the engine until we were barely drifting forward into the creek.

The creek wasn't clogged. It *was* narrow, and it didn't look like where the steamboat had come ashore. I guessed the grove had moved everything around.

But I could sense a path, and if I could, the African gods were okay with me coming in. Maybe.

We passed beneath the shadow of the trees on the bank.

"Damn," Bill said when I cut the engine, and he opened his eyes.

The rest of us joined him. We were drifting in an oddly clear pool of water, with barely room for us and the second boat, which had reluctantly nudged its way in after us.

Bald cypress and fat-trunked swamp tupelo surrounded the pool, leaning in toward the water and looming over us. They dripped trails of Spanish moss, which hung down like witch's hair to brush our faces. Roots like cathedral buttresses writhed out of the surface of the pool. Creepers were knotted around the trees' trunks and between their branches, providing an unending wall of leaves. Deadfall bobbed in the water, stirred into movement by our boats. Silted banks of mud were hidden beneath decades of rotting vegetation. There was a smell of plant decay, slightly sweet in the heavy air.

The evening chorus was getting going. Mournful hoots and screeches of owls battled against the sullen roaring of bullfrogs. Only the snakes were silent, fleeing from our presence.

"It's there," I said, pointing at the wall of greenery in front and to one side.

Bill swore softly in patois.

I'd gotten them this far when they couldn't see the way, but there were still grumbles as we got out of the boat and slithered around on the mud banks. I had to admit, this right here was no sacred grove. It was hot and humid and dark and smelly and slippery, and the plant life in front of us might as well have been woven together, it was so solid.

Yelena and Bian rooted around in the weapons bags and brought out some short swords and long knives that could double as machetes.

I could feel the trees squeeze in like I was being held in a bear hug.

"Don't you dare," I said. "No unsheathed blades, no fire."

"You not getting through that without chopping," Bill said, and others nodded.

"You and your friend stay with the boats," I said to him. "Rest of you, grab your gear and line up behind me. Hand on the shoulder of the person in front."

More grumbling. There was no room. Everyone was getting muddier and more irritated until Bian spoke: "You take me to some lovely places. This isn't one of them."

"Drinks are on Amber if this doesn't pan out," Mirela added.

Okay, so the truce was holding.

Yelena laughed loudly and a couple of others joined in.

"Hi ho, hi ho," Rita started, but the swamp seemed to absorb the sound, and she didn't go on. Too much like whistling in the dark.

"Close your eyes again if it helps," I said, and started to walk forward slowly.

"This is strange," Theris muttered. He'd been the quickest moving on the bank, and it was his hand on my shoulder. "There *is* something there. I've never felt anything like this before. I don't trust it."

"If you live with crows, the falcon's call sounds strange," Yelena said.

A snort from Mirela.

Rita spoke from the back of the line: "Damned Ukrainians and their sayings."

I let their chatter flow over me. It lifted them, and it wasn't as if we were sneaking up on the grove.

In addition to the swamp trees, I began to see scrub oak, pine and willow, showing it was becoming drier underfoot, despite the unending mud.

The wall of green we were moving through wasn't an illusion. The plants were there. They were real. I had to push them aside and I could feel them pushing back at me as I moved forward. But we *were* moving forward. Further than my brain told me it should take to reach the grove, but this *was* the right way. I could tell. I was getting that eerie feeling on the back of my neck, and my hair was standing up. There was a wind that had nowhere to come from, and yet it was suddenly cool on my skin.

After fifteen minutes of slow progress, trusting Flint and Kane to keep me safe from any connection with T-cat, I let my eukori and aura reach out into the forest around us, wider and wider.

Nothing specific from the sacred grove yet. Lots from my team. They were worried, but okay, except for Donatienne. She was terrified.

I stopped and called her forward. No other words were needed. With my eukori open, everyone sensed what I wanted and why. They shuffled places until it was Donatienne's hand on my shoulder.

"I'm here," I said. I couldn't say I'd keep her safe or anything, but just those words seemed to help.

"Thank you," she whispered, stumbling over the words. "I can feel her. She's here. Close by. She knows."

I shook off the feeling of dread her words brought. I put my hand over hers and lifted a foot to take another step.

But touching Donatienne made me feel the connection she had. And my connection added to hers. It wasn't just the queen. The African gods weren't much for actual words, but the sudden deluge of images from them seemed to coalesce into words as they'd done for me when I'd been in their grove before.

Join us. Here, in the forest of night. Let your passing phantoms slip away. Simply be.

My foot came down and the ground beneath wasn't swamp any more. It was dry and firm. A mist swayed between the looming shapes of great trees all around us.

We'd arrived.

Join us.

The siren song of the grove was new to the others.

It was new to me too. Not *completely* new. But definitely changed. Just like you can't step into the same river twice, the grove was a different place now.

How different?

137

I'd done the grove-that-had-been a favor.
Did that give me credit with the grove-that-is-now?

Chapter 23

We weren't just inside the grove. We were part of it. I'd spirit-walked my team into the gods' trees. We were rooted in the deep and silty soil. Our leaves fluttered in the rising wind and our branches shook to the thunder rolling up from the sea.

Become, be one, and we will heal the ills you bear. With us, there is no pain, no passing.

It was like standing beneath a waterfall of sensations. I'd spirit-walked with trees before and I'd met these gods; I was okay.

Flint and Kane had spirit-jumped to trees many times; they loved it. They were familiar enough with spirit walking to be able to keep control of their physical bodies. They chose a couple to sit against and drifted off to commune with them.

The rest of my party, one by one, were overwhelmed and sank to the ground. Bian's grip on me eased as she slumped against the nearest tree and slid down. Eventually, even Theris succumbed, although he managed to keep standing. When his eyes glazed over, it was just me and Donatienne left. Donatienne was shivering and clinging on to me.

There was a voice in the grove that hadn't been there before. It was clearer. Sharper. Using words rather than sensations.

The queen.

I see you, she said.

Donatienne had been right. She was *here*--not some abstract, fleeting echo of her, not some prisoner, but somehow the queen herself, in all her chilling presence.

Shit!

My hand stretched out and felt the wide trunk of a tree beside me. Not a Louisiana tree. A tall Iroko, an African tree, far from home. The tree that they said was the throne of the gods and the foundation of the mind. A hard tree, a strong tree, a tree with deep roots. A good tree to have at your back.

I sat against it and pulled Donatienne close.

It had become dark, too dark to see, and yet the darkness was full of watchful movement.

The old gods could hear me, I guessed, so I spoke aloud, thanking them for letting us in, and thanking them for the offers to join them, which I declined.

A silence. Breaths came, slow as the ocean's tides, slow as the moon's pull. In and out.

And with them there came a light in the limitless dark.

They know what you think you want.

The Queen of Diamonds, almost as I'd seen her when we fought, her body emerging from the roots of a cypress, the bark paling to show her skin, shadows falling to form her hair. She floated, sitting in a lotus position. A Chinese woman, so delicate. So powerful.

Hello, Amber. Hello, Donatienne, she said.

I pulled Donatienne tighter. She was shaking with fear.

Mirela's words of warning came back to me. The queen would seek fear. She'd find a weakness, and Donatienne and I were still connected through aura and eukori. I wasn't going to let Donatienne be the fault in my defense that the queen exploited to slip her icy fingers into my head.

"Focus on me, bitch," I told the queen. "Leave her alone."

I sank my eukori and aura deeper into Donatienne, to calm her. *I am here, Donatienne. I will not let the queen have you. Trust me.*

I *pushed* the fear out of her, but I pushed too hard. She slumped against me, unconscious. Not what I was trying for, but it would have to do. No time to think about it.

"Mine now," I said to the queen, a wolf's smile stretching my lips.

What a wide mantle you cast, Amber Farrell. As wide as the world, to have shapeshifters, shamans, a Vietnamese lover and Carpathian spies at your back, and the former leader of my Rougarou at your side. How powerful and well connected you have become. We have no interest in Donatienne, or anyone else in your group. Just you.

The politeness was just her way of toying with me. She'd been the same on her steamboat.

I couldn't go back and re-think all my reasoning that had brought us here. We needed the antidote, and I believed we needed the queen's power. We needed to be here. But I'd misjudged this. My instincts were good in the areas I was familiar with. The spirit world was still not my territory, and the queen wasn't imprisoned as far as I could see.

What if she'd moved *herself* to this grove when her trick to capture T-cat failed? What if Ash and my power were merely a cover for her to get in, and once here, she'd re-established her hold over the African gods? What if all she wanted now was a body to walk out of the grove with? One that was well-connected in the paranormal world. Like mine.

No fear, Mirela said. I breathed deeply to bring my heart rate down. Ignored the coolness of the sweat on my face. I was being distracted from the real danger. She could shift shapes; she didn't need my body.

On the other hand, just my face wouldn't fool people, so she might need my soul.

If she really was free, then I hoped she killed me, because that was better than the alternatives playing out in my mind. If not, then I had a job to do. I needed my wits about me if we were going to get out of this. And I needed to start with making sure I knew *exactly* who she was and what she was saying.

"You said *we*."

I am part of the grove. Their voice, if you like. Donatienne has nothing to fear from me.

"What did you mean when you said *what you think you want?*"

You think you want to cure yourself of what's killing you and harness the powers I wielded to aid you in your fight against Matlal and Vega Martine. Few know what their desires will cost until the price has to be paid. Fewer are willing to pay once they do.

"I definitely want to cure myself and my friends. The rest? Now that is dependent on price."

Ah. The difficulty is this: it's all the same thing. The Serpent's kiss is neither poison nor venom. Think of it as the doorway through which you could pass to a higher level of perception and a different state of being. A great gift.

"Sounds like dying to me."

No, truly. Your fear holds you back. You have the gift of the fourth Serpent, the Serpent of Air, the Mistress of Breath, and the Guardian of the First Tower, the transcendent level that lies beyond dreaming.

"Why would you smear it on your blades, if it was a gift? And I *am* dying."

I could feel it here, like a darkness in my body and a despair that threatened to choke me.

The Serpents wanted it, so that there would be a path, whichever of us survived. They didn't expect you to do what you did. She smiled. *It's one of the things they most value in you, your unpredictability. Your capacity for choosing good outcomes.*

"Yeah. Very interesting. Did I mention I'm dying? Are we going to be able to deal? Are you going to tell me what this price is?"

Yes, I'm glad you remembered there's a price to pay. You fear my answer. You fear I'm going to say you have to free me. You fear for your friends. You fear for yourself and your soul. But it's your fears that you must fear. The truth is you have what you need already, but you are not ready, and the path is hard. There is no royal road to the powers I held. I cannot grant them to you and neither can I snap my fingers and make you the Queen of Serpents. And you must earn the right to learn.

She stood, and I struggled to my feet, using the hard trunk of the Iroko to lever myself up. My legs felt weak. My whole body felt weak, and I tried to cover it.

"How do I earn the right? Who's judging? What do I have to learn? Who would teach me?"

You've begun both tasks. You've convinced the Grove. You must convince the Serpents. You must learn to use their powers.

She began to move, and I followed.

I earned the right and failed to learn, yet you spared me. Do not expect others to spare you. If you fail the test, you die. If you pass the test and fail to learn, you die.

"Did I mention I'm dying? Can we get on this path already?"

You are.

Chapter 24

There was a rushing and swirling around us, battering me.

And at the center of this storm, it was just the queen and me now. Everyone and everything else had disappeared into mists and howling winds. The ground beneath me lost its firmness. Now it shifted from side to side. I took a step forward. Whatever was beneath my feet moved and the swaying got worse. To either side were rough ropes, like the cables of a rope bridge. I gripped them.

Do you trust the old gods of the Grove? the queen asked.

"I do," I said, through gritted teeth, even though I wasn't so sure about them now. Then: "Wait, does that include you?"

Yes. In a way.

"Then that's how I trust them. In a way."

You trusted them to deal with me, so now you must accept their solution. Believe me, I am not what I was. I am not the Queen of Diamonds. The grove decided parts of me had to die. You trusted the gods of the Grove, but they have their agenda. They have their price. You'd do well to remember that everyone has their agenda, all those connections you have, and whether you think of it as a price or not, there is a cost for everything.

I needed to understand, and I knew she was being deliberately obscure, but concentration was getting difficult. It wasn't ground I was stepping on, twisting and swaying beneath my feet. I knew this, just as I suddenly knew where I was. I was on a primitive rope bridge across a gorge hundreds of feet deep. The gods of the grove had found an old memory of mine from an Ops 4-10 mission. A flimsy bridge that had been built for people to cross in bare feet and without baggage. I had been on it with full kit. It had sagged and twisted beneath me. I had been sweating with fear then, and I was again now.

I squeezed my eyes shut and tried to erase the memory, to *think* myself back to the grove.

Back to safety.

No. Mustn't let the fear drive me. Accept the fear. Use the fear. I was still on the bridge, but this was some extension of the grove. And it wasn't my combat kit weighing me down.

Ahead is what you think of as the plantation, the queen said. *It is the place of the Temple of Serpents. It cannot be reached by anyone but those who carry the Serpents' gifts.*

"Given I don't even know what these Serpents are, how am I getting there?"

By moving forward. By having some of me in you. By bearing the Serpents' gift. These are part of the price.

No! I didn't want the queen inside my head. My heart surged, and the bridge swayed sickeningly from side to side. I was going to fall right off it into the gorge below. I felt sick, dizzy.

Careful. You carry your entire team. They would die with you.

"You bitch," I managed to gasp.

This is the path of your desire, Amber. I warned you there would be a price, just as I once warned you that if you killed me, you would replace me with you.

She *had* said that, when we'd fought.

"I didn't kill you."

No, not exactly, and you're also not exactly me or a replacement of me, either. Not yet. But to do what you desire, you have to learn. And to learn, you'll have to become like me. And to become like me, you'll have to walk a mile or more in my shoes. Then you'll have to persuade the Stone Serpents not to kill you. You'll see, I did it. It's your turn now. You must go on. To go back is to die. To stay where you are is to die. To walk onward is at least to discover.

I felt her leave. I was alone on the rope bridge, weighed down with the lives of my team.

Worse than that. I was weighed down with the lives of Diana and Salar as well.

Even worse. Far worse. Everyone else I loved. This path, this bridge, might lead to the way to defeat Vega Martine, and Matlal. I didn't know how that might be, but with fever clarity, I saw that if I didn't find out, or if I failed, Matlal would win.

The gray mist had thickened 'til it seemed I was breathing water. At some point mist became rain and it began to fall, harder and harder. I could feel the rope steps beneath my feet getting slicker every moment.

I took one tentative step and it slithered beneath my foot. I panicked and grabbed hold. The bridge swung wildly.

I fell to my hands and knees, gripping the slippery ropes and steps of the bridge for dear life, the weight on me dragging me down.

It was unfair.

Why should I be the one?

I had to get off this bridge, but every step threatened to pitch me over the side.

And it would be all for nothing. If I succeeded, it was only by becoming something I hated. To win, I would have to lose everything I believed in.

Easier to simply let go now. To stop striving.

That's not you speaking, Tara said. *We'll find a way. We have to move.*

"I can't," I yelled at the rain. "Even if I get off this bridge, I'm a shitty Adept. I can barely do my own workings. I can't *learn* to be powerful. Not in the time it'll take before Matlal lets Quetzalcoatl loose."

You managed before. You beat Weaver. You beat the Threefold Spiral. You beat the queen.

"Tricks. I can channel power. That's all I'm good at. Stealing power."

I crawled forward anyway, one wooden slat at a time, with nothing to tell me how far I had to go. It was freezing cold, and my hands and feet were becoming numb.

On top of that, I could feel the poison moving again, like cold fire, sidling through my veins. Again, it brought a peculiar clarity of vision—as the queen said, it wasn't just a poison or venom. It was something of the Stone Serpents, something of the queen. I could feel it opening perceptions in my head. She'd called it a gift, one that would kill me if I turned aside or stopped.

Not tricks, Tara was saying. *You used Kane's power. You used Ash's power. You shaped their power. You used it for what had to be done. For what they couldn't do.*

Yes, I'd used Ash's power. I'd stolen her reservoir of power too. I'd weakened her. All that hate and anger the coven had kept alive so that their curse wouldn't die. Raw power. I'd taken it to stop the curse and because I could and because I'd thought I might be able to use it somehow, sometime. But I didn't really know how. A lot of good all that stored power was doing me.

At least the queen had provided something to be angry at while she spoke to me. Now all I had was the rain and my own negative emotions.

And the bridge. Which was so badly made and so loose, I was making it sag. The way forward was becoming more like a climb the closer I got to the end. Naturally. It wasn't enough to make it wobbly and slippery, but it had to be like climbing a ladder with no idea how long it might take, and whether I'd run out of strength before I reached the end.

There was an inevitability to what I felt next. The bridge came apart behind me.

Instinct made me loop my arms and legs through the strands of the bridge as I felt it give way. I couldn't see anything. I had to be swinging over the gorge, but here there was no sensation of movement until the very last moment, when a cliff of rocks seemed to leap out of the mist, and I crashed into it.

My fingers slipped. I barely kept hold, even with my limbs twisted through the ropes.

Blood ran down my face.

It made me angry, and I lifted my head to scream curses at the rain, the queen, the Serpents, even the old African gods.

Screaming made me feel better. Anger made me feel better.

There was light ahead.

A blur, as if I were looking at something from underwater. Vibrant green and white and blue, waving like a flag in the breeze, mocking me in the watery gray.

More anger boiled into my muscles. I swore and began to haul myself upwards, one step at a time.

I was going to do this. I'd find this damned Temple and I'd strangle the freaking Serpents, take their powers, cure everyone *and* work out how to use T-cat's power to defeat Matlal without becoming his slave or his route back to the physical world. Then I'd probably go back and have words with the queen, to prove I'd won. And make her take back whatever that 'some of her' was.

I let the anger fuel me, closed my eyes and climbed through my nightmare.

Chapter 25

"Amber?"

Bian was slapping my face.

"Amber?"

I jerked into awareness, heart pounding, out of the cold rain and into warm sunshine, my cheek stinging from Bian's blow. The bridge was gone; the cliffs and the rain and the gorge were gone, and I was standing on a grassy lawn in the sun.

But my team was here, safe. They were spread around me, dressed in costumes from the eighteen-hundreds and carrying the swords from Bian's hoard.

I blinked, trying to orient myself. "What the hell?"

Bian said, "We're at the plantation."

We made it.

I looked around. It was so bright and fresh I had to squint. The contrast to the nightmare of carrying them across the bridge was jarring. It was full daylight, hot and humid. Spanish oak lined a wide, wide lawn, spreading low and lazy branches in all directions. Behind us were willows, providing climbing frames for fragrant honeysuckle that misted the air with their perfume. Behind them, I could feel a river, and somehow, I knew that through a gap in the trees there would be a glimpse of a narrow bridge made of rope that descended into the water.

It was a good reminder that the nightmare was still going on. No matter how peaceful it looked, the danger was just beginning.

I turned to see more lawns, edged with flowerbeds, and centered around stone fountains, which rose in great steps up towards the house. Or rather, the temple. I was pretty sure that there wasn't a warm welcome waiting inside.

I checked myself. I wasn't a man dressed as a major of the Confederate cavalry this time. I was in a pretty, but hugely impractical hoop-skirted dress that swept the ground and would be impossible to run or fight in. Across my back were four swords: Bian's gifts, Onibi and Nekotsume, and the queen's dao and jian swords. They were all sheathed in ornate scabbards, and I was also carrying a parasol, because of course I would be.

Four arms might be useful. Or five even.

I frantically scrubbed that thought from my head. I was in the spirit world, and anything I thought hard enough about could easily become real.

There was a ripping sound, startlingly loud in the peaceful garden.

Bian. *Of course.* Tearing her skirts off.

"Grew up wearing this sort of shit," she growled. "I was done with it a long time ago."

The other women were laughing and joining her. I did too. No way I'd be able to fight in these clothes, and I didn't think we were just going to walk in and out.

Donatienne was excused the ripping. She was dressed in the formal uniform I'd seen her wear as the captain of the *Queen of Diamonds*. She shrugged, and didn't seem happy to be wearing it again, but the trousers were fine.

The men were better off, but they still shed their jackets. I shared Bian's view of our clothes, but I had to admit I liked the look of Flint and Kane in their formal finery. Even Theris. All of us cast an appreciative glance or two.

They may have returned the favor when we were down to chemise and pantaloons.

I snapped back into the right frame of mind when I noticed the gardeners. They were scattered over the property, kneeling down and working on the plants.

"Rougarou," Donatienne murmured. "The queen sent them here if they displeased her. It's not just Rougarou, I think. There are others here, too."

She shuddered.

"They aren't interested in us," I said. "Ignore them. Come on."

"What happened?" Bian asked as we started to trot up the endless gardens. "How did we get here?"

"I had a talk with the Queen of Diamonds." I grimaced. "Who's no longer the queen, and no longer what she was because she's part of the grove. The grove want us to visit the temple." I rubbed my head. "The temple also wants us to visit, and they're the reason the queen poisoned us, but it's not a poison. It's their gift which I might benefit from if I can survive their tests and learn how to use their power. Everyone wants something, and has an agenda. And we're all running out of time."

"Clear like tar in a bucket," Yelena muttered.

"Yeah. Made more sense while she was telling me. A little more, anyway."

It was strange. Things happened in a substantiation which made less sense when you returned to the physical world, like dreams when you woke. It seemed that also applied to a substantiation within a substantiation, like the queen talking to me.

Maybe it would make sense after the 'tests', whatever they were.

I studied the temple as I led everyone toward it, running now with the urgency that infected me. The side facing us had the general design of the ritziest of plantation houses. Glaring white in the sun. Regular. Symmetrical. Graceful. Greek columns under wide, triangular pediments. Deep, cool porches. The palest terracotta slate roof. Tall windows with the shutters opened.

I didn't fall into the mistake of calling it the front of the house, because I knew there were seven identical sides to the building. One for each of the Stone Serpents. The one facing us was the fourth side, the doorway of the fourth Serpent. Naturally.

The Serpent of Air, the Mistress of Breath, and the Guardian of the First Tower, the transcendent level that lies beyond dreaming.

Whatever the hell that meant.

I could see, even at this distance, the door stood wide open. It was too dark inside to make anything out, but I could almost feel the coolness reach down across the expanse of gardens and speak to me.

Come. Enter.

"This is the Temple of the Stone Serpents," I said. "Somewhere inside of that..."

"The antidote?" Mirela said. "The queen told you it was here?"

"Among other things. Yes. I think I am the potential antidote somehow. But we're going to have to earn it."

Nothing happened as we approached the house, but the feeling of menace grew. I heard Theris draw his weapon and move in closer to me. We stopped at the threshold.

The building was even larger than it had looked from the bottom of the gardens. Marble floors and a wide, classic-style portico stretched out from the door in welcome.

From here, it didn't seem dark inside, but full of light from the huge windows.

Good. I like to see what's coming for me.

I said, "Everyone, be ready for anything," and stepped inside.

The Temple of the Stone Serpents was much larger inside than I'd expected. A scent like incense hung in the air. A waiting hush. Light streamed in. It was cool. There were no halls or walls, staircases or furniture. Across the huge space I could see the other six doors, but the interior was an empty space—except I knew it wasn't. For some reason I knew how it looked depended on what you came for. I knew things about this place without knowing how I knew them.

With little else to look at, the floor took my attention as I walked forward to let everyone else get inside.

It was a mosaic, and the designs made me dizzy.

A few yards inside each door there was an image of the world, a blue-green circle centered on a snake's eye. Surrounding each doorway's world were patterns that stretched out in all directions, flowing to the others. The patterns were like fractals. The more you looked, the more they seemed to replicate themselves, in smaller and smaller sizes.

I felt the venom in my Blood go still, as if it were listening to a song that the silent floor tiles sang.

That snake's eye called to me.

Come. Learn.

Distant sounds floated in on the heavy air. I had no idea where they came from, but I knew they meant that was something wrong. Something was going to happen. Soon. Some*things*.

I took a step. Another. My foot came down on the eye of the world.

And I fell through it.

Chapter 26

Training kicked in. I hit the ground and rolled. Everything seemed to be a confused blur of harsh sounds and vibrant colors that suddenly snapped into focus.

A battle. Struggling people around a chaotic column of rough-made carts, pressed against a city's fortified wall. Choking red dust rising in clouds from hundreds of stamping feet, partly obscuring a huge, powder blue sky and a searing midday sun. Dry heat. The stench of open sewers and recent death. Screaming, fighting men whirled around me, all dark, some bareheaded, some with ragged turbans. Swords clashing, wielded with strength and desperation but not much skill. Blood rained on the thirsty earth. Men fell wounded. Some died.

Definitely not in Kansas, anymore. Or Louisiana, for that matter.

I had my back to tall iron and wood gates, which had been closed against us…

I blinked.

…to keep the bandits who were attacking the convoy from entering the city.

We'd get in, *after* the bandits retreated. If any of us were still alive.

I had swords in my hands and these bandits were keeping me from the city I'd sought for the greater part of my extended life.

I ran at the tightest knot of them.

In my left hand, the curved dao sang the great circle of the moon, wide and silver and cruel. In my right, subtle and deadly as a serpent's bite, the straight jian flickered and returned, time and time again. *This* was how they worked together; a web of death, woven of many silvery strands.

Those I fought were stronger than me, but not quicker. Therefore, I was smoke and mist to their attacks; never where they struck.

I knew this.

I knew this art of fighting. I knew it in my bones, in my muscles, in my whole body. I had trained a lifetime in it. Longer than a lifetime.

The bandits fell back under my attack. Some tried to flank me, but the other convoy guards, the *sarthapala*, knew a good opening when they saw it. Abhik and Vibhu joined me, fighting on either side. More and more came as they saw our success.

These types of bandits lived on a knife edge of chance. In their world, there were only smart bandits and dead ones. Smart ones were those who could see when the odds had turned against them.

As the bandits broke, the city's sally ports opened, and their guards streamed out to slaughter the wounded bandits and those that couldn't flee fast enough.

Practical. Necessary. Expected. Yet their cowardly glee was sickening. I left them to it.

Where the hell was I? What was going on?

This wasn't 'me'. I was spirit-riding on someone's memories. These scenes had happened centuries in the past.

Whoever it was, she was in a hurry—definitely *she*, even if her companions didn't realize it.

The city gates opened, but the cluster of carts in front of it was so tight, no one could move. Drovers split their efforts between calming terrified mules in their harnesses and screaming at others to let them pass. Their delays didn't matter to me now. My duty to the convoy was complete, and I could see the convoy chief had managed to squirm his way into the city already.

I leaped up onto the nearest cart and began skipping over them as they churned and struggled with each other. This upset the mules again, and the drovers' curses that followed me made me laugh. What did they know of curses?

I landed lightly on the city's paved courtyard and caught the convoy chief before he could slink off. I'd already cleaned and sheathed the jian, but the dao was still in my left hand, smeared with blood. He chose not to argue about my promised payment, so I was able to get my money and leave him before the other *sarthapala* caught up. Abhik and Vibhu had seen what I'd done and had wisely followed my example.

"Himadri!" they called after me.

It was a name they'd given me because I'd come from the north, and everyone who came from there was called after the legendary great mountains under their turbans of snow.

At that time, down in the Surparaka, on the southern Malabar coast of the land that would become India, in the state that would become Kerala, the far distant north was a vague and fearful thing. People there lived in the cold and must be possessed by evil Raksha spirits to be able to endure it. In the same sort of way, in the mountains of the north, they thought themselves in heaven and called this region hell.

"Himadri! Wait!"

I waved to my former colleagues with the rag I was using to clean the dao and kept walking. I discarded Himadri as easily as I'd discarded every other name I'd been called on my journey.

I hadn't come down from the Himalayas. I had skirted their foothills, coming from the east, passing through the areas of the Hmong and Shan peoples. I'd lived many seasons among the Naga. I'd sailed the mighty Red River and the Ganges and the Padma, down to the great bay, where I'd listened to wise teachers arguing in the shade of trees beside the lotus temples. I'd talked with the Athanate Houses and fierce weretiger clans of the steaming delta, trading magic workings for the stories I sought. And I'd talked even to the Adepts: the witches and wizards. Those last had been the most dangerous and difficult; they'd been suspicious, slow to trust, but they were deep in the knowledge I needed. I'd had time. I'd been on this journey while months had stretched into years, and years to decades, but I was *busi, abomination, cursed,* and the years did not touch me.

I feared the truth catching up with me. I feared the suspicions of powerful paranormals, but that wasn't what drove me on. All that knowledge and all those tales I gathered, woven together, was what had drawn me ever south, down the length of the mighty subcontinent, sometimes guarding ships, sometimes guarding merchants' land convoys, always chasing the heart of the legend of the Stone Serpents.

And now I was finally here, where the truest of the tales had guided me— in the city of Kallamada Mala. But that was not the name in the tales; in them, this was the City of Serpents. This was the city where the Serpent Temple stood waiting.

This was my aim.

I knew this.

I knew all these things. All these fragments of another life.

This was a true memory, a memory from the life of the Queen of Diamonds.

I *was* the Queen of Diamonds, and I was not. Not the queen as I'd known her, but before she was queen. We were together, here in this place. A memory for her, but something more for me: a trap and a test.

All is maya. This is that which is not. This is only another illusion of the world.

That was the queen's philosophy, voiced in her mind. It seemed I could hear her thoughts, just as I could see through her eyes.

Why?

There had to be a reason I was here, but it seemed that to understand, I would have to walk a mile in her sandals, as she had said I would.

The queen again, following her own aims: *Here, in the City of Serpents, I will learn, or I will not. I will live, or I will not.*

I couldn't tell where the border between us was, but somehow, I knew that assessment of the outcome applied equally to me. I could die here.

If this was a memory, something from her early life, she must have made it through. She'd found the Stone Serpents. She'd passed the test that the Temple had given her.

Could I?

In front of me, I could see Kallamada Mala had been laid out with good intentions before being overtaken by the pressure of its success. The center was a pleasant, broad boulevard between busy markets, tree-shaded, with fountains and paving. The far end of the boulevard stopped before the king's palace and grounds. Very deliberate. Every visitor to the city would quickly see his magnificence and they'd know who ruled here.

They'd think they knew who ruled here.

They were all wrong, from the exalted king down to the lowest beggar.

Around his palace, the king's ancestors had built temples to every god and goddess whose favor they sought. Each temple was set in its own wide courtyard, and the area resembled a hive, as if humanity could cultivate fortune with the gods like they cultivated honey from bees.

I glanced to the left and right. Away from the palace, those temples, and that spacious boulevard, the city was crowded, chaotic, and full of people who were only here because they preferred the city's taxes to the countryside's bandits.

I'd seen many like it, and the sooner I was gone, the better I would feel. But what I had to do couldn't be hurried.

I found an inn with a bathhouse because I couldn't go directly to the Temple. I needed to clean a month of dirt and sweat from me. But more importantly, I needed to prepare myself, because I would die here, or I would not.

The landlord named a price to rid himself of this blood-spattered, sweat-stained, stinking apparition. I halved it and brought out the coin from my pay.

"You've come in with the merchants," he said, nervously eyeing the sword hilts showing above my shoulders. "But you are no merchant. You are *sarthapala*. I will have no fighting, no drunken—"

I shook my head and cut across his babble. "I served as a guard rather than pay for passage in the convoy. I'm here on a pilgrimage, not to fight, and I want no drink but water. I must prepare myself to visit the Temple."

He bowed his head then and took the money. It would have been bad fortune for him to impede a true pilgrim, especially if the temple which this self-proclaimed holy man sought happened to be one of the stronger deities. Best not to tempt fate. And also, he had the money now.

He wanted a name, and I took Himadri back as easily as I'd discarded it. My true name would mean nothing to him. I thought of myself as Nai. It meant *to endure*, which was entirely fitting.

I gave him more of my pay to ensure my privacy in the bathhouse, claiming it was part of my holy obligations on this day to see no nakedness and in turn, not be seen. The lie tripped easily off the tongue. I'd had a lot of practice. It worked.

With my occupation as *sarthapala*, and my swords in plain sight, it was easy for him to believe that I was a man, and that men of the north were smaller and slighter than the men of the south. Easier to believe that, than the truth; that this strange, foreign warrior-mystic with the light skin and folds in her upper eyelids was actually a woman.

Lying saved so much time.

When I was sure that I was away from any watching eyes, I stripped and scrubbed my clothes swiftly. They were threadbare. The soles of my sandals were as thin as the skin of a mango. It didn't matter. Today, I would die, or I would not. Clothes would not matter, either way.

I scrubbed myself after that, and by the time I'd finished, my clothes had dried in the heat.

I dressed slowly, concentrating on a deep and even cycle of breathing. I murmured chants in languages no longer used. I drank a bowl of water. Gradually, all else began to recede and my mind began to clear, to be as pure as the water. To flow like an invisible mist through the city and see it as it really was.

It was time.

"Himadri-yatri," the landlord called after me as I left the inn, naming me Himadri the Pilgrim. "Which temple do you seek? I may guide you."

I ignored him. I didn't need him, and I'd paid him enough already.

In my mind's eye, the Temple I sought stood like a towering rock in the sea. I knew all the paths to it. I could *see* the way, as clearly as if it were strewn with blossoms and lined with swaying crowds.

It was the temple in the middle of them all, unregarded and overlooked.

The Temple returned the favor. It knew its worth and it didn't care what anyone thought.

Chapter 27

As we walked, the not-yet-queen and I, I sifted through her memories to try and understand how we'd come to be here and why she'd gone through so much to get here.

I got a cascade of glimpses into her life.

Nai, as a young girl, an Adept in training among the secret societies of Shizhaishan, in the Dian kingdom which was now Yunnan in southern China. Young and gifted. Brilliant and impatient. *A bad mixture* said her teachers and tried to teach her patience by tasking her with learning how to weave workings. To take small magic created by others and make something greater from the parts.

There was a vivid memory of speaking about weavings to her teachers. "They're ugly and weak, because they can only be as beautiful as the ugliest part, and only as strong as the weakest part. They only work until the least powerful Adept is exhausted, and they only work as well as the least effective. There must be a better way."

She'd been punished for her arrogance. Sent to labor on the farms in the foothills of the mountains for a year.

And there, while her body did the work she was forced to do, her mind, freed from her teachers' restrictions, became calm and it *reached*.

How far it reached!

To make the smallest part of a working beautiful. A miniature working that was *right*, that didn't need constant attention. That absorbed the power it needed to carry on. A circle. A snake that swallowed its tail. A *ring working* she called it.

Then to weave, not by interlacing straight lines of poor workings that began and ended wherever their designs took them, but by linking each perfect ring working with other ring workings, interlocking them. Each remained a small working, but supporting others, building and building, one onto another until it was all a working of beauty and elegance.

Vindication. She would create this thing of beauty. Her teachers would have to acknowledge she was right. They couldn't help but see how perfect her method was.

At the end of the year of banishment, she was ready, but there was nothing on the farm that she could take back to her teachers worthy to be used to impress them with her new skill.

Nothing but herself.

Oh, shit! She'd turned her Adept skills back on herself; made herself the object of her workings. Made herself...

Another vivid memory forced its way to the fore. The moment when her teachers understood what she'd done.

Instead of praise, anger and fear.

The shouting. A word she'd never heard used before: *busi.* Deathless.

Not unkillable. That would not have been possible, but Nai had found a way to recreate a form of immortality like the Athanate had.

Busi!

And a*bomination.*

And *cursed.*

Escape. Running. Hiding from Adepts. Using her poorly developed powers to defend herself. Travelling further and further to keep ahead of the news about her. Any Adept who heard that news and knew who she was would try and kill her.

She was resourceful beyond her years; she managed to outrun the immediate associations of her teachers, she outlasted their lives, but the death sentence on her head would not die. It became like a snake behind her, sometimes distant, sometimes close, always pursuing. Slithering from Adept community to Adept community. *Find the abomination. Kill it.*

One day she knew she would wake to find the snake had caught up, so she learned what she could to defend herself. Studied workings and adapted them with her outcast methods. Developed her own style of sword fighting.

And then she heard the legend of the Stone Serpents.

A way to break this cycle...

The flow of memories was abruptly cut off, though I was still walking in Nai's shoes. We were back in Kallamada Mala.

We'd arrived at the Temple.

Like all the temples of the city, the Temple of the Stone Serpents had a wide courtyard, surrounded by high rough-brick walls, blank and undecorated. There was a single unguarded gateway without a barrier. Unlike many of the other, older temples, which had tall, shady trees in their courtyards, the Serpent Temple and its courtyard lay uncovered to the sun.

Yet as soon as I walked through the gate, I could feel a coolness, even in the searing heat of the day.

The Temple itself was a large dome, mounted on a heptagon, of course. Seven serpents, seven pillars, seven sides, seven tall archways that opened into the darkness inside. It was all built from great blocks of maroon sandstone, dark as old blood, carved intricately with a pattern that flowed down the sides of the building. That diamond pattern looked like hundreds of trickles of water. Or the scales of serpents.

Nothing moved and no one called a welcome. There were no patient gurus, no singing priests or incense-waving monks, no supplicants. Not even monkeys came into this courtyard to listen to the wind whispering over the walls.

The coolness that defied the burning sun came from the Temple itself and it lodged like a stone in my stomach.

Busi they called Nai, *deathless*, but she could be killed and death was here, waiting, wound around the columns of the Temple like an invisible, choking jungle plant. But that risk was also an opportunity. Power lay in the inhuman perfection of the working that the Stone Serpents had made.

For the first time, Nai felt an understanding of the horror her long-forgotten teachers had felt when they'd seen her work.

To have come so far and to hesitate seemed foolish, yet each step towards the gaping thresholds was slower than the last.

Finally…

This was the Caturtha Sarpa doorway. The fourth Serpent, the Serpent of Air, the Mistress of Breath, and the Guardian of the First Tower, the transcendent level that lay beyond dreaming.

I knew this.

I couldn't see much inside. Some light reached down, in tiny, bright fingers, coming through holes in the roof so small I hadn't seen them from outside.

No monks inside, but there was incense. Smoke rose slowly and swayed like cobras dancing in the beams of light.

The Temple *seemed* empty of anything else.

I raised a tentative foot and brought it down into the darkness inside. The floor was cool through the thin leather of my sandals. Clean, but not smooth. Rippled, like pebbles.

It didn't feel *real*, whatever that meant here.

Another couple of quick steps and I was out of the stinging sunlight.

Absolute silence. Nothing I could smell but the tang of incense. Nothing I could see but an empty space stretching out to the other archways, each blazing with the outside light.

I tried to reach out with Nai's inner eye, and failed. We'd parted ways. I was just Amber. I was alone.

I knew this.

Chapter 28

In the gloom, I realized was back in my own body as well, though still dressed as Nai had been, right down to the sheathed swords across my back.

Did that mean this was the start of my trial by the Serpent Temple?

"No," Tara said aloud, as clear as if she was standing next to me in the dark. "*All* of this has been part of a trial. I think it started when you spoke to the Queen in the grove."

"You think riding along with Nai was a test?"

"Or a learning experience. Come on; you're calling her Nai and not the Queen of Diamonds. We were cheering her on."

"Yes. Even though we knew she had succeeded, and whatever happened it eventually made her the Queen of Diamonds."

"A learning experience and a warning."

Tara was right. It had been a learning experience, all the way back to the grove. Talking to the queen, crossing the bridge, spirit jumping into Nai so I could walk a mile in the queen's shoes, literally. Reliving a memory of hers that must have been a thousand years old or more. I'd found out that she hadn't created the Stone Serpents as Mirela and I had assumed; that they were even older than the queen and she'd sought them out to increase her powers to allow her to escape the death sentence of the Adepts. I was seeking them out to increase my powers to be able to fight against the Lost Gods. And escape the death sentence of their venom.

It was all vaguely similar, but the real difference was the queen was a gifted Adept who'd developed methods with workings that were clearly at the level of genius. I was a magical damp squib in comparison. What did I have to offer the Serpents?

And, yes, it had been a warning too. If I succeeded, would I change as much as Nai? Would I become something that I would despise? Replace the threat of Matlal, Quetzalcoatl and Tezcatlipoca with the threat of me?

I didn't know, but what I *did* know, was if I turned back now, there was the small problem that I would die, along with Diana, Bian, Mirela and Salar.

If I went on and failed… well, I would be dead then, too, and not just in this place.

I was waiting for my eyes to adjust to the darkness. Nothing seemed to be threatening me immediately, but there didn't seem much point in moving when I couldn't see anything.

Standing in the dark wasn't any kind of a test, was it?

"What do you think the Serpents are?" Tara asked.

"Soultrees?" I shrugged. "A different set of Lost Gods? After all, why would there just be one group? Or maybe they're just Adepts who also became immortal. 'Busi' as Nai called it."

'Deathless' sounded very much like 'undying'. Did that mean busi was the same thing as Athanate?

"If they were Adepts, why didn't she join them then? For that matter, Alice Emerson is some kind of busi, but she doesn't seem to know anything about the Stone Serpents."

Good point. Alice was outcast by the Adept community because she worked with the Athanate and challenged Adept orthodoxy. I'd originally thought she was kin, but she was too old for that. According to Bian, she was nearly five hundred years old. Alice must have found a way to extend her life as Nai had, and yet the workings I sensed Nai had created were different from anything I'd sensed before. Clearly, there were different ways to extend your lifespan.

"The more important question is why they're considering allowing me access to their power," I said. "Or why they allowed Nai access to it."

"Assuming they are genuinely considering it and not just toying with you."

I laughed. My twin sister was good for keeping me focused.

I peered into the darkness, but my wolfy eyes weren't adjusting to low light levels in the shadows. It was unnatural. Unnerving. Light from the doorways should have revealed the inside of the temple. But at its center, there wasn't low light; there was no light. No heat.

Still, there was *something* here.

It seemed long ago, in another life, that Tullah's mother had given me a wolf's eye bracelet with her own workings woven into it. Workings that she'd said would help warn me of danger. Workings that would eventually weave themselves into me. I wasn't wearing the bracelet, but the skin where it would have been on my wrist began to tingle as if I'd been slapped.

There was danger, whether I could see it or not.

The swords were in my hands instinctively without me even having to think about drawing them. I didn't know what the next tests would be, but maybe it would be better if I was ready for physical attacks.

As I stood, tense and searching the shadows, I realized not all Nai's skills had left me with her departure. I knew those swords, the jian and the dao, as if I'd lived with them the way Nai had.

Was that what the Queen meant by 'some of her' in me?

Impossible to tell. I could ask her, *if* I survived and got back to the grove.

Which I probably wouldn't do by standing here. There had to be some clue what I was supposed to do, so I closed my eyes and submerged myself into my spirit senses—aura and eukori.

There was a sensation, a little like falling. A little like spirit walking.

I could hear things I hadn't before. I could feel things.

The wind blew through the doors and tiny gaps in the roof. I heard it speak in many tongues. It chanted prayers and whispered promises. It pushed at me, as if urging me to move deeper into the temple. I inched forward and let the blades of my swords weave through the air, sensing workings that parted and reformed like smoke. Workings that could snap closed on me if the Serpents commanded it. Workings that seemed more solid behind me than in front.

Okay, I got it. Move forward to the center.

I couldn't see the floor, but it felt peculiar. I pushed off my sandals and stepped forward barefoot. The floor seemed to be pebbles set in mortar, like cobblestone. Smooth and slick with moisture, but stranger than those purely physical perceptions. As if the floor was there and not there, at the same time.

On instinct, I pressed down with my foot. *Down.* Through the floor I couldn't see, into another depth. I touched another surface. Wood? Narrow. A step? A staircase of some kind?

Heart in my mouth, I moved forward blindly again, toes searching out the edge of each step. Down, step by step, until I knew I had to be below the level of the temple floor, in utter blackness. I reached a point where there seemed to be no more steps. I still couldn't see. Not even the doorways behind me.

What was this test? To see if I could fight without eyes?

No. If the temple wanted to kill me, there would be a thousand easy ways while I was blind. This wasn't about a physical attack. Not right now, anyway.

I sheathed the swords.

And felt a stir in the workings around me in response.

As Tara had said, everything was part of the test; even *understanding* the test was part of it.

All is maya, Nai had thought as she made her way through the city. *This is that which is not. This is only another illusion of the world.*

With that understanding came the first hint of light on my eyelids. Not so I could see well, but enough for my wolf eyes to be able to make out the heat of human bodies, live and warm and moving all around me. I didn't need wolf hearing to make out their voices. My name was being called. That wasn't the only sound, or the loudest. No; the loudest would have been the sound of the orgy.

What the hell kind of a test is this?

A hand caresses my calf, and someone reaches up to plant a kiss on my thigh. More hands brush my hips, lingering. On top of the sounds and the touch, there's the scent. Athanate can put out sex pheromones, but no Athanate ever put out this amazing richness. Pure, hundred percent lust. Yet these Athanate are my House.

Stunning.

Join us, the lovers sigh. My House calls to me.

If I had breath to laugh, I would, but they've stolen that along with half my wits.

And my body's responding. My legs feel like jelly. Hands steal up my shirt, trace exquisite circles on my breasts. Lips kiss my throat. A tongue runs the length of my spine. My body lights on fire. I stagger. Another second and I'll fall and never get up.

No!

All is maya! This is that which is not.

I pushed my foot down. Somehow, I found another step between the traps of flesh.

Another. Another. Down. I ignored the voices. I was shaking. Every cell in my body urged me to go back.

No.

Finally, silence. Cool. Dark again.

I dragged air into my lungs and let it out in a wobbly laugh.

"Some hell of a test," I said aloud. "I'm assuming I passed by not succumbing."

"Feint," Tara said.

"What?"

"When you're fighting someone, you feint. How the opponent reacts tells you about them. Gives you an indication of their strengths and weaknesses. That was just a feint. You weren't ever going to fall for that."

I snorted. Easy for my spirit twin to say. The flesh was weak.

"It's going to get harder," she said.

"That is so comforting."

"Nah. You got this."

My feet crept forward again, searching for the next step.

"What do you think would have happened, if you'd stopped there? I mean apart from great sex."

"I think that was just a simple trap," I said. "There wasn't anything there that was a real benefit."

There was light ahead.

"But the next one…"

People. Fully clothed this time. Busy. Walking fast. A flickering of bodies rushing backwards and forwards, moving with urgency. A sound like surf. A balcony with some kind of podium and microphones, screened by bulletproof glass.

Bernie, my campaign manager, rushes up.

"Astonishing. Utterly unprecedented, but it's confirmed." He's unshockable, that was why I hired him, but he's looking shocked now. He shakes his head in disbelief. "You can write your own ticket. Everything on your wish list just went solid gold."

There's a roar from outside that seems to shake the foundations of the building.

"Results have gone up on the screens out there," Bernie says.

AM-BER! AM-BER!

A call like waves crashing over the balcony. Crashing through me. Drawing me to that podium.

Some journalist whose name I've forgotten is in front of me.

"Can I have a first reaction, Ms Farrell?"

"She is incredibly humbled by the trust of the people. And you can quote her on that." My press secretary slips between us.

The Emergence legislation can start tomorrow. It'll be a march through hell, but it will happen. It will. We've done it. Humanity will welcome the paranormals as equals.

They'll be trusted because the people trust me. Today, as they've shown their trust, I need to talk to those people directly. I need it. I have to do it. I feel it in every cell of my body.

I take a step toward the podium, but my shoes don't feel right.

The shoes don't fit.

And I remember. Maya. Illusion.

This is Skylur's job. Not mine.

Another step, but this one was down again. There were shouts behind me. They faded.

"A political solution?" Tara says. "You reckon the Serpents could deliver that?"

I let out another shaky breath. It had seemed so real. "There's that old saying about a lever long enough can shift the world."

"*Long* lever."

"Yeah. But not my lever in any case."

But if it *could* be… That thought doesn't want to go away. Was this something the Serpents wanted or needed? Or simply another diversion to lure me away from what I needed? Or a trap?

It was getting brighter again.

Almost blinding. Hot and dry. The heavenly fragrance of Tuscan lemon trees floats in from the garden.

Tara and I hurry in beneath the shade of the long verandah. As always, we're dressed identically because we like to mess with people. It never works with the kids of course.

"Mom!" That's Sarah's voice. Shrill with excitement.

"And Aunty Tara, too!" And Amy.

My twins. My life.

"You're here!"

"At last!"

Of course, right behind my twins are Tara's, Stephanie and Frances.

"Mom!"

"Aunty Amber!"

Twins produce twins, of course. A double wedding and a couple of years later, four bundles of joyous mischief, who are now approaching ten.

Instinctively, Tara and I kneel to brace ourselves for the onslaught.

They break around us like the unruly ocean and wrap us both up in unselfconscious hugs.

It's hot and they've been playing, so they're grubby and sweaty, but there's a clean, sweet edge to their scent. An innocence. A purity that cuts my soul.

"There's a pool! With a slide!"

"Grandpa said we couldn't go swimming 'til you got here."

"Pleeeeaaase."

My heart is breaking. I can't see for the tears. This, too, is an illusion. This cannot be.

Tara is shaking her head, but no sound comes from her lips.

"There you are. At last." Dad emerges from the house, pretending to be exasperated. "They've been so difficult, these four terrors."

Mom's just behind him. She's laughing, in a way that says she knows we haven't a real care in the world.

I stand unsteadily.

"Mom! The pool!" my twins sing in chorus.

It's not real. Dad and Mom and Tara. Husbands and marriages. Children. Holidays in a villa in Tuscany. Normalcy, safety and security. Family and love. It's not real!

I feel for the next step with my feet. It's back out into the sun.

"Amber!" Dad says. "Wait! It's too hot out."

It's worse than hot.

I welcome it. I need it. I need this pain to burn this illusion out of me.

I get the pain.

It's as if flames are running up my body and leaping outward to scorch the others.

There are screams behind me, and I put my hands over my ears, because that sound is tearing me apart.

I staggered and I would have slumped down to cry, but it wasn't wooden steps beneath my feet.

It was burning coals.

Chapter 29

An arrow-straight path lay ahead of me, laid with compacted coal, glowing red. I couldn't see the end.

And I was barefoot.

I'd fire walked before, for a dare, on R&R with Keith during my days in Ops 4-10, but that hadn't been in a magical underground temple and my life hadn't been on the line and my heart hadn't just been ripped out of my chest.

I was staggering forward automatically. I could barely see for tears. Searing hot air fought with choking sobs in my throat. Grief made squeezing bands like iron around my chest.

A fire walk seemed a trivial test in comparison to the last. Even as I thought it, I knew that was a potentially fatal assumption. And it was hurting.

Just go, but 'walk' is only a suggestion.

I sprinted down the path.

The air above the flaming path was as bad as the coals themselves. My clothes threatened to catch fire. My hair crinkled, my feet blistered, and the lining of my nose felt like I was snorting the flames directly. Even my lungs burned.

Faster.

On either side of the path were pools. Deep, cool water beckoned me, but every paranormal sense screamed at me not to try it.

There was no end to this path that I could see, and there was no option but to keep going.

The pain had reached a steady level and I needed to *think* about the tests rather than just linger on my feelings about them. I was getting a sense of them. They all meant something, whether I fully understood them or not. Even standing in the dark had been a test of understanding that it was a test. The Stone Serpents didn't seem to do anything in a simple way. Tara was wrong to dismiss the orgy as only a feint, for example. It did that as well, but it was also a test of strength. And a warning. Same with the rope bridge earlier. Strength. Determination. Resolve. The politician illusion: well, that was testing how well I knew myself and my purpose. This test was about pain. Pain of the body, as opposed to pain of the heart and soul.

The family...

I couldn't avoid it, and I couldn't push it away like the others.

I *hated* the Stone Serpents for what they'd just done to me. I hated them with a fire stronger than the coals beneath my feet. I hated them like the wordless scream of rage that seemed to rise in my belly and force its way out of my mouth.

They'd dug into my soul and found a dream I'd never acknowledged—even to myself—and then they didn't just rip it out from under me. They forced me to destroy it and walk away, or lose everything and everyone I cared about now.

But I couldn't let them defeat me—especially not this way. They'd used my family against me, and I couldn't dishonor the people I loved by letting that break me. The Stone Serpents had taken nothing from me, I told myself. They hadn't killed my sister with a curse, or caused my father's death from cancer. They hadn't made me Athanate, taking away my ability to ever have children or a normal life.

And yet.

There would now *never* be a time when I couldn't hear their voices, my twin daughters that *never were.* Never a time when the pain that they *never were* would completely go away. *Never.*

The burning hatred of that cruelty surged inside me, so fiercely it opened the strongbox where I kept my most violent emotions locked away.

And I got a glimpse of purpose that I couldn't fully grasp, as I realized I'd reached the end of the fire test.

I was scorched, my lungs and throat raw. My burned and blistered feet were in agony, but I didn't dare sit. I needed to be ready for whatever the Serpents were going to throw at me next.

I stood on the cold stone floor of a huge domed temple, gloomy as a mausoleum, big enough to build an airship in. The curving walls looked like sandstone, the color of weathered bronze. They were lined with dozens of pale columns that rose toward the invisible ceiling with the same curve as the walls. They made me think of ribs, seen from the inside of a body.

Was this the heart of the illusion? The actual Temple of the Stone Serpents itself?

*No, because there **is** no heart to the illusion.*

I stood and panted, feet still burning, feeling another piece of the puzzle fall into place. I had the venom of the fourth Serpent in my Blood, and I could sense it throughout my body, like a shadow in my veins and a fire behind my eyes. While the venom was killing me, it was also elevating my consciousness to see beyond the veil of illusion. This was what the Queen of Diamonds had meant by calling it a gift, a transcendent level beyond dreaming. The venom in my Blood was what had allowed me access to this spirit world, and given me a hint of the workings that made it.

Including the knowledge that I was running out of time.

Just as that thought crossed my mind there was a pulse of sound, so low it was no more than a measured rhythmic pressure on the ears, like the heartbeat of some gigantic beast. A whispering came from all around—the sort of sound a snake might make on a stone floor.

There was a structure below the surface of the floor in front of me.

A few steps forward and I stood on the brink of a circular amphitheater surrounding an arena of sand lit by braziers around the edge. In the center of that sand, a single candle burned.

Oh, shit.

It was a Mandaviran, one of the sacred arenas where ancient Athanate had ended disputes by dueling when all other means of resolution had been exhausted.

They'd tempted me and tortured me with my most hidden, most unacknowledged dreams. Now, finally, they were giving me someone to fight. It was almost a relief.

I limped slowly down the steps to the arena, wincing from the abrasion of the stone on my sore feet.

The amphitheater was split into seven sections, naturally, each section separated from the next with a tall stone statue of a snake. The statues seemed to move in the flickering light, and the gems they had for eyes twinkled.

As I got to the bottom, the dimness seemed to clear—or my discernment became sharper. A jade throne came into view, on the steps above the sand at the far end of the amphitheater.

A few moments more, and I could make out the figure of a large man lying on the step immediately beneath the throne, his back to me, apparently asleep. He was covered by a cowled black robe.

My opponent?

As I descended, the figure stirred, sat up and turned around to face me. His face stayed in the shadow of the cowl.

The menace that seeped from him seemed somehow familiar. I reached with eukori and aura, and the shock of recognition almost brought me to my knees.

"Greetings, ehvasi," he said.

Chapter 30

Everyone has *that* fear, the one that's always lurking in your nightmares, just at the edge of your vision. One you can't even acknowledge or name, because just doing that might force you to confront it.

And then you have to.

House Chrysos was my fear made flesh.

That fear flooded through my body, paralyzing me. My heart refused to beat. I was powerless, just like that night in the looming shadow of Hacha del Diablo, hidden in the jungles of South America.

Powerless.

In the arrogance they'd trained into me in Ops 4-10, I'd believed there was no person on Earth that could have done that to me. Then he had come screaming out of the night and shown me how wrong I was.

He was the first truly powerful monster I'd met, and I saw now that he was all monsters to me, the one from which all fears sprang. He'd been so terrifying, so effortlessly overwhelming that I had locked his effect on me into my mental strong box and never examined it.

That safe was torn open now and the thing I couldn't face, now faced me.

Was this the Temple of Serpents' test? To face my fears? Or to confront this terror of being helpless and overcome it? Or was this more, a test inside a test?

Whatever it was, I was no longer that helpless woman.

My voice was a dry rasp, my throat still painful from the long fire walk. "I killed you, House Chrysos."

"And I killed you," he replied. "Yet here we are, and you are my ehvasi, child. You should address me as Kyrios."

His voice chilled me down to the bone. It was a deep, arrogant voice, a voice trained for command with none of the insanity there had been that night when he bit me, and I had silenced his insane screams by cutting his head off.

"You *tried* to kill me. You didn't succeed. I'm alive. You're…"

"What? I'm a figment of your dying imagination? Or are you a figment of mine? Or are we some combination of memories captured in this place of power?"

"I didn't die from your wounds. I've been very much alive for over two years since we fought."

He tilted his head up and the cowl slipped back, revealing a frowning face.

"I sense truth in your words." He stared at me. "Can you not sense the truth in mine?"

I was no Truth Sensor, but as far as I could tell he wasn't lying. At least, he didn't think he was.

All is maya. He didn't have to be real, and this didn't have to make sense. It was whatever the Stone Serpents wanted it to be.

The question was, why him? Did I need to exorcise my greatest fear by killing him? But I'd already killed him. Was there something else to be learned here?

"You don't seem as insane now as you did then," I said, trying to ignore the trembling in my body at the same time as keeping it from my voice. "I mean back when I killed you."

He laughed. Genuine, free laughter. "Yes, I was insane, wasn't I? But this place is guarded against him. I can't tell you how wonderful it was to wake and lie here, half asleep, waiting for you, without the constant struggle, without hearing him all the time."

"Who is *him*?" But I knew before he spoke.

"The same god that speaks to you."

Tezcatlipoca. Of course.

Was this another illusory choice—between killing him and ridding myself of the fear, or sparing his life and hoping to learn the key to harnessing T-Cat's power?

I felt the weight of the shadow in my Blood. Time was pressing.

I'd try getting information first. "Why do you think you're here?" I said.

He turned it on its head. "The most profound philosophical question we all ask ourselves." He snorted. "You didn't mean it like that, but in asking, you've answered it, if you can see."

I shook my head.

"The concept of maya, the theories of existentialism, the power that enables the paranormal races... it's all one. Belief. *Belief.* What do you believe can happen here and now?"

I took a deep breath and tried to put my scattered thoughts in some kind of order. If we were going to fight, I needed to win the mental fight first.

"This is a test for me," I said, speaking to him, but really to the Stone Serpents, who I knew were listening. "You are an illusion, taken from my mind and set against me. There is nothing for you here. If I win, I pass my test and you cease to be. If I lose, I fail, and you cease to be anyway."

It was a good try, but he didn't disappear in a puff of logic.

He nodded somberly. "I, too, believe this. The powers in this temple want an agent. As you believe your test is to overcome your fears, I believe mine is to destroy that which I created. To erase the stain, so House Chrysos can once again be a beacon in the darkness. Do you not see the significance of this arena?"

The ritual of the Mandaviran was from ancient Athanate history. No one used it any more. Only very, very old Houses still practiced the skills.

Luckily, the oldest of them all, Diana, had taught me. But I still wasn't understanding him, which meant I was failing the test. The fear returned, and I didn't trust my voice. I shrugged as if I didn't care.

"Belief stands at the end if it all." He stood, and his voice took on that hypnotic rhythm of the Athanate oral traditions, saying the ritual words Diana had taught me.

"*Beyond emotion, there is reason.*" He added, "You have moved beyond your fear and tried reason. I do not accept your reasoning."

I swallowed to clear my throat and quoted the second line of the Mandaviran incantation. "*Beyond reason, there is logic.*"

"But I do not accept your logic, which seems to be that, because you believe you have memories of experiencing life after we fought, therefore you must be the center of this illusion. Which takes us to: *Beyond logic, there is faith.*"

"We can only have faith in what we believe, because without it, we are illusion." The words tumbled from me. They seemed right.

He let the robe slip from his shoulders, revealing a naked body in the peak of condition, and armed with the traditional Athanate weapons: the left arm encased in the segmented armor of the pelea, and the right holding the kinirak, the sword with its extended hilt that was braced and strapped against the forearm.

"Which leaves us with the ending of the ritual words," he said. "*And beyond faith, there is only iron in the Mandaviran.* Faith is belief, and the Athanate way is the stronger belief will prevail."

I cleared my throat. "The Athanate have moved away from the idea that might is right."

"Maybe that was a false step. Even in my remoteness, I hear the Athanate have descended into futile argument, where strength and singleness of purpose is required."

He lifted his chin, gesturing. On a step to the right of me lay a pelea and kinirak. I knew they would fit me perfectly.

I still felt weak. I *was* weak, and tired and injured and poisoned. Seeing him move with the weapons told me that he was a master of the art of the Mandaviran. Even being trained by Diana didn't raise me to that level. If I tried to use his tactics and weapons, he'd win.

But there had to be a way for me to beat him, or there was no point to this test. I didn't think he'd ever come across the Queen of Diamonds, and her style with these Chinese swords—the style I seemed to have inherited from her—would be unknown to him.

I'd start there.

I drew the jian and the dao, discarding the scabbards. These swords felt a part of me, where the kinirak did not. The sensation of their weight in my hands eased the trembling of my arms. I felt Nai's muscle memory seeping into me. I knew how to use these blades. Nai would have considered herself far more skilled than Chrysos, but even with her knowledge, I was not Nai.

He began to pace counterclockwise.

The ritual forbade us from fighting until the candle at the center burned out. It was guttering. Not long now. My body flooded with adrenaline. I began to walk to keep on the opposite side to him.

Walking was painful. My feet hurt, my calves ached, my whole body was sore. The venom flared in my Blood, reminding me once more that time was slipping away.

In contrast to me, Chrysos was rested. He had no injuries, no poison in his Blood. Even without those advantages, he out-massed me by fifty pounds or so. He was much stronger. He had a reach eight or nine inches longer than mine.

And he was watching me as keenly as I watched him.

"This will not be much of a test," he said.

He was trying to put me on the back foot mentally, which was half the struggle in any physical fight, so I ignored him.

I focused the way Bian had taught me, feeling her words resonate with Nai's skill.

> To be aware of everything and know the one right thing.
> To be whole in body and weapons and purpose.
> To not **be**, other than that purpose.
> And to move without thought or hesitation.

The candle at the center of the Mandaviran went out. Time to fight.

Chapter 31

He started with a bull rush, as if he were going to charge across the arena.

I just watched it. It was a feint. He was seeing if I would react in panic, and I needed to conserve my strength.

I walked on the sand, got used to the feel. It was firm. Abrasive, and the pain in my feet belonged to someone else, far away. The same person who owned the fear and helplessness. I was no one. I was a weapon. I was a purpose.

His first genuine attack, when it came, wasn't fully committed. He thrust and swung the kinirak high and low, but never with his full force behind it. I deflected them. Let his blade slide off mine. He was just probing to see any obvious weaknesses.

I learned too. I had to be careful. His kinirak was heavier than my swords. Probably as heavy as both together. Given his strength and weight, it would be very difficult to stop a blow directly. I would have to depend on deflecting instead, trying to draw him off balance, so whichever of my swords wasn't busy deflecting I could use to strike back.

He knew this.

Feints aside, we began the song of steel.

Slash, return, thrust. Again. Again. He fell into a rhythm. Three, six, twelve cycles. Then he broke off.

I was sweating. He wasn't.

I was lighter on my feet, but I was already tired. I would slow long before he would.

He was far stronger than me.

He knew this too.

"Contend for honor, for duty, for responsibility, for dignity. Do not submit needlessly, nor in cowardice, but to sacrifice oneself foolishly is not true valor," he quoted some ancient text. "This is the way."

I snorted and he slashed high, at my head. I ducked. He reversed. Slashed down with frightening speed. I jumped to the side and circled.

He went on with his little speech, as if nothing had happened. "To contend without hope is to turn aside from the path, to abandon true destiny. This is not the way."

He came again, in the same pattern. I estimated he was fighting at half the speed he could. I was holding back as well, but the problem was, I wasn't going to be able to double my speed.

Difficult as it was to split my attention, I tried eukori and aura, but I couldn't feel anything. No way to sense his intentions. No path of aura out of this Temple. No way to call on the strength of others. No power to channel. I was alone. I couldn't even sense Tara. I had no underhanded surprises I could spring on him.

And I had to concentrate, as he swooped in to attack again.

Slash and return in scything movements, then thrust. Back to the earlier pattern. Tempting me to exploit the predictability of his movements.

I deserved to die if I fell for that.

But in the middle of the fourth repetition, I feinted and, sure enough, he broke the pattern to lunge when he should have been moving to the side.

Slick. Well executed.

I was waiting.

Crouch. Weight low. Step to the side. Stab with the dao rather than the jian. The pelea knocked the dao aside, but his weight was wrong. I whipped the jian up to rake his gut. Quick, quick.

But he wasn't there.

Oh, he was good. Very, very good.

I'd gotten so close. Close enough to force him back.

I pressed forward, switching the lead between my blades. An all-out attack with the dao, defense with the jian, then the reverse. Quicker than thought. One with my weapons. Solely my purpose.

He retreated, eyes widening.

Again. Again. Yes! Forcing him back.

Then the subtlest change of his weight. He seemed to fall to one side, with his pelea desperately held in front, to protect his vulnerable chest.

I leaped away, as his arm whipped back. I felt the wind of his mailed fist passing an inch from my face. If he'd landed that blow, he'd have shattered my skull. But Diana had taught me well; the armor of the pelea was a weapon of attack as well as defense. I was also expecting the kinirak that followed behind, sweeping up in a blow that would have gutted me if I'd been there.

He was better than very, very good. Much, much better.

I was panting. He was barely breathing heavily.

I had magically learned so much from Nai, but it wasn't enough. I hadn't earned Nai's expertise. My body was different. We moved differently.

I had no time to learn to adapt, and I was already weakened.

He paused his pacing.

"I was wrong," he said.

I was surprised enough to respond. "Yeah?"

"I thought my test would be to kill you. I thought that your continued life would be a dishonor to my House." He shook his head. "You've shown that you have what it is that makes House Chrysos great. My test is to overcome you. To convince you. Submit to me, and together we will make the strongest Athanate House that the world has ever seen."

"Your beliefs don't seem deep rooted if they change that easily," I said.

"This is the only way."

He moved seamlessly from speaking to attack.

Five strikes. Break. Then three. Break. Then he moved so fast, the kinirak seemed to blur.

I kept it out, barely. The blade grazed my arm, my thigh, my belly, and I bled. I was Athanate; I healed quickly, but another few attacks like that and my self-healing wouldn't be quick enough.

No question—other than Diana, and maybe Bian, Chrysos was the best I'd fought. Whatever Nai's confidence suggested, I thought he was better than her, which didn't bode well, since I'd decided to use her weapons and skill. Not that using the traditional weapons would have got me any further.

He came again. Seven strikes, each heavier than the last. I had to use both swords to defend. I felt the strength draining from me and the fear returning.

I was too weak. Too tired. Sweat and blood were already making my grip unsure. My vision blurred and my head swam with the Serpent's fever.

I was sinking in a nightmare. It would only get worse.

Fate has a day marked for each of us. Maybe today was that day for me. I'd never thought it'd come in a fight with bladed weapons.

In this nightmare, all that seemed left was to take him with me. Force him to close with me, and kill him as he killed me.

I needed strength, just a little more. Strength to stand and strike back as I died. Was that too much to ask when the odds were so stacked against me?

The strongbox in my mind groaned and I felt the escape of the hate and anger I stored there. They burned. *That* could fuel me.

I didn't need to wait for him. *In death ground, fight.* I launched an attack.

Spin the jian around and hold it like a dagger. Get inside his reach, so he had no advantage there. Hit him with everything. Everything. Hilt, fist, knee, forehead, blade. No pause. Be crazy. Crazy. Crazy! Get the jian between us, cutting both of us. Don't care. Dare him to try and grab me with that blade there. Stab at his belly and thighs while he didn't.

The anger burned in me as brightly as a flare.

The way the kinirak attached to the arm meant he couldn't use it effectively while I was so close. He was still hitting at me, even cutting me, and I didn't care while that fire inside erased everything beyond the narrow purpose of killing him.

Pain! Like fire on my body.

We were close as lovers. I bit him. I couldn't reach his neck, so I bit his chest, felt the shock of the Serpent's venom in my fangs.

He broke away, tearing his flesh as he ran backwards.

I wasn't going to let him. I lurched forward, but the crazy burn that had carried me this far was gone. It had been twice as bright for half as long, and where it had gone was now a sickening emptiness.

My right leg nearly buckled. It had been cut deep. An artery. I'd been so focused, I didn't even know if he'd done that, or I had. I staggered. My guard sank down.

I could see the shock in his eyes. He was panting now. Sweating. Bloody from dozens of cuts. More than the injuries, the mindless ferocity of my attack had unnerved him. He was scared. I could smell the sudden fear, coming off him like a mist.

On top of those injuries, I'd broken the strapping on his kinirak; the part that braced it against his arm. As that came loose, the kinirak would become much more difficult to control.

Too little, too late.

My whole body was shaking. My chest was heaving. I couldn't get enough air. I was bleeding out quicker than I could stop it. My sight was dimming, but still I felt the surge of exultation.

I could have taken him.

And the pride was followed by a wave of bleak despair. Yes, I could have won. If I hadn't been exhausted to start with, and injured, if it had been a fair fight, I *would* have won.

All that's left is to finish it.

But I'd hurt him badly enough he was too wary to close with me again. He didn't need to. My wounds would do his work for him soon.

He knew this.

"Submit, ehvasi," he said, but his voice had lost its deep authority. "You're dying anyway. I might be able to save you."

Damned if I would.

I tasted the Blood in my mouth and spat. I managed a chuckle and raised the jian to point at his chest where I'd bitten him.

"I've killed you again, Chrysos. Can you feel the venom yet?"

He shook his head as if to dismiss the thought that any venom would kill him.

I was running out of time. Certainly, no time to wait for the venom to act. I couldn't chase him. I needed him to come at me again, so I could see him die before I did.

But how? My legs wouldn't carry me. I could barely see for the Blood and sweat in my eyes and the flames of the venom in my head. The effects of the venom were getting worse. I could see the venom *inside* him. I could see his doom in the form of a cloak that seemed to wrap him up, inch by inch.

I shook my head to clear the double vision. I had another way to close with him. My voice felt as if it came from another person.

"You spoke of the *way* while we fought. You spoke of honor and duty, of responsibility and dignity. You spoke of a stain on House Chrysos. I tell you, there is no ocean that can erase the stain on your name, and that stain is you."

"You are dying," he shouted. "You're delirious."

He was right on both counts. I was dying and delirious. The venom, the gift of the fourth Serpent to transcend the veil of maya, flared in my Blood and behind my eyes and I *saw*, even as my eyes failed.

"We're both dying, but even your second death won't restore the honor of Chrysos, that was once the Golden House. You know this. Your anger betrays you." Blood spilled from my mouth, evidence of some catastrophic internal injury. I spat it away. "Tezcatlipoca is your fault. And Quetzalcoatl. You tried to get the people to worship you, and your interference in their religions corrupted their gods. What your meddling created... they are abominations. They are monsters. And they are your true ehvasi. By that deed your name will be known."

He screamed, and it was the scream I'd heard in the night beneath the shadow of Hacha del Diablo; the scream of insanity.

He attacked, and as my death rushed toward me, the last moments of my life slowed down.

Why this fight? What had this proved to the Serpents—that I couldn't win an uneven fight? That I could kill him by the force of my will while I died?

Would I ever have been able to understand what they'd wanted? The queen had said I couldn't know the mind of the Stone Serpents, but if that was all this fight proved, why use Chrysos to do it?

No. Looking at it the wrong way. My old sensei speaks to me—this is not the way.

I had to be aware of everything and know the one right thing.

I could feel the venom scorching my veins, searing my mind.

Think!

This is maya. This is that which is not. This is only another illusion of the world. Wake! Escape the nightmare. Transcend the dream.

Transcend the dream!

That was not Chrysos charging me. I killed him long ago. No one comes back.

Both of us had *almost* understood the Stone Serpent's minds. The Mandaviran was a test of *belief*. A contest between irreconcilables. Who was stronger?

Which belief was stronger?

Which illusion?

I knew. I *saw*. The one way. My belief was stronger than this illusion of a contest. The man trying to kill me didn't exist.

No more time. *Move without thought or hesitation.*

I'd automatically raised my swords in the guard position, crossed in front of me. Now I swept them down to my sides, leaving myself unprotected.

"You are that which is not," I said, words jarred loose by the explosion of realization. "You can't kill me."

I saw the shock in his face. Even in his insanity, he feared a trick in my unguarded pose. A moment of doubt, too late. He was committed to the strike.

The point of the kinirak struck me on the chest. There was no pain beyond what I'd have felt being punched. Far away, I felt ribs break and the cruel blade pierced my heart. The blade was too sharp for the strike to do anything more than rock me back. There was a sensation of utter cold, of flesh parting, of death rising and darkness falling. I couldn't see. Blood flooded my mouth. Both of us were screaming.

Chapter 32

Wrong! Wrong! I was wrong!

Too late.

His attack had halted with his kinirak buried in my chest and his face inches from mine. I had dropped my swords and grabbed him at the last moment. We stood, holding each other up, pinned together by the blade between us, each staring at the other with unbelieving eyes.

Incredibly, his legs were buckling first.

No. It wasn't just his legs, it was his whole body, which was becoming loose and shapeless, like a discarded coat.

Our eyes remained locked together. I saw the ripple of shocks, and the awareness of his death in his face.

"No," he whispered.

He slipped through my fingers and sank down, down, but there was no sand, no Mandaviran, no arena to receive him.

"No."

There was no kinirak in my chest, though I could still feel where it had been.

"No!"

His body became shapeless. It spread out soundlessly across the tiled floor. It evaporated like winter's breath on a frosty morning.

I'd killed the real Chrysos down in South America. This was something the Serpents had created, but they'd created it from the real thing. This ghost had been all the real Chrysos had been. He'd know all the real one had. As Chrysos, he'd known what he'd done—that he'd been responsible for the true abominations that threatened the whole world from the City of Lost Gods.

I'd made him confront that, and it'd driven him crazy, just as it had in the depths of the South American jungle.

I felt sorrow for the ghost. He hadn't been real, but he'd believed in himself, and that's as much as any of us can say.

But he'd won. My earlier wounds didn't heal with his disappearance. Only the final killing blow was as gone. Almost. I could still feel the aching cold metal piercing my body, even if it wasn't there.

Nothing remained of the arena except the braziers holding back the dark. And the throne.

Some kind of prize?

I tried to step towards it. This time my leg buckled completely, and I would have fallen if Tara hadn't caught me.

"Thought you were gone," I said, Blood in my mouth bubbling through the words. "Now you're here physically?"

"Hush. A substantiation like this has power for me to manifest a body."

She carried me to the throne and sat me down.

"Is it over?"

I had meant the testing, but I could see Tara thought I meant my life. Maybe I did.

"This is bad," she said. "Much as I've enjoyed these few seconds, I have to abandon the body to try healing you, from the inside."

She disappeared and I felt a gentle warmth spreading through me. I closed my eyes. It wouldn't be enough. The end was coming and, in the meantime, the throne was more comfortable than it looked. I hoped it was easy to clean, because I was still bleeding all over it.

And the fire in my Blood was gone. The venom wouldn't kill me. I began to laugh, dribbling more blood over my jaw and splattering it down my chest. Even if the venom was still killing me, it wouldn't have had the time to finish the job.

Enough.

Rest.

Dying like this was so comfortable. Who would have guessed it?

Just like falling asleep.

I'm back on an Ops 4-10 mission, doing things I understand and have been trained to do. It's night in the Sahara. We've had to shelter from the sandstorm. The khamsin wind, the bearer of dreams and the voice of the spirits, sings against the fabric of the tent, a song of a sea that is no more. I'm slipping deeper and deeper into sleep, and I feel sad, because I know when all the sand has blown away, there will be nothing left.

But the song doesn't fade away. "Trust thyself..." it says.

"...and another will not betray thee," I whispered and coughed.

I felt like I was coming around after an anesthetic. Drowsy. Heavy. Unfocused. But there was someone here, and I opened my eyes. The fact that I could open them, that I could see, and I had breath to whisper or cough, all surprised me.

What I saw belonged more in my fevered nightmares.

A snake. A snake with a body three feet thick and hundreds of yards of tail coiled up in front of the throne. A snake that ended in the torso of a beautiful woman with a strange headdress, poised above the coils, watching me with eyes that glittered. The fact she had four arms seemed the least bizarre thing about her.

"It seems you do trust yourself, under threat of death," she said. "Even unto death."

Her voice... she had one mouth, one tongue and, I had to assume, one throat, but there were seven voices speaking. Her arms floated up and down independently, like a dancer, as she spoke.

I coughed again. No Blood.

"I guess you're the Stone Serpents," I said.

She dipped her head.

That *wasn't* a headdress. It moved. She had snakes for hair.

Shit!

That shock got through the sensation of floating, disconnected from everything.

"Is looking at you going to turn me to stone?" I asked. "Are you Medusa?"

"Not exactly. We are no more the Gorgon Medusa than we are the goddess Manasa, or Lilith, or any other myth associated with serpents. The same way you are not a vampire, at least not in the way that myths portray the Athanate."

I could only agree with the rest of it, but that *not exactly* response to my question wasn't comforting, so I looked down. I hadn't turned to granite, but there was a green glow inside my naked body that was unnerving. It seemed to come up from the jade of the throne, all the way through me, as if my body were part of the jade. Sort of not exactly stone, but not exactly flesh either.

But the glow showed my wounds were gone.

It also showed that I had snakes for jewelry. Live snakes. Warm bracelets for my wrists and ankles, around my waist, my neck, and if I wasn't mistaken, my head. Seven serpents. Jewelry or restraints, I couldn't tell. I couldn't get up, couldn't even lift a hand.

My heart began to race again.

Was this the next test? What the hell was I supposed to do? Escape? Talk my way out?

"Calm yourself," the woman said. "You're healing. There's no immediate threat to you now."

She did more than just speak. I sensed she was using magic on me in the way Athanate can use pacific pheromones to calm someone.

It didn't dull my urgent need to know things. "The test is over then?"

"Over? All life is a test and a trial, a learning experience and a warning. It's always training for the next thing that happens to you. That's how you become the sum of all the things you ever did."

I shivered but couldn't let her leave it there. "And all the things I will do."

She nodded again.

"So, this is more maya." I looked down at myself and then over at her. "Since you're here to ask in this illusion, what did the last test mean? The Mandaviran?"

She paused before answering. "What do you think it meant?"

"You made me face the worst fear that underlies other fears I have."

"Yes, partly, the fear of being helpless in the face of an attack. You needed to confront that fear and overcome it. You did, and you'll need to do that again to face the enemies we have. Our enemies are strong enough as it is. We cannot give them more power over us, and that is what your fear would do. Understanding that was an important part, but only one of many aspects of what you call our test. We don't have time to explain them all. We can't explain them all, for they came from within you. More importantly, you will learn best and most profoundly what you discover for yourself. You have what you need to do that."

It sounded like some of the obscure mantras that Diana had taught me, and I recited them. "Knowledge that is easy is not knowledge. Belief that is just there is not belief. The strength that is others' is not your strength."

"Truly spoken. What is learned, what is found, what is nurtured, this is what is truly yours."

She touched me where the kinirak had struck. "This is knowledge learned, but now we have run out of time and our enemies gather."

I wasn't sure if my enemies and their enemies were the same, but mine were definitely gathering. I wondered how long I'd been here.

"I thought time was what you made it in a substantiation."

"Not quite. Time can slow here, but once we reconnect to the physical world, there are many things about to happen nearly at the same time. One of those is an attack here, from the physical world, and we cannot delay that. There are important things you need to do for yourself and your friends, and then there are things you need to do for us."

Still that uncertainty about who she meant by *us*, but it seemed we had reached the negotiation stage I felt suddenly optimistic, since it appeared I'd passed their test.

"I came here partly to find a cure for the effects of your venom," I said. Before she could answer that, I added, "and partly to ask for your assistance to defeat Tezcatlipoca and Quetzalcoatl."

"And those are the same aims as ours, just seen from a different perspective. We must come together in understanding swiftly. Listen to us." Her hands floated down and joined in a sort of double namaste briefly, and then began their hypnotic dance again.

"We speak the truth as much any of us can perceive it. What you call venom is our Blood in yours, even though you received it through the Queen of Diamonds. It will do you no harm now, and Blood calls to Blood, so you may gather it from your friends. It is the part of us in you that welcomes you here, and it will lead you back to us when it may be safe to do so. As you have already worked out, it is the gift of the Fourth Tower that allows you to see beyond the illusion of maya, and now you will begin to learn to use this."

I had so many questions, but she went on before I could ask any of them.

"As our Blood is your Blood, our enemies are your enemies. This Temple exists in the spirit world, alongside what you call the City of Lost Gods, ruled now by Tezcatlipoca and Quetzalcoatl. We have always been able to defend the Temple, but now the City is becoming too powerful. If Tezcatlipoca and Quetzalcoatl break through into your physical world, their power will be overwhelming, and they will consume us. Already, Quetzalcoatl is close to that point. If they break in here, and consume us first, then they will need no other path into the physical world."

I couldn't let her go on without interruption.

"Then our enemies are mutual, but why can't *you* do something? Why do you need me?"

"We're strong here, but not that strong. The City of Lost Gods has always sustained itself by consuming others in the spirit world, gaining their power, where we sustain ourselves here without that predation. Unfortunately, that means the City has grown stronger while we have stayed the same. Already you have helped us, but time is not on our side, and our only hope is to strike from inside their defenses, the way you did with Chrysos."

"Why am I the person you would choose..." I stopped. "Of course. Because of my link with Tezcatlipoca."

"Yes. And no." Medusa dipped her head, and the serpent-hair stirred. "But before we talk about that, other things are about to happen, and you urgently need to attend to your kumemnon and retrieve your gift from her Blood. She and the woman with her are on the point of death. Go now, and you'll have just enough time. Then it will be just as urgent to return here afterwards. Outside of this Temple, time is pressing."

Her arms started a movement that I sensed had purpose.

"Wait. How do I retrieve the gift?"

"The Athanate way. Blood calls to Blood. Call your gift and it will return to you. But first, you must make Kaothos let you in. The dragon has become very powerful, and she cloaks the whole of Haven from the spirit world. Do what you have to and don't linger, we need you back here. Go!"

The darkness around us began to make swirling, half-seen patterns, a moving mandala forming from shades of black. The serpent-woman's arms floated up and down to the changing of those patterns. Released from the embrace of the serpent bangles, my arms imitated hers. This wasn't only the Serpents' magic; this was *my* magic. *Our* magic.

The Temple faded. With an image in my mind of reaching out to Diana, I spirit jumped effortlessly, and I found myself flying above Haven, the former home of House Altau, now House Trang, and probably my home in the future, if I had one. Diana was down there.

It was night, and I could feel a spirit barrier preventing me from getting closer.

At a loss to do anything else, I shouted for Kaothos, and was amazed that she answered.

"Amber?"

"Yes."

"With a cure? Diana—"

"I am the cure. Too much to explain. Need you to let me in. Quickly!"

I felt the air change and I dropped down toward the house.

I had only a moment to wonder if I'd been completely lied to. Was this an elaborate scheme for the Stone Serpents to gain access to Haven? Who better than me to act as their Trojan Horse?

Too late for those thoughts—I was there.

Chapter 33

I stood in Diana's darkened room.

I was aware of her in the bed, Salar lying by her side. They were both unconscious, sweating and lost in a feverish coma. I could sense the Serpents' venom pulsing in their bodies. It was a darkness that nearly filled them, and it pulsed, creeping into the last pockets of light. The venom worked more swiftly for older Athanate, and Diana was oldest.

And Salar had taken that swiftly developed poison into herself.

The lights came on and Kaothos was there, her body filling the room with coils and frustration.

"I haven't been able to help them," she hissed.

I was too late. I could save one, but not both. Simply not enough time.

There was no decision I could take other than saving Diana, but the thought of Salar dying felt like a weight crushing down on me. A decision I would have to bear forever. The thought of what Diana would say…

But the Serpents had said *just enough time*.

They'd also implied that everything I did might be a test.

That meant there was a way around this.

I felt Tara stir suddenly in my mind, and we both reached the same crazy conclusion.

"Yes!"

Two of us could save both Salar and Diana.

Kaothos' shield around Haven was a substantiation. A light one, very close to the physical world, but it was still a substantiation. Just like the Temple of the Serpents. Linking into the shield was like catching a wave. That was the easy part. Riding it, working with it, that was something else. It was a roaring, incomprehensible maelstrom.

Bad decision. We weren't powerful enough for this.

But a bewildered Kaothos was there with us.

The dragon spoke, and the whole substantiation seemed to ripple with her words: "*What* are you trying to do?"

No time for complicated explanations. I *showed* her. I showed her what had happened in the Temple of Serpents. Then: "Here, this thread of the shield working. Make it the same way you do for you to manifest outside of Tullah. Like this."

And she did.

Tara manifested beside me. A full physical form, mirror image of me, capable of everything I was doing.

"Hurry," we both said at the same time.

I literally fell onto Diana. Placed one arm beneath her shoulders to tilt her head back and stretch her neck. Gripped her hair to keep her steady. Sank my fangs into her throat.

Blood calls to Blood, the Serpents had said.

The shadow of the Serpents' venom paused, as if sensing me. No, *not* venom—my *gift*. *Mine.* My heartbeat matched Diana's, and we synced. I sustained her body as the shadows gathered in her throat. Then I closed my eyes and *pulled,* and the Serpents' gift came to me. The Athanate Blood channels that had manifested in me sang with exquisite pleasures, familiar and new. I *pulled* again. Again.

The gift redoubled inside me as it shrank and finally disappeared from Diana.

Tara was copying me, bite for bite, with Salar, who was easier to heal. Although she'd been as close to death, the shadow of the gift in her Blood was lighter, and taking it back went quicker.

Tullah came storming into the room, having been called by her dragon. "Really? Really healing?"

Kaothos was almost dancing. "Yes!"

"Oh, Amber! Tara!"

After feeling earlier like we were being thrown around in Kaothos' working, We were now riding it. Surfing the wave. The intricacies that created the substantiation made sense to us. It still required more power than we had. But now we could see, if we channeled power, how Tara and I would re-create something like this.

All this we saw while we had healed Diana and Salar.

I withdrew my fangs and licked Diana's throat to seal the skin. I looked up into the great lamp that was Kaothos' unblinking eye.

"How did you—" she began.

I interrupted her. "Did anyone else follow me inside your shield?"

Kaothos looked puzzled. "No. Should I expect them to try?"

"Maybe." I shook my head. "Or it's just my paranoia. If getting in here wasn't a trick, I *think* I really have some kind of a deal forming with the Stone Serpents."

"Is that why you have marks?" Tullah said, and touched my wrist.

I disentangled myself from Diana, lifted up my hands and looked. I had marks, like henna tattoos, on my wrists. Exquisite, intricate images of snake bangles. Tara had the same.

Tullah gently touched my forehead and my throat.

"Seven," I said. "Head, neck, wrists, belly and ankles. Their sign."

"Sign of what, exactly?"

"Something along the lines of *look out, here is a rank beginner trying to learn to use our power.*"

Kaothos steamed with laughter. "Hmmm. I'll grant you seemed to have learned *something* about workings, Amber Farrell. But not enough. Not the most important part."

"What is that?"

"That you shouldn't meddle with them. Not with mine anyway."

I laughed. And then I tweaked the structure of the dragon's substantiation.

"There," I said. "That's neater and more efficient isn't it?"

"Miserable human," Kaothos hissed, but a little trail of steam still escaped from her nostrils. The dragon could almost hide how surprised she was that I could change her substantiation, but Tullah couldn't. She wanted to know everything.

I shook my head again. I could feel the Serpents' words as if they were part of my pulse: *don't linger, we need you back here.*

We'd done what we needed to do. Diana had been more affected by the 'gift', and she'd fallen into a deep, repairing sleep. But Salar was struggling to wake up.

She tried to rise, and I pushed her back down.

"Rest," I said. "Summon some kin, feed and rest. Sorry for the poor bedside manner, but I have to go."

"Mistress," Salar mumbled. She was still having trouble focusing, let alone speaking. "Have to report. Attacks on Matlal's Atrax teams…"

Tullah enfolded Salar in her arms. "Hush." She looked at me over Salar's bowed head and took over. "They're going well. Salar's very worried to hear that the Atrax team in Houston weren't there. We can't find any sign of them. She's worried where they might have gone instead."

Houston. I closed my eyes for a second. The domain of House Young. Iudah Young and Diakon Trelawney. I'd never met them in person; they were apolitical and avoided meetings. They'd vested their Assembly vote in Skylur and never attended. They were mildly unconventional: for one thing, everyone in the House was a full member of the security team. If there was any House that Matlal's teams would balk at attacking, it might very well be someone like House Young.

"I'll tell Mirela," I said, and leaned over to kiss Salar's forehead. Without her, Diana would have been dead long before I arrived.

Tara vanished, and I felt her rejoin me.

She was worried about Salar. Nothing to do with recovering the gift. Something to do with Salar's mental turmoil.

No time to discuss.

I turned to Kaothos. "You're doing a reasonable job, lizard. Now I need you to open your shield to let me out. Or should I just push my way through?"

"Go! Take care."

She flooded the room with steam, that swirled in patterns. I was plucked out of there and back to the Temple in the time it took to blink.

But not to the strange underground throne. I was back where I'd started, in the Temple above, the plantation house, stepping on the floor pattern that depicted the eye of the world.

All I'd been through, and no time at all had passed. No. *Almost* no time, and that was part of the problem. It was getting late.

Chapter 34

"Amber? You okay?" Bian, alongside me, looking worried.

She would have seen me disappear for a second and I'd stumbled when I'd returned.

"I'm fine. Diana and Salar are fine. I have the antidote. I *am* the antidote. And we have an emergency."

"What? And what's that on your head? Your neck? Damn, on your wrists too."

"Magic weirdness. They're signs that I've made a deal with the Stone Serpents, and the first payment is coming up. No time to explain. We're about to be attacked."

The feeling of wrongness I'd had when I first stepped into this place—just moments ago, here—coalesced into knowledge. Someone was here who didn't belong.

This substantiation surely had to be as powerfully shielded as Haven was by Kaothos. I'd been allowed in because I carried the Serpents' gift, and they wanted me here.

But whoever this was, they had something that breached those protections.

The sounds I'd heard when I first arrived were growing.

There. Across the Temple. The Sixth Door.

I reached for the blades strapped across my back. Not the jian and the dao this time. I reached for what would feel better, wishing for the sheer weight and attacking options of two katanas. What emerged over my shoulder *were* two katanas. Bian's gift, Onibi, already glowing as I drew it, and a nearly identical sword without the light show. No sign of Nekotsume, the smaller wakizashi.

Do *not* wish for four arms in this place, I reminded myself, as I sprinted toward the Sixth Door.

The others ran after me, swearing, but readying their weapons anyway.

As we ran, our bodies became draped in chain mail.

The enemy was almost at the door, and the Serpents' Temple couldn't stop them. They needed us to fight. The invaders were forcing their way into the substantiation, and the Temple had responded with fire. The result looked like a lava flow. Inside that flow, I could see the intruders had come prepared for this substantiation. There were no firearms. Instead, an outer ring of men held interlocking shields together and followed the wall of magic that was pushing the Temple's fire back. Some of them had swords, some had spears.

It had to be hellish for them—their clothes and shields were smoking in the heat—but they were advancing in a steady, disciplined way.

Behind them, at the heart of their formation, was Vega Martine.

The Temple was now my place of power. I knew that Vega Martine had something that belonged to the Temple, and I knew that was the source of the problem. The Temple couldn't fight against itself. Both sides tapped the same power. Inside Vega Martine's sphere of magic, the Temple's magic would not work, and that sphere was being carried forward by the invaders. It was down to me to find a way around that, to stop before they reached the inside of the Temple.

I looked with the Temple's sight and *saw* the invading group; the whole structure, down to the way they'd arranged themselves in three rings. The outermost was the shield wall, and the innermost contained Vega Martine, well protected by guards. But it was the middle ring that was the strangest to my Temple-enhanced sight. This was the source of the workings that were breaking into the Temple's substantiation and forcing the fire back. I could see an aura like a boiling cloud that focused on one man, an Adept, at the front of that middle ring. But it wasn't *his* aura. Bizarrely, he had none. The aura around him was a projection of something far more powerful. The Temple told me that what I sensed was Quetzalcoatl's power being loaned to Vega Martine through that one aura-less Adept.

The Lost God's power wouldn't have been sufficient by itself. The man with no aura, the vessel for Quetzalcoatl's force, he held something that belonged to the Temple. A key. Without it, their attack would fail.

Then I realized what we would have to fight to get that key. There were *children* in that middle ring. Children like those we'd found in that lonely farmhouse outside Denver last year. Innocents bent into Matlal's sick purposes.

My stomach rebelled, but I knew we couldn't hold back. I had to stop this, whatever it took. Regardless of what Vega Martine thought she was doing, Quetzalcoatl wanted the power of the Temple for himself. The power *and* the connections.

Oh, shit! I'm part of the Temple, he'd get my connections as well.

Magic like that worked on lines of association. Even if he couldn't leverage my personal connections, there was a direct link between the Temple and the grove, back on the bank of the Atchafalaya, back right into the physical world. *I had created it by coming here. By taking part of the grove and the Temple into myself.*

That's what the Serpents had meant. Quetzalcoatl wouldn't need Matlal to open a path for him. If he took the Temple, he'd have the grove in the physical world.

I shut my mind to all the potential horrors and looked at what we could do.

The Temple's guardians had rallied to its defense. The Rougarou gardeners were also fighters, and they were large and powerful. They were armed with metal claws on one hand, like some Hollywood superhero. Many shifters and human Temple attendants were also running to join us, armed with swords and spears.

And what Donatienne had described as *others* with a shudder. Swamp wraiths, like patches of rotting darkness floated up from the borders of the Temple's grounds.

But the invaders' magic defenses and the Temple's lava fires kept them all back.

As I thought it, the fires died.

My team was too small. I needed the Rougarou to attack, but they had never trained in this sort of fight, and attacking individually they'd just get in each other's way. They'd die against those steel shields.

There has to be a way!

I forced my combat-trained instincts to take over, and saw a way.

From inside their defenses.

The invaders were disciplined, but they were unfamiliar with medieval weapons and the tactics that went with them. I had Nai's experience to draw on—and so did Theris.

Even if we were blocked from using magical powers, we had Athanate physical capabilities.

I yelled to him, "Right into the center!" and took a running leap over their shield wall, passing through their magic shield as well. Bian landed right beside me, then Theris, a stream of curses erupting from his mouth. Then Mirela and Rita and the rest of them, loyally following me into a type of fighting they'd never experienced.

Nai's instincts had shown me the flaw in the shield wall. All of those shields were held in place by interlocking clasps, and they were double strapped to their bearer's arms. The ones we'd landed behind panicked at the thought of a threshing machine of blades at their undefended backs. Each man rushed to free himself as quickly as possible, struggling to extract their arms from the braces, grounding their shields, halting their advance and making their impregnable line buckle.

I stabbed and slashed with both blades.

Flint and Kane had joined us, turning the invaders' trick back on themselves. We were inside their magical defense, protected from magical attack in the same way that they were protected from the Temple's. A sort of Russian doll of nested substantiations.

They were fighting back, but it seemed their whole wall of shields was going to fail when I hear a yell from Theris: "They're attacking us from behind. Form a circle."

Her troops didn't, but Vega Martine *did* have experience in ancient fighting techniques. She'd held back a company of men in case there was a breach of the shield wall. We were now being surrounded by them. Not ordinary men, like her shield wall. These were Were.

We had the advantage of the reach of long swords. They had numbers. Lots of stabby, little swords eager to make up for their shortness, and much smaller, lighter shields.

I swung high with one katana, at their heads. They ducked the dreadful arc of the blade, and their shields lifted involuntarily. I slashed at their exposed thighs with the other katana.

And staggered back in pain as one of them struck out blindly and connected with my head. There was blood on my face. Another stabbed my thigh.

I forced a gap between the two of them. Drove Onibi into one, then had to leap back as more short swords reached out to replace the ones whose owners I'd killed.

As the first few died, there was a hesitation. They were afraid to come within reach of our katanas, and we couldn't break through their line without getting cut to pieces. But I felt a pressure in my head. A Were Call. Urging them. Forcing them forward as a pack.

Not good.

They swarmed us, no longer individuals. They'd become crazed, and the melee descended into a raging sea of blood and sweat, flickering blades and waving shields, curses, wordless screams and dying Were.

It got worse.

Vega Martine had a small group of bowmen behind.

We were so pressed together, they hesitated to fire, but only for a second. There was someone ordering them, and arrows began to hiss through the gaps. Not every arrow made it through the gap. Vega Martine's Were died, killed by their own side, but it only served to spur the rest of the pack on.

An arrow hit my chain mail. Another.

"Got to break through and get those bowmen," I yelled.

But there was no way. The same roiling wall of Were that protected us from some of the arrows prevented us from getting through.

The world shrank. We were squeezed closer and closer together, hampering our ability to wield our swords in the wide arcs they were designed for.

There seemed no end of the enemy; snarling faces, shields trying to crush us, blades kissing my flesh. I was covered in blood and much of it was mine. Athanate or not, there was a limit to this, and it was bearing down on me, as unstoppable as a train.

Nearly lost the katana because my grip had become so slick with sweat and blood. I had a dozen wounds on my arms and legs where the mail didn't protect me.

The end was near. All I could do was take as many as I could with me.

The howling that came was fit to wake the dead. A new call. A Rougarou Call and a cry from a hundred throats.

I realized Donatienne hadn't joined us in the center. Instead, she'd gathered the Rougarou behind her. She was a Rougarou alpha, she'd been the alpha of *all* the queen's Rougarou. She had alpha dominance in spades, and they acknowledged her. She'd formed them into an arrowhead shape and led them on a running charge against the weakness we'd caused in the shield wall.

It was like a Mac truck running flat out and hitting plastic crowd control barriers. The Rougarou broke the shields' locking clasps, they flattened defenders under their shields and slammed right into the back of the reinforcements, a howling Donatienne in the lead.

The whole body of invaders shuddered at the force of the Rougarou's charge.

And in a second the situation changed.

Lines collapsed and dissolved. There was no formation, no discipline and the Rougarou were supremely equipped to fight like this.

I turned and carved my way deeper into the broken invaders. I was after the key that got them here and held them in place while it cancelled the Temple's magic.

I reached the lines with children in. They weren't armed with swords. I couldn't kill them. I hit them out of the way, interrupting any magic workings they were attempting.

The vessel of Quetzalcoatl's power knew I was coming for him. He was flanked by well-armed guards, and he tried to take a step back, deeper into their protection.

I didn't let him. I lunged at him with Onibi.

The result was spectacular. Onibi was trailing blue-white sparks even before it hit the cloudy miasma that was Quetzalcoatl's aura. Once it touched that, everything exploded in violent light and screaming.

I followed Onibi with the second katana in an all-out assault. I hit something, but I couldn't see—my eyes were still recovering from the flash of light. One of the Adept's guards was in better shape than me. He'd been facing away from the light show, and he could see me well enough to stab.

His thrust wasn't good, but it didn't need to be. I felt the tip break the mail and pierce my side. I would have been dead in another moment, but the man lost his entire arm to Bian's vicious strike before he could push any farther. On my other side, Theris lunged and killed the other guards, his sword whirling like a propeller.

Leaving me with the man in the middle. The man with no aura.

He *was* insane. This close, it was obvious. Matlal was struggling to find a way to use Quetzalcoatl's power without paying the price, and this was one of his attempted solutions.

I could sense what the madman was carrying and where it was—in a bag hanging on a strap around his neck. My second sword slashed the bag open; I dropped the sword and snatched the contents before they hit the ground.

It was nothing more than a little stoppered jar. The sort of handmade kitchenware you might put cooking oil in, except it wasn't oil inside; it was the antidote to the Serpents' venom. The bit of the Temple the queen had given to Vega Martine. And it answered to the shadow in my Blood as if it were the venom itself.

Still acting on instinct, I bit the stopper out and drank the contents.

I heard Tara's voice in my head. *Shit! What are you doing?*

I had no idea.

There was a sound so low I could only feel it in my body. A *thud*. The whole substantiation seemed to shake. There was a short silence and then we had storm winds shrieking around us.

The invaders' magical defense started to retreat back onto itself. The middle ring of Adepts, children and adult, collapsed toward to the inner ring in terror, as the outer ring continued dying under the assault of the Rougarou. Vega Martine's breach of the Temple's substantiation shrank like a punctured balloon.

And then their dead began to rise. They struggled to their feet and attacked, throwing themselves onto the points of their former comrades' swords.

Vega Martine cut her losses. I could see her ordering a retreat.

If I could kill her…

Using only Onibi, I redoubled my efforts, slashing at the men between me and Vega Martine. Bian and Theris matched me stroke for stroke, our blades singing.

Yet even as they died, crammed together as they were in a shrinking circle with other guards and children, the dead had no room to fall, and still protected Vega Martine by getting in our way. It was taking too long. In desperation, Mirela grabbed a spear from a fallen guard and hurled it with deadly accuracy at where Vega Martine stood alone.

The mad Adept leaped up into its path. The spear took him through the chest.

Vega Martine's power source collapsed.

In the last moment, her eyes filled with an implacable hatred as she took in all her opponents, and then she and the survivors remaining within their shrinking bubble of magic were sucked back to wherever they'd come from.

Chapter 35

My team was left alone, breathless and battered. The Rougarou, the wraiths, the other defenders, including those invaders who'd been dead a few seconds earlier, began cleaning up the debris from the attack, as if it had been no more than damage from a storm. They ignored us. Our chain mail vanished.

Bian lowered her weapons and turned to me. "What the *hell* is going on here?" she demanded. "You blink out, and then a second later, you reappear and tell us Diana's okay, but the Temple's under attack and we have to fight for it? Then you just leap into the middle of their formation and expect everyone to save your ass? What the hell is going on? And what possessed you to drink whatever it was that madman was carrying?"

I opened my mouth, and no words came out for a minute.

Explaining what had happened to me between what appeared to everyone else to be one moment and the next was like explaining dreams the morning after. What makes sense in the dream doesn't work in the daylight. I wasn't even sure what I was remembering had actually happened. Things I thought I understood were slipping between my fingers.

"I was gone a long time," I said finally. "At least, it was a long time for me. I want to tell you about it, and I will, but right now I think we're on the clock again. So, short version—the Serpents tested me, and I guess I passed. They gave me the ability to cure the poison, and I spirit-walked to Haven and back. Diana and Salar are okay. Really. It works."

They all stared at me, clearly wondering if I was as insane as Vega Martine's madman.

"It's real," I said quietly, reaching out and gathering Bian and Mirela to me. I opened my eukori, inviting them in. "Diana and Salar are fine. I left them sleeping."

I felt the returning touch of their eukori. Both of them were relieved, but Bian was still angry. She felt things were sliding out of control. She wasn't a person who liked that at all. Neither was I, but this particular wild ride didn't care, and I couldn't see a way off without simply giving up.

I took a deep breath and let the pair of them go. I wasn't able to fix anything yet with them. In fact, I needed to tell them more things that would make them angry.

"The catch is, that capability makes me part of the Temple," I said.

Out the side of my eye, I saw Theris twitch, but he just grimaced and continued cleaning his blade.

"I'm *so* grateful to them for the solution to a problem *they* caused," Bian snarled. "Why use *us* to get rid of this invasion?"

"Yes. Why didn't they fight it themselves?" Mirela asked. "Why did they need us?"

"It's complex," I began, and Flint came to my rescue.

"I think that little jar was the antidote that the Queen of Diamonds gave to Vega Martine. Difficult to explain, but it's part of the Temple's working and Quetzalcoatl could use that like a key to break into this substantiation and then as a counter to defend against the Temple's power."

Kane took over. "It's good that they haven't got it anymore, but if Vega Martine and Quetzalcoatl work together, they can probably break into this substantiation again. They've made an initial connection. The only thing in the Temple's favor is they wouldn't have the protection they had this time."

"Well, it makes sense for all sorts of reasons to break up Matlal and Vega Martine," I said. "But first things first. I got news in Haven about the Atrax operation. Generally seems to be going well, but the Houston Atrax team have gone AWOL. Salar was worried."

Mirela looked thoughtful.

"Let's look at it this way," I said. "You know the team. You know their objectives. If they felt their primary objective was compromised for any reason, would they call HQ? What fallback orders would they have? In the absence of orders, what initiative would they take?"

"I know the team, of course. House Basynia. They're tough and capable. They know to keep communications to a minimum. Their overarching orders are to damage the structure of Athanate government in the southern states. If they felt the House in Houston was a no go, they probably wouldn't call home. Instead, they'd look for another opportunity to present itself."

"Even if it wasn't to the same schedule as the other attacks?"

Mirela nodded. "Obviously, the attacks on the Panethus Houses were intended to happen simultaneously to prevent time for warnings to go out, but if the right opportunity presented itself..."

My gut feeling about where the Houston assassins had gone started to form, but I didn't want to influence Mirela.

"None of our other teams have reported any sign that the Houston Atrax team arrived in the cities they were assigned to. So where could they go in keeping with their orders, and where we wouldn't see them?"

Mirela's face looked grim.

"New Orleans. They've worked out I'm no longer in place. They've monitored the movements, and they've found House Labastide is in New

York with all her security team, leaving the remaining members unprotected. It's a perfect opportunity."

"Shit," I said. "That's what I was afraid of."

I was the reason House Labastide was vulnerable. And through our new association—dokaria—I was obligated to protect them as if they were my own House. I *needed* to protect them.

"The rest of House Tucek are hiding out in Louisiana?" I asked.

"Yes. I'll call them as soon as we get back. The safe house is remote though. It'll take them some time to come in."

"There's another thing. Marguerite left the House under the management of her new Diakon, Solange Dupuis. Solange and Diana exchanged Blood."

"Solange is probably sinking into a fever right now. She may be making poor decisions. What time is it in New Orleans?"

"I don't know. I'm assuming it's the same night we came here. The way time can slip when you're in the spirit world means we won't know until we're back out. Better get going."

We started to look around to make sure everyone was ready to move.

"No," Mirela said suddenly.

Her eyes were fixed over my shoulder.

The Rougarou had gathered where the fighting had been thickest. Where Donatienne had been.

"No," she said again, her voice fading, and I could hear the despair welling up as she sprinted over.

For everything, a cost.

Donatienne's charge at the head of the Rougarou had saved us and the Temple, but she'd taken point, the place of greatest danger. She'd received a dozen vicious cuts from the short swords and kept fighting to make sure the breach held. Two or three of her wounds would have been fatal on their own. It was testament to her Rougarou strength and ruggedness that she wasn't dead already.

The Rougarou didn't want us to touch her. They snarled and slashed at Mirela with their metal claws.

I snarled back at them with all my alpha dominance behind it, and they grudgingly let me pass. I had to snarl again for them to let Mirela in.

But not even two Athanate working together can repair severed arteries.

She knew. She smiled faintly at our failure, and whispered something in her native French to Mirela, who kissed her forehead.

Her hand gripped mine. "Not here," she whispered to me, her eyes losing focus. "Pas ici. Donne-moi à la rivière. Laisse-la me laver, me rendre propre et pure à nouveau. Promets-le-moi. Promets."

I understood. Jen had taught me enough French to answer her.

"I promise. Je te le promets. Tu descendras vers la mer. Tu redeviendras sans tache. Entière et pure. Et la mer sera ton seul linceul."

I promise. You will go down to the sea. You will become unsullied. Whole and pure. And the sea will be your only shroud.

She heard. Another half-smile, a sigh, her eyes closed, and she was gone.

She was still wearing her captain's uniform from the *Queen of Diamonds*, and I knew she wouldn't want that. I cut the clothes from her and picked her up. The Rougarou didn't want Mirela to carry her. I didn't think they wanted me to either, but they let me pass.

We walked down the endless lawns back to the bridge, my feet sinking into the soft ground. My House followed. Rougarou walked on either side of us, making a noise deep in their throats, a wordless song of grief.

No one spoke.

Donatienne's face was turned slightly into my shoulder. Her eyes were closed. Her copper hair brushed my arm. She could have been asleep.

The bridge was there, repaired, but it angled down, and after a dozen yards or so, it was under water.

I stepped carefully onto the slats, wary of slipping. Everyone but Mirela stayed on the bank. Another step. Another. The water rose and Donatienne's body became light in my arms, as light as a dream. The water tugged at her, lifted her arm behind my back, so it seemed she patted me clumsily. Comforted me.

The water washed our wounds. Blood flowed for a short while like flags waving behind a veil.

Mirela cleaned her face and kissed her, then we set her free, and our last sight of Donatienne Gaudreau in this life was the bright copper of her hair growing dark as it slipped below.

Chapter 36

The Rougarou left, walking sorrowfully back up into the gardens of the Temple, leaving my team staring at me from the bank.

I had to speak, even if I sounded crazy. I waved my hands to indicate the whole river, which probably made me look crazy as well. "I carry the power of the fourth Serpent, the Serpent of Air and the Mistress of Breath. Trust me. You will be able to breathe." I looked at each of them in turn, meeting their eyes, trying to instill them with confidence.

The Temple had a purpose to this. The bridge didn't need to be underwater, but my team needed to believe in me.

It was difficult. This *was* water. This *was* the Atchafalaya.

I walked backward until only my face was above.

Mirela's jaw tightened, and she walked to join me, just ahead of Theris, who'd decided he either had to save me from drowning or follow me into whatever craziness I was heading into, but couldn't do either from the bank.

Everyone got on the bridge.

"It's slippery," I warned them. "Hold on."

I turned and walked deeper.

I was panicking, but I was driven forward by the thought of House Basynia attacking House Labastide, and as before, if the Serpents wanted me to die, there would have been a lot of easier ways to do it.

The water around my face softened.

Breathe. Just breathe.

My hindbrain was screaming at me to get back on the riverbank, but one terrified breath later, it was no more uncomfortable than if I was walking along the bridge in a tropical downpour. Another step and it was no more than breathing humid air.

Currents I could no longer feel peeled away and dissolved the ruined clothes I'd been given. That left me wearing the practical gear that I'd arrived in, right down to the cross hatching of swords on my back.

A glance over my shoulder showed my experience shared by the others. They were dressed as they had been when we'd reached the grove. Theris, Flint and Kane seemed comfortable breathing underwater. Bian just looked angry, and Mirela sad.

It also showed me a ghostly Nai, walking on nothing beside me. She was in the clothes she'd worn as a sarthapala when she'd sought out the Temple in the City of Serpents.

"We didn't expect you to *drink* it," Nai said conversationally. "You know, it would have worked just as well if you'd only broken the jar. And it's not an antidote in the sense it will cancel what you have in your Blood."

"Drinking it felt more my style, but a little more explanation earlier might have helped if I shouldn't have done it."

She smiled at that. "Yes, it would all be easier if we told you everything beforehand, but we cannot see everything that's going to happen. And it's not what we're trying to achieve. We don't want to tell you what to do and how to do it. We want you to discover knowledge, to arrive at a true understanding, not believe whatever you've been told by us."

I snorted. "Yes, you're trying to harness my unpredictability or something while I thrash around to find out what's going on."

Mirela broke in: "Who exactly is this 'we' you're speaking for?"

"That's a clever question, does Amber have the clever answer?"

I took a deep breath. Remembering we were underwater, that made my heart skip a beat.

"It's not clever, but I think I've untangled it." We must have been halfway across the bridge because I felt I was starting to walk upward. I still couldn't see the far end. I pointed at Nai's ghostly form. "You're now part of two entities, the Temple of Serpents and the Grove of the African Gods. But you weren't before."

"Very good," Nai said. "Go on."

"The Queen of Diamonds was part of the Temple. When I defeated the queen and sent her to the Grove of the African gods, they split her in two. Let's call one part Nai, which is the good bit, and the other part the Queen of Diamonds, which isn't. They did this to keep the Nai part because they needed your abilities."

Nai nodded encouragingly.

"But they broke one of those abilities, the bit that was able to connect to the Temple, because that was the Queen of Diamonds. But you were smart enough to know I'd come back to the Grove and sneaky enough to hitchhike on me and re-establish your connection with the Temple."

Nai smiled. "I did warn you that the Grove had a price for their help, and an agenda. I even warned you that you carried part of me in you. And that part of me went through the testing as before. We are both connected to the Temple *and* the Grove, sister."

I scowled. I'd kinda worked that last bit out, and sometimes it sucks to be right.

Theris was getting agitated. "You're connecting the Temple and the Grove?" he called out from behind.

"Yes," I said. "The Grove was trapped in the physical world. It needed a trusted connection to the spirit world that avoided the City of Lost Gods. The Temple has been self-sufficient in the spiritual world, but needs more power to defend itself from the City, which can only come from the physical world while the City remains so strong."

"You've opened a fixed connection between the spirit world and the physical world?" Bian snarled. "Like the one we're trying to stop Matlal doing?"

Nai nodded. "The Temple existed with connections to the physical world since I first found it. It hasn't used those against humanity. The person I became, the Queen of Diamonds, did, but that was her fault, and only shows an error of judgment on their part. The Grove, meanwhile, has no ambitions other than to not fade away."

"All of which is just talk," Mirela said. "It doesn't make me trust you."

"I don't trust either of you," Bian muttered.

"Can we try and resolve it *after* we save House Labastide?" I said.

Nai disappeared.

Silence. Not good. A ball of dread that had been forming in my stomach grew another layer. I had a very tough time coming up with all of them. Bian. Theris. Mirela.

But Nai hadn't gone completely. I could sense her.

I tried a silent conversation.

We could spirit-walk right there, where we need to be.

We could, Nai responded. *And Tezcatlipoca would see it.*

Okay, so we need Tezcatlipoca to be kept in the dark. For the same reason, I'm guessing I must hide any powers that your venom has given me.

At least until you absolutely need it. Your Blood is also the Blood of the Serpents now. You will understand. Until then, let your mind's eye guide you.

Invisible lips kissed a spot in the center of my forehead. It burned cold, like the touch of dry ice.

The growing light ahead of me was shining right through the water. We were near the end of the rope bridge, and I could see the tall trees of the Grove take shape, as if emerging out of a mist.

Every task is a test, a lesson, a warning, a clue, Nai said. *You will not become the Queen of Diamonds. Or the Queen of Serpents. Or the Queen of the Grove. But you must become something new. What you need to be is more… the Paladin of the Temple.*

I have no idea what that means, I thought. *What would make me a paladin?*

Doing things a paladin would do.

Like what?

But she'd gone, and I was speaking to myself in the stillness at the heart of the Grove, on the banks of the Atchafalaya.

Paladin. Another thing I had to find out for myself. Everything that had happened was beginning to feel like a dream. Not a dream of random events, but a meaningful dream. One where I could grasp what it all meant if I simply had enough time.

We didn't. *That* bit I knew already.

"Hurry," I called to the others.

When we'd been searching for the right part of the river, I'd noticed the swelling of clouds in the south. A storm was gathering over the Gulf, and I could sense it was a mean one. We had places to be before that broke.

We forced our way through the forest and back along the path toward where Bill Patout waited with the airboats. Ten minutes later, when I got to the muddy part I realized was near the hidden pool, I yelled ahead for him to get the boats ready.

We broke out from the vegetation and rushed aboard with Bill and his friend in the second boat looking confused. They pointed rifles back the way we'd come, thinking we were being chased.

"We're not running away," I said. "We have another emergency, back at New Orleans. We need to get to the helicopter as quickly as possible."

We clambered onto the boat.

Bill looked at the state we were in and back down the way we'd come.

"That everyone?" he said quietly.

I nodded.

He was smart enough to hold off his questions, and as he piloted us out onto the dark flow of the river, I allocated tasks.

"Bian, get me Diakon Dupuis on your cell, please. Mirela, soon as we know where House Labastide is, call your House. Rita, get hold of Jo. Yelena, take over steering from Bill. And Bill, can you find us some backup from the packs down near New Orleans, as soon as we know where to send them?"

Yelena took the wheel and sent us racing toward the field where we'd left the helicopter.

It was Jo who answered first. Rita handed me the cell.

"We're at Maison de Dance on Bourbon," Jo said, once she'd got outside so she could hear me. "How did it work out? You have an antidote?"

"That's all okay, but we have another problem for you and House Labastide. The Matlal team that was assigned to attack House Young in Houston has disappeared, and we're worried they're coming to New Orleans. I'm trying to get through to your Diakon now, and in the meantime, I need you to stay away from any Labastide property. Find somewhere to hide."

Mirela waved at me, indicating she wanted to join in the conversation.

I tilted the cell her way. "There's a safe house I set up in Algiers Point," she said. "Only my team knows about it. If you're sure you aren't followed or tracked, you'll be safe there."

I left her telling Jo how to get in as Bian handed me another cell with Solange Dupuis on the other end.

"Solange?"

"House Farrell," she said politely.

I could convince myself I could hear the fever in her voice, but it could just be tension. I was a newcomer, an upstart abomination, and she was Diakon to one of the proudest, most traditional Houses in the country. I'd saved her House from being swept up in an investigation, and she resented that she had to feel grateful for that. Now Diana would have told her about the Serpent's venom, and she'd probably be blaming me for that. And using that as an excuse not to listen to me, just as the venom in her Blood compromised her judgment.

As the leader of a House associated at the level of dokaria with House Labastide, I officially outranked her. I *could* give her orders, but I didn't push it. I outlined our worries and asked what she wanted to do.

"Paranoia has its benefits," she said. "I already closed the town house and called everyone together at Talleyrand. No specific information that made me do it. Just precautionary."

My first reaction was immense relief. We weren't in a nightmare scenario of chasing down members of House Labastide out in the city while House Basynia could attack at any minute. The second reaction was that, being well out of town and an old design, Talleyrand had its drawbacks.

I'd spent some time there, recovering from my fight with the Queen of Diamonds. I hadn't had a lot of time to look around, but my impression was of tall, airy rooms with large windows and wide balconies. Lots of points of access. Not ideal for defending.

"Is there any part of the mansion or grounds that's big enough to get everyone in and better for defense than the main house?" I asked.

"House Labastide has always had plans in the event of attack, and Talleyrand is no exception," she said. "Thank you for the warning, House Farrell, but we are more than capable of looking after ourselves in this instance."

Her tone told me she would take it as a personal insult that I might have to rescue her House a second time. She didn't want my help. That was stupid, given her security team was in New York with Marguerite.

"Solange, wait. There's fever in your Blood. You're not thinking clearly."

She'd ended the call, and when I tried to get back to her, I discovered she'd switched off her cell.

"Shit."

I didn't have anyone else on hand who was knowledgeable about what capabilities they might have at Talleyrand. I didn't want to call Jo again until she confirmed she and the party of New York kin were safe.

"Yelena, try calling Marguerite."

I had more to worry about because Bill was having problems rounding up support quickly. His own pack was too far away. The nearest pack needed time to assemble and prepare. The only werewolf in the locality was a cub, both young and only recently become a Were. I wasn't surprised he sounded eager, but he had no support. He didn't even have a firearm.

"Hold the cub back," I said to Bill. "Close enough to report to us, not close enough to be caught."

Bill nodded. "Okay, he can bird dog, but there's not much he's gonna be able to see. Way I recall it, that place's got a screen of trees 'tween it and the road."

He was right. While he spoke to the cub, I pictured the layout of the estate in my mind. Twenty acres of grounds, maybe. A thick barrier of trees and bushes lined the edges. Wide lawns around the main house in the middle. A couple of smaller side buildings like garages and sheds. The road ran along one side and the river on the other, hidden by the levee and the trees.

The middle section of the house itself was a central hall or ballroom. Kitchens, dining rooms and other utilities to either side. Smaller halls at the front and back. Living rooms and bedrooms on the top floor, which had a balcony running around the outside. The middle floor had a patio with an enormous pair of symmetrical staircases down to the formal gardens on the river side.

I had to assume the worst, and Basynia attacked before we got to Talleyrand. On that basis, if I were Basynia, how would I attack?

Talleyrand had lots of rooms people *could* be in. They wouldn't be, because we'd warned Solange about the attack, but House Basynia wouldn't know that. They'd plan for people to be all over the mansion and grounds. They'd quickly see something was wrong, and work out their attack was expected. Would they stop there? If they didn't, how would changing plans make them vulnerable to my attack, coming in behind them?

Too many variables. We were going to have to split our own forces, and without a tactical comms system, I'd have to rely on everyone having a really simple overview and flexible options that wouldn't conflict with each other.

It was shaping up to be the worst kind of operation.

"Bill, how far are we from the helicopter?"

He squinted. "Five minutes, tops."

"Kane, how long to fly there?"

"Pushing it? Five minutes to warm up, and fifteen to get there," he said.

If House Basynia struck now, I had to hope that whatever defenses Dupuis was using could hold for the half hour it would take for us to join them. I'd have to brief everyone in the helicopter. In less than twenty minutes.

Damn.

And despite arriving by helicopter, we weren't going to be the cavalry. We had nothing more than the assortment of weapons and Kevlar vests that Bian had brought with her from Denver. Not ideal, not by a long way.

Bill had to stay to organize the packs. I couldn't spare anyone else.

Theris wouldn't let me go without him anyway. Bian, Yelena and Mirela were essential in a fight. Kane had to fly the helicopter and Flint had to come to keep me shielded from Tezcatlipoca. Whether I could deploy their Adept powers in a fight was unsure. I had a task I needed Rita to do, which meant she had to join us on the helicopter ride, but would keep her out of the main attack.

Mirela had said that if House Basynia put all their team into this one attack, there would be sixteen of them. They'd be well armed, but lightly, for a raid, not a pitched battle. They might have explosives and grenades.

There would be a lot more of House Labastide inside Talleyrand, but I had no information on their training or weapons. Their experienced members, the security team, were in New York. Most of the remainder would be kin. They could be as much of a handicap as an asset. What if Basynia took some as hostages? Or just opted for a suicide mission when we turned up?

My brain churned over the possibilities.

"You got marine flares in this boat, Bill?"

"Course."

They'd be useful, but this was still really, *really* not ideal.

The riverbank loomed out of the night, and we were half an hour from finding out how bad it was going to be.

Chapter 37

It had been eight minutes since we'd swooped down and dropped Rita on the road far enough away from Talleyrand that it wouldn't alert the attackers.

Seven minutes since Kane had become tense at the way the winds were rising, and gusts were starting to shove the helicopter around.

Six minutes since Bill's cub had reported that vans had unloaded in front of the house and that now there were the sounds of gunfire from the plantation.

Five minutes since Jo had called to say the New York kin were all safe, that Talleyrand had a basement under the floor of the ballroom which was defensible if Solange chose to fight there, and that she would call others who she knew were at the mansion.

Three minutes since Marguerite had called to say briefly she'd get through to Solange.

Two minutes since Rita had reported she'd linked up with the cub and they were ready.

One minute since Kane had taken the helicopter down to a level that seemed to kiss the very surface of the Mississippi, with half of us outside the cabin, standing on the skids and clinging on.

"Five seconds," Kane yelled.

"Flare," I shouted into my cell, and Rita fired a marine distress flare directly at the front of the mansion.

Then Kane whipped us up and over the levee and set us down on Talleyrand's well-kept lawn in the space of a heartbeat.

We scattered like ants from the helicopter and sprinted for the positions I'd assigned.

This was our point of maximum vulnerability. Basynia were bound to have night vision goggles and at least a couple of guards posted to keep their escape route clear. I was gambling that because they'd picked the road to come in, their escape route was on that side of the building, and that's where they would be guarding. We'd come in from the river.

The flare was intended to confuse them while Kane had landed the helicopter right beside the house, where the two matching flights of steps prevented a clear view of the helicopter from inside on the ground floor.

But the rip of automatic fire that I'd been afraid of didn't come from inside the house. Basynia had posted a guard on the river side as well.

Gunfire and muzzle flashes *behind* us.

Shit!

I spun around, stumbling and falling back.

My wolf eyes could see the spray of glass from the helicopter's canopy exploding across the lawn. Kane, last to exit, scuttled away. Flint turned to help. I saw the heat glow of the barrel and the body of the guard behind it. Saw his submachine gun turning to track my two shamans.

No!

I'd picked up a pair of Walther automatic pistols from Bian's luggage. 9mm. 10 rounds.

I fired both as I fell over. Three shots each. Saw the guard's body jerk and swivel with the impacts.

Mirela had a Glock pistol. She knelt, aimed and fired half a second after me, and hit the falling guy in the head.

Scratch one guard.

I finished falling over, rolled back onto my feet and sprinted up the steps to the house's patio with Yelena, Mirela and Theris right behind.

A second flare went off in front of the house—Rita and the cub had achieved the goal I'd set them.

Objective one.

My next objective was to get into the top floor. Solange had ordered the shutters closed on the lower floors.

Yelena boosted me up. I hung on to a balcony balustrade while the others climbed using my body as a ladder, then hauled me up after them.

I picked one of the bedroom windows and shoulder charged it at full speed. I was inside and running through the room before the shattered glass finished falling, my Ops 4-10 training ringing in my ears.

Speed is the key. Ride the shock wave.

Hit the enemy before they can react.

My wolfy senses felt urgent movement in the mansion. They were reacting too damn quickly.

And worse, House Basynia had the same type of training I had. Even before the man fired, I sensed an alert guard had been posted on the upper floor.

As I ran out of the bedroom, I was already turning to where I sensed the threat was. He fired. Shockingly loud. Muzzle flashes in the darkened building.

I caught the bullets high in the chest. Two rounds flattening themselves on the Kevlar, not killing me, but delivering a double punch like being kicked by a horse.

I got one wild shot off before I went over the gallery's balustrade and down two levels into the darkness of the hall below.

There was a burst of gunfire above.

Best thing you could say about my landing was I landed on my feet. Second best was I was right in among the Basynia: I couldn't miss, and they couldn't shoot for fear of killing each other.

It would have been neat if I hadn't just been shot and was collapsing in pain.

I fired and then I had to stop because Theris was there, holding me up and shielding my body with his while he took over the shooting.

Yelena and Mirela came down that staircase like a pair of avenging angels, just as Flint and Kane lit up the small hall with spirit fire the color of a welder's torch.

The four Basynia went down.

Reinforcements rushed from the main group of Basynia in the ballroom.

And skidded to a stop as Tara, in full fire wolf form, manifested. Flint and Kane redirected their spirit fire to support Tara.

But at a cost. Their concentration on their workings made the shield they'd been maintaining over me slip.

Tezcatlipoca found me.

My priestess does not need to fight this scum.

I could see a ghostly overlay on the shadowy shapes of my wolf vision. Every person in the ballroom lit up in flames. Not friendly flames, but *fintyne*. Magical napalm.

No.

Using Tezcatlipoca's power would mean losing part of my soul to him. Another part.

Then it would take no more than a few of those urgent, well-intentioned uses, and Tezcatlipoca would have his permanent connection into the physical world.

I blinked his vision away. If my plan worked, I didn't need his power.

Right about now...

Bian burst open the doors of the hall at the other end of the ballroom and poured shots in at the Basynia until they returned fire.

Which was too damn quick. They were well trained.

Bian ducked out of sight, but now the Basynia knew their way out was cut off at either end. They didn't know how stretched we were, and that a concerted rush would get them through. Until they worked that out, we were in a standoff.

Others had different ideas.

"Rush them!" Mirela yelled, charging toward the ballroom.

I wrenched myself out of Theris' grasp and launched myself into the air, catching her with a tackle that would have featured on the Superbowl highlights.

We crashed into a chair, and I dragged her out of the way as bullets scoured where she would have been. My whole upper body was screaming in pain at me. I could have done without this.

"*Tucek*?" A disbelieving female voice called out from the ballroom as the gunfire eased. "What the fuck are you doing?"

I clamped my hand over Mirela's mouth.

"Talk her into standing down," I hissed quietly.

"You are insane," she hissed back when I let her go. Then loudly: "Pinning your ass, Basynia. Time to quit."

"What are you talking about?"

There was an explosion in the ballroom. I guessed Basynia had just blown up the entrance to the basement which had been hidden in the floor. They followed Ops 4-10 procedures—a couple of people leaped straight into the hole to attack while the defenders were recovering from the blast.

There was a thunder of shotguns being fired in a constricted space, then silence.

"You've just discovered that basement passage is a steel tube, and lined with murder holes like an old-fashioned castle, only with shotguns instead of boiling oil or pikes," Mirela called out. "You haven't got the strength or equipment to assault it. You can't achieve your objective, and we're pinning you in, front and back—"

"If there were enough of you, you'd be in here already," Basynia yelled.

"On top of which, your escape vehicles are no longer available to you, and we have local Were packs on their way."

I could imagine Basynia's Diakon would be hurriedly trying to get the guards on the trucks to respond. Thanks to the efforts of Rita and Bill's cub, they weren't going to.

"You can't call werewolves," Basynia said.

"I can't, but my new boss is also high in the werewolf league. She can, and she has."

"You mean *Farrell*? The *freak*? You've turned coat for that abomination?"

"I am a sub-House of House Farrell, who's right here beside me, by the way."

Basynia stopped calling out, but my wolf ears could hear whispered discussion.

"She's planning to try a breakout," I said. "Convince her not to."

"The mission has failed," Mirela called. "All the Atrax teams are being rolled up. There's no point to what you're trying to do. It wasn't as if this really was Vega Martine's plan anyway. We were just doing Matlal's dirty work for him."

I could hear Basynia spit. She wasn't denying whose plan the Atrax teams had been, and she didn't like Matlal.

"What are you suggesting?" she said.

"Surrender," I replied. "A Blood oath to keep out of it, and we'll let you join the non-aligned Athanate in Ireland."

I got a bitter laugh in reply.

"Being in Ireland wouldn't shield us from the Lady's revenge," she said.

She wasn't buying it, but she wasn't killing anyone either. I just needed to find the right argument.

Compel her, Tezcatlipoca hissed in the back of my brain. Then Flint and Kane got my shield back up, and the Lost God faded out.

Small mercies.

Unfortunately, Solange didn't know what I was trying to do and wasn't smart enough to stay put in the basement.

There was an eruption of gunfire from the ruin of the entrance to the basement, and an equal amount directed back down.

Shit.

Nothing for it now. We'd have to charge or risk more House Labastide deaths. Basynia would be reeling.

But we didn't have the chance to attack.

"*CEASE FIRE.*" Theris' voice was dramatic just in volume, and I'd entirely forgotten he had Adept abilities. I didn't know how long it might last, but his shout had the same effect as a stun grenade. All shooting stopped.

I used the opportunity to add my voice in. "Everyone, put your weapons down. Attend to the wounded."

They did. It was over.

Damn! If I'd known we could do that, I would have had Theris yell at them sooner.

Or would I? Had I put compulsion in that order? Or was it just Athanate dominance? What was the difference?

I didn't want to get to the point where I thought it was okay to use compulsion—even to save lives.

We moved forward to assess the situation.

There was a bloody mess around the entrance to the basement. Members of House Labastide and House Basynia together. Some dead already, others heading that way.

House Basynia herself was in the latter group.

She lay in a spreading pool of Blood, unable to get up.

Her Diakon was already there, bent over her, desperately trying to keep her alive.

She saw me looming over her Diakon's shoulder and, from the look in her eyes, I could tell she suspected I was there to finish her off.

"This is not what I wanted," I said. "Help me to help you."

I bit her wrist, trying to add my Athanate aniatropics to hers and her Diakon's, even as I reached for her with eukori and aura. But she was already slipping away.

No.

I'd done this before. In El Paso I'd kept House de Socorro and his Aspirant, Carrizal Ribera, alive. I'd retrieved them when de Socorro had tried to sink into madness and death. I could get House Basynia back from the brink. I could.

There was a moment when I wondered why I would. Basynia was the enemy, wasn't she? She'd come here to kill members of House Labastide, a House I was profoundly connected with. And yet... *doing things a paladin would do.*

Was this what Nai meant?

Was this what the Temple and the Grove wanted me to do?

I *wanted* to do it. There had been too many dead, and many more to come. Basynia had surrendered, so not keeping her alive was as bad as killing her. But I could already see how this would cause more problems.

Stop arguing with yourself. Think about it later.

I redoubled my efforts. I would not lose this fight.

"Amber!"

Someone was screaming in my ear. Physically and mentally pulling me back.

No! I had her. Just one more moment. One more reach. I could feel Basynia's hands in mine. I could feel her looking up at me, as if from a great darkness.

I could—

Abruptly, there was nothing there but a spiraling emptiness, descending into that darkness.

And arms around me. Holding me. Drawing me back.

Bian and Yelena. Theris and Mirela.

All the others. Willing me to rise back up.

"She's gone," I said, blinking as someone turned the lights back on. "I failed."

"Idiot," Bian shouted. "You came here to rescue House Labastide. What the hell did you think you were doing?"

"I failed," I said again, looking at Basynia's Diakon, a heavy-set man kneeling beside me. He looked as if his life had ended, despite being barely wounded by the gunfire.

"You tried," he said. He bowed down in front of me, head to the floor. "No one could have saved her. I was there beside you. I saw. I felt your aura. No one could have tried harder. You spoke truly and dealt fairly, House Farrell, but House Basynia is no more."

He took a shaky breath. "I offer my life as korheny in exchange for sanctuary for the rest of the House."

It shook me. He wasn't accepting my offer for them to run to Ireland. He was offering the survivors to me, to take into my protection, and he was offering his life in exchange. Typical Agiagraphos.

Shit. I should have realized when I tried to save his leader that this had all the hallmarks of screwing my own life up. Even more.

But it didn't feel as if there were other acceptable options. If life was going to hand me Agiagraphos problems, then I was going to have to use Agiagraphos solution.

I pulled him upright and gripped his shirt.

"I accept your life," I said, pulling him closer, forcing him to look at me. "But not for you to throw it away. You will take up the mantle of House Basynia and you will offer your Blood oath to House Tucek as a sub-House of hers."

Behind me, Bian swore in Athanate.

The new House Basynia's eyes didn't seem to be able to focus.

"House Basynia?" I shook him.

"I... yes." His Athanate brain caught up and started sorting out the Athanate relationships. Basynia to Tucek, Tucek to Farrell. "Yes, Mistress."

I let the formality pass. "The rest of the House have a free choice. Blood oath to you and Altau, or go and stay in Ireland."

"Yes, Mistress." His voice was stronger, even if he still looked dazed and alarmed at the change in fortunes.

"What the hell are you doing?" Bian hissed in my ear as he began to check what the rest of the old House Basynia wanted to do.

"You mean I could have just killed them after they surrendered?"

"No! The right thing would have been to send them all to Ireland."

"Another death sentence," Mirela said. "Preceded by a brief period of looking over their shoulders all the time. Vega Martine does not accept surrenders. This way, they have a chance."

Bian and Mirela glared at each other.

Luckily the new House Basynia interrupted us before they took it any further. The survivors had heard the offer, and no one wanted to hide in Ireland.

"Actual Blood oath to wait until I've cleared the Serpent's gift from Mirela," I said to the new House Basynia.

That alarmed look redoubled in his eyes. It must have sounded like I was talking gibberish to him. I didn't have time to explain. It wasn't only Bian who had an issue with the sudden increase in the broader House Farrell. Yelena's tight-lipped disapproval was telling me even she was starting to feel I'd gone too far.

But before that could develop, Solange emerged from the basement. She had a call from Marguerite, who was also *not* happy with her, and had ordered Solange to put her on the speakerphone.

"You will shutter up Talleyrand, dispose of the bodies and then all of you will accompany House Farrell to Denver, where we will meet," Marguerite said, speaking in Athanate. "And until we meet, I place House Farrell in command of House Labastide, and you will obey her as you obey me."

If she'd been in full control of her faculties, Solange might have made a token argument, even against Marguerite's anger, but as it was, she was flushed with fever and grudgingly accepted it.

Marguerite wasn't happy with the hint of reluctance in her tone of voice.

"We have, over many years, put all our efforts behind the Eastern Seaboard association," she said, her voice rising. "It's time now to transfer ourselves completely and place those efforts at the disposal of House Altau and his sub-Houses; Farrell, Trang and Ionache foremost among them. We will do so happily, and with enthusiasm, and we will ensure we become indispensable to them, because the stain of our association with the Eastern Seaboard will linger like the stench of unburied bodies. Do I make myself absolutely clear, Diakon?"

"Yes, Mistress." Although Marguerite couldn't see it, Solange bowed her head as she spoke.

At Solange's final meek acceptance, Marguerite softened a fraction.

"My last Diakon blinded me to the dead-end situation we were in. Don't be like him, Solange. You're better than that, and I should have realized it long ago. I trust you."

"Thank you, Mistress."

They completed the conversation, and Solange bowed to me.

"Mistress," she said.

She wasn't going to be able to comply with Marguerite's orders to be happy about the changes, but I'd let that slide for now.

Rita came in, leading the cub and the local pack which had just arrived.

The werewolves seemed upset to have missed the fighting, but they were cheerful enough about helping clear up the mess and hammering boards over broken windows and shutters.

Their alpha offered their pack's disposal methods for the bodies.

"No," I said, my mouth getting ahead of my brain. Again.

I hadn't had a problem before. The paranormal world had kept to the shadows, and that included discreet disposing of bodies. The Denver pack's dead... well, some of them were buried, but others were made into fertilizer. I'd never objected, and bodies were just bodies. But it felt wrong now. We were coming out of the shadows. There should be some sign of that, in the rituals we'd adopted to remain hidden.

To my surprise, it was Bian who spoke first. Marguerite's handling of the situation with House Labastide had made an impression on her.

"Solange will make arrangements for the Labastide dead, but as our Houses are dokaria, they would be welcome at Haven," Bian said. "Basynia are now a sub-House of Tucek, which makes them sub-Houses of Farrell and Trang, and within our mantle. Whatever arrangements are chosen by House Basynia, as far as possible, they will be in Denver, at Haven."

Bian had a way of saying things. No one argued.

But her face told me how upset she was that I'd pulled *another* House into our association without involving her. She wasn't going to start an argument in front of others, but her eyes promised a difficult discussion I couldn't put off.

I had two urgent tasks. One—retrieve the Serpent's gift. Two—resolve the growing situation between Bian and Mirela.

I took off the Kevlar vest and rubbed my painful bruises thoughtfully.

Apart from the continuing pain from being shot in the chest, I was distracted by the feel of the gift in my Blood. It had been stirred up by the fight. It sensed Bian. It sensed Mirela. It sensed Solange. It slowed my heart and made each pulse like the beat of a drum.

My vision blurred. I was tasting the aura of everyone in the room. Seeing the physical world overlaid with the spirit world. Solange, Mirela and Bian were edged in light. I could see the Serpents' gift coiling in Bian's Blood and in Solange's, eager to be released to me.

Why wasn't Mirela's reacting the same way?

No time to investigate now. I had to recall my gift and then I couldn't put off that discussion with Bian and Mirela.

"You three." I pointed out Bian, Mirela and Solange. "You have the Serpents' fever, and your necks have a date with my fangs."

Chapter 38

I ushered them out to the patio that faced the formal gardens and the levee.

I got the three of them to sit on the cushioned cane chairs. Theris came out as well but didn't join us. He went to sit on the steps down to the lawn, facing away. Flint and Kane stayed inside, but close by to keep the aura shield in place.

I found the item of furniture I needed, an item that I was sure would be somewhere on the patio. To a human visitor it would simply be a broad, narrow chaise longue; well padded, without sides. To an Athanate, it was the *aimious*, the seat that allowed two Athanate to sit side by side, facing opposite ways, to exchange Blood in comfort. A polite and civilized Athanate accessory.

I hauled it in front of them, sat down and tried to relax.

The plantation had gotten quiet, the way a place does after violence, and that quiet had gotten more noticeable when the doors to the living room had been closed. Even the thunder as the storm from the Gulf crept closer seemed muted.

The patio was lit only by lights from inside the main house, and the occasional distant flash of lightning. The Louisiana night seemed so dark, so vast and full of threat as we sat, expressions hidden from each other, wrapped in shadows.

"Solange, please," I murmured and patted the seat next to me. She came. "I take it that you've been updated about the fever in your Blood?"

She nodded. "Tricks our Athanate immune system. Fatal."

"I'm the antidote. I can call the venom from your Blood."

"By biting me?"

"Yes."

Solange huffed and slipped her jacket off to leave her throat bare.

I put my arms around her, and she leaned into me. It should have been intimate, but she was tense as a bowstring, and her eukori was closed like a shop with steel shutters down.

Although she was much older than me, my Carpathian-forged eukori was stronger: I could have overwhelmed her. And I was senior: I could have just ordered her. But I didn't do either. It was perverse to refuse to share the pleasure, but it was her choice.

Her neck held Diana's scent and reminded me that Diana liked her. A point in her favor. Marguerite trusted her. Two points.

My fangs pressed against her fevered skin, making her shiver. Even at the very last moment, I expected her eukori to open to me. I was wrong. My anticipation of pleasure in biting felt tainted, but she'd die if I didn't, so my fangs broke her skin and found her artery.

In any case, the Serpents' gift, the shadow of the venom in her Blood, responded to my call. It gathered, it *wanted* to be taken, I *pulled*, and I'd cleared it from her Blood in less than a minute.

I slipped my fangs free and licked the wounds.

She thanked me, as if I'd given her a present she didn't really want, and she was just being polite.

I sighed and sent her off with a warning to rest and to delegate to others. She had time and opportunity. Buses were being organized. Jo and the New York kin were being picked up. Aircraft were being chartered to take us all to Denver. Solange couldn't make it happen any faster.

I put her out of my mind. Finding a way to work with the Diakon of my dokaria was an issue for another day.

And then there were two.

Bian and Mirela. A far bigger problem. A *huge* problem.

The storm had been creeping closer while I dealt with Solange. Winds gusted in from the south, carrying the scents of fresh rain and ozone from lightning. It blended with the acrid tang of nitro from the gunfight and all together, it smelled like unfinished violence. Like there was electricity in the air, searching for a fault line, waiting for me to make a move, seeking a path to discharge the power of the storm.

Too much of the Serpents' gift in my Blood.

I reached out with my eukori, but neither Bian nor Mirela opened fully. We were just connected enough that our hearts and lungs could sync. And that we could all feel how tense this had become.

No way forward but to call down that lightning.

"I'm sorry I've put you both in this position," I whispered in Athanate. "Everything that led to this... well it felt right at the time. Good intentions, I guess."

I paused and rubbed my face. I felt better than when I'd had the fever, but I was scared and I was tired and I was distracted by the Serpents' gift, and I was a long way from as sharp as I needed to be.

"I failed you both, in different ways. I know I got us into this position, but I need your help resolving it," I said. "What do you want me to do?"

"First, listen," Bian replied, staying with Athanate. "Both of you. I know you hate the Agiagraphos, Amber. Some of it is brutal and senseless. But

221

some of it is simply the expression of what the Athanate are and how we work inside."

Her voice had risen with frustration and anger.

She ran abrupt, angry fingers through her hair and only continued when she got herself under control. She deliberately leaned back in her chair to give the appearance of calmness.

"You're my fiancée, in your own words. It's a human term. The Agiagraphos doesn't really have a translation for it. What it does say is that whether we formally merge our Houses or not, we are *associated* within the laws and customs of the Athanate. What we each do reflects on the other. I cannot reverse these decisions you made on Tucek *and* Basynia without breaking that association."

I swallowed hard. Breaking association in the Agiagraphos would mean I had to remove myself and my House from her territory. I couldn't live in Denver. The absolute earthquake of personal heartbreak aside, I had responsibilities to the Were community that meant I *had* to be in Denver. And I had growing Adept responsibilities to the Denver coven.

All of which Bian knew. Just as I knew she loved me, and I hoped that meant she wouldn't push me away like that.

"A long time ago, before I even came to America, I had associations. Not like we have," she gestured at me, "but they were still deep, Athanate associations. Basilikos killed them all, and I made oaths." She slammed her hand down on the wooden armrest of her chair, making us jump. "Oaths against people like the Queen of Diamonds, who helped Basilikos, even if I didn't know her name, and oaths against people who followed the creed of Basilikos. Oaths against Basilikos itself, because that was what killed the people I loved."

I knew it had hit her hard when Skylur chose Livia as his new Diakon. Skylur had actually required Livia to retain her Basilikos creed. But they were in New York, half a continent away, and Bian could rationalize it, telling herself that it was a canny political maneuver.

Then I offered Mirela sanctuary, and I'd accepted her return offer to become a sub-House. All Bian really knew of Mirela was the evil she'd done. And *then* I'd made deals with Nai, the spirit of the person who'd become the Queen of Diamonds. It meant I'd become involved with the Temple and the Grove, spirit entities which Bian didn't trust. And to top it all, I'd just taken House Basynia into House Farrell as well, through Mirela.

This wasn't something half a continent away that Bian could ignore. This was bringing it into her mantle. Into her *home*.

How would *I* feel if Bian had done similar things without consulting me? What if she'd made a deal with the Were Confederation, for example?

And for that matter, how was Marguerite Labastide going to react when she found out what I'd done with Basynia, who'd been trying to murder her House?

I'd earned that sick feeling in my stomach.

"These." Bian stroked her throat, though we couldn't see the leopard tattoos in the darkness. "I had these done to symbolize those oaths. They are bound up as part of those oaths, and that's why they don't fade. Why they will not fade, until Basilikos itself fades from the world."

She stopped and I couldn't let the silence grow.

"You've seen the broadcast from the conference," I said.

Bian nodded, a movement in the darkness. Even my wolfy eyes could make out her expression.

Mirela spoke, very quietly but her voice was firm. "I was Carpathian. Then I was Basilikos, as I was ordered to be. I'm now Panethus, as I'm compelled to be."

Neither of them had opened their eukori to each other, but Bian *should* have been able to sense the truth through my eukori. Putting the barbs about compulsion aside, whatever Mirela had been, she was Panethus now.

"It's not what you *are*," Bian said. "Or how you came to be there. It's what you *were*, what you *did*. Yes, today, you and Salar made choices to save Amber and Diana, and those choices could have led to your deaths. You don't lack the capacity to make noble gestures. I thank you for those actions. But nothing you do can erase what you were."

Mirela still refused to open her eukori to me, but even from outside, I could feel her writhe at the sting in Bian's words.

Stung or not, Mirela wasn't one to take a step back.

"Tell me, Mistress, that the oaths you've just told us about have never bound you to commit unspeakable cruelties."

Oh, shit.

I didn't have time to react. Athanate develop the ability to move quickly. I knew Bian was far quicker than she should be, but Mirela's words had barely sunk into my brain and Bian was *there*, holding a knife against Mirela's throat.

"Stop," I shouted.

No one moved. I couldn't breathe. My heart didn't beat. No time to act. But I *saw*. I saw that Mirela *could* have reacted. She might not be as quick as Bian, but she was a formidable fighter. And she hadn't moved. She was sitting perfectly still, arms at her sides, looking straight into Bian's eyes. Calmly looking at death.

That's what kept her alive.

"Stop!" I said, quieter, trying to take the anger out of it. "This isn't getting us anywhere."

"Her or me?" Bian said.

Shit.

"*Both* of you."

"Why?" Bian's voice had lost all the earlier anger. She could have been talking about what to eat for dinner. Her knife stayed touching the top of Mirela's throat, angled up for a killing blow into the brain.

"Because I love you," I said, "and I owe her, and all those cursed Agiagraphos associations tie us all together, and it's simply the way we work inside."

She scowled at having her own words quoted back at her.

"I can understand an alliance with her when you were trapped on the *Queen of Diamonds* steamboat. I can understand you feeling an obligation to protect her afterwards, even if I don't agree. But *then* you take her into your House. You save her life inside," she gestured where the firefight had happened. "That dumb move could have gotten you both killed. As soon as we stop shooting, you try and save the dying woman who'd been trying to kill you, and *damn*, but you would have died right there if we hadn't been quick. We just manage to pull you back and *then* you go and take Basynia into your House."

A flicker of lightning revealed all of us frozen in position, edged in the harsh light, burned into my eyes. Thunder growled.

"I don't understand," she said, and her voice took on a tone I'd never heard from her. "And I'm frightened. All this spirit world and aura shit is scary. You leaped right into the middle of Vega Martine's troops in the Temple. It's as if this woman has infected you with her own death wish and I'm scared you'll carry each other down."

My heart seemed to be beating inside my throat.

"I'm sorry. It scares me too. But I'd have saved you in exactly the same way I saved Mirela inside. It's a *life* wish. As for taking people into the House, I saved them—"

"You can't save everyone!" Bian's voice was angry again.

"It *is* the Carpathian way to try." Theris's voice came from the darkness where the steps descended to the lawns. His voice was deep and measured, carrying its own persuasiveness.

Didn't persuade Bian.

She laughed bitterly. "Say the Carpathians, who've killed every Athanate who's stepped into their territory for the last couple of thousand years. That's some 'saving', House Zalissia."

"Not true, actually, although it would have appeared so from outside. Almost all of them joined us, wherever they came from. Those that wouldn't, I admit, we killed. We have been that security conscious. Those that joined us have remained inside our domain, of course."

"You're saying this collecting everyone is some kind of Carpathian thing?"

"Yes, but it's not an imperative. All I'm saying is that it is an instinct in our Blood."

"Amber and I share Blood, but I'm not into collecting Basilikos leftovers."

All the time, Bian's knife hadn't moved.

I cleared my throat. "Bian..."

She turned her head to look at me. If that was a test to see if Mirela tried to move, Mirela passed. She stayed completely still.

Bian took a half a step back. The knife retreated, and my heart stopped trying to break out of my chest.

Mirela remained still. The knife hadn't retreated that far.

"I apologize for my comment," she said to Bian. "That was unwarranted and a false equivalence. I don't have a death wish. I think."

Bian said nothing, but maybe we weren't on the very edge of the precipice any longer.

"It doesn't help any of us if we're fighting," I said. "It sabotages what we're trying to do. Maybe we can—"

"You can't fit every person inside the tent," Bian cut across me.

"That's exactly what Skylur is trying to do with the Assembly."

"He's reaching out to the Hidden Path," Bian snapped back. "Ignore what Livia calls herself. She's not Basilikos in the way we're using the term now. What Skylur *isn't* trying to do is to bring Matlal and Vega Martine onside, and for good reason."

"Mirela isn't with them anymore, and she isn't Basilikos." We were going around in circles. "Anyway, it's not fitting people in for strategic reasons. It's not because I'm driven by oaths. It's because I'm me, and I owe Mirela. I need to make this right."

"I can't understand why you think you have to save everyone."

"I don't, but I *compelled* her to change. Forced her. Honoring that change is the least I can do. And Basynia... well, he surrendered the House."

"And you feel obligated because of that?"

"Yes."

Mirela stirred.

"You have something to add?" Bian asked.

"Yes." The wind gusted through the patio, cold, slippery, oily-rich with river scents.

There was a long pause.

I braced myself. This could go many ways and most of them were bad. How could I stop Bian killing Mirela? Without losing Bian? Was it only possible to choose one or the other?

Chapter 39

"Among the other benefits of being trapped in Amber's substantiation, it gave me time."

Bian shifted her weight at the implied criticism of me, but the knife remained where it was, a couple of feet from Mirela's neck.

"I had time to think. The mission I was given by the Elders of Carpathia was finished, obviously. What next? And there were two sides to that question. What would we do and where would that be. You could probably tell, from what I said in the Assembly, going back to Carpathia wasn't in my list of choices. Justified or not, their mission was a betrayal of me and my House. It felt much more profound a betrayal than being compelled to shed the Basilikos creed that I never wanted. That I'd taken because I'd been ordered to, and I'd sworn to obey those orders."

I nodded, and maybe she saw the movement in the darkness.

"What did I want? What would be best for the House? What was possible, given what we'd been?"

Of all of us on the patio, I saw clearest with my wolfy eyes, and even I couldn't really gauge the expressions of the other two women. Theris was little more than the glow of his body heat, facing away into the night. Maybe that difficulty with seeing loaned weight to the words we heard. And Mirela, like any Athanate, had learned the ancient cadences of speech which ran like roots through the language.

"To live, and not to merely count the days, but to live as I had wanted to live when the world was fresh to me. To return, renewed, to the beliefs and passions I once had. And yet... to not be owed or owned. To not be bound by base obligation only, and to hoard no reluctant credits of gratitude. None of that! To be free to strive again for such virtues as all the world would acknowledge as excellent. For my duty to be harnessed entirely by my heart and my head and my soul. And to bring my enemies down into the dirt. These are the things I wanted. And nowhere did I see a harbor for my desires."

I shivered. The world had shrunk to this darkened patio and the words which hung in the night air between us.

Mirela slipped into a mixture of Athanate and English. "You know the truly terrifying thing about compulsion? It *feels* right. It gets under your skin, and you start to think *yeah, this is the way I want to be*. And once you realize that, how can you trust yourself again?"

I shuddered. I knew just how that felt.

In the shadows, I could make out Bian was frowning.

"I was so angry about being compelled," Mirela continued, falling back into Athanate. "And I struck out at Amber for it. I apologize for that, too. Once I stopped reacting, once I thought about what had to happen to get to where I wanted to be, it felt less bad. In fact, there comes a point when it all feels the same: compulsions, oaths, persuasion, peer pressure. The whole process. The de-programming I'd have had to go through if I had returned to Carpathia would have been worse than what Amber accidentally did to my House in her substantiation."

"All very moving," Bian said. "But it doesn't erase what you were or what you did."

"Maybe nothing can," Mirela admitted easily. "You hate Basilikos, Mistress. You swear oaths to drive them from the face of the earth. You wear your oaths on your neck, so all may see. You hate me because I had to be Basilikos to spy on them. What do you think drove me to do that mission, knowing what I would need to do? Do you have the hate I had, strong enough to do what I did?"

Another flare of lightning and rumble of thunder, making the silence on the patio all the deeper.

"I don't have a death wish. I said I saw no harbor for my desires, and that was the truth, until the moment Amber spoke on the floor of the Assembly. I saw it then, even if I already knew that there is nothing without a cost. Even though I was still angry with her. I saw a chance of belonging for my whole House, a *hope*, and I took it."

"What cost?"

"To undo what being Basilikos has done to us, is to hold up an unpitying mirror to ourselves. Believe me, that's a cost that has to be met. However harshly you judge us, however well my House may hide it, you could not judge us more harshly than we judge ourselves. But we will go forward to this *hope*, we will do everything we can to be worthy of it, to prove ourselves. Not everyone will succeed, but in time, some of us may come to terms with what we were. Will you?"

I could hear from her tone, she ended with a peace offering of a small smile, which I knew Bian didn't return.

But she'd had an effect.

"Both of you need to figure out how to make this work." Bian's voice was tight with control. "You have my support. For the moment. Understand that this is a fragile thing."

Mirela bowed her head.

Bian turned to me. The knife was gone. "Now get rid of this venom."

Chapter 40

She sat on the aimious next to me.

I didn't want this to be like Solange, which had felt as impersonal as a nurse taking a patient's blood sample, but I wasn't sure how engaged Bian would be. Or how relaxed she'd be with Mirela watching.

I nuzzled her neck. Inhaled.

Felt the rush of pleasure through my body and I didn't care if there wasn't an exact Athanate word for fiancée, or that everything seemed so tangled.

I kissed the lobe of her ear and mouthed the words "I love you."

Got rewarded with a huff of air that wasn't entirely exasperation.

"How fortunate I love you too," she murmured.

I had no doubt Mirela's eyes were rolling in the shadows, and I was way beyond caring.

I kissed Bian until the tension left her mouth and she gave in to me. Allowed my teeth to gently close around her wantonly loosened bottom lip. Allowed my tongue to tease hers.

We groaned, both of us. Half from the furnace of our desire and half from regret that this wasn't the time for everything we wanted to do.

Still. She was in a better state of mind. I took what pleasure I could from that, and grabbed a fist of her hair to pull her head back and make an offering arch of her neck.

My lips came to rest on the pulse in her throat, and I felt it jump to my touch. Blood and gift both called to me. There was a hitch in her breath and her arms pressed me closer. A feeling of her eukori shield dissolving. The sharp joy of anticipation as my fangs manifested.

It felt like my heart had swollen to batter against my ribs and my whole body was throbbing with that pulse as I broke her flesh.

I didn't even need to *pull*. As soon as my fangs found her artery, a mixture of Blood and the Serpent's gift shot through my taryma, to explode into my chest.

We both groaned again.

Joy.

How it was meant to be.

The gift swirled inside me, and Bian could feel that through our bond. The way the night seemed to sway around us. The feel of the Mississippi moving past behind the levee. The murmur and movement inside the house. The weight of the gathering storm above. The feel of us in each other's arms.

"That aura shit is downright eerie," Bian whispered as my fangs disappeared and I licked the wounds I'd made.

"Mmm."

I wanted to keep holding her and kissing her, but the gift had shifted its focus to Mirela and Bian tensed at the withdrawal.

I opened my arms reluctantly and let Bian stand up.

"I'll go check how we're doing with the logistics," she said.

She paused by Mirela's chair, reached down to lift Mirela's jaw and silently stared into her eyes for a full minute.

Then she slipped through the patio doors and left us together.

"Do I get the kissing and the tongue first, too?" Mirela spoke as she sat in the seat Bian had just left.

Trying to project... what was that Frenchy word Jen used? *Insouciance.*

I chuckled and sobered up.

"Don't actually need any of it," I said. "Don't need to bite."

"What?"

"Open your eukori."

She did, slowly and carefully. Nothing like the feeling of dissolving that I'd had with Bian. More a gradual retreat.

"Going to have to trust me," I said.

She huffed, but the retreating mental shield thinned and evaporated.

I didn't engage. I sat there and waited for her eukori to come to me, which it did, slowly.

"What are you afraid of?" I asked.

"Your aura." She rubbed her face. "Sorry about the dumb-ass behavior in the fight."

"Forget it. Trying to prove yourself? No need."

She snorted. "Yeah, but that stuff is real for my House. Like Donatienne." She looked away and went silent.

"I'm sorry about Donatienne. You looked very... close."

I winced. 'Close' was a pathetic word.

"She was katikia. I was thinking about asking her to become kin, but I wanted her to understand what she might be getting into first. That it wasn't all going to be a holiday on the beach." She sighed. "And sure enough, it got lethal again. So fucking quickly."

Lightning flared, its harsh light revealing to me the grief she'd tried to hide in the darkness.

"*You will become unsullied. Whole and pure,*" she whispered. "That was perfect. That was what she wanted to be. Thank you. But how did you know what to say?"

"I don't know. It just came out of my mouth. I think the Temple helped me."

"Yeah." She cleared her throat and straightened her back. "Anyway, what do you mean about not needing to bite? How else do I get rid this?"

"I'm not sure you need to. It's supposed to be the gift of the Serpents to me, but I don't think it can tell the difference between us. You're not running a fever. When we shared auras on the *Queen of Diamonds*, maybe we ended up with enough spiritual similarity that the venom could be a gift for you as well."

"No! Please." She shivered. "It's freaky enough becoming like you, but there's a line I need to draw. And that *aura shit,* as your fiancée calls it, is on the other side of the line from me. Get it out!"

"Okay, okay. Just making sure."

She grabbed my head and brought my lips to the pulse in her neck.

It still felt completely different to every other time I'd called the gift. It coiled like smoke in her Blood, as if hesitant to gather. No urgency. Yet I wanted it.

Mirela could feel all that, through our bound eukori, and I sensed her trying to visualize pushing it away. That worked.

My fangs found her carotid, and I *pulled* lazily, once, twice, slowing down, feeling the gift expand inside of me. Third time and there was no gift remaining in her Blood. It was all in me, and I felt as if my mind was stretching like an elastic sheet.

I barely remembered to lick her wounds closed, and afterwards, I simply rocked back where I sat, with my eyes closed.

There was too much to feel. The whole night. The black horizon. The storm.

And like fireflies in the dark, the flickering light of souls in and around Talleyrand.

"Amber?" Mirela whispered. "Are you okay?"

Chapter 41

"I'm fine," I said. "Just give me some space. It's weird."

"I'm not going anywhere while you look like that."

Like that. Shadows pulsed in my Blood and fire flickered behind my eyes. I saw the aura of every person in the house, like bodies on infrared. I was tempted to reach out and see more, but I could also feel the Lost Boys' shield above me, and the blackness beyond.

Theris had come up from the steps at the worry in Mirela's voice.

I opened my eyes to see them both peering into my face.

"This Serpent stuff takes getting used to," I said.

Around each aura, there was a seething of possibilities and what-ifs. Like catching up a handful of snakes.

And Theris.

Ah. Theris. Yes. You are not quite what you seem, are you? But you are what I was beginning to suspect you are.

And Mirela.

And me.

Too much. Too quickly. Too difficult to process.

The aura vision faded, and I was back on the patio.

"Mirela, it's time for you to get Basynia's Blood oaths. I'm okay. I'm just going to get a bit of air in the gardens before the storm breaks."

She looked at Theris. He nodded, reluctantly.

"You'll need to hurry, then," she said. "That storm isn't far away. I'll warn Flint and Kane you're moving."

"Tell them, but there's no need for them to come with me."

I tasted the shield they had built, looked at it with Nai's knowledge. It was okay. It had its own flavor, as wild and eccentric as my shamans were. I wasn't ready to try out a working of my own as complex as this, and yet, I felt a push from Nai's love of neatness, beauty and efficiency in spells. It made me tinker with it. Just *there* and *there* and *there*, and suddenly it was my working, my shield, and one I could maintain by myself.

The patio doors burst open to reveal a startled Flint and Kane, wondering what the hell was going on.

I waved them away and Theris backed me up again. Of course, his Adept skills had been sharp enough to sense what I was doing and how effective it was.

That was probably why he was looking sideways at me the way he was.

I stood up gingerly, still a little dizzy from the spirit vision.

The gift was too powerful and unpredictable for me to use it yet. Too unknown. Nai and the Serpents hadn't given me powers, they'd given me a way to discover them for myself. I'd have to keep it switched off and then I'd have to find some quiet time to experiment and learn.

The thought of finding quiet time made me laugh, and Theris gave me another questioning look.

I shook my head and descended the curving steps he'd been sitting on, down to the well-tended lawn where I strolled toward the river, with Theris a half-step behind.

Even with everything shut down, I could sense auras. Not just people.

The river. The approaching storm. The night itself.

We climbed the levee, and I unbound the braid in my hair to let the rising wind wave it like a ragged flag.

The storm was almost here. I could smell the rain and the ozone. Feel the electricity in the air, still searching for that path to rush down. The river had swollen in anticipation, it seemed to sway, as if it were reaching up to a lover.

There were old gods loosed upon the world tonight.

I paused and turned my head.

"Kyrios Pelea," I said, joking again about the mistake I'd made when I'd first mangled his titles. "My Lord Protector."

He drifted closer. My wolfy eyes could make out his smile was uncertain. I looked harder at him, and the whole world seemed to slide and drift in slow motion. As if I was *seeing* him the way I'd seen with spirit vision.

I'd been told his real title when the Carpathians arrived in the Assembly.

"Kyrios Kryfokratos," I corrected myself. "It means 'Lord of the Hidden Fortress', doesn't it."

He looked away. "You know the Carpathian dialect."

"Not well, but Diana had to give me help when we were looking at older texts." I looked toward the river, back at the house, and judged we were far enough away from any ears that might be listening. Still, I started walking again, slowly. "There is no literal fortress, is there? It's a title. In fact, it's the one the Carpathians give their spy masters, isn't it?"

He matched my casual, rolling walk, but I could see the tension in his body.

"Yes."

I laughed. "The Domain of Carpathia, one of the four most powerful groupings of the entire Athanate world, thought it would be nice to look after little ole me, and assigned the man who runs their entire spy network to be my pelea."

"A great many of Altau's strategies, whether intended or not, come to a focus in you. It seemed a reasonable precaution, given we support his intentions on Emergence."

I snorted.

Bullshit.

The gift of the Serpents told me that was an illusion. Without the gift, maybe I wouldn't have been able to tell for sure: the Carpathian spy master was also a master of disguising his emotions.

"No," I said. "It's not that."

I hesitated. I was about to start paddling in some very deep waters. The Carpathians had pulled my ass out of the fire in the Assembly, but they weren't my friends. It struck me then, they were like Skylur—who'd once told me, minutes after thanking me for saving Diana's life, that nothing and no one would be allowed to stand in the way of a successful, controlled Emergence. And he'd meant me, as well as everyone else, in that 'nothing': if I threatened Emergence, he'd kill me.

In the same way, the Carpathians had plans, which they considered vital and which they weren't going to share with me. They had people on the ground who would not hesitate to act in the way that Skylur had implied. If I threatened the Carpathians' plans, Theris would kill me, even if it meant he lost his own life.

If I could work out the real reason he'd been assigned to me, and I revealed it, would that be a threat to the Carpathians' plans? Would he kill me for that?

Ah!

Yes. That was the key to it all. Killing me. Theris was *there* to kill me.

The last veils of illusion blew away.

I rounded on him, standing in his way and forcing him to stop.

Away from the lights of the plantation house, he was a solid wall of darkness, a hot glow to my wolfy eyes, a thumping heart to my wolfy ears. He was a big man. He blocked the line of sight. No one in the house could see me out here. No one could save me.

But...

"The Carpathian Council of Elders trusts you, where they would not trust anyone else," I said.

He didn't respond. His breathing was deep and even, yet his aura boiled, and his body was a hair-trigger away from violence.

"You're here, guarding me, because you have four great attributes which the Council recognizes. You're skilled in magic. You're skilled in killing.

Your loyalty to the Domain is beyond question. And your commitment to the Domain's objectives is unshakeable."

Unbidden, our eukori merged. We were as close as lovers in the darkness beside the Mississippi. Our hearts fell into sync and made it all feel like a dream. But it was still a dream that could end in death.

I was right, so far. I had named the attributes which made him the Council's choice for his task. I knew because he'd opened his aura to me. He was allowing me to see into his soul. He was a very strange man, Theris Zalissia, House Zalissia, Kyrios Kryfokratos, Elder-elect of the Domain of Carpathia. He was the rock on which the waves broke. He was the oasis that the desert could not claim.

I could trust him more than I trusted myself.

My voice felt scratchy. "You will protect me, Kyrios Pelea, from any threat within your power to defeat. You will face any horror for me. You will do this at the expense of your own life, if the situation demands it."

He would. Our eukori and auras had both calmed, almost to meditation levels, as if we'd hypnotized each other.

"Yet, there is one exception," I whispered. "The heart of your mission. The Sword of Damocles over my head."

A twitch in his eukori.

"You are oath-bound. If I succumb to Tezcatlipoca, you will kill me, even if you die in the process or aftermath."

So quiet, it was as if the wind spoke. He replied with one word. "Yes."

I looked up at the mass of him in the darkness. I weighed his aura, and I saw no illusion, no lie.

I reached out and took his hand, placed it over my heart, and then placed mine over his.

Felt the shock of the touch pulse through our bodies. Felt our heat like a beacon as the air cooled before the storm.

The wind blew his long, black hair so it caressed my face.

Our hearts beat deep and slow and even. As deep as the night. As slow as lovers resting.

I slipped into the Carpathian dialect of Athanate.

"Thrice welcome, Kyrios Kryfokratos. Thrice I welcome you, beloved Theris. First, to be the weapon in my hand. Second, to be the shield upon my arm. And third, to be the sword at my back, should I stumble."

I stepped around him and made my way back to the light.

A sheet of lightning tore the sky apart, and the world shook to the thunder that followed.

By its flare, I saw the arrival of Brynswere, the Valkyrie spirit guide for Gwen. It would have been difficult *not* to see the arrival of a seven-foot-tall woman in mail and leather, descending under the power of her two huge wings.

Others spilled through the doors onto the patio.

The wings disappeared into her back, and she stood there as I ran up, a second ahead of the heavens opening and rain beginning to lash down.

I knew the night was not finished with its sorrows. I could taste it.

Bryn had news of the Atrax operation: as a military operation it had gone very well. All reports back so far had said the Matlal teams had been surprised and neutralized.

"But there has been a price to pay," Bryn said. "Members of House Tucek insisted on leading the attacks. As Annie put it, they took point."

She paused, eyes on Mirela.

"How many?" Mirela asked, her voice very low.

"So far, you lost four. There were three more injured."

"*We* have lost four," I broke in. "Five, including Donatienne."

I opened my eukori to Mirela's grief. A moment's delay and Yelena followed me. Another, and Bian did too.

Into the stillness that followed, like a pebble dropping into a pond, a bus with Jo and the New York kin inside drove up to the mansion. They piled out, a contrast to us. A strange and beautiful kaleidoscope of high emotions and youthful optimism.

Denver
Chapter 42

It was a subdued group in the ground floor ballroom at Haven, attending the full debrief of the Atrax operation as the last teams reported back.

The management of the campaign had been classic Ops 4-10, and the debriefing was done in the same way. There was a large screen behind the debriefing area displaying the list of Atrax sites and statuses. All sites were now at least provisionally 'OS'— 'operation successful'. Most had been updated with the number of Matlal killed. Those with the stats also had a couple of other numbers, the injured and killed on our side, with names. There were a few numbers, showing where the Atrax squads had surrendered—all of them were Vega Martine sub-Houses, and they were being brought here. None of the Matlal squads had been open to defecting.

I tried to look at it as a vet of Ops 4-10. In that light, the numbers of deaths were low, or even very low. The campaign had been an overwhelming success. Not a single failure. We'd protected every House under threat, even the bastards who called me an abomination.

But my Ops 4-10 days were over, and I was House Farrell now. Those troops on that display were House Farrell, formally or informally, and among the formal sub-Houses was House Tucek. I was monitoring those numbers, because I knew how Mirela would feel. No number was 'low' when it was your own.

House Tucek was a medium-sized House. They'd had twenty-two Athanate. Six dead now. *Only* six. But that was over a quarter of the House, and it was a devastating loss. Another five wounded, of which a couple were injured severely enough to need prolonged recovery, even with their Athanate healing capabilities.

House Tucek had been both spies and troops for Vega Martine. They'd taken part in combat. They were used to loss, but not at this level. Not on operations which had taken the enemy by complete surprise. Not when the total of other fatalities on our side was a smaller number. I could see the thin lips, pale faces and lingering, wide-eyed looks among the returned members of House Tucek.

I could also see they weren't completely isolated. Atrax teams were mostly sitting together. I could see them in groups, including some of my ehvasi, some of my Denver pack, some of the Ops 4-10 troopers. Not everyone. But most of those who'd been with me in the campaign down to Mexico were staying, for support.

That was a positive to take away. Understanding teams was a major step.

I had Annie beside me. She had made sergeant in Ops 4-10 after my time, and she was now one of my ehvasi. Someone whose opinion I valued, and she was unhappy.

She'd been on the Atrax team for Phoenix, and she'd made it her job to speak with every Ops 4-10 vet on every other team because she saw something wasn't right about that death toll.

"It wasn't anything we did, Amber. It wasn't any one thing they did either."

I suspected I knew the answer, but I wanted to hear what Annie thought.

"What do you think it was then? Just a statistical anomaly?"

She shook her head. "No. There's something there." She grimaced. "Nothing as simple and obvious as a death wish, or not understanding the risks, but... they wanted to prove themselves. To us. To each other. To themselves."

She shrugged. "Maybe they were trying to compensate for having turned on former colleagues. I don't think it's a consistent thing. With some I think it was just a sort of... fatalism. And they don't seem to believe they're really an accepted part of Panethus."

"Did anyone say to any of House Tucek that they weren't an accepted part of this House?"

Annie waggled her hand. "Not in so many words, but there are some of us who can't get their heads around how former enemies can become trusted team members."

Bian for one.

I could hardly fault others for sharing my fiancée's view.

"You?"

It took her some effort to meet my eyes. "I'd be so ashamed if I gave them that impression, but I'd be lying if I said it was easy."

Her eyes slid past me to the group of Basynia, who were huddled together and obviously in as much shock as House Tucek, but for different reasons. They'd lost more, down at Talleyrand. They'd lost their Mistress. And they were looking at a display chalking that up as a victory.

"They're not ready," Annie said. "We got lucky in this op because we had good local backup and total surprise. But, with my Ops 4-10 hat on, I wouldn't want to take these troops on another mission. That's in two parts, Boss. Firstly, for the sake of the mission, because you can't run our kind of ops with people you don't completely trust. We managed this one, but it was a straightforward mission on our own territory, and my gut's telling me the next won't be. And secondly, specifically for the Tucek people, for their own sake, because they haven't got their shit together and that's lethal in our kind of ops."

She nodded at the figures on the screen. "Case in point."

That was damning, but I couldn't argue. I could taste it, like a scent on the air. Like a false note in the choir.

"Okay. Thank you, Annie. I see I have a task. And I may need to come back to you."

She nodded, tight-lipped.

We were both unhappy. Not with any one person, but with the situation that had developed, which was my responsibility to fix.

In the meantime, the debriefing was paused. The next team due back was an hour or more out. Mirela had taken the opportunity to get up in front of the group. She sensed her House, and the teams they were with, needed something to focus on. Something to snap them out of any spiral before it headed downward.

She chose to talk about moving on. About the mission in context of a covert war. Of what the next mission might be, which was something I'd been thinking about on the way back to Denver.

She was good, but it was too vague. She wasn't thinking clearly because she was suffering along with the rest of them.

A few of House Tucek chose to turn their grief to anger and wanted to argue.

Two voiced the opinions of others. I recognized Dosia, who'd been with Mirela in New York. Athanate Houses didn't have ranking systems like the army. House Tucek had Mirela as leader, and Salar, as her Diakon. The remainder were nominally equal, with some authority coming to older ones. I guessed, in a military style hierarchy, Dosia would fit as a sort of lieutenant.

Then there was Leyla. She was a long-standing member of House Tucek but didn't fall into any military hierarchy above private. She had a role, something between barrack room lawyer and union rep. She was barely five-seven, but she had six foot of attitude and the mouth to go with it.

Dosia's beautiful red hair was neatly captured in a ponytail, and she wore smart jeans and a glossy, deep-green blouse that complemented her hair.

Leyla's midnight-black hair was shaved in a band above her ears. She kept it long on top and it looked as if she had braided it back for the mission. Now it was unbound and a magnificent mess. She was still wearing what she'd worn when she'd led the squad to kill the Atrax team assigned to Bismark. All matte black tactical gear. She'd taken the shirt off to tie it around her waist, leaving her in a gray workout vest. It was the style Jen called racerback, with a single strap at the back splitting into two and leaving her shoulders bare. Which happened to be as beautifully sculptured as an Olympic swimmer's.

Maybe listen to what they're saying and stop checking them out? was Tara's helpful suggestion.

"We're hurting, Mistress. We're all hurting." That was Dosia.

"We're just back from the worst setback we've had and you're talking about the next mission?" That was Leyla, hands on hips, and she was barely a word or two short of a challenge.

It wouldn't be a challenge in House Farrell. I regularly had Yelena or others arguing I was wrong, but that wasn't House Tucek style, and everyone knew that. The tension that had been building suddenly soared.

I stood and walked to the front, still feeling the same out-of-body sensation I'd had since Talleyrand. I hated this political crap, but I was a leader here, and I had to lead. This was my House, and House Farrell did things differently.

The overt talking stopped, replaced by a murmuring.

"There's a need," I said quietly. I wouldn't shout at them. I'd encourage them to shut up so they could hear me.

Tara: Good political trick, non-political person.

"Emergence is happening now, people," I said. "Whatever your thoughts from before, whether you wanted it or not, whether you thought we could hide forever or not… all that's gone. Humanity was going to find us whether we hid or not. A whole regiment within the military knew the paranormal existed as soon as my last mission was over. No one can keep a secret like that. The knowledge has been seeping out. There are whole communities in places like New York that have already accepted that the paranormal exists, and bless them all, the reaction has mainly been 'whatever'. But what goes down in New York might play differently in DC. *Will* play differently. *Will* play badly for us unless we control it, sure as politicians lie, because someone is going to see that *otherness* as a way to gather support and get himself or herself up the greasy pole. And however that politician chooses to view it, someone else will need to take the opposite view for political expediency. The 'us and them' that drives the political process. Our difference will make us a target, as it always has, but now we'll be front and center. We've started the process of Emergence to get ahead of it. We're talking to the government, right now. We're working our way up the bureaucracy, and that bureaucracy has its own timetables. The timing's been taken out of our hands."

Silence.

I wasn't pushing out eukori, but they'd done the Athanate thing of getting in sync with everyone else, even those who weren't Athanate.

We had one heart, one breath.

Time for me to offer them one mind. I wasn't going to push. I wasn't going to compel. Despite the temptation I could feel like a phantom sweetness in my mouth.

"How do we control it? What is our role here?" Mirela had enough of her senses about her to feed me an easy one.

"Our role is *not* politics," I said, and got a breathy sort of laugh around the room. "But our role is as important. Our role is military. Our task is to remove Basilikos from the equation as far as possible. To stop people forming their opinion of all paranormals based on a bunch of sociopaths down in Yucatán. To do what we've been doing. We've dealt with Matlal's werewolf allies in northern Mexico. We've neutralized the Atrax assassination squads all over the US."

There were a few side glances at the small group of Basynia, but Yelena had gone to stand with them, and that gesture pulled in more support from Haven-based people. Simple move, but it made a visual image of Basynia not being so isolated.

But it was still an illusion. As Annie had said, I wouldn't want Basynia or most of House Tucek at my back in a fight. Not because I felt they might betray me, but because, in their current mental state, they weren't going to be any use and might be a hindrance.

"So we've hit them twice, hard. There's a campaign strategy I was taught in Ops 4-10 that applies to this situation," I said. "Any of my fellow veterans want to guess which one?"

"Ride the shock wave," Annie called out.

Good woman.

I nodded. "If you've hit them, hit them again before they recover. Keep hitting them until they can't recover."

There was a growl from the werewolves who'd been with me in Mexico. Some of them knew the temptation we'd faced when we'd destroyed Astilla de Luna, the headquarters of the insane alpha Mauricio Gálvez, near Villa Ahumada, in the Mexican province of Chihuahua. They knew there was a catch in the shock wave strategy—you had to make sure you didn't overextend and go beyond your planning and logistics.

"We can't strike against Matlal immediately. He's a harder target," Mirela said. "Vega Martine is closer. We know more about her, and House Vega Martine is responsible for the operations in North America, which has to be our priority area."

"Vega Martine wasn't in control of *all* Basilikos operations," I said. "Not even in the US. It was Matlal who insisted on the Atrax squads, and half of them were his Athanate."

Mirela conceded the point.

I hadn't intended to follow this line yet, but Yelena pushed it further. "Vega Martine only had to know about Atrax because it was her operation to supply and coordinate the assassination teams. I wonder what else Matlal is doing in the US that doesn't go through Vega Martine."

"That we know of?" Mirela said. "He's funding religious groups like the one down in Louisiana, the Church of the Risen Sun."

"That's in New York as well," Yelena said.

"All over the Midwest," Pia added. "And new cults in California."

"We know he's involved in the drug trade, and people trafficking too," Yelena said.

"Yes, and many other things which are generally targeted against the whole country. Apart from the Risen Sun, there's nothing else targeted against paranormals, though he may still be supporting the Central Mountain Confederation of werewolves against Denver and the Were League," Mirela said. "But it's too diffuse. There's no concentration, no military target that makes sense. Vega Martine is right there. We know exactly where she is. We know her strengths and weaknesses. Our defection and the defeat of Atrax has weakened her. And remember, Matlal's entire operation in northern Mexico just went up in flames, so he's going to be on the alert."

"So will Vega Martine be on the alert," I said. "She knows you've defected now. Of course she knows where you think she's weakest, and she'll be doing something about it. She's expecting you to lead our attack."

There had nearly been a little rebellion going in House Tucek, but the room had moved from disputing that we'd need to be doing more fighting to a discussion about where it would be best to fight.

Leyla cleared her throat.

"On a purely practical level, attacking Matlal makes more sense," she said. "With Vega Martine's blessing, we in House Tucek have war-gamed dozens of operations against Matlal, on the thinking that Matlal might betray our alliance. On the other hand, I don't think we ever planned an attack against Vega Martine, so that planning would have to start from scratch."

Good point.

Not just a barrack room lawyer.

She joined us at the front and continued. "*Matlal* doesn't know we've defected and joined Panethus. Vega Martine isn't going to tell him because it'll make her look weak, and no one wants to look weak in Basilikos. You know he's smart: if we attack him, he'll find out it's us, and he'll think Vega Martine has turned against him, because that's what will make sense to him. He knows she's wanted to take over for some time. Matlal and Vega Martine fighting each other is a big win for us."

"But if we attack Matlal, it has to be soon," Mirela pointed out. "Before he finds out from someone else that we're not part of Vega Martine anymore."

Leyla shrugged. "Okay. A small operation against Matlal."

I hadn't yet decided whether House Tucek was ready for any operation, small or not, but before I could say anything, it was taken out of my hands.

David had been here from the start of the debriefing. He'd been sitting with Mirela's Diakon, Salar, at the back of the room, and I'd been aware their muted conversation had become increasingly urgent, and was focused on something coming in on Salar's cell.

David swore, loud enough half the room heard him.

To someone else, I might have made a teasing comment about sharing what they found so interesting, but David I trusted absolutely. If he was disrupting things, there was a reason, and he'd tell us.

He stood up.

"Diakon Tucek has just received information that we think is core to this discussion," he said.

Interesting. *We* think. David was telling me he trusted whatever it was. And he'd called her by her formal title, to emphasize that this was House Farrell and House Tucek working together. He'd understood the mood, and he was doing what he could to help.

I liked that. What I didn't like was that he looked grim.

I gestured for them both to join us at the front.

Chapter 43

"We'd like to take over the screen, if we're done with news of the Atrax updates for the moment?" David asked.

No one objected. Getting those figures off the screen would actually be a relief for some.

Salar started to transfer information from her cell to the laptop that had been used to update the display.

"Give me a moment," she muttered.

David filled in.

"I've been working a lot with Diakon Tucek as she's recovered from the Queen of Diamonds' poison," he said. "We've been theorizing about what Matlal would aim for, in order to attack Panethus in North America. He doesn't have the sheer numbers to make a widespread, direct military assault possible. As I heard you discussing earlier, he's had specific projects. The Atrax squads were aimed at Athanate Houses. His Mexico plans were aimed at Were and Athanate on the southern borders. We've been able to stop those. We can't really stop the quasi-religious, anti-paranormal efforts he's made with the Church of the Risen Sun, or the rise of Aztec cults we're seeing in California. They look like long-term strategies anyway."

"He also has strategies to weaken the fabric of society in the US with crime. Again, that all looks like long-term. Matlal has to know that Emergence is coming. He's not stupid. He knows humanity would have discovered us soon, and he knows that Altau has a project to reveal our existence to the government."

He went on, "What's he doing about that? I've been wondering for some time. I've been searching for any clues, but his security is good. Very frustrating. So I turned it around and I asked myself what I would do, if I was an evil, psychopathic monster?"

That got a couple of laughs.

He started counting off on his fingers.

First finger. "Cults and internet groups which have the ability to influence people. Low cost, wide effect, nearly impossible to police, but slow to achieve the effect *unless* something pushes an issue out into the foreground. Something like Emergence."

Next finger. "Stockpiling mineral assets. Entirely legal, but high cost and an inefficient way to affect a country with as wide an industry base as the US… *unless* something causes a market shock in response to dramatic news. Like Emergence."

Next finger. "Acquire large amounts of decentralized digital currency. Yes, funny money. Again, I concede that as a tactic on its own, it wouldn't be effective in any reasonable amount of time... unless..."

He left the point there, because people were seeing the general case he was building: multiple attacks that might be insignificant alone, but would reinforce each other. Other than saying these would become more effective when Emergence hit, he hadn't really made his point.

He did now.

"Those would be the supporting acts, but the main events are a different league. Intelligence on some of these has just come in from House Tucek's information gathering assets that they've been running in Mexico."

I got the start of a chill. David understood these things, and despite his light delivery, I could sense how worried he was about whatever it was that Salar was indicating she was now ready to show.

"Matlal has been building competence in information technology," David said, and Salar put up a badly taken photo of an organizational diagram.

"Sorry about the quality, it was taken under difficult circumstances," Salar said. "This person's entire spying career over several years comes down to these images we're showing you."

David pointed. "Digital currency trading that I talked about is simply one section, there. But this section, over here, is the largest, and it deals with network viruses. The icons you see are allocated to teams. Utilities, healthcare, transport infrastructures, and over here, military."

That chill ran down my spine. Electricity, water, hospitals, air traffic control, highway emergency services, rail travel... they were all vulnerable to network attacks. Even the military was increasingly dependent on electronic communications.

In Ops 4-10, we'd targeted criminal organizations that had this sort of broad spread. It was amazing how many drug criminals had sophisticated technology. But Ops 4-10 had been a precision hammer. We took out criminals and locations, but without the knowledge of where these sites were, we would have been useless. There was nothing on the diagram to show the location of these teams. They might be spread all over the world.

"This next slide is worse," David said.

It was.

The same poor photograph and lack of location data, but I could make out an organizational structure involving research and production.

"This is Matlal's virology team. The biological type of virus. The sort of thing that could be released wherever his digital network viruses seize control of hospitals and emergency services."

There was an utter silence in the room. These attacks weren't aimed directly at us—certainly Athanate and Were had little to fear from human viral infections. But it made sense from Matlal's point of view. Humanity outnumbered paranormals. This evil Basilikos strategy addressed that.

"And it gets worse," Salar said as she put a third photo on the screen. Not an organizational diagram, but a scheduling diagram.

This one was clearer, and I could see the dates. I could also see someone had amended them with a pen, overwriting the dates for completion of 'stockpiling', 'transport' and 'delivery'. Completion of stockpiling was now scheduled for this week. Transport to target locations would start next week.

The delivery date was a codeword, but the shock of it was going to work its way into my nightmares. Sometime in the next couple of weeks, Matlal would have the ability to devastate the US.

My voice felt strained. "*Stockpiling*. Where?" I asked.

Salar brought up a new image, a map of Yucatán peninsula, covering four Mexican provinces and two bordering countries to the south.

"We don't know for sure. Matlal has three main sites here, and he regularly visits all three, so our argument is it'll be one or more of these. On something this important, he doesn't trust anyone enough to leave them on their own for too long."

She walked to the screen and pointed. "One here is his 'town house'. It's actually a gated estate the size of a town on the northern outskirts of Mérida, the capital of the Yucatán province. That's where he spends most of his time, but we don't think he stores things there. Access to the estate is too public, too visible for everyday use, but it's probably where he has a reaction force for emergencies."

"Lucky we're not going there," muttered Yelena. "We couldn't assault a place like that, surrounded by a city full of innocent people."

Salar pointed down in the south, where the next Mexican province bordered the little country of Belize. "He has a place out here. It's remote. Very inaccessible, hidden in the jungle."

"We don't think that's a good place for stockpiling," David said. "Too small, poor road access, and the transport schedules suggest somewhere less remote. It might be where he has the biological virus development facility. Which leaves stockpiling to site number three."

He pointed to an area on the border between the provinces of Yucatán and Campeche. "Still isolated. The property is huge and well defended. Surrounded by jungle with limited access, but there's one well-maintained road, and it has its own airfield, which is long enough for a jet to land."

"Shit," Leyla said. "You're talking about Xibalbá."

Salar nodded.

"For God's sake! It's a fucking fortress!"

Salar nodded again, letting the anger wash off her. "We already have the outline of a plan we produced for Vega Martine. Operation Xorso. Vega Martine authorized funding so the resources would be waiting if the button was ever pressed."

"If we're right," David said, "a successful attack could destroy Matlal's stockpiles of viral weapons and the control center for electronic attacks. If we have the extraction capability at the end of the attack, this might also be where he stores his stockpiles of precious metals. More importantly, if we can take his servers, that would be his digital currency funds gone." He turned to look at me. "And the identity of every Matlal spy and traitor in the world."

He knew. He understood.

In that moment, it felt like all the air in the room had been sucked out.

The meeting and everyone in it receded. I was back in Los Angeles. With Diana. In therapy. Making a list of enemies, so that my hate became a tangible, controllable thing. Something I could lock away.

Matlal and Vega Martine and the alphas of the Rocky Mountain packs. Colonel Peterson, who'd been put in charge of the Ops 4 group and had been the one instructing the scientists to experiment on me like a lab rat. They were known. I could put names and faces to them.

And then there was the one I could not name or put a face to. The one behind Peterson, because sure as shit, a colonel in the army didn't have the juice to do what he did without someone *very* high up in the government.

Askrynos, Diana called him. Or her. From an old Athanate myth: the Masked Demon. The hidden evil. The one who cannot be seen.

Askrynos. The name pulsed with hate in my stomach.

David was continuing, but it was as if he were speaking from the end of a long corridor, far away.

Yelena's arms slipping around me brought me back.

"I'm okay," I whispered. "I'm okay."

She didn't let me go.

"That's if we succeed beyond all reasonable expectations," Leyla was saying, but the tone of her voice said something different. She was starting to come onside—although not without a struggle. "And I gotta point out, an unsuccessful attack would leave us dead or worse; isolated in the heart of Matlal territory."

"Then we plan for that contingency and put in place emergency extractions," Mirela said.

That was whistling in the dark. Yes, it was the sort of planning we'd done in Ops 4-10, but that had been extracting small teams with an infrastructure in place to achieve it. We weren't going into the Mexican jungles to assault a fortress with 'small teams'. We didn't have the US military's infrastructure to call on.

But I wasn't focused on that.

Someone high in the US government had interfered with Ops 4-10 towards the end. Given what they did, Askrynos had to be someone *high* in the government. Someone who'd ordered people to do experiments on me that they probably wouldn't have done on an animal.

Someone who had to still be in a position to damage Emergence.

And if we got Matlal's servers, we got Askrynos.

David wasn't finished. He was still looking at me.

"Xibalbá is run by someone you know. Former colonel of Ops 4-16. Peterson."

Chapter 44

There were things on the good side. We had a debate going on that distracted the teams from their losses and provided a sense of common purpose. My husband arrived at Haven with a new contingent of El Paso Were to be integrated into the Denver pack and came down to hug me. The stale coffee got thrown out and the kitchens produced food.

On the bad side, I still didn't want House Tucek or House Basynia going into any kind of fighting situation yet, and hadn't worked out exactly what was wrong, let alone how to deal with it. And yet, I had to. There was no way we could pull this off without House Tucek's inside knowledge and expertise in the area.

"We'll use wolves instead," Alex growled into my ear when he heard that.

"As well," I replied. There hadn't been a way of persuading Alex that he wouldn't be part of whatever attack we came up with.

The discussion had split into streams, like some crazy paranormal convention. One stream was concentrating on how we'd go about assaulting a fort in the middle of the Yucatán jungle, as well as destroying his laboratory, which was even more isolated. I let them run with that one for the moment, because Mirela was downloading her original plan from the secure server she'd stored it on, and I needed to see that before I thought about the practicalities.

Alex was muttering that their transport system had to be the best target.

I disagreed. I was mainly listening to the alternate stream discussion about what Matlal was trying to achieve. The favored theory was blackmail—wipe out one city and threaten the rest. But what would he be demanding? Even if the US surrendered, Matlal didn't have enough people to run the country. If he killed too many, what was he taking over? It didn't make sense.

The trouble was, I could see the worst case make sense. Reduce the world to the point where Basilikos *could* take over, even if that destroyed almost everything.

And even that would be merciful compared to letting Quetzalcoatl into the world.

When Mirela and David had downloaded the outline plans House Tucek had made, Salar give us a picture tour of Xibalbá.

The locals apparently believed it was a military installation, and it looked the part.

It was a fortress, a square, measuring about a thousand yards a side and surrounded by a reinforced concrete wall and double fences of razor wire, twenty feet high. Each corner of the compound had an armored lookout tower with three heavy machine guns, each covering over ninety degrees with plenty of overlap. The ground the guns overlooked was bare of vegetation and flat for about a hundred yards before the jungle took over. There were more watchtowers at the halfway point on three sides. On the fourth side was the entrance, and it had a machine gun tower on either side of a barrier gate.

Entry to the compound was also protected by a sandbagged chicane—a road purposely constructed with bends so tight a large truck couldn't turn.

On the far side of the compound from the entrance, there was a concrete aircraft runway, lined with hangars. House Tucek's intelligence notes on the side listed them as containing aircraft and anti-aircraft defenses.

I raised my eyebrows as I read the list. They had a mix of surveillance aircraft, the kind used for inspecting pipelines or patrolling borders, equipped with lookdown radar and infrared detectors. A couple of them were manned, but the majority were drones. The notes said they patrolled up to twenty miles out from the compound, which was within the range of the radar and comms equipment I could see on a control tower alongside the hangars. So the area was patrolled from the air and on the ground. I could see the thinking behind the design of the defenses: it would be impossible for a body of troops, large enough to attack the fortress, to sneak up on it.

If anyone tried to use the airstrip as their point of entry, the defenses were even more extreme. In one of the hangars, they had a Russian anti-aircraft tank called the Tunguska. It had twin 30mm cannons on a turret and could also fire radar-controlled missiles. It was the sort of thing you'd use to shoot down a cruise missile. It was backed up by a couple of heat-seeking missile platforms. They were deployable in seconds.

This was all bad news.

I'd attacked a fortress before: Astilla de Luna, near Villa Ahumada, run by Mauricio Gálvez, the psychopathic alpha werewolf allied to Matlal. I'd left it in flames and rubble. But that had been a fortress designed by a madman. It had weaknesses. Poorly integrated defenses. Xibalbá had been designed by Colonel Petersen. He was evil, not crazy, and he'd obviously used the Ops 4 rulebook.

One last item of joy: he had Ops 4-16, the Nagas as we used to call them, to run the defenses.

The isolation and the surveillance would mean that it'd be impossible to approach with sufficient force without being seen. Once there, the design of that entrance meant that we couldn't ram our way in with a truck, the way we had at Astilla de Luna.

Ops 4 doctrine would have a lookout for HALO parachute attacks. The radar that swept the surrounding jungle for twenty miles in every direction would also have the capability to spot an aircraft flying overhead and might even pick up parachuting soldiers.

I wondered about a HALO jump from high enough and far away enough, using Ops 4 batsuits to glide in. Risky. But we didn't have that many suits anyway.

I couldn't see a way to breach the outer defenses, let alone take control of the site well enough to break into the 'bank', as the images called the building in the middle. That was where Salar said any stockpiles and computer systems would be.

One of many problems was that the bank had been designed to withstand attacks, and the entrance apparently had blast doors which would close within three minutes of an alarm sounding.

If you had already broken through, you could get to the bank quickly. There were roads inside the compound. It looked like a one-way system that ran from the entrance. I traced it out, turning right from the entrance. It went past a dining hall, covered recreation area and a medical center. At that point it split: a spur straight on to deliver fuel and ammunition to stores behind the aviation hangars, or a left to pass the bank, then left again to run past barracks and admin blocks, finally left to the entrance again.

But how to get to the bank in less than three minutes?

House Tucek obviously had some ideas. I'd wait and see.

In the meantime, I was looking at a picture of the bank taken from a stealthy drone some distance away.

"What are these structures on the roof?" I asked Salar.

"We're not sure. Their security is very tight. I think they might be air conditioning vents of some kind. They'd need something like that for their servers."

"Hmm."

It was possible. The structures were stubby towers and laid out in an odd pattern—it was as if the bank had four sections, and each section had one of these towers in each corner.

I didn't like not knowing so much about the layout of the target. In fact, I hated the whole idea of a rushed plan, but Matlal wasn't going to give us any time. We had to go soon, and we had to go with House Tucek's lead.

I shook my head.

"It's not impregnable," Mirela said from behind me.

I snorted.

"For instance, there's a delivery," she went on. "Every two weeks. Fuel, food and general supplies. They use a contractor. That contractor looks very like a normal trucking business, but it's ours."

I looked sideways at her. "Are you going Trojan Horse on me?"

"No. I'm more a Mad Max fan. I prefer leathers and guns to skirts and swords."

I rolled my eyes. "Okay, but you can get inside?"

She shook her head. "Not that way. All the trucks are stopped outside. The drivers stop the fuel tankers here." She tapped an area to the side of the gate. "They're not allowed inside the compound. They sit in a shed about fifty yards away and wait. The guards test it's fuel, then move some of the sandbags to allow another guard to drive the tanker in, unload the fuel and drive it back out again. Takes two to three hours. Entrance gets a double guard during that time."

She pointed to another area on the other side of the gate. "While that's happening, the container trucks stop here, up against the outer fence. Again, the drivers wait in the shed while a crane unloads the new containers. Once that's done, the empty containers from last delivery are loaded back onto the trucks. Takes about four hours. When everything's finished, the trucks form a convoy and leave. After they're gone, they come out with motorized trolleys to check and unpack the supply containers."

"They have guards overseeing the unloading?"

She nodded. "And they're vigilant. They run four six-hour watches— morning, afternoon, evening and night. They split guards up into crews, with each crew operating on a cycle that ensures they get a different watch every day, and watchtower duty gets relief after two hours. They've got good food, air-conditioned barracks and recreation facilities. They get four days to go off-base for R&R every other week. Once a month they're on patrol duty in the jungle for a week. They're fresh, alert, motivated and well-trained. They're not going to miss any of the usual tricks."

"Which means you have some unusual tricks up your sleeve."

She smiled, evilly.

"What do you know about triethyl borane?"

The name had featured in Ops 4-10 training on explosives. I frowned, struggling to recall the details. They gradually surfaced. "TEB to its friends. It's one of those crazy chemicals that explodes on contact with air. They use it to light up rocket engines."

She looked at me, and I looked at her.

"You crazy bitch," I said. "How the hell?"

"A membrane bag of TEB suspended inside the tanker. The membrane is too weak to hold the TEB unless it's floating in the fuel and supported by the liquid around it. When the guards test it, they'll think the tanker's full of fuel. But when the surrounding fuel is pumped out, the membrane tears under its own weight and the TEB comes into contact with the air. *Big* bang. It'll take out the whole fuel dump, and since the aviation bowsers are up against the wall there, it'll take out them *and* the nearest hangar. Also, since they're located in the blast radius, the control tower, their radar dish and their whole communications installation."

I laughed and looked back at the compound diagram. "But not the ammunition depot?"

"They have baffles between the two. Earth berms forty foot high. Standard practice for fire precaution. This isn't going to be a standard fire though. It *might* blow up the ammo. Still, we're not depending on the explosion to take the ammo dump out. Its primary objective is really the comms and radar. Its secondary is to provide a distraction."

"Hell of a distraction. I have an idea why the radar is an objective—you're bringing in helicopters to get us out."

"Right first time. But the first helicopter on the scene, in less than five minutes from the blast, will be a Hind."

I shook my head. She was using the NATO reference for the Russians' helicopter gunship, the Mil Mi-24. They were available on the black market, but to have acquired one, along with the expertise to fly and maintain them—deep pockets and a real long view.

These had all been part of Vega Martine's arsenal, but Mirela had been trusted with the storage.

"Followed by a couple of big transport helicopters to extract us with our loot, which we will have stolen from the bank," she continued. "After destroying the virus store and ripping all the drives out of the servers, of course."

"Whoa! Back up. Missing whole sections of this plan."

Mirela hadn't tied all the details down yet, but she started to outline an entertaining but seemingly incredible heist for me.

It was going to be difficult to make this work, even in the best of circumstances.

I had to stop Mirela when Pia signaled that I was needed elsewhere.

"You and your team have to lead the planning. You have the knowledge of the parts in place," I said. "But you're going to need help."

I called Annie over and told her to put together a team including David and three Ops 4-10 vets.

"David has a good feel for what resources we can put into it, and the vets have experience of these kinds of operations. Alex will coordinate for the Were. Use them all."

Mirela nodded.

I let Pia lead me away. Apparently, there were House issues for me to deal with.

More of them.

Chapter 45

"We have problems," Bian greeted me angrily as I walked in.

Diana held up one hand and everybody else was silent.

Everybody else being Gwen, Tullah, Tolly, Flint and Kane. I sensed Kaothos, but she didn't manifest. Pia, Yelena and Theris came in behind me.

"We have a series of interlocking problems," Diana said. She was staring at Theris, and I got the idea he was one of them.

He didn't wilt, like most people would have under that gaze. Instead, he moved forward to stand in front of her, knelt on one knee and then bowed his head.

He slipped into the older Carpathian dialect. "I am here seen. I am named Theris, House Zalissia, Kyrios Kryfokratos, Elder-elect of the Domain of Carpathia. Now kneels the Domain in the presence of the Kumemnon, and we are much honored by it. My Blood is yours."

He raised his head but remained kneeling.

"I am appointed an emissary of the Council, to call back to your mind that your Seat remains unfilled and our welcome undimmed by time."

Oh, hell.

Diana was an Elder of Carpathia?

She huffed.

"An offer unsought, unclaimed and undeserved, as you well know. I suspect a pretty compliment to distract me." Her eyes narrowed and she switched back to English. "I hear you have been appointed pelea to Amber. A position of great trust, with a need for great loyalty. Since it's a question we will all face in Emergence, let me ask you, Elder-elect Zalissia, how you might be loyal to two masters?"

And hell again. I'd seen through Theris' mission, and it was stupid not to think Diana would too.

I spoke before he could answer.

"I've talked with Theris about this. I'm satisfied by his replies about his position as my pelea."

And I'd rather not discuss them and get everybody else upset over something I regard as a vital benefit.

Diana saw all that. Her lips thinned and her look promised that the discussion wasn't over. But she didn't pursue the topic.

"Sit somewhere, House Zalissia. I might be interested in your opinions at some stage, in which case I will ask."

Ouch.

I'd never heard Diana being quite so sharp before. Theris didn't seem upset, to his credit. He just bowed again and sank into a comfortable lotus position, joining Pia and Tullah on the floor.

Bian was pacing, and there was no room between Gwen, Tullah and Tolly, so I got Flint and Kane to make some space on their sofa and sat between them. Yelena adopted Rita's habit of leaning against a wall and becoming so still as to be invisible.

"We've had the report of your visit to the Temple of Serpents from Bian's perspective, which leaves almost everything vital out," Diana said to me. "Let's hear it from you."

"I'm one of the problems?"

The fact that they all waited for Diana to respond told me I was.

"I hope not," she said.

She wasn't being subtle about reading my eukori.

I could see the issue. I'd been very inward looking. I'd taken decisions and trusted their outcomes without thinking about others.

Like the problems I'd caused Bian.

It was reasonable that they were concerned about what I'd gone through, how it might have changed me, and how it all might affect them.

Tullah confirmed it. "Kaothos was startled when you modified her substantiation. Now we've found out that you took over and changed the shield that Flint and Kane were running."

"Improved it," Flint said.

"Power *and* sustainability," Kane added. "Very neat. We learned from it."

"Elegant," Flint ended.

It seemed the Lost Boys were still fans. We were a tight fit on the sofa, which must have been why Flint's arm was casually draped around my shoulders, and Kane's hand happened to be resting on my knee. I concentrated on *not* thinking about teasing them, 'cos sure as taxes, that *arrangement* I conjured up last time would be sensed by everyone in the room.

Concentrate.

"Modifications you haven't been trained to make, and yet you performed without effort," Gwen said.

Her eyes were icy blue, so Bryn was in residence.

"I'm still me," I said. "And I don't have a great deal of power unless I channel someone else's. But I have new skills, and they've come to me from the Temple and from the person who eventually became the Queen of Diamonds." I hurried on. "Which is not as bad as it sounds."

I took them through, from the Grove to the Temple, up to the point we returned to rescue House Labastide. Like everything that happens in the spirit world, that part seemed even more of a dream now, but I told it as clearly as I could.

At the end, Diana turned to Tolly. "Thoughts? Anything in the Dark Library about this Temple or the Grove?"

"Nothing supported. Endless tales of magic temples and gods as trees. Nothing I can be sure is factual," he said, and turned his face toward me, as if he could actually see me. "Many, many tales of evil serpents."

"Athanate get called 'snakes', especially by the shifters," Tullah said, "so we shouldn't be leaping to associate serpents with evil."

"A dragon is a sort of serpent," I murmured.

Kaothos, invisible but present, heard me and hissed with laughter.

I got a 'not taking it seriously' look from Pia.

Diana intervened again. "We may proceed with humor, so long as we proceed, Pia."

"I would be *most* interested to talk to them," Tolly muttered quietly. "My library has gaps which must be filled."

I chuckled and then held up my hands.

"Homor aside. Look at my aura and my eukori. I'm not shielding myself. Bryn, Kaothos, Diana. Look. I'm me. No serpents in my head. If I could fool you about that, and they were evil, you'd have lost already."

I stared at Gwen, who nodded to concede the point. I could feel Bryn in my head, but it wasn't as scary as it once would have been. I trusted her, like I trusted Kaothos and Diana.

"There *are* things I'm worried about," I went on. "Without realizing it, I've managed to make a spirit connection from the Temple to the Grove, which they wanted and needed, but that means we need to help them defend the Temple. If Quetzalcoatl gets in there, then he has a direct path to the physical world and he doesn't need Matlal."

"If they're so powerful, why do they need our help?" Pia asked.

I shrugged. "They weren't clear. Maybe we're stronger together, and this is persuasion to enter this alliance. Maybe we have complementary skills."

"I think I understand how Nai, if she really is what the Queen of Diamonds was before she became evil, is complementary," Diana said. "But outside of the spirit world, you've entered alliances precipitously. I'm not sure what Tucek and Basynia add to our capabilities. And if they do, how trustworthy are they?"

I replied: "I have to point out, if not for Mirela and Salar, three of us here would be dead. And Donatienne saved us in the battle at the Temple, at the cost of her own life."

Yelena cleared her throat, startling those who'd forgotten she was there.

"Add me to your list. I was Carpathian. I became a spy against Basilikos. I was never under the scrutiny that Mirela was, but I had to appear Basilikos. I did things that trouble me still. Have I proved my loyalty? Is my worth doubted?"

She paused to let anyone argue against it. No one did.

"And Diana, you work in the same way. Labastide was part of the Eastern Seaboard, so was an enemy. You take Solange, Diakon Labastide, to your bed. And I think Salar, Diakon Tucek, no?"

Diana's smile was thin. She didn't confirm or deny.

Yelena continued. "I hear Jen and David, they joke about this. They call it 'horizontal integration'. Body and Blood. This is an old Athanate method to bind Houses together."

"It's certainly a well-established way to cement unions between allies or neutrals," Diana replied. "I wouldn't use it as an initial gambit on an enemy. Yet, from what I hear, Carpathians are claiming this sort of behavior is intrinsic."

She was looking at Theris, but he indicated Yelena should respond.

Yelena raised her eyebrows thoughtfully. "Intrinsic, like part of the attributes of our Blood? Maybe. Difficult to tell. On the other hand, it could just be wisdom accumulated over time. We have an old saying in Ukraine: 'No enemy so defeated as one who becomes your friend'."

That had a deepness to it, as Yelena's sayings usually did. I would certainly find it easier to argue that as a reason for my actions, than 'I'm expected to do paladin stuff'."

Diana was quiet for a moment, absorbing what had been said. And probably what had not. Then she turned back to Theris: "Is that how you think of Panethus, House Zalissia? An enemy that is defeated and now your friend?"

"We were never your enemies, Kumemnon."

"What's a little land grab between friends?" Bian snapped.

Theris shook his head. "It suits Altau to appear to be conciliatory to others in the Assembly, while it serves his purposes. Altau knew Panethus was over-extended in the Caucasus. This gave him an excuse to rationalize. Relocating those strong and well-established Houses improves your infrastructure in the US and removes places of contention between Panethus and the Hidden Path." He shrugged. "And if we really wanted those territories that have been ceded to us in the New York Assembly, we could have taken them at any time since Altau moved his base to America."

I'd pieced most of that together myself, but it helped me to hear him say it.

Bian didn't like it, but she didn't argue.

"This uncertainty of what we mean by 'us' makes our current problems more difficult to deal with," Diana said. "We'll come back to it, but we need to see it in context. Bian, Pia, please update the others."

For a moment, I was just completely focused that Diana had said 'what we mean by us', and then called them 'our' problems. It grounded me. It reattached me to Haven and the people in it. Pack. House. Coven. My family.

Bian spoke. "The last Assembly is officially over, and what we have now is a group of paranormals debating how to form a new Assembly. A lot of attendees left, ceding their voting rights to those they trusted in the group remaining. It has helped speed things up. We've had a warning they will reach the end of stage one deliberations in a couple of days. The outline of how all parties will form the new Assembly of the Paranormal will have been agreed. The existing group will then disperse, and the leaders of all factions will reconvene here, in Haven, to finalize and announce the new structure."

After all the delays, they had suddenly moved with stunning speed.

Bian paused while most of us reeled our jaws back up before continuing: "It's a nightmare. Haven is the only choice because it's the only venue that's both large enough and secure enough. But there's the catch, right there. Internal security will be bad enough making sure there are no incidents with former enemies together in one space, but Haven will become a major target for Matlal with that concentration of leaders here."

"Okay, but not something you haven't handled before," I said. "I mean there was an Assembly held here last year."

"At which point, as Diakon Altau, I was able to demand security details to be sent from each Panethus House in sufficient time to train them to coordinate." Bian hadn't stopped pacing. If she'd been a cat, her tail would have been thrashing. "No one dared question it then. Livia now has that title and sent the requisitions but tagged me to handle it while she stayed inside the closed sessions of the Assembly. Some Houses have responded, but *all* the traditionalists have refused."

"Giving what reasons?" I asked, afraid I knew the answer.

Diana spelled it out. "Lots of words, meaning nothing. It's clear they still regard you as an abomination, you are *epitre* and therefore Haven is in quarantine. They want their security details to guard their delegates against contagion, and not coordinate."

"The same Houses," Bian snarled, "who are *demanding* we send our Ops 4-10 veterans to bolster *their* security in *their* domains. They want permanent deployments. They want them as Aspirants and kin."

"Not even the end of it," Pia said. "All the committees that Correia set up? They say they have an authority that cannot be revoked except by the new Assembly, when it convenes. The one responsible for overseeing the experiment with your infusion abilities: they say we must move to the next phase. They are demanding all your ehvasi be sent out to Houses to evaluate immediately. Even with the traditionalists refusing, there are enough Houses demanding an ehvasi to account for all of them."

That did it. I'd come to the boil. "No!" I shouted.

Diana made a calming gesture. Kane squeezed my thigh.

It helped a little that I could see no one was in favor of agreeing to these demands.

"What are they all trying to achieve?" Gwen frowned. "It's contradictory."

Diana smiled thinly. "I know paranoia is a House trait, but I don't think there is a coordinated strategy here. It's just a lot of different idiocy coming together at the same time. *But...*" she looked around. "It demands a coordinated and politically aware strategy from us."

She focused on me.

"Coordinated because we must address all the issues. Politically aware because Skylur's position with the traditional Panethus Houses is shaky after his concessions to bind the Hidden Path into the deal."

"On security, the Panethus Houses from the Caucasus could help with teams," Yelena suggested. "They're already arriving, and they've had decades of conflict to sharpen their skills."

Bian shook her head. "Only their advance security teams, and all of them are focused on surveying their new domains. The arrivals of the full Houses will be a distraction more than a benefit in the timescales we're talking about."

She stopped pacing and sat on the floor next to Diana, who rested a hand on her back while she finished. "They will also have their hands full. Skylur has disbanded the Eastern Seaboard, and their domains are to be handed over to the incoming Houses. The junior members of the dissolved Houses will be taken in, while the senior members will be exiled back to Europe and absorbed into loyal Houses there."

Skylur had gone nuclear on them, and I couldn't say I disagreed, however much I'd tried to duck the problem when I'd been in the Assembly. I'd tried to be conciliatory, and Skylur's decisions told me the time to be conciliatory was at an end. Emergence was here, and we needed something dramatic to end the infighting.

Things fell into place.

"All of which leaves us with impossible shortfalls if we do as we are told," I said. "We need security, which needs to be in place and prepared for when the new Assembly's leaders arrive. We need troops for an attack on Matlal, which needs to be done now or we lose our advantage. We have concerns about some of us, meaning my sub-Houses. We need something Skylur can use, but we have no time for careful, gradual strategies."

Diana nodded, and I got an inkling that this entire meeting had been artfully managed by her, and with the aim that we were all of one mind about what I was going to say.

"So… the only option is to *not* do as we are told. I have recommendations. They are unconventional and confrontational. They affect everyone, so everyone here has to be on board."

Diana smiled.

Chapter 46

I walked back into the crowded briefing room. Silence rippled out.

An Athanate House was always aware of the mood of its Mistress. A pack sensed its alpha. Pissed off was not good. Shifters started that sub-audible growl that they do. Athanate eyes started to vamp out as if the threat were right here.

It was and it wasn't.

Diana's management of my 'problems' meeting brought me a clarity of thought I hadn't had in the last couple of days. I was still angry at all the things I'd been told in the meeting, but Diana had made me focus that anger usefully.

The silence wasn't rippling fast enough, so I jumped up onto a table and clapped my hands.

A few of the Were thought of making a joke about it but shut that down quickly.

"I know I have no right to demand the world makes sense, but what we have now is a bunch of completely contradictory orders, requests and responsibilities. What we used to call a clusterfuck in the army."

Snorts from the Ops 4-10 people in the room.

I outlined the situation. As I went along, Athanate and Were reacted differently to the emotion coming off me. Athanate went still and hyper-focused. Were began to stir as if they wanted to pace. Adepts... Gwen had followed me in, and she was as impossible to read as ever, but I could feel the spirit guides of others like I could feel the cool breeze coming in the French doors which were open behind me.

The first real swell of anger came from my ehvasi at being called abominations. But the good thing about it was it came from the whole room. Regardless of how splintered they were as a group internally, when the insult came from outside the group, they were a group.

"I take it literally. My Blood is yours, my community. What I am, you are too. I'll give them this: there's only one response possible to all this shit. We're not taking it."

A few stirred anxiously at that, which showed they were thinking ahead.

"We reject the Agiagraphos."

The Athanate in the room went into shock, and the rest of them were sensitive enough that they registered it.

"For the Adepts and Were who don't understand the Athanate laws, you can tell from your buddies' reactions that call used to carry a sentence of death," I said. "But even the Assembly has to agree the Agiagraphos has been put aside. Trying to keep humanity from being aware of us isn't working any longer. That was law number one, and the foundation of all the Agiagraphos laws and restrictions. The rest of it has a lot of stuff that used to be useful, and a pile of crap that no longer has any relevance. This House will not acknowledge any guiding philosophy that includes declaring us to be abominations and outcasts. The true situation is the Agiagraphos has rejected us, so we reject it."

The Were hadn't ever liked the formality of regulation that the Athanate had. I wasn't going to have to push hard to get them on side. Lots were nodding already. Yeah, I'd get to them later and see if they were still nodding.

"Pia is more diplomatic than I am..." cue laughs around the room, "so I'm going to let her message the other Houses. No ehvasi of this House will infuse the Aspirants of any House other than Houses that form associations with us on the basis of Blood oaths. This House won't even provide security for other Houses in their domains, let alone Aspirants for them to infuse, other than Houses formally associated with us. To that end, all the Ops 4-10 teams have been recalled. We will cease interacting with any House that continues to call us abominations."

I leaped down from the table and grabbed the nearest Were I recognized.

"Don't get to thinking this is just about the Athanate either, Ethan. We've made lots of friends, but most of the packs in the country think Were and Athanate shouldn't mix. That's before we get to what they think about skinwalkers."

Heads turned, and no one had difficulty picking out the towering figures of Nick Gray and Ursula Tennyson. No one would have any misunderstanding about what I meant. They were skinwalkers and I was proud they were Denver pack, whatever other alphas thought.

I rounded on an Adept I also recognized, a guy who'd come to join us from Tucson.

"And you, Mateo. How do you feel about being called an abomination because you're in a coven with Athanate and outlaw shamans?"

He pursed his lips as he thought about it, and I got a positive feeling, so I waited.

"Good," he said, looking up and grinning. "In fact, damn good. Vivan los marginados!"

"Vivan las abominaciones!" someone called back, then "Vivamos como vivimos!"

Others joined in.

Yeah. *Outcasts. Abominations.* And then; *let us live as we live.*

I'd take that.

It was getting rowdy, so I had to raise my voice.

"We're not in revolt. This is not a new political party. You all know that we've drafted a constitution, and it applies to everyone in our community. We'll publish it on the paranormal bulletin boards so everyone will know who we are and what we stand for, because it's time to draw those lines. The new Assembly has to untangle the Agiagraphos to incorporate the other paranormals and the new reality of interaction with humanity. They could take our constitution as a starter, but that's not why we made it. We made it because it will define us. And we didn't broadcast it to force others to be like us, but to accept us for who we are if they want to associate with us."

A voice called out: "What if the new Assembly orders us to do something?"

Leyla. Doing her union rep bit. It was a good question.

"We will obey orders that do not conflict with our personal rights. We'll provide security for the new Assembly. We'll go to war against Matlal. But we won't hand over members to Houses who consider us abominations. We will do what we know is right."

It got quieter. It was a difficult point, but I sensed I had enough of them on my side, and I didn't want this to go on disrupting work that needed to be done.

"Now, to each their tasks. We have to attack Matlal's fortress, and the plan we will use will be based on House Tucek's planning. Mirela will lead the planning, and the assault. Annie and a team of Ops4-10 vets will advise. Alex will provide coordination with the Were, and Gwen with the Adepts. My only real requirement is that Colonel Laine should be satisfied with the plan before we push the button on the mission. Bian will be selecting a group to plan the security for the new Assembly meeting, but that comes later."

There was shuffling and stirring.

"Those of you in the planning team know who you are, and you need to stay. The rest of you, I want you outside."

They streamed into the gardens, and I closed the French doors behind us to leave the planners in peace.

This wasn't the whole community, by any stretch, but about a hundred of them. Athanate. Were. Adepts. Humans.

Theris muttered about security, and I laughed. If we weren't safe here, there wouldn't be any meaning to the word for us.

As I led them away from the mansion, I started reorganizing them. They'd joined me in their little groups, and I didn't want that. Haven had terraced lawns, each successive one about four foot lower, and there were five of them. A path ran through with stone steps down. In the time it took to get to the last and largest lawn, everyone was mixed in.

Walking outside was good. Shoulders got less stiff. Deeper breaths were taken. People spoke quietly. Ther were some laughs. A little flirting went on. My wolfy hearing picked up one or two excellent put-downs that made me smile.

They were wondering what they were doing here.

"I do this with the packs," I said, as we finally came to a halt. "I mix them up and I make them look at the people standing next to them."

The werewolves knew this from the rituals, and they took the hint. They started introducing themselves along with the spiel I'd worked out for the pack ceremonies—*I'm your buddy. I have your back. If you stumble, I will lift you up. You have my word. You are my pack.*

It worked its way through the crowd, a little self-consciously. Some of them said 'House' or 'coven' instead of 'pack', 'oath' instead of 'word', and that was fine. All one thing to me.

"Are we gonna get naked and dance?" That was Ben, from the Cimarron pack.

I part-changed and snarled at him.

Despite being little more than a cub, he knew where he was with me, and he snarled back.

To an outsider, it would have looked and sounded real. It wasn't. It was the kind of mock aggression that the Were loved. The Athanate and the Adepts here could sense it was in fun. Even the Ops 4-10 vets were laughing.

Because they were all part of this one oddball community.

I changed my head back and laughed along with them.

"No dancing today. Or not right now, anyway."

This wasn't the right place for that.

Out in Bitter Hooks or behind the ranch at Coykuti, the ground itself would seem to shiver to the echoes of wolves. The cool air that flowed down out of the darkness of the mountains would have the pack's scent to it.

Haven wasn't like that, and the issue I needed to talk about wasn't just werewolves. This had to be for the whole community, and it was even bigger than saving halfies.

It was still spring, and the winds that slid down the flanks of the Rockies didn't have time to warm up before they reached Haven. I shivered, despite the bright sunshine. The mountains seemed so close and clear. I felt like I could see every face in the crowd around me, hear every heartbeat, every sigh of breath.

"War's coming," I said. They went silent and my words dropped into a pool of waiting. "Not because we want it, but because it has to be. Change is coming. We're about to Emerge to humanity and drop the secrecy that has guided so much of what we've done. At the same time our community, the one right here, is going to be the tip of the spear and there will be a cost."

No laughing now.

"When I was in Ops 4-10, we never left anyone behind. That's good. What wasn't so good was the dead came back and there was no one place where we could lay them to rest and honor them for their service and sacrifice, because Ops 4-10 was shrouded in secrecy, just as the paranormal world has been."

"That's changed. The field behind me will now be a cemetery and place of remembrance for those of our community who will give their lives. Unless they've indicated otherwise, those who died in the Atrax operation will be buried here. Others, like Donatienne, well, we'll respect their wishes as much as we are able, and their names will be on our memorial."

Some of them stared at me, some of them looked past me at the meadow drowsing in the spring sunshine.

My eukori reached out and pulled them all into a single shared sensation, the connection that the Carpathians called a communion. I'd felt it before, when I'd bound the Threefold Spiral Coven in Ireland to an oath. Today, I felt even stronger. I could feel my aura filtering into the eukori. Making my will stronger. Strong enough to bind every soul here to me.

It made me feel like a goddess. Powerful. Righteous.

And that made me understand why the Carpathians thought that their faith and their philosophy of morality was so important. Because they felt like this, in the depths of their communion. They tasted the power to make followers into blind believers, and they feared it.

Maybe I needed to talk to Vera again. To understand how to tiptoe on the brink of this power and not fall in.

I drew back my eukori, subsided, breathed in a lungful of crisp, clean air, fresh off the mountains, and spoke again.

"Haven will be your home. It will gather you, gather us. In time, it will become our testament: to what we were, what we are, and what we will be."

They were silent, Athanate, Were, Adept and human, listening to me.

"Those who chose this path, to be part of this community… some of them will come home to lie here, in the field behind me. Others may decide this community's not for them. They're free to leave. Those that stay, we'll be choosing what we are, and we'll be part of what we become. But to do that, we have to know who we are. And we don't yet."

"What makes us *us*? Oaths? Obligations to an Assembly that thinks we're abominations? Rules? Shared magic?"

"None of those are good enough. Look around you, at your House, your pack, your coven, your team. That's why you'll fight when we need to. For those you're standing with now. We choose today. This evening, Alex will take the wolves out to Bitter Hooks, and they'll get their dancing and running in. There will be one Call, one pack. Gwen will meet with the Adepts and taste their aura. There will be one coven, one purpose. I'll meet each and every Athanate and exchange Blood. We will be one House, one Blood. If you're not Were, Adept or Athanate, pick a group and join in. You don't have to give your Blood or your body, but you have to give your commitment."

"This is for real. If you can't do this, then you can't be in this community."

Chapter 47

As a group, it went down quite well.

For individuals, I expected it was going to be variable, which was why I asked for Leyla first. *Ordered* her, when she tried to evade.

Sometimes it's best to go with the top-down hierarchy, and sometimes you do it the other way. Mouthy trade union rep first.

"How do you want me?" she said, when she finally walked into my room. *Oooh.*

Attitude you could cut flesh with.

"Alive," I said, and thought a bit more. "Fulfilled. Valued by the House and reciprocating that."

She snorted. Flicked her untidy hair.

"For someone who supposedly hates politics, Kyria, you make some marvelously political statements."

"Amber," I said.

"No, *Kyria*. I'm Leyla, but you are very definitely Kyria."

"Why?" I patted the sofa next to me, but she was pacing like a wolf.

"Why? I know your opinion on the Agiagraphos, but we could start there. Kyrios or Kyria are titles that are a courtesy to those who infused you, but also a term of respect for the Master or Mistress of a large House."

I'd never thought of House Farrell as being large and I guessed that showed, because she went straight on, walking to and fro across the floor, waving her arms.

"Yes, large. Your original House was a couple of Athanate and some kin, but in the course of the last year, you seem to have picked up a Carpathian Diakon, Yelena Vylkove, with kin, the renegade diazoun House, Amanda Lloyd, with kin, and of course nothing straightforward about outlaw Adepts as kin, is there? And now House Tucek. Including me. And Basynia. That would make you a medium sized House, achieved in your first year, and probably worthy of the title Kyria on its own. But nooo. Now you also have twenty ehvasi. All of that's ignoring that you have half a regiment of Ops 4-10 veterans, most of whom qualify as Aspirants. You're co-alpha of the Denver pack, and you also regard your pack as being part of your House, to the extent that you have a second Diakon who's a were-cougar and isn't even Athanate."

She stopped, glaring at me, hands on hips.

"That, by any definition, is a *large* House," she said. "And that means the Agiagraphos says you have earned the title of Kyria."

I nodded. "You left out the coven, but of course I'm only a member of that, not the boss, so I'm guessing that wouldn't count."

She laughed. A short laugh, cut off abruptly, as if it had surprised her. As if she wanted to remain angry but wasn't sure why.

"I admit I'm blurring the lines between pack and House," I went on, "partly because I believe all my ehvasi are eventually going to turn out hybrid. But I think the Assembly has come down on the Agiagraphos title of 'Abomination' for me, rather than 'Kyria'."

That got another cut-off laugh.

"Really? All your ehvasi will be hybrid?"

"If it's purely a matter of my Blood, I don't see why it would work for some and not others, even if it takes more time or more belief. In fact, if you keep exchanging Blood with me, I don't see why you wouldn't end up being able to shapeshift. You already do an Athanate version of it, when your fangs manifest."

She blinked.

"Oh."

I hadn't intended that to come out until I'd talked to Mirela and others. It was just my theory. Or maybe it was just the Serpents' Gift showing me what lay behind the illusion that split the paranormal into groups.

I wanted more time to think about it, but I sensed a change in Leyla that I needed to explore.

"That got your attention. You like the idea of getting all furry and running with the pack, do you?"

"Nah," she made a dismissive gesture. "Seems like every shifter's a damned werewolf. Too many guys with narrow eyes, hard abs and excess attitude. Cougar... now *that* would be cool."

I managed to stop myself snorting at the idea she should be complaining about 'attitude'. I covered it with a shrug.

"I don't think shapeshifting is limited to one form of animal," I said. "If you're a shifter, you can learn new shapes. Don't see why you couldn't be a cougar."

I stopped. *Whoops.* More stuff I hadn't meant to talk about until I was sure.

"Errr... look, that's shifter heresy. I'd rather you didn't talk about that to werewolves yet. It needs—"

"It needs a careful, diplomatic, politically crafted revealing." She laughed outright. "Yeah. You're just the person for that. So, you're a heretic as well as an abomination in shifter terms. And I heard a rumor you've upset the Adept leadership because you not only have seduced Adepts into your

House, but they're the despicable, dangerous, out-of-control shamans as well."

"Strictly speaking, it was Amanda Lloyd who seduced them."

And it was the tip of the iceberg. Hecate Faith Hinton's real beef with me was more to do with T-cat.

Leyla was trying not to laugh.

"See, that's what's great about this. We're running through all these carefully maintained flowerbeds with our big, ugly combat boots on." She paused. "I started off saying you earned the title based on Athanate rules, but that's not why I'll call you Kyria. I'll use the title because I love what you're doing to all the stupid rules and institutions the paranormal world has built. Tear up the rule books. Seduce innocent Adepts to the dark side. Light the alphas' tails on fire. Bang the Assembly heads together until they see sense. I'm with you."

"It's a little—"

"Yeah. More nuanced. Got it. I'm a soldier, not a Diakon. Give me simple objectives, Kyria."

She'd stopped pacing and now stood right in front of me, hands back on hips, but body language all different. I patted the seat beside me again. It had gone better than I anticipated, so far, but I had a lot more necks to bite. Time to get it on.

"I'm not really one for polite side by side," she said. "Polite is for tea parties."

She mounted my thighs, knee to either side, got in my face, and while breaking eye contact for barely a second, in one smooth move, pulled her T shirt off.

No bra. No need.

Luckily, I'd been well trained in this deliberately provocative approach. Bian had done this to me. Didn't stop my heart stuttering, which I knew she knew, and was the probable cause of that little smirk.

Just normal Athanate business. Don't overreact.

Easier said than done, but I passed the test, it seemed. She broke eye contact, and I could trace the path her eyes took down my cheek and jaw, to my neck, as if it were her fingers instead. She lowered her head and kissed my throat.

Just a lamia. An Athanate neck kiss. A very, very sensual lamia. A very deliberately intense lamia.

She took a deep lungful of air. Tasting my marque. Tasting my reaction.

She whispered, and her voice had gone husky; all darkness, whiskey and smoke.

"I want," she said. "Mmm. I want your Blood, Kyria."

"I want you in my House, fully part of it, fully committed. Like I said, valued and returning that value."

Damn, but my voice had gone all raspy too. My jaws were aching.

She lifted her head and pressed my face against her neck. Fangs threatened to manifest at any second.

Slowly.

I inhaled. Took in her marque. Tucek. Hard-edged. Strong.

Want it.

Like two bubbles touching, our eukori merged. Sweetly, effortlessly.

"I give you my oath, Kyria. Body or Blood?"

For all her trashing Athanate traditions, she'd picked one more. An oath could be sealed with an exchange of Blood. Or 'body'. Sex basically. Or both.

"Blood," I said, with the sound of my heart and hers thundering in my ears.

"For now?"

She meant we'd get to the *body* bit later, but I turned it around.

"Forever."

I gripped her hair and pulled her back down until I could feel the dizzying thud of my throat pulse against her lips.

"Blood. Now and for ever," I gasped.

"I am yours to command, Kyria."

"Then bite me already, Leyla, damn you."

Her fangs sank into my throat. She tried to stretch it out, tried to linger over it, but she couldn't. She *pulled,* and our bodies burned with pleasure as she took my Blood.

Mine. Mine. Mine.

We were mirrored in eukori. Merged. House Farrell. House Tucek. Leyla. Amber.

In the same blind haze of pleasure, I took her Blood in exchange. Reached, like I had with the Threefold Spiral Coven, and pulled darkness from deep inside her. Pulled it out and locked it away where I could use it when I needed to.

It felt right. It felt good. It felt like our bodies rang like bells together, all clear tones and harmonics.

And we sat afterwards, bonelessly slumped, pressed together, unable to move until the feelings subsided.

That had gone far, *far* better than I'd thought it would. I felt a bit less worried about the rest of them.

My mental *return to business* thoughts leaked through our eukori.

She stirred slowly but drew out every moment. Stretched. 'Accidentally' brushed across my face as she reached for her T shirt. Which, it turned out, could be put on as provocatively as it was taken off.

She cleared her throat as she eventually stood up.

"That was... unexpected," she said, and her face took on a serious look. "Of course, the Mistress of the House should ensure the loyalty of the House at regular intervals."

"I will, but not because I need to."

That got a genuine smile and a blown kiss.

"I'll send in your next unsuspecting victim, Kyria."

Chapter 48

I'd found out previously that Athanate couldn't get drunk for long; the body metabolism was just too efficient. And even a mild drunkenness would disappear if the Athanate adrenaline equivalent, elethesine, started pumping. I was jumpy with elethesine.

Now I also found that sharing Blood with my House had a similar effect to drinking *lots* of alcohol. Each bite, giving or receiving, was such pleasure at any time, but taken together, one after the other...

That burning pleasure lasted longer and longer, until it overlapped to the next person, and then the pleasure level itself just rose and rose.

Blood rapture, it was called.

I lost track.

I was lying on the sofa, blissed out, drifting in a sea of sensation, when I heard Mirela's voice.

"You've seduced my entire House, Amber!"

"No, ish not right," I mumbled.

The opposite. They'd seduced me, surely? And it had been Blood, not Body. If Mirela was here, I must have bitten my way through all House Tucek. I could remember others as well. My ehvasi. All of them. My House. My whole House, or at least the Athanate part of it.

Damn!

"How long?" I said.

"You've been at it a day and a night. Long enough for us to finish planning the attack, which you put me in charge of, remember? As leader, I say I need you up on your hind legs and functioning."

"Mmm. Gimme a little time."

There was something I needed to remember. A warning. Yes, that was it. I'd been so dismissive of the lure of pleasure when the Serpents had provided it as a test. Easy. Walk on by.

What if it wasn't a test, but a warning? What if the test was whether I ignored the warning?

I groaned.

Bit of overconfidence there or what?

And I'd been playing at politics, which was another Serpents' warning. I had Pia deliver my ultimatum about how my House would work with the Athanate community to test my Blood.

Done is done.

I needed to get back into my role. Military. First steps. Attack Matlal. Sow dissent in Basilikos.

Right.

"You said you'd finished planning?" I asked. "Is the Colonel happy?"

"Happy? No. But we have the best of the situation. And a couple of unexpected assists."

"Such as?"

"I got a call from the Carpathians. Theris talked to them and made a suggestion which they've supported. They're being very mysterious about it, but apparently, they have 'assets' in the theater, and they've said they'll take out the laboratory. That means we get to concentrate on one target, with one set of infiltrations and extractions."

"Uh." I rubbed my face. The Carpathians again. I had to remind myself I was one, too. "Good. I need a shower. And coffee, food, sleep. Stuff like that."

"You'll have time for some of that, soldier, but I'll need you in the final mission briefing, and then I want you on the plane. Meanwhile…"

I peered up at her. The mirage of a shower seemed to recede. "Meanwhile, what?" I prompted.

"I have a couple of questions. For a start, why did you put me in charge of this attack?"

"I made a management decision." I winced at speaking a sentence which contained both me and 'management', but it was accurate. I *was* having to make management decisions. "Best use of time and assets. You did the original planning on this attack. No one knows it like you do."

She was thoughtful and her aura uneasy. "I have so many questions, and not enough time."

"Then ask the questions that are stopping you getting on with what you have to do."

She huffed.

"Okay, out of sequence and completely left field. How on earth did you know what to say for Donatienne? Did you mean it? About being whole and pure."

That was the last thing I expected her to ask, and like everything in the spirit world, it had become a little hazy.

"It was what she wanted," I said, hesitantly. "She said it."

Had she?

"She was asking for absolution. Redemption. You gave it to her. Did you mean it?"

You will go down to the sea. You will become unsullied. Whole and pure. And the sea will be your only shroud.

"Yes. I mean, of course I meant it, but absolution's not in my power to give. It was… a prayer, I think."

"Hmm. Okay. What about exchanging Blood with all of House Tucek?"

"And House Basynia, and everyone. Because I need them to realize they're all in House Farrell. One House. All of us. No need to wonder if everyone's in the same House. No need to expect others to prove themselves. Also, no need to prove yourself to others. Or to yourself.

Mirela looked thoughtful, then nodded slowly.

"Well, I believe you may have achieved the goal you've just stated, but I don't think it was limited to that," she said and ran her fingers through her hair. "I think all of them, I mean all Tucek and Basynia, will feel like it was an absolution, even if they never think of it in those words."

The craziest thing was what she said felt right. It felt like I had been doing paladin stuff.

She smiled, as if she could tell what I was thinking.

"Don't I get it as well?"

"You don't need it," I said. "We've shared auras. We are one House."

"I meant absolution."

"Consider yourself absolved."

That smile again.

"Hmm. Okay. Back to my original question. You don't need me only to attack Matlal, then?"

"I do need, just not 'only'."

I felt my response needed more emphasis, and I was still blissed out, so I said the first thing that came to mind, a quote from Athanate poetry: "To love without reserve forever."

She sat on the sofa next to me. "From the lamentation of Arunne. The gift and sorrow of the Athanate and so on. Diana won't even admit she wrote it, but anyway, that's for Panethus and their kin."

"I see no reason it shouldn't be Athanate to Athanate," I said.

"No, you don't, do you? I can see it in your aura. But you *are* a witch. I think maybe you've put a spell on me to make me think that."

"Or you've put a spell on me. We've merged auras, against every sensible thought. Seemed right at the time, just as it feels right now. But we did merge, and I think that means you're a witch as well. And a shifter probably."

She chuckled.

"We should still give each other oaths," she said. "Don't dismiss tradition just because of traditionalist extremists."

"Okay." My throat was an absolute pincushion. One more wasn't going to make a lot of difference.

"Throat looks sore," she said. Maybe sensing it through our eukori connection, which had kinda crept up on me while we were talking.

"Huh."

"Of course," she went on with a little smile, "the oath is 'Body and Blood'. It can be sealed with either."

"Leyla mentioned that."

"I bet she did. But I bet she didn't push it."

"No."

"But the words of the oath stand. And it's mutual."

"Well, yes, of course it is."

"So… my Blood is yours, just as your Body is mine."

Cunning trap.

Especially cunning in that she was absolutely right in traditional Athanate thinking. The bond between us meant I had the right to call on her for Blood, and she had the right to call on me for sex. And vice versa.

Not difficult for an older Athanate that had settled into the Athanate world and mindset. Difficult for me. Whatever progress I'd made, I'd been truly Athanate less than a year, and some parts of me were human. Human-ish, anyway.

"I hear your Diakon favors the thigh," she said casually.

Her deft fingers opened my belt. Undid the buttons on my jeans, one by one. She was taking her time. Teasing. Pulling the jeans so I could feel the strain in the material and the pop of the button releasing. Each pop echoed with a little explosion of lust in my belly.

"I could exercise my right." She leaned over me, lips brushing mine.

Checkmate, so to speak. She had every right.

"I won't deny you." I couldn't say anything else. Her Athanate rights carried more weight than my preferences.

"I know."

She kissed me. With tongues, and with fangs manifested. French kissing with fangs was… intense. Done with great care and crazily erotic.

She broke the kiss reluctantly.

"Trust me," she whispered.

It was an order, not a question, but I answered: "Yes."

I did, and I knew at that moment, there was a world of difference between her teasing to prove a point and making me do something I might later regret. I relaxed.

She knew it. Her mouth turned down as if I was spoiling her fun, then she laughed and tore my jeans off to see if I really, *really* knew it.

I let her. I let her push me around, and I didn't care that the touch of her tongue on my thigh made me shiver. Or that I groaned when her fangs pierced me. And nearly came when she *pulled*.

I didn't care she knew exactly how much I enjoyed it, and again when I bit her neck. Or my reluctance to let her get up off me afterwards.

"I hate to love you and leave you, but I have a final briefing to give," she said. "Your attendance is not optional, soldier. You have time to shower. Please turn up with your pants on."

I began to limp toward the shower, little sparks of pleasure still going off in my body, and my limbs not really working properly yet.

"Bully. I knew it would be a mistake to put you in charge of the attack," I shot at her over my shoulder.

Chapter 49

I was late.

I showered quickly and emerged to find Theris outside with a to-go coffee ready for me. I ran. Still had to sneak in the back like a bad schoolgirl, but I did have my pants on, and my mind out of them.

The room was full, and it felt different. The cloud of confusion and grief about to boil over into anger was gone. Everything had changed. The marque had shifted. It wasn't exactly one marque, but there was that elusive harmony to it that had been missing before.

And the pack had run. I could smell the forests on them, I could almost feel the winds stirring their fur. They'd returned energized.

The Adepts and Ops 4-10 vets responded to the atmosphere.

The House had settled, replacing uncertainty with a keenness, an eagerness.

And they were sitting in mixed groups. Athanate and Were and Adept and Ops 4-10 together.

There were some other indications. Despite alert focus on Mirela's words, I saw little by-plays any time she paused between sections.

For instance, the bad-boy wolves had decided cool-girl Tuceks were a worthy challenge. How could they not have a try? There were some fabulous sneers and teen-worthy rolling eyes being sent back their way, which didn't break their determination. I saw evidence of lolling tongues that really couldn't have been that long without a little shapeshifting help.

The banter was good, but it disappeared whenever Mirela started up again, proving that whatever distractions they allowed themselves, they knew this was for real.

David moved to join me and typed a link for a download onto my cell.

"I'll fill you in the rest when we can," he whispered. His eyes roved over the room, taking it all in, and came back to me. "Well done."

"Thanks."

Alex came over and sat on the other side, the afterglow of his wolf still in his eyes.

I rested my hand on his thigh and got his on mine in return.

Ooh. Growl.

Okay, not completely out of my rapture, but as I listened to the plan, my old Ops 4-10 mindset snapped into place and dragged me into the right zone.

With the Carpathians dealing with the remote laboratory, Mirela's attention was focused on getting us to Xibalbá as quickly and invisibly as possible. It was in the border area between Yucatán and Campeche. We were going in by air, as ordinary passengers, in small groups arriving at different cities so there should be nothing to raise an alert if Matlal had people watching transport data, which he would have.

For some of us whose faces were known and who were arriving on international flights, our departure would be held up slightly as masks and documentation were prepared. There was no way we could use our own names or have a facial recognition program scan us. Matlal would have people watching for that information.

On top of that, Mirela suspected Adept surveillance of some obvious places like the international airports. We'd go in with nothing-to-see-here spells covering us provided by the Adepts. Those spells would be reworkable as nobody-here once we were away from crowds and closer to the target. However, other than getting us through the border covertly, actual Adept involvement in the attacks was limited. That was understandable. Most Adepts didn't operate well when there was a fight going on. Flint and Kane were the exceptions, and they had been allocated to two different teams. I was on Mirela's team, where Theris and I were the magic cover, which worried me. Whatever power I had, I wasn't sure I was in control of it.

Also, there were four main attack groups, so we were short of one Adept.

Or not. Tullah had discussed this with her mother Mary, former leader of the Denver coven. Mary had agreed to go with the attacking force, at least as far as the point where the spell needed reconfiguration from nothing-to-see-here to nobody-here.

I would have preferred Gwen, but David muttered to me that there were advance teams from the Empire of Heaven and the Carpathian delegations scheduled to visit Haven in advance of the leaders arriving. Gwen would not leave Kaothos alone under those circumstances.

"The Empire and Carpathians will want to see you too," David said.

"If I'm available."

I had to stop talking and get back to concentrating: Mirela was going on with the presentation.

Once in Mexico, we'd gather into our teams. The attack on Xibalbá was going to be from four different directions to create maximum confusion in the defenders.

I saw the schedules and I felt more than a prickle of unease. *Everything* was timing. Even something as everyday as a delayed takeoff at the airport could turn this highly complex, multi-interconnected operation into an unretrievable, uncontrollable, blundering nightmare. But I had handed control over. Mirela's teams had done these operations before. She'd had input from experienced Ops 4-10 veterans. Colonel Laine had given it a pass.

And we had no time to do anything else—those deliveries of viral weapons were scheduled to start soon.

An hour later, Mirela halted and gestured at the clock.

"Inevitably, we don't have as much time as I'd want. I have to bring this briefing to an end."

The session had included sharp questions and good answers.

It was a long way from a cast iron plan, but Mirela had gone some way to easing my worries.

"I'll come back to the core of the mission," she said. "Our objectives are as follows, in order of importance: One, destroy the stockpile of biological weapons. Two, remove all server drives and destroy any available backups we can locate. Three, make Matlal believe this is a Vega Martine operation. Anything else we achieve is not a core objective, and the operation's success will be assessed on the objectives."

I bit my lip. I was sure that Mirela had an eye on some of those precious metals Matlal had stockpiled. But I was equally sure she wouldn't risk the objectives.

She looked around the room.

"Read the briefing documents. The Were are the first scheduled departure, and their buses will arrive any minute now. It's on, people, we're doing this."

She paused, and her face went harder.

"One last thing. I'm glad some of you are getting on better with each other, but it's time for your game faces now. We are going to Yucatán. We are going to Campeche and Mérida and Xibalbá. This is the heart of darkness. This is the belly of the beast. This is the home of Matlal."

"Any planning of an attack like this starts off with certainties and ends with compromises and guesswork. Even then, as all the vets out there know, the plan only survives until contact with the enemy. I'm sure we'll get to Yucatán without too many problems, but I'm also sure we're going to have to improvise from there onward, and it's going to get real, real quick. We are good. We are the best of the best. We will do it, but things may get ragged as we do. Extractions are at the end of a long list of 'if this, then do that' decision points. Extractions are everyone's most important part of the operation, and yet they're beyond the point where we can be certain how things will go down."

"Attached to the briefing as a separate, single page is a list of places and resources. These are fallback options, if everything else has failed. They're Hail Mary's. High risk. The only guarantee I can make is that, if you need these options, by the time you need them, one or more of them will be compromised."

"They can be taken at any time, if necessary. If your personal cover is blown. If the attack is discovered. If the plan fails. Whatever. Scatter. Pick an option. Make up your own. Approach anything with extreme caution, however good it looks. Remember, this is Matlal's territory. This is the most dangerous place on earth for you."

"And, if you're caught and taken alive, death will not come quickly enough for you."

Yucatán
Chapter 50

I arrived at Mérida's international airport the next day, early in the morning, with David, Yelena and Theris. We were disguised as two couples on vacation. It might have been funny, but I had Mirela's warning echoing in my mind: *death will not come quickly enough for you.*

Don't get caught. Tara's useful comment.

I was masked. A rubbery thing that had taken an hour to fit and was stretched over my whole face. It was horrible. And hot. It felt like my head was going to melt, despite the building's air conditioning, and I had visions of that actually happening as I waited in line to clear passport control. We were all wearing scents that disguised us, but it was confusing for us as well. My wolf especially wanted to get an impression of the place, and it felt wrong not being able to smell.

But that was a light relief in comparison to the sensation of being in Mérida, Matlal's HQ city. According to Mirela's briefings, Matlal usually lived on his estate to the north of the city, in a monstrous house like a cubist's wet dream. That was miles away from where we were, but I could *feel* his presence. Or at least, the presence of his House. The air seemed thin, my skin prickled, and every shadow seemed to be watching us. It wasn't entirely my overheated imagination; Theris got exactly the same sensations. It confirmed that Matlal had Adepts guarding the airport, looking for suspicious arrivals. What I was feeling was them probing with their auras and, hopefully, sliding unknowingly past the nothing-to-see-here spell.

On the human level, I guessed Theris and I looked like any other tourists to the customs and immigration officials: a tired, stressed and nondescript couple, but with documentation in order. They passed us through with barely a glance.

The paranoid feeling eased as we took a cab for the short ride down to the Catedral de San Ildefonso, where we were scheduled to meet up with most of the others.

It *eased*, but there was still something there: a wisp, a barely noticeable touch, as if there were the single strand of spider silk on my face which I couldn't brush away.

"I know it's good use of time to go see the cathedral first," Yelena was saying, "but I can't tell you how much I want to get out to the resort and shower."

The cabbie wasn't part of Mirela's preparations; he was just the first in the rank when we'd gotten outside, so Yelena was acting the American tourist part, and her voice had lost all trace of Ukrainian. She sounded like a mid-Atlantic TV news anchor.

I met Theris' eyes across the cab. I could tell he was sensing the same tracking tendril of a spell I was. Neither of us wanted to speak. We were concentrating on putting out the aura image of a small group of completely unthreatening, uninteresting tourists.

Our raid company been broken up into lots of groups, each with a disguising spell, but few of them included someone with Adept training. Would the others be tracked like this, or had the trackers sensed we were just different enough for them to keep an eye on us? How long would they track us? What information could they gather through this weak connection?

I had to assume the nothing-to-see-here spell was partially working, otherwise I was sure we'd be getting *much* more attention. But the spell would have to change once we were in position for the attack. It would have to become a nothing-here spell, and we couldn't make that change without the watcher noticing.

David and Yelena didn't have the same senses Theris and I did, but I briefed them in our sign language, so they knew something was up. David replied to Yelena with some background on the cathedral. I could hear the overtone of concern in his voice, but it was a short ride, so there wasn't much time for either of them to speak.

The cab dropped us in front of the plain, square cathedral.

It was a clever choice of meeting place from the point of view of a standard covert operation: it was swirling with tourists and guides. There was more than enough of a crowd to hide in and lose any stalkers, which was the reason Mirela had chosen it. I hadn't really expected to use it to try and shake off magical stalkers as well.

Could I attach this trace to someone else without the caster noticing?

I had to keep acting like a tourist for the moment, and we spoke to each other about the trip, the cost of the cab and the merits of this particular tourist attraction.

The outside of the cathedral wasn't inspiring. It was a dusty, sandy brown, and the maintenance staff had an obvious ongoing battle with graffiti; layer after layer sprayed on and cleaned off, never completely erased, relying on the oldest eventually fading into invisibility. Given that first impression, I didn't hold out much hope of it being worth a visit inside, but to keep our cover going, I linked arms with Theris, and we walked in.

Mirela had chosen this as the place to meet, but what she couldn't have known was the way the building itself would pull at me, or what would happen when it did.

In stark contrast to the outside, it was cool and pale and beautiful inside. Part of the visual effect was the austerity and simplicity of the design: white columns along the nave rose up to flow into smooth ceiling arches in the Moorish style. Part of it was the light: the dome over the sanctuary had windows in the top and sides, bathing the transept and chancel in glorious, numinous light. People standing there glowed, like an artist's rendering of a divine revelation.

But dramatic and lovely as it was, it wasn't the aesthetics that grabbed my attention. As David had been telling us in the cab, this church was *old*, the oldest in the Americas, and it had been built 'with the stones of Mayan temples, over their ruins'. Just words, until I had to sit abruptly on one of the dark wooden pews because I was sensing the building's foundations reaching into the depths of the earth, physically and spiritually. This cathedral fed on the forgotten faiths of a lost civilization, and I could feel spirits seeping out of the stones.

They gathered over me. A host of ancient spirits, near formless, blurred and blended by the years. Normally no more visible to normal eyes than dust motes in the air, yet still urgent with longings they had no mouths to tell. I saw them. I heard the distant echoes of calls in a long-dead tongue, smelled the blood and dust, felt the ghostly grasping of their hands... and I saw the brightening of a substantiation trying to form around me, a channel to the spirit world that threatened to pull us all in.

Theris' eyes widened in alarm. He could see them too.

We were attracting them. The pair of us. The fact we could see them gave them substance, and the nothing-to-see-here working fed them more. They were breaking it down.

It was *me* they wanted, though. Like even dust motes can catch the light, the air above my head began to take on the same glow as the chancel.

A woman at the front, turning around to walk back from the altar, did a double take and grabbed her friend's arm and pointed.

Shit!

I was going to become visible to Matlal's Adepts at the same time as I caused a commotion in the cathedral by appearing to have a nimbus over my head.

I leaped up, heart hammering.

What the hell could I do?

The traces from Matlal's Adepts. They were workings as well. The spirits could feed on them. Better. They were fresher. They linked directly into the watching Adepts. A live link.

Theris thought so too. I sensed him *pushing* the spirits; focusing their attention on the traces. Without understanding how or why, I saw what he was doing through his aura and joined in the effort.

Some of the spirits responded. Some were hungry for the type of working that the trace was. They latched onto it. Began to follow it back, where I hoped they'd emerge as a very unpleasant surprise for the watcher.

A small victory, in the middle of a disaster. Been in Mexico an hour and already the plan was falling apart.

There were other members of our raid here, in the cathedral. They hadn't called the spirits out, but their nothing-to-see-here workings were as attractive as ours.

We needed the protection of those spells against Matlal. After they got over their shock of spirits consuming their workings, those Adepts would be looking back at the cathedral to work out what had happened. Theris had come up with a clever move on the traces, but he didn't know what to do with the rest of the spirits.

I turned and ran outside, spirits trailing after me.

The others joined me, standing around to cut me off from view of the other people in front of the cathedral.

"Okay?" Yelena asked. "Boss?"

I nodded mutely. Held up a hand to stop them from talking to me. I had a glimmer of an idea. *Think. Think!* I needed to concentrate. I needed…

I needed power.

Flint emerged from the cathedral with his group. Kane was inside. So were Mary and Liu. None of them knew what to do. I didn't either, but at least I had an idea. First, I needed to channel some power through them.

How well did that go down last time?

This was blood magic. Despite compelling arguments that no type of magic was inherently evil, and the others accepting that in their minds, they didn't in their hearts. *I* didn't. This was my type of magic. This was why the spirits had been attracted to me. This was the legacy of House Chrysos.

But I needed power, and I didn't want to pull it through my friends, whether or not it sullied their souls.

You don't need to, my Priestess. This is your power. This is your inheritance and my gift. This is your right. I can help.

Tezcatlipoca. A moment's inattention and he'd found me. I had a sickness in my stomach. Ringing in my ears.

On the other hand, he was right. I had no doubt he could help.

I can't do this.

I *had* to. Just not with Tezcatlipoca riding my aura.

I tried to block him out. I reached back, down into the roots of the building. Down into the dark earth. And up into the beautiful columns and arches, the solid walls. Down in time. Back to where the stones that made this cathedral had run with blood.

What were they thinking, to build a cathedral from these stones?

But it worked.

There was my power; in the energies of all the blood that had been spilled. All I had to do was embrace it.

I lifted my head.

The spirits, all of them remaining, stopped attacking the workings and came to me. It was too late for the nothing-to-see-here spells. They were tattered fragments. Matlal's Adepts would now be able to see us clearly as soon as they looked.

My idea wasn't clever or complex. I'd seen those disguising spells formed. I had power from this place. Was it enough to capture the spirits and force them into the holes they'd made in our spells?

Time is running out, Tezcatlipoca said. *Use my skills that I grant to you.*

And that would mean letting him into my soul. Never being able to block him again because he'd have an anchor point in me. An unbreakable connection.

I clenched my teeth.

Alternatives?

How would the Queen of Diamonds have done it? Was that a better way than surrendering to Tezcatlipoca? What was the cost of using her skills, knowing they'd been honed in so much evil? Was that any better than Tezcatlipoca?

But Nai hadn't been evil. I'd walked in her shoes.

Was this another test of the Serpents?

I had run out of time. I could sense Matlal's Adepts' cautious return to the cathedral, like snuffling animals keeping just outside a circle of light.

I pushed and pulled spirit matter, trying to think like Nai had thought. To make little spells perfectly and connect them into a powerful wholeness. It was like trying to sculpt with mist. My spirit hands passed through their spirit bodies, feeling the chill of time and death.

But the spirits moved to my patterns. Reshaped themselves.

It could have been easier. I was *not* using Tezcatlipoca's sheer power. I wasn't even depending entirely on Nai's clever designs. It was a bit of both and more of me, and even some of the spirits themselves.

The nothing-to-see-here spells reformed, but they were different. They were all around us again, four groups, four spells. Disturbingly, I was inside each one, as if I had four pairs of eyes, getting dizzying, overlapping, multiple visions. Worse than head trauma. Worse than the fever of the Serpents' gift. Looking out of those spell bubbles with spirit eyes was like looking through agitated water. The real world lurched and wobbled and waved as the spell surface rippled back into place around the groups.

I was going to be sick.

I could hear Theris talking calmly and quietly to get my attention.

"That has worked, whatever it was you did. Well done, Amber. Enough. Time to come back. Focus on my voice. Follow it. Follow it back to us."

Yes. Time to go back. I was skimming the spirit world, and that was dangerous. Almost as dangerous as letting Tezcatlipoca inside my soul. I would go back, but sick as I felt, I needed a few moments more to absorb what I'd done.

These new spells weren't like the old ones, even if they did the same job. They felt different. They felt like they belonged here, and I saw that made them stronger, better, because the original spells might have alerted a powerful Adept just by feeling out of place.

It wasn't all an improvement: the new spells wouldn't last as long as the originals, because they reacted to the power of any probing spell. They burned magical energy to match the magical energy used in any spells that probed at them.

I didn't want to try and fix that, given I barely understood what I'd done in the first place. This was a lesson learned. It had worked, but unless you grasped the completeness of what you were trying to achieve, you would end up with unintended consequences.

We'll be fine, Tara said. *Doesn't need to work for very long. We've avoided alerting Matlal's Adepts any more than they were already.*

She added her voice to Theris'. *Time to stop.*

It wasn't easy. These were *my* workings, with *my* imprint. They had something of me in them. They resonated. This was how Nai had reacted to her spells; the pleasure she had felt at her achievements. The urge to do more. I could tinker. I could perfect. Just a little more time.

You have to stop.

So difficult. I wasn't feeling sick at all now. The spirit appearance of my spell was hypnotic. The surfaces rippled, and as they did, images floated up and pulsed in the air, reflecting the raw energies I had used to create them. Mayan designs. Spiraling patterns. Glyphs that I could almost read. Nightmare faces. Fantastical headdresses and helmets.

Mine. My body glowed with pleasure in time to the throb of images.

Flayed jaguars. Staring eyes. Spreading wings. Tongues. Pyramids that seemed to float on darkness. Black-bladed knives. The sun and moon. Still beating hearts clutched in bloody hands.

Yelena slapped my face.

Chapter 51

Flint and Kane were holding me up, despite orders that we should all remain separate groups.

It meant our new nothing-to-see-here spells overlapped, making them shimmer and pulse together. But Yelena's blow had brought me back. From outside, the spells weren't so hypnotic.

"What the hell just happened?" Kane asked.

"Not completely sure," I said. I was back, but not firing on all pistons and I was talking clumsily. "Lurking spirits. It's like Queen of Diamonds' steamer, how it made a kind of breach between here and the spirit world. Spirits get called to it. These spirits are my wheelhouse. Blood magic. Just put them to use repairing their damage."

"Go back a moment," David said. "A *breach*. You were the breach? Just by being here?"

"Not exactly Amber alone," Theris said. "We did go into an ancient place of worship with powerful workings operating *and* Matlal's trackers snooping around us. Each of our four groups has someone personally attuned to the spirit world. All of that could call spirits."

He was right as far as it went, but despite Flint, Kane, Mary, Liu and Theris himself being strong Adepts, they hadn't called the spirits like I had.

They'd come to me. The Blood Witch.

I kept silent.

Theris went on about how we'd been feeding the nothing-to-see-here spell since we got in the cab. He thought that activity might also have contributed to what attracted the spirits.

I let him keep talking.

"But we have our disguise spells back and all the traces gone, yes?" Yelena said. "This is exactly what Mirela was saying would happen: things go wrong, and we fix them."

She was putting a good face on it.

"No Ukrainian proverb?" David asked, grinning. Trying to lighten the mood.

"No, but an old English one instead: *sufficient unto the day the evils thereof.* Give thanks and get our focus back on attacking Xibalbá."

"What about the fact that Matlal's Adepts put a trace on us?" Flint said. "Should we be worried?"

I let them discuss it. The consensus was coming down to the same conclusion I'd reached. If they'd really known it was us, we'd be in the middle of a battle right now. And losing.

"He can't have his Adepts put out many traces like that," Theris said. "Each one takes effort and needs a very skilled caster. As for the cathedral spirits destroying the traces, I don't know that it would be so unusual that it would raise the alarm. It's probably happened before, if they are scanning this area with magical workings. The whole peninsula is full of old temples, and they'll be full of collections of ancient spirits. They might even have had the same effect with someone visiting the cathedral before. But in any case, reconnecting a lost trace is much more difficult than setting it in the first place. The original trace felt like a standard precaution to me, rather than a genuine concern. It does confirm Matlal's in a heightened state of alertness."

David's mouth twitched. "He's just lost his entire werewolf alliance in the north. Of course he's on the lookout, but from your comments, he doesn't even know where to look. He's going to be spreading his forces thinly. Still, if I were a cautious Adept, working for Matlal, and my job was to check arrivals, I'd send someone down here to cast an eye over all the tourists who'd picked this cathedral as their first site to visit."

"All the more reason for us to be on our way," Yelena said.

Mary and Liu joined us.

Mary wasn't happy at the new nothing-to-see-here spells.

"These are dark," she said, unconsciously wiping her hands.

She was right. Even without taking much from Tezcatlipoca or Nai, I'd reached down into blood magic to achieve this. I might have compromised my ability to keep Tezcatlipoca blocked. I might be being influenced by Nai. I didn't know. What I did know was that doing Blood magic felt good. It felt like something I wanted to do a lot more of.

Not unless we really need to. Tara.

We will need to. Me.

I tried to wave it off. "I had to use whatever was in range. We got lucky this time. I hope we haven't used up all our allocation of luck on the first step of this op."

Theris looked sideways at me.

"The old spells had to change function," David said. "Is that the same with these?"

"Yes," I said. Although the new spells were different, they had the same scalability. While we were here, in the middle of the city and surrounded by tourists, they allowed Adepts to *see* us, but made us look uninteresting and unmagical. Once we were all in position to march on Xibalbá, the spell needed twisting so that we were completely invisible to any searching Adepts using a working to scan the area around the fort.

I opened my eukori to the others and let them see me reach into the workings and demonstrate how the power should be shifted from *here* to *here*.

Which meant I was inside the spells again. *Look how beautiful these workings were.*

I pulled myself back abruptly.

Flint and Kane had gone narrow-eyed with concentration. They didn't like the magic, but I knew they could handle it. We'd worked together before. They had a feel for my workings. They trusted me. It gave them confidence they could do it.

Mary and Liu didn't have that confidence, or that trust.

Liu exchanged a look with Mary, and I saw an intense communication, wordless, all in the flicker of eyes and firming of mouths.

"Mary will return home now," Liu spoke carefully. "I believe I can achieve all that is necessary with this working, but I'm afraid I will need to stay with it. I will need to remain with the group during the approach to Xibalbá."

Mary blinked and turned her head away, agreeing to Liu's proposal and incidentally, not meeting my eyes.

I knew.

Liu was coming along to keep an eye on me. He and Mary didn't trust my use of magic, or rather, didn't trust the effect it was having on me. Liu was going to be like Theris, a knife at my back if I should stumble and fall into evil.

I felt the coldness, like Chrysos' blade, striking into my heart. An ache. A presence that pierced me and would not go away.

Yelena started arguing the practical aspects, but Liu cut her off. Neither Yelena nor anyone else was able to run the Adept defenses for Liu's group.

Mirela was in charge, but she'd have to agree. Yelena was overruled.

We were saved from any further argument when David pointed across the wide road where a convoy of tour buses with tinted windows was parking as we spoke.

When House Tucek had planned something for Vega Martine, they hadn't held back.

Mirela had set up a tour company when the idea for this attack had started over a year ago. It was a genuine company, with employees, offices, and buses. The tourist business was booming; it had done well. So well, the management had sent the entire staff of the company on a cruise holiday for the next few days with a 'temporary maintenance staff' taking over. Those temporary staff were House Tucek and these buses were our transport into the jungle. All put in place 'just in case' the plan ever came to be executed.

I wasn't complaining.

Mirela emerged from the first bus and crossed the road. She was dressed in a loose cream blouse and skirt, her face shaded by a wide straw hat with a badge identifying her as our tour guide.

"We're in the first one," she said as Salar walked past us into the cathedral, leading a little group of Tucek Athanate, each of them holding little tour guide signs to collect the remainder of their flocks.

"All our equipment is waiting in the buses," she went on. "The windows are tinted so we can take our masks off and change inside, as soon as we're clear of the city. Get on board; they're a lot more comfortable than standing out in the sun. We'll go as soon as everyone's boarded."

"Yes, boss," I murmured, but we got ourselves into the air-conditioned buses without any hesitations or arguments.

Chapter 52

Thirty minutes later our little convoy turned south, out of the city and I peeled the mask off my face with a sigh of relief.

Theris was sitting next to me. As his face was completely unknown to Matlal, he'd avoided having to wear a mask, and I gave him side-eye for his amusement.

"You could have shifted your features," he pointed out.

He was probably right. I was coming to the realization that all magic was one thing. Athanate shifted like Weres shifted, only Athanate limited their shifting to the specific modifications required for Blood. I believed Were could shift to any animal, given a bit of training and belief. It wasn't something only skinwalkers could do. In terms of shifter capability, surely a human was just another animal. I sensed I could shift to another human form, given practice. And as for Adept levels of capability… the Queen of Diamonds had been able to change me into a man.

On the other hand, I did not want that bit of news coming out during Emergence. Humanity would have enough to worry about. And I had more pressing concerns now.

"That working back at the cathedral. I found it difficult to stop."

I didn't know exactly how to phrase the question, but Theris had been waiting for it.

"You're familiar with Athanate Blood rapture?" He was smiling as he asked it. He knew very well what I'd done back in Denver. He'd been guarding my door the whole time.

"Yes."

"Spirit rapture is the same thing." He raised his hands up as if he were holding something between them. Then he twisted. "Just a different perception."

"So, not something special to Blood magic."

"Not special to any particular type of magic, but Blood magic resonates with users very strongly. It's probably the reason that Lyssae become what they do. They are lost in a kind of Blood magic spirit rapture."

I huffed. "Another thing to be wary of, then."

He nodded, suppressing a smile. "Yelena won't always be there to slap you."

I settled back to think about that. I could sense my workings at a distance, each covering a different group in a different bus. If I looked at them *this* way, like another Adept would see, there was nothing there. A group of tourists on a tour coach. But if I looked at them *this* way, I could see the working itself.

Two of them were active, the surface flowing to my spirit sight. Flint and Kane were experimenting, to make sure they had control when they needed it. Liu's was static. Either he didn't want to touch it until he had to, or he was confident.

I used little towels to get rid of the masking scent we'd worn to get through the city, and then distracted myself by reviewing Mirela's plan of attack again.

The coaches were as comfortable as Mirela said, but not really designed with enough space for changing into combat uniforms. She'd designated the back of the coach as a changing area, and we had to split up into pairs to use it.

About an hour into the journey, it was my turn, and my changing partner turned out to be Leyla.

What a surprise, murmured Tara.

I was embarrassed to realize it, but most of the memory of biting my way through Tucek, Basynia and my ehvasi had blurred a little. My exchange with Leyla wasn't blurred at all.

Maybe because she was the first.

Or maybe she thinks you have some unfinished business, was Tara's take.

"Mistress," Leyla said quietly in greeting, and did the demure, downcast eyes bit that was about as convincing as an alligator's smile.

"You know," she muttered as we swayed and bumped into each other with the movement of the coach, "if you need to get away from your pelea, and you ordered me to distract him, I guess I would have to do it."

I grinned. Theris had changed earlier than us, and there had been some quiet nudges and glances back when he'd gotten out of the shorts and shirt he'd arrived in. Man had a fine body, I had to admit. House Tucek was all female, deliberately so, but that didn't stop them from appreciating men. As long as the man wasn't a pushy werewolf, maybe. Pushy Carpathian hybrid Athanate-Adept? That was okay, apparently.

The coach took a bend just as Leyla was standing on one leg to put her combat pants on, and I found myself holding her half naked body up. Her eyelids raised and lowered in that way I never could manage.

"On the other hand, if it's you that wants distracting, Kyria…"

I laughed. "Behave! We're too busy for that. And it's Amber."

But I took the opportunity to kiss her on the throat where the marks of my bite were still visible. I filled my nose with her marque: still definitely Tucek, but blended with mine. *Mine.* The glow that recognition caused spread through me like a shot of good rum. She returned the kiss, though how she knew exactly where she'd bitten me among all the marks on my neck was a puzzle.

Our hearts skipped a beat together.

A double dose of rum. And a very good rum, too.

I didn't need wolfy ears to hear a few chuckles from the nearest seats.

I shoved her back upright and laughed at the cat-got-the-cream smile on her face. I probably had the same.

She retrieved her pants, back to looking all demure.

By the time we finished, whispers had rippled up the coach. In the way that whispers distorted the facts, people were looking around, expecting us to be making out on the floor.

Instead, Leyla stood at attention. Shoulders back, chin up.

"Do I pass inspection, Sergeant?"

She'd done up her shirt buttons out of sequence.

Oh dear, oh dear. How could that have happened?

It was flirting and teasing, but it had other levels to it. I knew this game. It had no name, and it turned up everywhere in a different format. It was a 'finding out' game.

Push. Find out what happens.

A wolf might nip at another. Did the nipped wolf just ignore it, or nip back? A fellow soldier would get in your face, or even shove you. Did you shove back or laugh it off? The woman across the table saw your bet and raised you, even though you knew her hand wasn't strong.

House Tucek knew about me at the most important level—they were my House, but what was my style? Leyla had elected herself to find out. How would I respond to this? Was I all relaxed and confident even though we were heading into combat?

I sighed and shook my head.

"Come here," I said.

"Kyria," she murmured.

Fortunately, no one else had taken up the title. Whatever the Agiagraphos said, I needed to earn it.

She slunk closer.

Eye contact. Up close enough to kiss. *Concentrate. Hands steady.* Fingers working well.

I undid a button and refastened it in the right hole. Another one. Worked my way down.

You can't bluff me, girl. I'm not fazed.

I couldn't hide the effect though; especially since our eukori had merged. I could feel the tug of fabric on 'my' body as distinctly as I could feel the hard buttons between my fingers. We were both very aware of our breathing and heartbeats, and at the same time, our awareness of the rest of the coach seemed to drift away.

I didn't think she'd expected quite this level of intensity.

Last button.

She had that cat-got-the-cream look on her face again.

What to do?

I leaned a little closer and she mirrored me, her lips opening, expecting a kiss.

"I'll see your sexy buttons," I whispered, "and raise you a bit of *tucking*."

I kept eye contact. Hooked my left hand into her belt. Pulled. Then very slowly and deliberately tucked her shirt into her pants with my right hand. Enjoyed every sensation both of us felt. The pull on her belt, my knuckles raking against her belly, the slip of fabric against the back of my hand, all mixed together.

Oooooh.

Her eyes vamped out and her breath hitched.

I suspected I could skim the spirit world and maybe make a little time slippage to explore these feelings. Wouldn't really count as casting a spell, would it?

No.

I broke the gaze. Gave her a once-over.

Cleared my throat and steadied my voice "There. Much better."

She licked her lips. Lowered her eyes, but only to raise them again as she leaned back in, her voice oh so smoky.

"Body and Blood, Kyria. I am yours to command."

She managed to make the space at the back of the coach seem very small and intimate as she eased herself past me.

I let out a long, slow breath and shaken-up chuckle.

My little bite orgy with all my Athanate had worked. Yes, they were my House. It had also created another set of issues about how that worked moving forward. I would have to ponder that in my copious free time.

Leyla was getting fist bumps and low fives as she went back up the aisle. The whole coach thought that had been an excellent show. Much appreciated.

Look, Tara said, and opened my spirit eyes.

My nothing-to-see-here working had become riled up. In along with the pulsing Mayan designs there were now writhing bodies, like some drug-fueled animation of those erotic statues some Indian temples had.

I blinked and brought my sight back down to earth.

Body and Blood.

The heart of the standard Athanate bond.

I was a Blood witch. All that Mayan stuff was on that side of dark magic. Was I also a 'Body' witch? Or, skipping the tactful Athanate evasion, a Sex witch.

That was gross.

No, Tara said. *Don't be dense. Blood magic's strong suit is all the powerful negative emotions like fear and hate. You use it in anger. Why can't you use powerful positive emotions. Like love.*

Why not indeed?

But, how, exactly?

That made me blink again and yes, it would have to join that pile of things to think about.

Not now.

I had a quick check of my own clothes to make sure nothing had come undone accidentally during the little brush with Leyla. They were fine. The combat uniform and boots fit well.

Then it was my turn to walk back to my seat.

Eyes on me. What was the image I'd thought of, back in the jet on the way to New York? Ah, yes, the way a pack of wolves watches a limping moose. Completely different kind of hunger in this case. My House. Body and Blood.

Farrell, Tucek, Basynia, Ops 4-10—*my* House.

It was Rahaimon on steroids and, disturbing or not, I was *loving* this.

"Halfway there," Theris said in a matter-of-fact voice as I sat back in my seat.

Our bus was now alone on this road. The others had split off. Each team would approach Xibalbá from a different direction, so there would be no build-up in any one place. Smaller groups reduced the chance of Peterson stumbling on us.

I was sitting next to Theris on a section with four seats facing each other. Yelena and Mirela were sitting opposite me.

"Let me guess," I said. "There's a betting pool going in House Tucek on who gets me into bed first."

"Whole House. Farrell, Tucek, Basynia," Yelena said, face deadpan and with her Ukrainian accent back. "Senior like Diakon excluded because unfair advantage. Also stops during operation. That was last chance. Was good attempt."

I laughed. It had really diverted me from worrying about the operation, which might have been a good thing. But it was time to get back to thinking about attacking Xibalbá with an insanely small force, one way out and no reinforcement options.

"Everyone's boots fit well?" I asked them sweetly.

"Well enough for a few days," Theris answered and waved it away. "Given your background, what's your professional military opinion of the operation so far? Let's say from a perfectionist, theoretical point of view."

I snorted. He was stirring it. "The army isn't always a gold standard of how it should be done, if that's what you're trying to imply. Not even Ops 4-10. Anyway, I'd say the logistics of this op are incredible, and well thought out."

I hesitated and Mirela prompted me. "But..."

I didn't want to bring out a list of what I would have done, given infinite resources and time and the benefit of some hindsight. It would serve no purpose for me, and might undermine Mirela's authority. I had put her in charge, and she *had* to be the person in charge; she was the one who'd worked on the plan from the start.

I took a second too long, and Mirela's eyes narrowed.

"You'd expect your House to give their honest analysis if you were running this op," she said. "Why can't you do that for me? Criticize away."

"I'm not sure it'd be useful. Any raid like this is always a series of compromises and guesswork, but you've had sign-off from the Colonel and Ops 4-10 veterans. I don't know enough of the background detail to come up with something that would be better."

I could see her jaw tighten, and she made a come-on gesture.

She wasn't going to let this go. I sighed and said, "Ignoring the ideal situation, which we don't have, of much closer target and more support, the main thing that worries me is it's too complex. There are too many moving parts. But the most worrying point, the worst problem, is that the entire attacking force is in groups, each of which has to wait for the others, at our point of maximum exposure and discoverability, for an event we have little control over. Ideally, we should—"

She interrupted me. "Yes, we should arrive at Xibalbá simultaneously, with a squadron of fast attack helicopters for close air support. We should have an artillery battalion to soften them up first. And tanks. And more troops. We have what we have."

I grinned. "Touchy, touchy."

She scowled and then grinned back. "You're looking forward to it," she said.

"Wouldn't say that, but I couldn't sit in Denver and wait for updates."

Theris' turn to snort.

"How did you learn the skills to run this kind of operation?" Yelena asked Mirela.

She laughed outright. "You really have no idea what Basilikos is like on the inside. It's not a creed, it's a civil war. I've had a lot of practice." She shook her head. "Never this size of operation though. Or this level of prize."

But Yelena wasn't happy with that response. "This operation was planned while you were on Vega Martine's side. Even if you didn't use any of the expertise in her House, you used her funds. You stockpiled equipment and resources in Yucatán and members of your House had to visit to organize and maintain. And yet you say Vega Martine knows nothing."

"I was successful for Vega Martine, and because of that, I had license. I had freedom to act. I didn't need any assistance from her House. Of course she knows I had an attack on Matlal planned. Of course she's looking for more information now, but there's nothing for her to find in any place she knows to look. And if she found out, would she warn Matlal? Why the sudden cold feet?"

"As soon as we came to Yucatán, Matlal's Adepts put a trace on us." Yelena raised a hand as Theris started to interrupt. "We got rid of it by luck in the cathedral and by Amber being skillful. But we only knew about the traces because Amber and Theris have the skills to detect them. What about others? What if they put a trace on Bian and Alex and his Were when they came through earlier? You say if Matlal really suspected something was happening, it would have been a much stronger trace, or more of an attempt to keep it going. I say, if I were running Matlal's security, I'd be keeping traces so light you wouldn't be able to sense them, and they'd stay that way until I knew where you were going."

"You're saying it's a trap. He has a trace on one of the others, and he'll have worked out where we're headed as soon as we left the city?"

"I'm saying it's a possibility that we shouldn't dismiss. Peterson may have been warned and we could expect ambushes on the approach which would stop the whole assault."

Theris cleared his throat. "I think Matlal is suspicious that something's happening, but I don't think he knows who we are, where we are or more importantly, where we're going."

"What's your reasoning?" Mirela asked.

"I'm beginning to sense Matlal's Adepts doing a spirit search."

He looked at me.

"You've locked down your aura," he said. "Let it out a little."

I sat back and closed my eyes. This was more Tara's role than mine. She'd been the one who learned the techniques when she'd been Tullah's spirit guide, and they'd had to hide away from exactly this type of searcher.

It wasn't a good idea to relax too much into the memories, because Tara and Tullah had been skimming the spirit world, and if I did that, Tezcatlipoca would find me.

Just a touch.

Desert dust. Cold nights. The spirits floating in on the night breeze.

And the searchers. Blind monsters. Spidery feelers stretching out. Reaching. Seeking.

I slip between the worlds, neither one nor the other.

I am not here.

I can feel Tezcatlipoca stir. God of sorcerers, and lord of the night. To invoke his name and titles is to call him.

My priestess? Your need?

I blinked.

Yelena was reaching across and holding my hands, looking worried.

"I'm okay," I said. "Theris is right. I sense there are searchers looking for us, but some are near, and some are far away. I don't think they know where we are. On the other hand, I'm sure they're Matlal's people, and so they'll concentrate on the places he's most worried about. Including Xibalbá."

"Will they be able to find us?"

Theris and I exchanged looks.

"I think my workings will keep us invisible from Matlal's Adepts until we're actually involved in the attack. I think we're divided into small enough teams that we can avoid Peterson's patrols."

"You *think*."

"Yes. And as for getting out... that's another nightmare."

"Five minutes to the drop-off site," the driver said and turned down a dirt track.

Chapter 53

Our journey had been long enough for us to get used to the air conditioning in the bus, which was a bad idea, because it really hit us when we got out. The temperature was into the 90s *and* it was humid too. It covered me like a hot, wet towel, but not a clean one.

Suck it up. This was life for the next few days.

The bus had backed off the dirt road. Out of sight of anyone passing, we picked up backpacks, checked our weapons and ammunition, and smeared camo on each other's faces. In Leyla's case, the sides of her head as well, where she'd shaved her hair. She asked me to do it, but the focus was on business now.

Then we added body armor, helmets and Tac-Net headsets for when the attack started.

This was the largest team, assigned to take the front gate and the four watchtowers on that side. Most of us had the same firearms. The primary weapon was a Heckler Koch UMP submachine gun. Secondary was the Swiss-made Sig Sauer P226 handgun. Both were 9mm. I had a couple of bandoliers, each with a dozen 30-round magazines for the machine pistol and another half dozen 10-round magazines for the Sig. Mirela had never been in the army, but apparently, she'd learned the same wisdom that I had from Top and Ben-Haim: *The only time you have too much ammo is when you're on fire. Or drowning.*

Our team had four snipers with long-barreled sniper rifles. Since we weren't going to be a mile away for their shots, those looked like overkill, but I remembered my Ops 4-10 instructors again: *You can go in with overkill or underkill, but you probably won't survive the latter.*

Grenades. Explosives. RPG launchers.

No heavy machine guns.

We all had some bladed weapons, and they were more varied. Mirela had found some way to smuggle my katana, Onibi, into the country. It was securely strapped on the side of my backpack. Some of the others had standard machetes, but House Tucek favored Gurka kukri knives.

And a heap of stuff like small drones.

All cellphones were off, and batteries removed. The only comms option we had during the march was a satellite phone in Mirela's pack. It was a clever piece of kit that encrypted and compressed the message before transmitting. If Peterson was monitoring bandwidth, and I was absolutely sure he was, all he'd hear would be the occasional crackle or hiss.

Still, another single point of failure. I fretted but kept it to myself.

Once we attacked, we'd go to tactical headsets, just like any Ops 4-10 mission.

With Theris shadowing me, I made the changes to our shielding working. If any Adept had been spirit-watching us at that point, we would have vanished suddenly. Nobody here.

The working seemed fine. Stronger than I'd expected it to be.

I should just double check it. Run through and tidy the structure again…

No. Leave it be.

I came out from the spirit trance, and the physical sensations of the jungle rushed back into me. Hot, humid, thick with smells and ringing with distant animals' calls, at least to my wolfy ears.

We were ready, and despite the hiccup at the cathedral, we were on time. As of their last communications, so were the other teams. In the next hour or so, they would all be set down to begin their march toward Xibalbá, so that tomorrow morning, each team would be at its assigned side of the fort, at the points of the compass.

Our bus driver was an inexperienced cub from the former El Paso pack, and he wasn't coming along. Mirela made sure he understood he was going to drive straight back to the company depot, leave the bus and get the hell out of Mexico. He glanced at me, all pleading eyes, but I shook my head.

He wasn't happy, but he'd obey.

As soon as he'd left, we started walking and the jungle swallowed us.

We moved quickly and made good progress. This far out, we were outside the range of Peterson's patrols, and there were lots of paths.

Theris caught up to walk beside me.

"I can feel your body react whenever someone mentions Peterson," he said.

"That's such a classy conversational opening gambit," I said.

He was right. I reacted when I heard the name, but just having him make that comment made me angry.

"If you'd rather not talk about it…"

It was the same game as Leyla had played earlier on. He wanted to know how personally invested I was. Whether my obvious hate for Peterson might lead me to doing something I would later regret. Or something that would threaten the success of the mission.

So he gave me the equivalent of a little shove and watched what I did.

"I hate him," I said. "I hate him at a very deep level."

My mind seemed to split at that point. Formed several parts. One watched the nobody-here spell, at a safe distance. One was alert to the jungle around us. One spoke to Theris. And one opened the strongbox in the depths of my mind and rifled through things best left in there.

"Colonel Peterson, as he was then, was the person responsible for imprisoning me after I was infused. He put together a team of scientists and convinced them I was no longer human."

My voice was even. It was as even and dispassionate as the voice I could hear in my head saying: *The subject is distressed.*

That *subject* was me. That was when they were experimenting with breaking my bones and searing my flesh to see how long it took my body to repair itself.

"What they did to me was torture," I said. "All of them deserve to face justice for their inhumanity. But Peterson…"

As if in response to his name, as if by naming him I'd invoked a demon out of hell, a fragment of Peterson talking floated up out of my strongbox.

Is it viable for reproduction? he'd asked.

It.

That meant me. His voice had been even too, but my senses were already acute enough I could read the tone. He'd been excited. About the thought of creating a little army of super-soldiers, even better than the Nagas in Ops 4-16. About how he'd go about it. And about raping me.

He'd completely misunderstood how Athanate are created, but I doubted he'd changed his mind about what he wanted to do to me until I started eliminating his Naga thugs.

I'd left the sentence hanging too long. Theris was looking closely at me.

"Peterson deserves a special place in hell," I said. "I would be happy to be the person to place him there. I would take pleasure in it, which I would later feel bad about."

Theris grunted.

"But it didn't stop with Peterson," I said. "Because Peterson didn't have the political clout to put himself in command of the Ops 4 group. So, there's someone I hate even more than Peterson. Someone whose name I don't even know, but who's probably still there, in the government, maybe even the Department of Defense, wheeling and dealing and doing Matlal's work for him. Askrynos, Diana named him. Askrynos is responsible for all those things that happened to me. And you see, Theris, I'll only get to him if this mission is a success. So you can stop worrying about me letting my hate get in the way of the mission. My hate is stronger than that, and my hate needs the mission to succeed."

I closed the strongbox. Sealed it.

Theris grunted again. "Askrynos, the Masked Demon. The unseeable evil. As good a name as any."

While I had him on the back foot, I quizzed him about the mechanics of magic. Why using magic made me more accessible to Tezcatlipoca. How I could use magic and keep my soul.

We talked long and hard.

While we talked, a spirit search by the Matlal Adepts passed over us. It sent shivers down my spine, but it didn't pause. It didn't even hesitate. There was nobody here.

Shortly after that, we entered the range of the Xibalbá patrols, and we went silent.

We weren't hacking our way through the jungle. In fact, although there were fewer paths here, they were more open, because Peterson's patrols used them.

There were risks being on such frequently used trails. We changed to having two pairs of scouts probing ahead, leapfrogging each other, and our drone operators took turns scouting even further.

There were no patrols *visible*, but hurrying made for an anxious way to proceed.

We weren't worried about defeating any standard patrol we came across, but there was the risk they'd be able to call their base. Even if they didn't manage that, their base would be alerted when the patrol didn't make their regular report.

We were trying to avoid them entirely.

A couple of times the Xibalbá surveillance aircraft passed overhead. Thanks to our drones, we had warning. We were split up and hunkered down out of sight while they passed. It was simple for a few of us to hide from aircraft, because of the density of the foliage.

The problem Peterson had with aerial patrols was that they were a good preventative measure against a force too large to easily hide. The sort of size of force that would be necessary to attack Xibalbá, in his thinking. He hadn't factored in an insanely small force split up and creeping in from different directions.

However, the same issue made it difficult to be sure our tiny drones were able to spot Peterson's patrols while keeping far enough away that the patrol wouldn't see it.

It slowed us down. We were behind schedule, and my tension came back to ratchet up with every step.

As a way to distract myself between shifts on the scouting teams, I imagined what it would take to modify the nobody-here spell into a spell that also reported if there was somebody on the path ahead. I imagined and fiddled with the spell.

Not straightforward. The way it was set up, the spell wasn't designed to 'see' humans. It was a sort of reciprocal feature. If the spell needed to be invisible to humans, then the reverse applied. It wasn't a fundamental problem with workings, it was simply the way it had ended up this time.

It could look ahead and see paranormals okay, but again, because of the way it was constructed it would be discoverable in return. An Adept would sense there was something there.

The patrols were humans from the Nagas, so my design ideas went nowhere...

Right up until it turned out to have been a very good idea that I was experimenting with looking ahead, because just as the scouts warned us there was a patrol coming, I warned Mirela there was a Were with them.

Putting aside the danger of him sensing my spell, which he probably couldn't manage, there was the stone-cold certainty that a Were would smell us.

Chapter 54

"We hide downwind of the path. Now," I hissed, berating myself that there hadn't been enough time to teach Mirela our hand-talk. I didn't want any noise now.

Mirela accepted my order, and using her own elementary gestures, ordered our team off the path in the right direction. We spread out and effectively vanished into the undergrowth. Far enough away to not be seen. Close enough to get back and kill the patrol if we were discovered.

At which point the whole attack was a bust.

Theris understood the issue about the Were sense of smell.

Before we'd even hunkered down, he'd conjured up a strong wind that scoured the route we'd come along, then died down to a steady breeze as the patrol approached.

How long would our scent linger on the path? Would the rich layers of a million different smells from the jungle mask it?

I had my UMP in hand and the safety off in case his efforts didn't work, even though I couldn't actually see the patrol through the jungle foliage.

I strained my wolfy senses. Took deep breaths.

Over the multi-layered, intricate smells of the jungle, there was the smell of humans. Hot, sweating humans. They weren't noisy, but not in silent mode like we'd been. There was the odd bit of equipment that creaked or a ticking sound as metal kept touching metal. Heavy footfalls.

They marched past. Reasonable discipline. Paying attention. A larger patrol than we'd been expecting. There could be all sorts of reasons for that, so I didn't focus on it.

The Were was at the back of the patrol. The last one. I was straining to listen, and my aura reached out as well. I could sense him from eighty yards away. Then, with the wind blowing toward me, I could smell him.

Not what I was expecting.

Rougarou.

Not just a were-hyena, but the unmistakable sense of *rabioso* came off him. Like one of the were-hyenas created in the stinking hellhole beneath Galvez's fortress in northern Mexico. This was *not* on the intelligence briefing. There had been no mention of Weres working at the Xibalbá fortress.

Mirela was an arm's length away. She wanted to whisper. I shook my head minutely and held my finger to my lips, then spelled out Rougarou in standard sign letters with my fingers.

She nodded and I returned to concentrating on the Naga patrol.

They kept moving. There was no change in their movement or the level of alertness I could sense. An agonizing wait, and they were past us.

But another thirty yards on and the Rougarou slowed. I could hear him sniffing. Turning. Sniffing again.

Shit.

I made signs for Theris to get the wind blowing again, and signs for Mirela to stay still. The rest of the patrol was moving on, which made this my kind of situation to fix.

The jungle is never quiet, not even when humans are about. There's a skill to using those background sounds to mask movement that I'd learned in Ops 4-10. I'd slipped my backpack off, I had Onibi ready in my hand and I was just twenty yards away from the Rougarou when I had to freeze.

A couple of guys from the patrol were coming back to check on him.

"What's up, Yaxi?" Low-voiced, but not stressed.

"Smell something."

If they'd left him behind, I could have killed him silently and had him away from the path before anyone noticed or came back to check where he was. Of course they'd raise the alarm, but I wasn't sure they'd assume the likeliest reason for the Rougarou disappearing was enemy action. The were-hyena's aura was writhing like a snake in his head. Rabioso were borderline crazy, and I was laying big bets they'd had runaways before.

Not an option now. One I could handle quietly. Three—nope. And no way they'd think the three of them had decided to bug out together.

"*Feel* something," the Rougarou said.

I could hear the creak of their harnesses as his two buddies crouched, and I could visualize them looking outwards, trying to see through all the densely packed leaves.

Other than Onibi, my weapons were with my backpack, and anyway, fighting was the absolute last resort. This whole layered, tottering, complex plan depended on Xibalbá *not* being alerted. And right now, that depended on two Naga troopers only twenty yards away not seeing me or any of the other members of my team.

I was in a crouch. My muscles were tired. My heart was beating so loudly I thought they'd have to hear it. Sweat was trickling down my face, inside my clothes. Flies landed on me. I kept still and waited.

Two minutes passed.

Theris' wind still brought the scent of the three to me. The two humans weren't alarmed. The Rougarou was harder to read. His insanity fed changes in his body chemistry that masked normal responses.

Five minutes.

I twitched when one of them spoke.

"Nothing."

The other human echoed him.

"Hank," the first one said, "you and Yaxi catch up with the others. Keep the lookout going, okay? You did good, Yaxi. Rather a false alarm than miss something."

Two of them moved off, including the Rougarou, and the third remained. Another five minutes.

I heard him take something out of a Velcro pocket.

"Base, West Ten, Delta 5 here. Reading?" he spoke quietly.

"West Ten, Base. Go ahead." The radio was turned all the way down. My wolfy ears could just make it out.

"The Rougarou thought he smelled or sensed something at my current position. Dropped out of formation and just stood here sniffing."

A pause and a different voice from the radio, someone higher up: "Base 6 here. He's been solid?"

"Yeah. Takes orders, does his stuff. Better than the last one."

There was a snort at that, then: "Your take?"

"Dunno. I'm thinking there's been someone along this path more recently than the last patrol."

"Locals?"

"Could be."

There was a pause.

"Keep to your schedule. We'll send a double team to cover and put another bird over there."

They closed the conversation, and the last patrol member went off at a trot to catch up.

I relaxed and took some deep, deep breaths. Nagas might be evil, but they were well trained and competent. We'd gotten lucky again. *Very* lucky.

I slipped quietly back to Mirela.

"Gotta move," I said in a low voice. "Very quietly, very quickly. They're suspicious. Got another two patrols coming this way, and an extra aerial snooper."

As I spoke, I was already thinking ahead. In the jungle, you could generally be quiet or quick, but not both. In fact, 'quick' would be more like 'not slow'.

"There's a parallel path," Mirela said, wiping sweat off her forehead with one arm. "More open than this path. We could force our way through to it. That'd set us further back on the schedule, but we won't be where they're looking, and we could make up the time by going through the night."

"Okay, but I have some fine tuning to that plan. We won't be forcing or chopping our way through, making a lot of noise and leaving a clear trail."

"Going to fly, are we?"

I laughed. Quietly. The jungle was thick, but it had paths through it, kept open by animals.

"Wait and see, but first, we need to contact the other parties and warn them."

Mirela got her radio out of her backpack. The compression and encryption made it awkward for conversations. I had to dictate a message and press transmit. The actual transmission would sound like a short burst of static to anyone listening with a radio receiver unless they had the decompression and decryption keys.

It took several minutes to get the other groups to reply to me.

Flint and Kane were happy to experiment with using the spell to look ahead specifically for paranormals.

Liu wasn't happy. He didn't want to touch my nobody-here spell any more than he'd had to, and however skilled an Adept he was, he'd never faced a situation like this—making complex workings while running through the jungle under threat of being ambushed by Nagas. Worse, the wind in their area was behind them, blowing their scent ahead.

He reluctantly accepted there were no alternatives and signed off.

I sighed. We'd arrived at this point with a series of decisions that had seemed to be the best choices at the time. They were on the point of unravelling, but I needed to trust the others and concentrate on our own situation here. The good thing for the whole attack was we had Peterson's attention focused on our direction, and the others *should* be safer for it. The bad thing for us was we had Peterson's attention focused on our direction.

If we were moving fast, I had to take point, and I needed to be able to detect humans as well as Were beyond my line of sight.

"Theris, I'm going to need a breeze blowing from whichever direction I'm heading in. Can you do that without it damaging the nobody-here spell?"

He grimaced. "I can do that for about a quarter mile ahead of us, and I'll need to stop if one of Matlal's Adepts looks this way. I can warn you if that happens."

"That's a plan," I said, and started stripping. "Now, someone needs to carry my gear."

There were a few amused complaints, and some comments when I was naked.

I ignored it, reached inside and changed.

Oh!

I hadn't shifted in too long. I felt dizzy and uncoordinated. Maybe it hadn't been a good idea to try out something new under the circumstances, but jaguar seemed to suit.

Theris picked up my backpack and stuffed my clothes inside.

Leyla, on the other hand, took the chance to scratch behind my ears.

I snarled and turned as if I was going to take her arm off. I wasn't going to bite her, but I needed to remind her I wasn't entirely Amber in this form.

"Fierce pussycat," she said. "Pretty."

"Back in the zone, Leyla," Mirela snapped. "Time to go."

I loped a short way down the path until I found the first animal track crossing it which headed in the right direction. Narrow. But if I could get through, so could the others. I was just glad they had the backpacks.

I dived into the seemingly impenetrable jungle, and the rest of them followed behind, with muffled cursing quickly silenced.

Good thing we got under cover; there was a drone overhead about five minutes later. It flew up and down over the path where the patrol had stopped, and then spiraled out in a search pattern. Luckily, it had no hope of seeing us beneath the thick foliage, but drones might be a problem later, when we were more in the open.

I'd have to talk to Theris.

Like I'd have to think about where the Rougarou were coming from. It certainly wasn't the horrific factory under Astilla de Luna, Mauricio Gálvez's headquarters. That had been destroyed along with everything else.

Later. All for later.

Right now, I was being swamped with the sensations of being a jaguar in the jungle.

The first stage took far longer than we'd hoped: it was late at night before we finally broke through onto the parallel path.

That was just another complication in an already difficult situation. I felt more and more uneasy. There was no way back, and yet it seemed to be slipping out of our control—a feeling like the point where your tires lose traction on ice.

There was no alternative and no opportunity to rest. We couldn't get any further behind schedule. The delivery to the fortress which triggered the whole assault was due to be made in the morning, and every team *had* to be in position.

The problem of the moment was the path we'd reached was more open, and we'd have to follow it to catch up. It was dark, but we'd still be visible to a drone with an infrared camera, and if we were hurrying, we ran the risk of not noticing that one of Peterson's drones had line-of-sight on us.

Theris had to create a working that increased the heat our bodies shed. It did the job. It felt odd, like we'd gone from running through the Yucatán jungle to running through cold woods in Alaska. It didn't destroy the heat, it just discharged it. Any infrared scanner would see the area around the path was warmer than expected, but there would be no glowing blobs showing hot, sweaty bodies.

It was the best we could do, given the hurry we were in.

I ran ahead. If I came across a patrol, I was just a jaguar, and I'd have time to make a noise to alert the others before disappearing into the jungle.

We still had twelve miles to run.

Chapter 55

Dawn.

We were hungry, tired and dirty, probably smelly as well, but damn, we were in position. We were a hundred yards away from the front gate, still well-hidden in the jungle, and peering at the monstrous, threatening bulk of Xibalbá emerging from the night.

I was back in human form. Being a jaguar through the long night had been strangely calming, but that was gone now.

It was showtime.

Or it would have been, but everyone else was late.

Mirela's smart satellite phone also had a secondary function as a status indicator for each team. We got a green because we were ready. The delivery convoy had been spotted by a team placed for that purpose at a village thirty miles away, and they'd passed through an hour ago. They got a green. Even though the roads were bad, they *should* be here any minute.

Bian, Alex and the werewolves had a green.

The other three teams in the first wave were still showing amber, which meant en route, short of position, as of their last automatic update through the satellite connection.

The others being late wasn't the end of our worries; the guards on the gate had been doubled.

Mirela and I were talking in mutters. "They know something's up, but sure as hell don't know what it is," she said.

"It could just be based on the Rougarou that smelled us. Do you have any information on how they respond to general suspicions?"

She shook her head. "Nothing that specific."

The jungle around us was a cacophony of birds and insects, but then there was something else. I strained my ears.

"I can hear a truck."

In the still, cool dawn air, mechanical noises carried a long way.

One of the amber lights on Mirela's status page turned green. Rita's group, with Flint, on the north side of the fortress, so on our right.

"We've still got time," Mirela said, almost to herself. "It takes them half an hour to get the fuel truck inside from the time it arrives, and the shorter the time we spend in place, the lower the chance of being detected."

I snorted. There was nothing like putting a positive spin on it. Yesterday's feelings about my loss of control returned, but there was nothing that could be done about it now. Mirela trusted her House. Since that was also my House, I had to trust them too.

Another green. The team from the south, Kane's group, on our left.

"One more. See, we're getting there."

"Still late," I said. "Here are the trucks now."

They came into view on the dirt road leading to the fort, and lumbered toward the gate, slowing down as they approached.

There was a stirring in the armored watchtowers. Machine guns swiveled, without ever actually pointing directly at the trucks. They had enough firepower to cut the trucks in half. I felt my insides shrink at the thought of being in the sights of those guns.

A squad of Naga soldiers came out from the sandbagged entrance to check the convoy. Half kept looking out at the jungle, rifles pointed down across their chests where they'd be easy to bring up. The other half moved to check the trucks.

"Doubled up that as well," Mirela muttered.

These men didn't look bored or complacent. Their equipment looked well maintained. Their discipline was good. They looked relaxed, alert and damned efficient.

The only positive was, if they thought we were actually here, they'd be acting very differently.

The last status on Mirela's satellite phone remained stubbornly amber. That was Liu's group. What had happened?

I shied away from imagining what I'd say to Tullah if Liu didn't make it. I couldn't think like that. If his team had been caught, Nagas wouldn't be out casually inspecting the trucks.

Think positive.

The guards had brought out a camera system mounted on an inspection trolley and a pair of them pushed it underneath the fuel truck, painstakingly checking for anything that was out of place. Two sets of eyes. Good practice. Other guards looked over the containers and the other trucks. Only when they were satisfied did they motion the drivers to climb out. A couple talked to each driver, while another couple inspected their cabs. They had a handheld monitor of some kind, presumably looking for any trace of explosive.

"You *sure* the drivers know nothing?" I asked, imagining one of them starting to act nervously under the interrogation.

"Yes," Mirela said. "All they're told is it's a dangerous job. They're always nervous. They're told not to mess with the soldiers, and if anyone starts shooting, lie down on the ground."

"Which *might* keep them safe."

"Only thing that would. And yes, I have someone tasked with getting them out of here afterwards."

I wondered whether that was something she'd put in place because she knew I'd be unhappy about the dangers these drivers were exposed to. If she'd carried out this attack for Vega Martine, what would have happened to those drivers?

I'd ask her later.

We both kept glancing at her satellite phone.

At this stage, there was no turning back. We'd have to attack anyway, even one team short.

It wasn't completely suicidal to go ahead, but the missing team were the ones assigned to the east side of the fortress. It was their responsibility to take down the eastern watchtowers. The ones next to the airstrip.

If they didn't... well, our escape plan would be little better than 'scatter, run and pray'.

The guards were finally satisfied with the fuel truck. The driver was sent off to wait in the lean-to. One of the guards drove the truck into the chicane. Even with the sandbags moved back, the bends were so tight he couldn't turn, but instead had to drive forward up one part and then reverse down the next.

It would take him about twenty minutes to get the truck to the fuel depot at the center of the fort, about five minutes to connect it and start pumping. Shortly after that, the fuel in the bowser would drop sufficiently so it could no longer support the inner membrane bag of TEB suspended inside the tanker. The bag would split, exposing the TEB to the air and then the show would begin with a bang.

Thirty minutes. Maybe forty if they were being slow. The last group had to be in place. We didn't have spare capacity to cover their targets as well as our own.

We *might* get lucky, but I felt we'd already gotten all the luck we were going to on this mission.

The guards were now focused on the container trucks.

All these trucks had been used in deliveries before. They were unusual trucks, but the guards had seen them several times, and out here, no one had fleets of identical trucks. There was no reason to worry that the guards were inspecting them more thoroughly than they had before.

Mirela's satellite phone blinked. Incoming message. From the missing group.

Shit.

She held the phone where we could both hear it.

Salar's voice. Mirela's Diakon was the team leader for the group with Liu in it. She kept it short: "Had to eliminate a patrol. They didn't have a chance to report in, but we don't know where they were in their reporting schedule. We'll be in position in about half an hour."

Mirela swore under her breath and then got herself under control. She pressed the button to prepare a transmission.

"Understood. Fuel truck is twenty minutes from connecting up to the depot's pumps. Make the best possible time and expect to engage immediately."

She pressed the transmit.

They was a delay before Salar came back. "Will do."

"We're cutting it fine," I said.

Mirela nodded. "As long as they're in place and suppressing the anti-aircraft batteries before the helicopters come."

The helicopters bringing Bian, Alex and the rest of the Were would be sitting ducks for the anti-aircraft batteries.

"If the dead patrol's report is due earlier than the fuel truck explodes, we're going to have to attack anyway," I said.

Neither of us knew what Peterson's protocol was for a missed report. They'd try a couple of times before raising an alarm surely? We didn't know. What *did* we know? If the alarm went off, the fortress went on lockdown and ten minutes later, every single Naga soldier inside would be on duty, at which point it would be suicide for us to try and attack. We knew about the response to an alarm because Peterson had them practice it once a month.

Mirela updated the others—if the alarm sounded: attack. She told Alex's team about the potential problem. It made timing almost impossible. Alex's helicopters couldn't take off and hover while waiting—all their fuel was needed for our escape.

Twenty-five minutes.

The guards finished the inspection of the first two container trucks and waved them forward. The drivers parked them nose-in to the left of the main gate, where they always parked, and then went to join their companion in the lean-to.

A crane would come and remove the containers when all the trucks were parked. Then it would load the trucks with the containers from the last delivery and the drivers would be sent on their way.

Except that wasn't going to happen today.

Twenty minutes.

The other two trucks were waved on.

The four of us armed with RPGs double-checked our weapons and spread out. Snipers melted into the undergrowth.

I checked my UMP, made sure Onibi was secured on the backpack.

Fifteen minutes.

"We've got minutes left," Theris whispered.

"Yes, but quite a few of them," Mirela replied.

An SUV with six Nagas threaded its way slowly through the chicane. The Nagas were out of uniform.

"Time off," Mirela whispered. "R&R."

"What do they do?"

She shook her head. "Just about anything they want. The only rule is don't get caught. The local police don't count." She sighed. "The nearest villages are almost empty. Certainly, any young women have gone far away."

The SUV drove off toward the road, and the crane started removing the containers from the trucks. That was earlier than they usually started.

Most of the guards returned to their positions in the chicane. A couple watched the unloading. A couple watched the jungle.

Alert but not alarmed.

Ten minutes.

Every second seemed to drag out longer and longer.

I felt myself slipping into my old Ops 4-10 mindset. There'd been a time when I thought I was through with it. I'd left the army, and tried to make a conscious decision that my life wouldn't involve war and battles and death.

Some hope.

The old mindset had come back down in Mexico. Only reasonable, I guessed. That had been an operation very like Ops 4-10 had run. And now, here it was again. A sort of distancing from what was about to happen. My brain analyzed things. Kept them abstract. Kept them away from my gut reaction, so I wasn't affected. So that the horror of what was about to unfold didn't feel so much like a horror that we were unleashing. Because modern warfare *is* horror and hell on earth.

It wasn't like the Nagas didn't deserve it. But how could I be free of all the anger and hate locked inside of me if I was feeding it?

Still…

Five minutes…

Mirela's satellite phone blinked just as someone at the gate started shouting. Guards immediately began to trot backwards to the gate, rifles up and pointed outwards. The watchtowers became active again, machine guns roving back and forth.

Shit!

A siren began to shriek.

Chapter 56

Four RPGs lit off.

The military jury is out on using RPGs against well-prepared tanks, but RPG vs watchtower had only one winner. Each of those rockets we fired first only weighed about the same as a couple of six packs of beer. It would cover the distance to the watchtower in a blink and strike it at a fraction below the speed of sound. The head was designed to pierce tank armor a foot thick before exploding.

The steel plating on the watchtowers was no defense.

Every team had RPGs. They came from every direction and blew every single armored watchtower right off its scaffolding in a shocking burst of flames. In a second, all the murderously effective heavy machine guns with overlapping fields of fire were simply gone.

The second wave of rockets my team fired was trickier.

These were a different type of RPG: airburst fragmentation grenades. They converged into the space above the sandbagged chicane, where the guards were protected from us. Time to explode was much harder to get right. Two of the three which fired successfully intersected laser beams which the team had aimed to cross overhead the chicane. The rockets exploded, directing the force of the blasts downwards.

Each had a kill radius of fifty yards, and body armor wouldn't stop the shrapnel.

The single concrete pillbox, which was immune to shrapnel, received a rocket from the last RPG, right through the slot.

We were up and running before the sounds of the explosions had died away.

Classic Ops 4-10 tactics. *Hit them, and then hit them again before they recover.*

As we ran, a remote control signal was sent to one of our odd trucks. It fired up its engine and powered the hydraulic jacks that tilted the flatbed.

Suddenly it wasn't just us, sprinting across the undefended open ground.

Mirela's answer to how to get into the middle of the fort within the three minutes it took to close the blast doors on the bank was simple. Flying motorcycles. It was like a scene from some dystopian apocalypse, as she'd hinted. The side of one of the containers banged flat and a dozen lightweight, high-powered motorcycles came snarling out, ridden by leather-suited maniacs.

They skidded in the dust, spraying clouds from their back wheels, wobbled, lined up and, one by one, they hurtled toward the tilted flatbed of the truck, which made a great ramp, pointed over the fort's wall.

Before the first was airborne, two other containers from our delivery blew off their tops.

What emerged was like the nightmare realization of some child's robot toy. They were steel racks, each forming a rocket matrix, mounted on a platform. Beneath the two platforms, powered scissor jacks raised them quickly above the level of the fort's walls.

And then the rockets ignited and shot howling towards their targets.

These were another level of horror entirely: thermobaric warheads. The initial, smaller blast flooded the buildings they were aimed at with an unignited aerosol cloud of very high explosives. Then the second explosion lit that cloud. It burned so hot it sucked in air and collapsed buildings *inwards*, before the flames expanded in the final blast and blew everything back outwards, in pieces.

We ran past the remains of the sandbag chicane in time to see the barracks, food hall, gym and offices crumple and then vanish in violent explosions.

Even at that distance the heat prickled against our exposed skin.

But violent as those explosions were, they weren't in the same league as the fuel dump going up.

The earth itself rang with it. We were hurled to the side. My ears and eyes went into shock and when I could finally look up, I saw hell itself. A peculiar, brutal hell of flames, scouring dust storms, choking stenches and insane noise.

Mirela was shouting, but it sounded like she was in the next state.

I leaped back to my feet. Theris and Yelena were with me. Working mostly on instinct and muscle memory, I checked my UMP and then ran after Mirela through the smoke and dust and falling debris. It was raining burning bits of fuel dump.

I could hear more explosions ahead. It was difficult to tell, but I thought they had to be on the far side of the fort. That would mean Salar's team was doing their task and had launched their wave of drones. Clever design. Carbon-fiber, no radar profile. Electric engines, not hot enough for the automatically launched, anti-aircraft, heat-seeking missiles to lock onto. Just big enough to deliver explosives right onto those same anti-aircraft batteries.

I'd been so jarred by the intensity of the fuel dump explosion, I'd lost track of time. That had never happened to me in Ops 4-10. It felt like we'd been running forever, but I knew it had to be less than a minute since the alarm went off.

Somewhere ahead, the motorcycle team should already have prevented the blast doors at the bank from sealing. As we ran, I saw a motorcycle lying on the ground, front wheel still spinning slowly. Either the rider had been knocked off by the explosions, or there had been an attempt at a counterattack. No sign of the rider. A couple of Naga bodies lay to one side.

I vaulted the motorcycle and ran on. This had to be in the right direction.

A couple more staggering Naga troopers loomed out of the dust cloud. I didn't have time to shoot them. Yelena fired and then we were past them.

Theris fired behind me. I didn't turn. No time. There was a wall in front. The bank? It had to be. The next buildings were on the other side of a berm, and the fuel dump certainly wasn't still standing.

Follow the wall.

My ears were recovering. I could hear lots of shots from different directions.

And the sound of running coming out of the dust cloud. A body of troops, spread out as far as they could while still able to see each other. I recognized the one on point.

"Rita!" It came out as a croak and I coughed.

She heard me. We joined up.

We were at the entrance to the bank. There were three discarded motorcycles. Two of the team were down; another was giving first aid.

We swarmed in, and others joined us, at which point I realized my TacNet headset and helmet had been torn off in the explosion.

We got inside just in time: Salar's second wave of drone bombs hit the ammo dump and it felt like the world had come to an end.

Chapter 57

I was trying to get off the floor, again, with my ears shut down.

Yelena helped me up. We helped Theris up.

Focus.

We were in the bank. Along with about twenty others and more dust than all the deserts of Africa.

We hadn't come in through blast doors. The intelligence about the design of the bank was wrong.

I fumbled in my webbing and brought out the powerful flashlight I'd been issued with. The beam showed everyone in the same state, staggering to their feet and shaking their heads.

Where were our objectives? The store of viruses? Matlal's secured servers? *Think.*

The bank was divided into four sections. I'd seen the aerial photos of it. The strange, squat rectangular shape with the sixteen peculiar towers on the roof. Yes, the towers, whatever they were, were grouped in a way that implied the building had four sections. And thinking about it, dividing it made sense. We knew Peterson had some method of sealing it off in an emergency. Sealing each part off separately was a better way to achieve security. Certainly, sealing the virus storage from everything else was a sensible precaution.

So… we were inside the building, but what was where, and which parts had we got access to?

Through the clouds of dust, I could make out a central hall, big enough for a small truck to get in.

I couldn't see the far end of it, but nearest to me, there was a short passageway which had to lead somewhere.

I ran down it, Yelena and Theris on my heels. Mirela had reached the same conclusion. She was there.

It was only about fifteen yards deep. Our flashlights caught a tangle of metal where two motorcycles had jammed the blast doors of this section open.

"Which part is this?"

"We find out."

We climbed over the motorcycles and our flashlights showed us a warehouse structure, with rows of racks. Most were empty, but the nearest rack had a rank of about thirty sealed metal containers with black and yellow biohazard labels. One of the two from the motorcycle team was inspecting the labels while the other stood guard.

We'd found the viruses.

"Team Virus," Mirela was calling on her headset. "First entrance on the right of hallway."

We were still assembling. A couple of the team clambered over the motorcycles and began to take the canisters down. We hadn't known how many we were going to find, or what size, but it didn't matter. Some of Team Virus would have explosives that would burn at over 3,000 degrees. The containers themselves would vaporize. The racks would vaporize. The whole room would vaporize. We needed to be a long way away when that happened.

Objective 1 was on its way to being achieved. I couldn't do anything more here.

I made my way out and back to the central hall.

The dust and smoke had thinned some, but I still needed the flashlight.

More of us were coming in all the time. I was just about to start cursing my lack of a TacNet when Theris grabbed my shoulder and handed me his.

"I don't need it," my pelea said. "I only have the one task."

Yeah. To keep me alive by whatever means. Just so long as I didn't succumb to Tezcatlipoca.

Despite my being too distracted to shield myself, Tezcatlipoca was out of my head at the moment, which made me uneasy. What was he planning?

Listening to the TacNet was hardly less confusing than not having it at all. I tuned it out and went for the second hall on the right.

The blast doors at the end had closed on another couple of motorcycles, so we had at least another section of the bank open to us.

Some of the motorcycle team were just inside, firing at guards who'd taken refuge here.

I took a fast look—head around the door and back out again quickly. This was Xibalbá's vault. The warehouse that Matlal used to stockpile his rare metals. Open-plan layout. Pyramids of ingots. Gold, platinum. Millions or billions. I didn't care. Not my priority.

I made a call on the TacNet. "Team Metal, second hallway on right. Resistance inside the vault."

We couldn't take all of it. We didn't have the carrying capacity. I didn't care what Team Metal managed to shift. I knew they had enough explosives to vaporize what we couldn't take.

I was already sprinting back to the central hallway.

Gut call. The servers were in the second hallway to the left from the entrance.

I was on Team Server so that's where I ran, shadowed by Yelena and Theris.

Alex's voice came over the TacNet "Team Wolf is on the ground. Your ride home is here."

He was getting ahead of himself. First, Team Wolf had to suppress any counterattack to ensure we had a safe exit corridor to the airstrip. Meanwhile, we had to ensure we had what we'd come to take, but I liked hearing his voice and I chuckled at his delivery.

The clouds of dust and smoke were thinning slowly.

I had to stop running and pick my way carefully. The motorcycle team had made it to here as well. But they hadn't made it in time.

The blast doors to the server section were closed and sealed.

Chapter 58

Mirela was already there.

She ushered me back. "Back around the corner. Explosives."

We backed up, and found David, surrounded by his protection team. I really hadn't wanted to include him in this op—he didn't have the fighting skills we'd been developing with the packs and our Ops 4-10 volunteers. But he was the tech expert, and it was imperative to get the information on those servers. We needed an expert on the ground.

We'd assigned two Ops 4-10 and one Tucek combat expert to be with him at all times. So far, so good. They'd gotten him here unharmed.

Rita skidded in to join me, just as the team working on the explosives came scuttling around the corner.

Our cue to cover our ears and hunker down.

Another explosion. This one was unimpressive in contrast to the destruction we'd unleashed on Xibalbá already. A sharp crack and a spray of debris into the main hallway.

We turned the corner again, flashlights playing on the damaged wall.

They hadn't tried to blow holes in the blast doors themselves. They'd gone instead for the seam between the roof and wall above the doors. Smart.

"Didn't want to risk a bigger charge to get through the doors," Mirela was saying. "This building's structure is already compromised."

"Look like it worked," I said. "I can see enough space above the blast door structures to crawl through."

"You're not going first—" Yelena started to say, and stopped.

The building was shaking.

As if synchronized, our flashlight beams went upwards, through the continuing dust and smoke, to check on the ceiling.

It was shaking too. A fine rain of dust from the edges joined the swirling after-effects of all the explosions.

There was a banging, mechanical noise. The sound of gears and motors and wheels. Not like a truck. More like a...

"Shit," I shouted. "The whole damn section is on an elevator platform."

The strange structures on top of the building suddenly made sense. Four sections. Sealed by blast doors from the main hallway—that was one level of security, but Peterson had gone further. Each section could sink underground. Those structures on the roof contained the pulleys.

"Alex!" I shook my head as I called into the TacNet. Not Alex. I needed to talk directly. "Team Wolf. Is the Hind still in the air?"

"Affirm." The voice that came back wasn't Alex—it was a female. From background noises, I was talking to the Hind pilot. She was one of House Tucek. Ophira. Smoky eyes. Silky black hair. Even though most of my memories of biting all of House Tucek were a little hazy, my throat remembered perfectly. The two points where her fangs had broken my skin throbbed pleasantly.

Mind back on task.

"Ophira, on the top of the bank building, there are towers. Sixteen in total. Four in the middle of the building. I want those middle four destroyed without blowing the ceiling in on us."

"Wilco, Mistress. Applying some cannon with due care and attention."

She sounded as calm as if she were out for an afternoon stroll. I was sure pilots practiced that.

The Hind carried a 30mm cannon for ground attack work. Each round weighed only a bit more than my cellphone, but it arrived at three times the speed of sound. That made it about the same destructive power as being hit by an SUV at 30 mph. For *each* round. She had a couple of hundred of them.

The building shook and shuddered. When the thunder of the cannon died away, there was no longer the sound of those winches lowering anything, anywhere, ever again.

"*Excellent* job, Ophira," I said.

"I aim to please, Mistress."

In the meantime, Yelena decided the best way to keep me from going through the breach first was to beat me to it. Milena and Rita followed her. Theris allowed me to go in front of him, and there were more from Team Server behind him.

Once we were past the damage, we reached a gantry designed to allow maintenance of the blast door mechanisms. It joined up with other ceiling-level gantries in the shape of a room-spanning 'X', which were designed to allow access to the elevator towers in the four corners.

It was difficult to be sure of what we were seeing. There was less of a dust and smoke cloud in here, but no light except through the damage done by the Hind to the tower on our left.

The gantries themselves had taken some damage and they swayed alarmingly as more of us came through and spread out, looking for a way to get down to the platform with the server room.

It was impossible to tell how far the platform had gone. Over a hundred feet at least. Far enough that we couldn't jump. I went to the left, to see if the damaged tower could provide a way down. Mirela and Rita were ahead of me. Theris was right behind me, with David, but Yelena had gotten on the other side as we came in, and she was being pushed further away from me as more came through.

"Mission timer," a pre-recorded voice spoke from the TacNet. "Ten minutes remaining."

It felt like we'd been here *hours*.

"Clock's running down," Mirela grabbed my arm. "We've got the virus stores, and this is taking a lot longer than we planned. We quit now."

We *were* short of time. We didn't have precise information on Matlal's reaction force down in Campeche—readiness, deployment delays, actual transit time. My gut said if Matlal was as much on the alert as we'd seen he was, his reaction force was already on the way. The trucks would be hours. The helicopters, however, would be here in another ten minutes. That's why we'd set the timer.

Of course, they wouldn't be expecting to come up again a Hind attack helicopter, but we'd just emptied its most formidable weapon. And I wanted our exit to be clean. I didn't want to make our escape while fighting off Matlal's forces.

But I couldn't pass up a chance of finding Askrynos *and* destroying Matlal's online resources if there was a way…

"There's a way down inside this tower," Rita yelled.

"Five minutes," I said to Mirela. "It's what we planned anyway. Start the evacuation process, but we search for another five."

"It'll take us longer than that," Theris said.

"Maybe." I argued as we went. "But those server drives down there rip the heart out of Matlal's whole organization. They're right there."

"With Peterson and an unknown number of guards," Theris said.

He was testing me. It was *likely* Peterson was down there.

"It's not about Peterson," I said, as I climbed carefully over the rubble and peered down into the body of the tower, "it's about those drives."

I wasn't lying, exactly. I had rationalized the strategic view, and I did hate Askrynos, but that demon had no face. Peterson had a face. And a voice. I remembered them well. I remembered what had been done to me on his orders.

Without the need to open up my mental strongbox, the hate was seeping out, filling my body with fire. All the battering I'd taken from the explosions faded away and my focus became sharp and clear.

There was a set of rungs inside the tower, all the way down, and an open door at the bottom with a dead body propping it open. Lots of tools lying around him. The maintenance man had chosen the wrong day to work in the towers—the fuel dump blowing up probably made him fall.

Even protected by huge berms, the explosion had done a lot of damage. The whole gantry structure was lurching and coming away from the remains of the tower. Theris, trying to climb from the gantry to the tower, cursed as the whole structure swayed.

"The explosion to destroy the virus store is set for ten minutes," Mirela said. "Five minutes to start evacuating is cutting it fine."

I was about to make a joke about nothing ever getting done except at the last minute, but I heard Leyla and Yelena yelling, immediately followed by gunfire and explosions.

Theris swore again as I dodged past him on the rungs and stuck my head up to see what the hell was going on.

We hadn't dismissed the Nagas, but we hadn't expected them to stick around or put up much resistance after the first wave. They were a bunch of mercenary psychopaths. While they'd had a good thing going, they'd kept it going, and they were well trained in how to do that. Hit them with the ordnance that we'd used, and the dumbest of them could see their good thing wasn't going to be good any more. Xibalbá was finished. They had no deep ties of loyalty, not to Peterson, and not to Matlal. Probably the opposite. They'd expect Matlal to blame them for this disaster and wanted to be far away when he did.

But not all of them had bugged out.

A group had emerged onto the gantry from the tower diagonally across the room and were charging toward us, firing submachine guns and throwing grenades.

Crazy. A damaged gantry, swaying like a branch in a gale, made aim impossible and the grenades just fell through the grating. But they still had their guns.

Nearest to the tower I was poking my head out of were Leyla and Yelena, firing back.

Leyla leaped across to get in front of me.

"Get down, Kyria!"

A submachine gun is hard to aim when you're stationary on solid ground. It's impossible on a rocking gantry when you're also running, but if you put enough bullets into a limited space, some are going to hit.

Leyla staggered. Fell against the gantry rail and nearly went over.

Yelena grabbed her webbing, one handed, still firing with the other, but her shots went wide.

Two more Ops 4-10 troopers burst out from the entrance we used, which was one of the only parts of the structure that was still stable. They raked the Nagas with lethal fire.

And then the remainder of the ammo dump exploded.

Chapter 59

Ammunition dumps don't usually explode all at once.

Xibalbá's was no exception.

The early strikes had set the place on fire, and it chose the worst possible time to start cooking off—where the fire explodes the rest of the ammunition. And this wasn't just any ammunition. The fire must have reached the stores of anti-aircraft rockets. One went, and the rest of them followed.

The building we were in was protected from the direct effect of the detonation by the huge earthwork berm between it and the ammo dump. It wasn't protected from the concussive effect transmitted through the earth itself.

The building shook. The gantry, already loose, bucked and then buckled. There was a scream of metal and sharp cracking sounds. The tower I was in was already damaged, and the gantry's fastenings pulled away from the wall. The entire diagonal walkway tore free. All the Nagas, dead or alive, plummeted down.

Then the crossbar gantry running along the top of the blast doors, the one that had the rest of my team on it, began to twist and sag.

"No!" I screamed. "Yelena!"

She dropped her UMP and hung on. One hand on the railing, one hand in Leyla's webbing.

I tried to go to them, but the tower I was watching from was crumbling underneath me. I lost my grip. Fell. At the last second Theris grabbed onto my webbing and I came to a bone-jarring halt, losing Theris' TacNet headset and my helmet. I could hear the remaining gantries detaching and it felt like my heart was coming apart. With Theris' help, I scrambled back up.

The tower was five feet shorter, and the cross gantry was floating free, hanging down and held by no more than two tortured steel tubes.

Yelena was still holding on grimly.

Those above the gantry formed linked chains to reach down and pull their team members up.

Yelena started to climb, but she wasn't even looking at what she was doing.

Her eyes were fixed on mine. Wild. Staring.

My stomach felt like it was still falling down the tower. We were separated by about fifty feet, and it might as well have been a hundred. For all my skills and powers, I couldn't turn into a bat and fly. I couldn't jump across that distance. And while I could think of a dozen ways we could be rescued, none of them could be achieved before the virus storage explosion took the whole building out. In fact, none of them could be achieved before Matlal's reaction force started to threaten us.

My priestess…

No! Even if Tezcatlipoca *could* make me fly. And Theris didn't kill me.

"Yelena! Listen to me," I shouted. "Mirela's with me. Salar's out at the airfield. You're my Diakon. You're taking over command here. You evacuate *now*. You get everyone away."

Chains of teammates had reached her and taken Leyla.

She barely seemed to notice, swinging by one hand.

"I can't leave you." The pain in her voice cut into me.

"You have to. Go now. I can't let my whole House die trying to save me. And anyway, there's a way out for us, and a chance to get the drives."

She was being pulled up off the gantry. Pulled into the breach we'd come through. Everyone had been taken off the damaged gantry. Everyone was safe, for some definitions of the word, and for a very limited time.

"Climb on the roof," she yelled. "I'll get the Hind to pick you up."

"No, Yelena! No time. The Hind has to cover your getaway. You can't risk it. Look, Peterson's down there with the servers, and he has to have another way out. We *will* find it. You have to get out too, or it's all meaningless to me. Go! Now! Hurry!"

She gave curt instructions and people went, leaving her alone.

She spoke, trying to say something to me. I could see her mouth move, but more ammunition reached its critical point and another explosion drowned out the sound of her voice. It also broke some more of the tower. Theris was shouting urgently at me.

We had to go.

I kept my eyes on her, and took the first, deliberate step down.

She took a half step back.

Theris grabbed my webbing and pulled me down.

Keep them safe, Yelena. Protect my House.

Chapter 60

At the base of the tower, we had good news.

The damage the Hind's cannon had caused to the mechanisms for lowering the platform had prevented it from going all the way down. It was stuck, like an elevator between floors, with only half an opening.

Turns out, that was two good bits of news.

The first was we could crawl out beneath the floor, praying that another shock wave wasn't going to unstick the platform.

The second was that we learned, as we crawled, that the platform being stuck had ruined Peterson's emergency plan for the servers.

We could see the trollies lined along one side of a hall that the platform should have opened onto. We could see the feet of people rushing backwards and forwards. From the shouting we could make out that the idea had been to offload the entire server system, rack by rack, onto the trollies so they could be wheeled to some safe location.

But then the platform jammed. People could squeeze through the opening. The full six-foot computer racks couldn't.

They'd had to change the plan; they were stripping drives out and collecting them.

And I heard that voice.

The one giving orders. That same flat, cold tone that had given orders to scientists to experiment on me. The one that had asked: "Is it viable for reproduction?"

Peterson was here, telling them to hurry. We'd caught the bastard.

Rita, David and I spoke in hand signals. We whispered to Theris and Mirela. The four of us got in front, UMPs at the ready. David would stay behind us.

The building above us shook. With a groan and squeal of metal, the platform began to descend again, and my blood ran cold.

Clever plans to leap out and surprise the enemy were dropped. We all began to scuttle like frightened cockroaches toward the narrowing exit.

The same shaking made one of them stumble and he dropped a drive. I could see him reach down. I was a couple of feet from the entrance, a couple more from his face as my frantic movements caught his eye. He saw me and froze in disbelief or fear.

I shot him.

We propelled ourselves out from under the platform like orange pips squeezed between fingers. David was last out, and he made it with less than a second to spare.

We had the advantage of knowing they were there. Most of them were Nagas, but they'd holstered or put down their weapons to help extract the drives. A few tried to rush us while drawing weapons. They died.

A handful of the people in the server room on the platform were techs. None of them tried to do anything beyond raising their hands or dropping to the floor. Tara manifested as a fire wolf and snarled at them, which kept them from trying anything else.

Peterson ran, carrying a bag and ducking into a side passage along with the surviving Nagas. I chased them with a few shots, but I didn't pursue immediately. Most of the drives were still in the racks.

The server room was slick and *full* of equipment. It could have been from a multinational, hi-tech company. A few minutes before, I was sure it had been spotless, with temperature controlled and filtered air. The air was still chilled, but there was nothing the filters could do to remove all the dust and smoke of our attack. The power was still on, supplied by batteries that ensured any accidental loss of electricity didn't affect the servers.

The techs had been powering systems down before extracting them. David got in there and flicked the master power switches off. The racks were designed for ease of access to the drives. In a couple of minutes, he'd ripped out every drive and dropped it in his backpack.

Then he flicked the power back on to the inner set of doors.

"Get the techs in there," he said.

Tara herded them in.

David set the doors to close and walked out with the main power cable in one hand and a fire axe in the other. The cable got caught between the doors and he cut it with the axe.

"They've got plenty of wire in there," he said. "They'll patch it up and get out in an hour or so."

"Good," I said.

Even Theris nodded before we turned our attention to the hall and passages.

The main passage led straight from the hallway. It had been made with industrial techniques. Huge circular concrete pipe sections formed a smooth passageway into the distance. The floor had been leveled. Somewhere down here, a motor generator was running, powering lights and pumping air down from above.

It had been damaged in the explosions. Water leaked in at some seals and dust fell like a fine rain from the roof.

There were side passages, like the one Peterson and his guards had ducked into for cover. These were natural formations, with a bit of enlargement and rough and ready planking to provide some level surface between outcrops and obstructions. There was lighting in them as well.

Why? What are the side passages for?

"That's the way out," Theris said, pointing down the main passageway when I paused.

He was right; it would have been too difficult to take trollies down the side passages. But I wasn't ready to leave yet.

"Peterson has some of the drives, and while we're here, he's trapped," I said.

Under fire and in extreme danger, Theris had been moderately imperturbable. Now he was getting angry. "Unless the cave system doubles back," he pointed out. "We don't have time. Matlal's reaction force is on its way. We've achieved most of what we set out to do."

"Most, maybe, but not all," I said. "I want those drives."

David spoke: "He'll have taken the most important ones first."

"You're fixated on him," Theris said to me. "You told me the mission was more important than Peterson."

"What I said, pelea, was that my hate for all the people involved was stronger than my hate for Peterson alone, and that greater hate needed them all identified. It's also that list of contacts that will tell us all of Matlal's networks, and we need that. Peterson may have the one key drive of data. Or the one drive that gives us what we need to crack encryption on the others. Whatever it is, I'm not willing to risk not having *all* the drives we can get."

"But you don't know —"

Rita hit him on the shoulder.

"Like Yelena already told you, you're Amber's pelea, not her Diakon. She decides. We obey."

"He's right, Farrell." The voice came out of the side passage. That same voice that lived in me, sealed away. It reached into me and confirmed the decision I'd already made.

But there's more than one way to get what you want.

"It's a standoff," Peterson went on. "You don't want to chase us down here, where we have good cover. Matlal's on the way, and you're dead if he catches you. Better get out now. Might even get one of your helicopters to pick you up."

I laughed. "When Matlal gets here, you're dead too. He won't be pleased you lost his stockpiles and viruses and digital currency. What do you reckon you've lost him? A billion? Ten? Twenty?"

It went quiet. I could hear some urgent, angry whispering.

None of which changed the even tone of his voice when he called out to me again. "Fair point. We're both dead if we're here when Matlal arrives."

I was distracted by Rita. She'd gone to that eerie cougar stillness and focus, looking down the passageway. I took in a long careful breath and let my wolfy nose taste the air. Not as sensitive as I'd be if I part-changed to wolf, but I didn't need to.

It was faint, but I could smell Rougarou down there. Not the everyday smell of were-hyenas. The stench I associated with rabioso, the rabid ones. The same stench I remembered from the pit hidden beneath Mauricio Gálvez's fortress.

Now I knew where Peterson was getting Rougarou from. Matlal had set up another 'factory' here.

I hadn't answered Peterson, but silence is a negotiation tool. He called out again.

"Your colleague was right in your assumption about the drives. I have the key drive, and without it, it'll take you a *long* time to decode the others. I'm betting that won't suit you." He paused. "I'm assuming neither of us wants to die, so I propose a temporary truce until we both get back to the US. We part ways. You get all the drives."

That achieved the mission objective. If I could trust him, which I knew I couldn't. He could be trying to work out a way where he delivered me to Matlal in exchange for his life.

Our attack's farewell message to Xibalbá detonated in the building directly above us. Another thermobaric explosion which was designed to guarantee that no virus could possibly survive.

We might as well have been in one of those snow globe toys you pick up and shake. The shockwave lifted us off the ground and then slammed us back into it. Wary of Peterson recovering faster than us, I was up on all fours and reaching for my UMP before the floor stopped shaking

I was just in time to see the main passage, our only way out, collapse with a roar before the whole tunnel disappeared in a cloud of dust and the lights went off.

Chapter 61

We were alive for the moment.

We checked on each other with flashlights and fashioned temporary breathing filters with our shirts.

We'd kept out of any possible view of Peterson and his Nagas down in his tunnel. I put my flashlight around the corner and carefully stuck my head out there for a moment. I could see nothing but dust further down. Closer to us, some of the floor planking had splintered.

"We'd be dead if we'd headed down the main passage," Theris said quietly.

"We might still be," I answered cheerfully, "but until that's confirmed, we have a job to do."

He snorted. "The drives?"

"Yup. We gotta move on the Nagas, before they can sort themselves out."

I led them into the side passage, guns in front, flashlights blinking on briefly to light our way, and then off to keep us from being targets.

We'd prepared for an assault. We had lots of ammunition and useful equipment like flashlights. Peterson didn't. Everything was on our side.

Well, apart from that we had no idea where the passage went, or how it got there, or how many Nagas there were and what defensive positions they had.

First obstacle. The floor of the passage followed the contours of the cave system. It rose up a couple of feet. They hadn't bothered to even it out, they'd just made a couple of steps to get over the bump.

The sort of bump someone could take cover behind.

Check. Look. Pull back.

No one on the other side.

We went over, smooth and quiet and slick.

Got to the next one. Same layout.

There weren't any further noises from detonations or ground movement, so we could hear the Nagas up ahead. The dust cloud was thinning.

Rita put her hand on my arm and indicated her nose.

The stench was stronger. Strong enough for human noses.

Someone ahead of us knew it too, and they knew it was *big* trouble.

"Shit! The holding pens have breached!"

"Fucking Rougarou are out! We gotta go!"

"Wait!" That was Peterson.

"Stay down," I said to the others and stood. Wolfy eyes were keen in the dark, but only minimally useful seeing through the veils of dust which still hung in the air. I fired in the direction of the voices. Three very quick shots, refining my aim by the light of the muzzle flash. I was back down in a crouch when they reacted by spraying bullets where I'd been. Only just.

Good reactions. Nagas were well trained. But I might have hit a couple, and I knew I had their attention now.

"Not good odds," I shouted. "Rougarou coming up behind and us in front, with flashlights and plenty of ammunition. Here's the deal: drop your firearms and leave, with your wounded. We're only interested in Peterson and the drives. We'll even give you a flashlight and wish you luck."

I could *feel* Mirela frowning at me, but I wanted this over quickly.

Damn, but it worked.

Nagas *were* well trained, but they weren't loyal.

Two shots. A grunt of pain and scrabbling noises.

"You got it. I'm coming out," a voice spoke cautiously from the darkness. "I got the drives. I got no firearms. My hands are above my head."

"Me too. I'm carrying one of the guys you hit."

"And me. Got my hands up."

"Seven of us."

I popped up and straight back down, in case it was a trick.

Nope.

The guards were shuffling forwards, emerging from the dust and darkness with their heads down. Three had their hands up. Two were carrying comrades. The first one was holding a messenger bag.

Rita and I stood, flashlights on and UMPs aimed.

"Hold it there. I'll call you one by one," I said to them. "Theris, check them for weapons. Knives are okay. Mirela, anyone with a gun gets shot."

I was watching carefully. None of them twitched, or looked like they were getting any second thoughts about surrendering.

"First one, with the bag, come forward. David, take the drives and give him your flashlight."

They came, one by one, climbing over the hump in the floor and being patted down by Theris under Mirela's watchful eye.

When they'd all been processed, I asked: "Any more back there?"

The one who'd taken the lead shook his head. "Just Peterson. And sick monsters."

"Peterson alive?"

"Probably. 'Bout seventy yards on the right."

I snorted. "Okay. You have your truce until we get out above ground, so long as you don't try anything against us."

He nodded.

"The snag is that last explosion collapsed the main passage," I said.

He blinked, and his eyes swiveled to the others before coming back. "We'll get out by the Pool of the Dead."

There was something in that glance at the others, but I had no time to investigate. I had to depend on their instincts of self-preservation.

"Which is where?" I asked.

He pointed with David's flashlight to what looked like no more than a crack in the wall.

"Difficult?"

"Long scramble. Some tight spaces. Long swim underwater at the end."

Definitely something he wasn't telling me.

There were snuffling, shuffling noises coming from the darkness and the stench of rabioso got stronger. The Nagas knew what was coming. Their heart rates were already high, and they kept going up.

"Go."

They hurried away, following the guy with the flashlight, turning sideways and squeezing through the crack.

"That was stupid," Mirela muttered.

"I gave my word," I replied and turned to David. "Does that look like all the drives, and is there any indication you have the key one he was asking for?"

He shrugged. "Looks like the right number, but they're all the same. It *could* be one of these."

Theris looked at me and groaned. "You want to check, right?"

"Yeah. That guy didn't take the time to search Peterson."

He swore then, but it didn't count; it was in a language I didn't recognize.

With that out of his system, he got in front of me, and we started walking in a battle crouch, towards the stink and noise of the rabioso.

About thirty yards in, the dust cloud got thinner as it finally began to settle. We could see movement just beyond the reach of our powerful flashlight beams. A shadowy, churning mass. No individuals. All in their four-footed form.

I didn't understand how the pit worked for rabioso, other than some died violently, and others were finally able to come out as functioning, if highly disturbed, Were. For all I knew, these were on the point of becoming sane Rougarou, but they didn't look it. They were salivating and snarling, eyes crazy-bright where the beams caught them, and only just sane enough to not charge us, knowing we had guns.

I'd never heard Peterson's voice with any emotion in it. Always that flat delivery, until any normal person would begin to wonder if there was any emotion in him.

It turned out, fear undid that. He screamed as our beams picked out what was coming for him. What was *right there*.

And the screams triggered the predator instinct in the pack, overcoming caution. They seemed to swell and fall on him like a wave.

I flicked the UMP onto full auto and emptied the magazine. Snapped the empty one out, slammed a fresh one in. Emptied it again.

Everyone followed my lead, and we literally couldn't miss—the Rougarou filled the width of the narrow cavern.

The pack shuddered and cringed. Tara manifested in fire wolf form, flames licking around her. They retreated, inching back, growling and slavering. They wouldn't hold once they saw how few we were. There were more arriving behind, pushing the ones in front.

I ran forward. Theris followed, running beside me, swearing again as he fired down the passage. Rita was on my other side. She helped me pull dead and dying Rougarou bodies off Peterson.

Finally. Face to face.

Peterson was bleeding out from a hundred bites and a couple of bullet wounds. There was nothing I could have done for him, and I wasn't going to try. I felt no sympathy. I didn't let myself feel *anything*. I was here because I had a mission. Emotion would be a distraction.

His clothes were half torn off. He'd been wearing a tactical vest, and it gaped open, the strapping broken. It had Velcro pockets. I ripped them open. The third one was paydirt. A drive. Checked the others. Two sets of truck keys.

"Fuck you, Farrell." He managed to say with effort.

I stood back. He *might* have nothing more to give me. He was nothing to me. Nothing.

His eyes flickered. "Don't leave me for them," he said.

I didn't owe him anything. Not even a quick death. Unless he had something to bargain for it. Something that might speed up justice when we made our way back home.

"Who's the big man in the US, Peterson? Who got you to run Ops 4?"

His eyes narrowed.

"If you lie, I'll know," I hissed at him.

He knew enough about Athanate to believe me. "Then hear this truth. I don't know. Someone very high up. That's all I know."

"We'll find it on the drives. We'll work it out."

"Then you'll do better than Matlal. Not even he knows."

His voice had fallen back into its normal tone, despite his breathing being labored because of his wounds.

That same voice. Hearing it seemed to trigger something in me. I felt it all rushing back then. Lying on the gurney. Naked. Strapped down. Blindfolded. Clenching my jaw to stop screaming. Listening. Always listening. Sick with fear. Desperate to find a way out of the nightmare.

"Can it hear me?"

"The senses are working normally, sir. It's safe to assume it hears, but we can make no judgment on how it's processing information."

"Oh, if it hears, it knows, I believe. It fears. That's good. It'll be very useful."

The months of hate and fear and pain and insanity as they'd experimented on me came back in an avalanche, a bursting of emotion that I'd suppressed for too long.

I wrenched him around, so he was looking down the passage to where the pack waited.

"Fuck you, Peterson," I said.

Then I blew his brains out and screamed into the darkness where the monsters lurked beyond the light.

Chapter 62

The pathway to the Pool of the Dead was a long, *hard* scramble.

Unlike the other passageway, this one hadn't been modified in any way. There were no wooden planks to walk on, no cutting of the sides to expand it into a tunnel.

Rita took point, chasing the scent of the escaping Nagas who knew where they were going.

The path alternated between damp, echoing caverns so big our beams couldn't reach the sides, and choke points so small we had to take off our packs and bandoliers to wriggle through.

Potholer's dream, except this was a nightmare and we were being chased by monsters in the darkness.

It was cold and we were sweating and panting.

I was running on automatic. I felt nauseated. No one said anything about Peterson.

Mirela and Theris pushed me and David in front of them. They were moving in leapfrog. One would cover while the other ran forward, and then they'd swap. If they could see movement behind us, they fired.

They couldn't miss, but there were always more. The only thing that seemed to slow them down was that they paused to tear apart any of their number that was wounded.

It got worse in the second big cavern. They spread out and rushed us, leaping over boulders and howling.

Bad enough to snap me out of my funk.

All of us had to turn and fire into the mass. We spaced it out, did more of the retreating leapfrog. As one of us emptied a magazine, they'd trot backward, reloading, while the others continued firing.

Even worse; the rabioso might be mad, but they sensed their opportunity and stopped turning on their wounded, so they could concentrate on us.

And the cavern ended in a choke point.

Rita's turn to reload. She called the choke point out and I heard her go through, dragging her pack and weapons.

Shit.

This was going to be a bitch for the last one through.

We backed up, bunching closer as the cavern narrowed.

David's magazine ran out and I shoved him into the hole we had to go through.

Theris stole my UMP while I was distracted.

"Go. Go!" He barged me, pushing me toward the crawl space.

The UMP is not designed to be fired one-handed. Not by a human. Theris was strong, even for an Athanate, and his targets weren't making it difficult to hit them. He fired both UMPs with double the effectiveness, but he was going to be in trouble reloading.

I scuttled through and turned as soon as it widened out.

I still had the Sig, and it would be as good as a submachine gun in the narrow gap. Just ten rounds in the magazine though.

Mirela joined me and got on the other side, so we bracketed the passage.

She was dragging her gear and Theris'. Now he couldn't reload.

He had switched both UMPs to single shot, but he still had to keep firing. He only had thirty rounds in those magazines, and he had to have fired half of them. The choke point was too narrow for us to shoot around him.

The mass of rabioso surged closer. He'd fixed his flashlight to the barrel. We could see just beyond him. It was like there was a wall of snarling, salivating fur and fangs.

He was trying to back into the gap feet first. It wasn't going to work.

I expected Tezcatlipoca to whisper in my ear, but he'd gone silent.

What the hell did that mean?

One of Theris' UMPs clicked empty. The rabid pack lunged.

Tara manifested beside Theris. She was in full firewolf form, flames billowing out from her, making Theris stumble.

"Crawl! Now!" I yelled.

The pack couldn't kill Tara, and the fire scared them, but the sheer weight of those behind was unstoppable.

Theris dived into the gap, throwing the backpacks and submachine guns in front of him and crawling.

Behind him, were-hyenas screamed as they caught fire, but it wasn't stopping them.

Theris dragged himself past us and began to turn, swearing or trying to make a working, I couldn't tell which. Neither was going to work in this situation.

Tara disappeared and suddenly the pack hit their end of the choke point like a wave of fur and fangs.

Mirela fired.

"Hold fire," I screamed.

Those she'd hit were shoved out of the way. The rest flowed like lava into the narrow gap.

"Hold," I yelled again.

Mirela was swearing, but she held fire.

I could see the madness in their eyes and smell the stink of their breath. Their fangs gleamed in the beams of our flashlights and their claws scrabbled the rock like a heavy surf on shingle.

"Hold!"

I could reach out and touch the first of them. His jaws were snapping, spraying me in saliva.

"Fire!"

We both fired. Theris joined in with the remainder of the magazine in my UMP.

Point blank. Full auto.

They tried to come around the side of the dead in front. We killed those as well. The ones who could see what was going on tried to get back. The weight of the pack pushed them forward and we killed them and killed them. Our bullets were passing right through the ones in front and killing them in the second and third rank.

Mirela snapped one magazine out and another in. Emptied it right into the mass of dying bodies, sweeping it left and right. Fur and blood. Screams like the sorrowing depths of hell overrode the snarling of the pack behind.

"Stop!"

I felt Tara's presence again.

She stood in front of us and breathed fire into the jam of bodies. She was no dragon, but in this restricted space, it worked. The choke point was sealed with dead and burning bodies. The stink of rabioso was lost in the stench of burning flesh and fur.

"Go, go, go," I shouted. "This won't hold them for long."

I got my UMP back. Swapped out the magazine. Grabbed my backpack. Counted spare magazines as I ran, missed a loose rock, tripped, caught myself. Lost the flashlight as it shattered.

Shit.

"Ammo?" I called out. "I have three mags for the UMP and five for the Sig."

One hundred and forty bullets.

"Two and six," Theris replied.

"Same." Mirela.

"Five and six," David.

"Three and six." Rita.

Much less than half of what we started with. The ammunition could be shared. We could load up UMP magazines with Sig rounds because they'd been chosen for that. But only with time and even then, it wasn't enough for another stand in an open cavern. And I did *not* want to resort to bladed weapons against a pack of rabid were-hyenas.

Despite all the problems explosions had caused us in the last hour, I'd have given a lot for a handy bit of C4 when we reached the next choke point.

But rather than narrowing, the cavern we were in was widening.

I could hear the pack behind us. Not clearly enough to tell me whether they'd cleared the obstruction, but enough to tell me they were still coming after us.

"Pool ahead," Rita shouted.

She was maybe fifty yards in front and the cavern split into two. She was following the scent on the right fork, and it was heading down steeply.

Do hyenas swim?

There was a climb down to where Rita was standing at the top of a subterranean cliff.

We didn't have rope, but neither had the Nagas we'd been following.

"Ha! This'll stop them," Mirela said.

Theris shook his head and pointed. "Those rocks," he said. "You can jump from one to the next. I suggest we do."

"Wait one second." I turned and looked around, paying more attention to my nose. "The Nagas jumped carrying their wounded?"

They hadn't.

One was dead. The other they'd left. He'd crawled behind a small outcrop, as if that would save him from the pack.

Theris unclipped his Sig.

"No," I said.

This was madness. I owed this man nothing more than a clean death. Mirela and Theris told me so, in no uncertain terms. I couldn't hear them.

I'd been killing were-hyenas by the dozen. I'd killed Nagas. I'd killed Peterson. But I couldn't leave this man shivering in shock at his wound and the fear of what was coming for him.

I picked him up.

Chapter 63

Trust and jump. But the first jump is the worst, they say. Certainly applied to parachuting in my experience.

It didn't apply to descending an unstable cliff with a backpack and weapons and carrying a wounded man. I nearly managed it.

It was the last jump, from a relatively stable rock to a scree of loose debris. It felt like it tore my shoulder joints out and landed me on my butt.

I got up, staggered to the edge of the lake and put the Naga down in an ungainly heap.

Theris knelt beside me.

"You've shown you're willing," he said. "But Amber, you cannot swim while you hold him. The Nagas knew that. They warned us this was a long swim, and they knew they wouldn't be able to do it carrying their comrade."

Yes, maybe that was the reason for the glances between them when they'd spoken of the way out. They'd never intended to get their wounded out. I was surprised they'd carried them as far as the cliff. Maybe they thought it might delay the pack descending. Give them more time to make their escape.

On cue, the sounds of distant howling floated down the cliff face like a gloating, evil mist.

The pack had chewed and torn its way through the choke point. They were minutes behind us.

Again, do they swim? Can they hold their breath underwater?

I wasn't going to bet against it.

But here we were, sitting by the Pool of the Dead, and Theris was thinking about knocking me out and dragging me. If it hadn't been exactly the same issue as we had with taking the wounded Naga underwater, he'd have done it. Actually, it was worse, because I couldn't be told to hold my breath if I was unconscious.

That made me laugh, which got me worried looks.

The 'pool' was an underground lake. The limestone bedrock of the Yucatán Peninsula was riddled with cave systems that flooded like this. Hundreds of miles of it. Somewhere ahead, the ground had caved in, creating a sinkhole, a cenote, open to the sky, where the sun was shining on the water. I could see the distant glow.

How distant?

If the Nagas had gotten out, so could we. Just not with a passenger.

I reached out and touched the water.

Cold. Deep. Clear. Mysterious.

A cold beyond physical sensations. A deepness also in spirit. And the answer became clear to me.

Oh, yes. There was a reason for the name. It wasn't the original name. That would have been more like the Lake of the Gods' Messengers. The Nagas had called it the Pool of the Dead because this was another ancient place of sacrifice. The bottom of this lake would be littered with skeletons who'd been sent to bear messages to the God of Rain. The water stirred with their spirits.

They called to me, and without meaning to, I called to them.

I straightened my spine and drew a long breath in.

Nai was prompting me.

I spoke in whispers, and the words that came from my mouth were sibilant as the serpents' hiss.

"I have the gift of the fourth Serpent, the Serpent of Air," I said. "I am the Mistress of Breath."

I came to my feet smoothly.

"Pick him up and follow me."

I did not look back.

The water was so cold. Shocking. *Shocking!* Enough to make me wonder if I was deluded as it reached higher up my legs, my body, sent icy fingers into my heart.

"This isn't the spirit world, Amber," Theris was saying urgently. "We don't have the power to create this working here."

He was right. This *Mistress of Breath* had worked in the spirit world. I didn't have the power to make it work in the physical world, not even with his help.

But Nai was insistent, and the pack had reached the cliff's edge above us. We had seconds before they started the descent.

"All is maya. Trust me and hurry."

I could not tell who spoke those words. It was me, or it was Nai. Or maybe it was the fourth Serpent, who transcended the illusion of the world.

Trust me.

They came to me, the spirits of the dead of this underground lake. They came in ones and twos, hesitantly at first. They came like the half-heard notes of a distant choir, snatches of music carried on a fickle wind, pieces that hinted at a massive anthem of longing. They rose like a fog before dawn, bright, as if lit from within. More and more. A multitude so that the lake itself was glowing.

Time had worn them down, this legion of the sacrificed, but it had not erased their last need; to tell their tales.

I was a Blood witch. My Blood was strong. My call was true. They came to me.

Among them there were more recent victims. Peterson had used the lake to kill people. Local people who'd objected to the way the Nagas treated them, or who'd simply been caught hunting in the Xibalbá area.

A couple of the Nagas who we'd let escape hadn't made it either.

I walked through them all as if they were clouds. I breathed them in. I felt the touch of their ghostly fingers and I heard their tales.

But I could not delay with them, because were-hyenas, it turned out, could swim after a fashion.

There was no scent trail of the Nagas to follow now, but I didn't need one. I walked toward the light, where the sun beat down on the restless water. I had to crouch in places where old stalactites had grown down from the ceiling before this lake had flooded. Beneath my feet was only sand and bones.

And as I walked, I breathed, even if there was a part of me panicking at the thought that I was surrounded by water. No time to panic. The others were right behind me, and right behind them was the ravening pack.

I walked on, Nai beside me.

We weren't in the spirit world. I'd created a piece of the spirit world here, in the physical world, using the spirits. It was good because we could breathe. On the other hand, it lit me up like a beacon. I could feel Tezcatlipoca and Quetzalcoatl, darkness and light, sensing the disturbance I made, swirling around me, seeking me out.

There was no way to hide. The song of the spirits had swollen with every step. From distant, hesitant notes it had come to be the thundering noise of an organ in a cathedral. The sound battered me and drove all other thoughts away.

I barely noticed the light changing in front of me. How the water waved like sunlit veils in a morning breeze.

I felt solid rock beneath my feet.

Some cenotes were so steep-sided, you needed ropes to get out. Not this one. We walked up a slope until our heads broke through into the air.

I was in two places. The spirit place where I was aflame with energy. The physical world, where the sun would slowly bake some warmth back into our freezing bodies.

I was aware of the others. Words of congratulation and disbelief. Frowns from Theris. They asked me if I was okay. I nodded. They shook the water from their weapons and checked their magazines, preparing themselves for the pack to emerge from the chilling depths of the cenote.

It wasn't necessary. I wanted to tell them, but I couldn't find the words in the physical world yet. It was too insubstantial. The only thing that was real to me, that had substance, was *energy*. It was dark and thick and vital, and I was pulling energy from the underground lake.

The rush of spirits didn't reduce. The cenote's surface was at the foot of a hill, and down that hill came a landslide of spirits. The whole place seethed with them.

That was what they'd now call a sorcerer's hill. It was an overgrown temple, once associated with the cenote. The whole arrangement had been one place of ancient worship. It bled spirits from every stone.

All Blood magic. All resonant with me. All power I could use.

It was intoxicating.

Flint and Kane had given me the idea of what to do about the pack snapping at our heels. Amanda had told me the story of their escape from the criminals pursuing them in Michigan. They'd turned a road into a sheet of frictionless ice, because *water is crazy*, the Lost Boys had said. *One moment it's solid and another it's liquid. Or even gas.* And the power to do that, even to a whole lake, was less than the power I'd used to be able to breathe underwater.

I reached out and spoke to the water.

Rita and David were hastily sharing their extra ammunition with Mirela and Theris, while all four of them were firing at the Rougarou who were already struggling to escape the cenote.

Some were only able to half emerge before they got stuck in ice. Most were no more than shapes in the depths, moving in a frenzy beyond the call of the hunt. Fighting futilely to escape as the water got colder and heavier and thicker.

I could *feel* it change. I could hear the cracking of stalactites as the ice set through the whole passage we'd swum. The grinding of bones in the sand. The dying gasps of Rougarou. The frustration of hundreds more, trapped inside the cavern.

All of it, the shots and the howls, faded away to a shocked silence in the physical world.

Even the spirit world grew quieter.

I was filled with spirits and their power. Intoxicating no longer covered it. Using that power was my mine by right. By *birthright*—I'd lived because of the sacrifice of my twin. I could feel how perfect it felt to shape the energy, to use it. I would always want to use it. I couldn't let it go now.

In the spirit world, I could see the whole peninsula. I could see Quetzalcoatl and Tezcatlipoca watching me, assessing me, weighing me. Wanting me. I could see Matlal and his coven of Adepts. I could see my House, fleeing in helicopters, chased by Matlal. I could taste their fear, every one of them, Bian and Alex included. I could see it all in patterns of darkness and light, sound and silence, air and spirit and stone.

And I could see my death in the battle to come.

Theris was beside me, speaking too quickly, about how I had to put away the spirits while I could, how we needed to leave, to make our way to where Peterson's escape vehicles were hidden.

"No," I said. The words fell so slowly from my lips, as if my tongue had nearly frozen. "I can see Matlal and his coven. They're too quick for the others to escape, and too strong to fight. I need to stop him, or he'll kill them all. I need him to come after me instead. Here. Now."

I pointed up to the top of the temple hidden by the jungle. At the stone altar. At the place of sacrifice.

"Up there."

Chapter 64

I didn't need to do anything more to attract Matlal's attention, but I needed a way to pull him back from his pursuit of my House.

A working.

Something he'd see as a challenge.

As we climbed the hill that was more than a hill, I called up power and scoured the vegetation that had grown over the temple steps and altar. I left the stone bare and cold to warm in the sun. I repaired where roots had broken and moved stones.

I could feel the tread of countless ghostly feet on the steps I climbed. I could taste the rich tide of blood on the stone, washed down with water while sacred chants hummed in air.

The temple steps were like the bare chest of a sacrifice about to be offered to the sun god.

I was already lit up like a beacon to Matlal's spirit-sight, and this working just made it flare higher. I had his attention all right, he slowed his pursuit, and my House slipped further from his grasp with every passing second.

Dangerous, my priestess. My brother sees you. You need me. You need my protection against him.

It was past time for Tezcatlipoca to whisper to me again. He was right. Even boosted as I was, I might not be able to take Matlal. I knew I couldn't face Quetzalcoatl, and if Matlal was losing, he'd let the Lost God slip through.

My heart hammered at the thought. What if he didn't? What if I *could* take Matlal? I could finish this, right here and now. Quetzalcoatl would lose his bridge to the physical world. All I would need then was to *not* provide that same bridge to Tezcatlipoca.

Who already had his claws in my soul.

Not the same thing, Tara said. *And barely one hook of one claw.*

I snorted and reached the top.

This hadn't been one of the great temples of the Mayans. No archaeologist had tracked it down and marked it. They should have; it reached even deeper in history, back down to Olmecs. It had been added to, layer by layer over time. That ancient Olmec temple was buried in the heart of the Mayan temple. Despite its secondary status, it was also full of power, which now channeled through me.

I shed my backpack and sat cross-legged on the stone of sacrifice.

The others were with me. They'd seen the temple unveiled by my working. They'd seen vegetation torn away, trees uprooted, and stones shifted. They could sense the presence of the spirits, but only Theris had some inkling of what I was seeing.

Theris might be of some help. The others...

"Trust me," I said. "And hunker down. Close as you can."

My working had already created a partial substantiation around me. I grew it, till it covered all of us.

Tara manifested in her own body. My twin sat back-to-back with me.

Not enough.

Theris sat, and there were three of us back-to-back.

Sacred three.

Not enough.

I felt like the fever dream had returned. My mind darted in different directions but gathering glimpses rather than understanding anything.

Tezcatlipoca was hissing in my ear.

That I was called the Abomination of the paranormal world. The thing that should not be. The breaker of rules.

You owe them nothing, Tezcatlipoca said.

And I would be an Abomination to the Adepts as well. I would be a multitude. I would take my strength from many.

Yes, Tezcatlipoca said. *Take their strength.*

Tara spoke: *And use it wisely, and for their benefit.*

There were three of us. I called to Ash: tree of dreams, tree of life, soultree of the Threefold Spiral Coven.

And Ash came.

Four of us.

Still not enough.

I reached, and the formless African gods came from their sacred Grove.

But my thirst for power grew even with the increase.

Still not enough. More. More. More.

I called, and the Stone Serpents did not come. Somehow, I knew that they wouldn't. I knew that Medusa, the snake woman who spoke for them, would say to me that they had given me everything I needed, if I had the wits to see it, and if I needed more, then I wasn't the person they would give it to.

But Nai came. Or maybe she'd been with me all along and just waited for me to call.

You aren't trained for this fight, she said. *Allow me to take over.*

The African gods pushed inside my head like a heartbeat. They wanted control, too.

No. This must be enough. I must be enough.

A substantiation formed and inside it, I was a multitude. I had forms and I had none. I had wings like night that I spread around the temple altar and held those I would protect under their shield.

I was an abomination, a monster, a winged human with the face of a wolf and fangs of a vampire, but despite that, my House trusted me.

Not the wounded Naga. Crazed by fear, he tried to crawl away, his hands reaching, scrabbling at the worn stones, clawing his way out of my circle of protection.

And Matlal arrived.

Chapter 65

Matlal was on top of a pyramid temple, like me.

But his temple was flying, and it stretched from horizon to horizon. It reached into the sky. He was crowned with stars, and lightning danced around his altar. His temple was a vast mountain, uprooted from the depths of the earth.

It wasn't just Matlal and his coven. They weren't *that* powerful. This display meant he'd brought Quetzalcoatl to the fight.

That knowledge reached into my chest and froze my heart. Against Matlal, I maybe had some chance. Against a Lost God…

No! Tara shouted in my head. *Don't let him have this power over you. Matlal hasn't let Quetzalcoatl take over yet. He's posturing to scare you.*

I understood what she was saying. Fighting 101. Let the opponent scare you and you're halfway to losing the fight.

I got echoes of my Ops 4-10 instructor Bar-Haim whispering in my ear before a similarly one-sided contest during my martial arts training: *Laugh at his display. It'll make him angry. Angry people make mistakes.*

Hard to do, but I laughed.

It unfroze my heart, just in time, because I angered him alright.

He lashed out with fire. His strength. Quetzalcoatl's strength. A sun god's specialty.

Fire. Hotter than fintyne, that Adepts could use like napalm. As hot as the heart of the sun. He hurled it down like a spear of flame aimed at me.

I swelled up to shield the others as it struck.

Pain!

Pain enough to blast any thoughts of resisting out of my head. Pain that stabbed through my eyes and into my brain, flayed the flesh from my bones, and boiled my Blood.

No!

Nai and Tara and Theris screamed warnings at me.

Nai: *He can't do that. It's illusion!*

Tara: *Hidden Hand. Hidden Hand.*

It was Tara's call that jump-started my brain from the paralysis of terror. Ops 4-10 training again. *Kakusareta-te*: an attack in two parts. The obvious part distracted attention from the Hidden Hand strike.

And this was still Matlal's attack, using Quetzalcoatl's power, not the Lost God himself.

I had a chance.

Gather. Center.

Difficult. My substantiation and my great dark wings were protecting us, but the heat was still appalling, and it was still me in the end. My skin wasn't flaying, but it was blistering.

Soft chanting rose like cool fountains around me. A thousand voices. A language I didn't speak, but words I understood.

Light vanquishes darkness.
Yet the night is boundless,
And even stars grow cold.

The spirits of the temple sang from the cold stones beneath me, and my spirit wings grew wider and deeper, absorbing the flames, sinking the heat deep into the earth.

Blisters still burst on my skin, sweat blossomed and stung, but the ferocity of the attack receded. And I caught the Hidden Hand. A simple spear. Such a primitive weapon. So unexpected. Lethal when Matlal hurled it at me with Athanate strength. I twisted and caught it as it passed, but if I had still been distracted, it would have punched through my heart and out of my back. No amount of Athanate healing would have fixed that.

A vital lesson. With spirit powers concentrating on defending against spirit powers, the physical world can make its way through.

I was learning, but every lesson emphasized what I already knew: I had no real idea what I was doing in a battle with magic. No experience of fighting using spirit energies.

Even the shield that protected us, the dark wings, and chanting spirits, must have come from Nai. She was inside me, and the only thing that comforted me was that I knew it was *not* Tezcatlipoca, even if Nai was somehow using some of his power as the God of the Night.

Theris stirred, but he didn't kill me.

The chanting was still going, and the words focused the energies into absorbing Matlal's fire.

Dust and ice.
All will fall into the endless darkness
Beyond the death of suns.

Whatever language they were singing in, there was something mesmerizing about the words. A promise of sweet surrender. I had to wrench my attention away before I was sucked down into oblivion.

But I learned from what Nai was doing. I felt the way she wove energies and directed them. I learned from what Matlal was doing. It was impossible to fight with magic and conceal how he was making it work.

I reminded myself that I had beaten Matlal before. I had touched him with eukori and channeled the rage from my strongbox down that connection. Of course, he knew that. He might keep his eukori shielded.

He might have learned something from it too, Nai warned. *He might have a way to feed on your rage, unless you catch him unprepared.*

It was still worth a try. We were fighting with auras, but if I could just sneak a thread of eukori past his guard. Aura and eukori were different aspects of the same thing. To attack me with aura *might* mean he'd neglected his eukori shield, like concentrating on spirit defenses might mean he neglected his shield against physical attacks.

I saw how Nai took the chants and used them to fashion power.

Focused on what was needed and just let the energy bind into that.

For me to achieve something like that, I needed to visualize what I was trying to do.

My katana, Onibi, flowed into my hand. I'd thought the light display in the Assembly had been spectacular, but it was nothing on the violent eruption of lightnings from the blade as it encountered Matlal's aura, as I thrust the katana blindly in his direction.

There, where his spear had passed through.

I visualized my eukori flowing down that blade, through the breach, leaping toward Matlal and his coven.

I felt the others join me. Tara and Ash. Theris, hesitantly. Nai remained focused on preventing his firestorm from breaking through.

My eukori arced like an electric discharge and struck Matlal's coven.

And died in horror.

Worse than him feeding on it. Far worse.

It was like plunging my hand into a bucket of maggots. *Things* squirmed away from my strike, and I had the sensation of them slithering up my arms. The eukori of the coven, their whole aura, it was *wrong*. Wrong like the feel of rabioso. Sickness of the mind.

Worse, some of them even knew they were mad.

The children didn't.

Matlal's inner shield was children. Maybe I could force my way through the insane Adepts, killing some of them, but I couldn't strike through the children. I'd have to find a way around that, or lose.

My attack died, and as I faltered, my protecting wings shrank a little. Everything was connected through me – attack and defense. I couldn't let my concentration or resolve fade, even if I felt my energy draining away.

The wounded Naga had crawled too far away. He was outside the protection of my wings, and I couldn't get him back without exposing the others to Matlal. I yelled at him, but that just drew Matlal's attention. Spirit arms shot out from Matlal's coven like striking snakes. They snatched the man up and pulled him away.

"No!"

The Naga floated up into the air, kicking and shouting helplessly.

"I swear on my Blood, hear what I will do to you, Farrell," Matlal roared at me, his voice distorted by the crackling of magic. "I will make you my slave. You will be utterly mine. You will want nothing except to please me, whatever I ask. Every day I will tell you to kill one of your House like this. You will do it eagerly, to please me. When you have no House left, I will make you find more. I will make you bind them to you and when they are bound to you with your ties of love, when they trust you completely, you will flay them alive like this to show me how much you love me."

The Naga's flesh quivered and bulged as if there were rats running beneath his skin. A scream erupted from his throat, a scream of the utmost pain and utter despair as his flesh began to peel off him in strips.

I couldn't save him. I couldn't get him back. I could only spare him his pain.

I wanted to kill him, and my only thought was it needed to be quickly, but I was in a substantiation, a place of power, skimming the spirit world. Nai whispered warnings in my mind. *The thought and the deed are joined by different rules here.*

I ignored that. I needed to do something. I'd seen how Matlal had snatched him.

With barely time to think, spirit arms erupted from my body. They formed like huge scorpion stings over my head. They were flesh and stone, water and sinew, blood and ice, and they ended in great claws that struck out at the Naga. One broke his ribs and wrenched his living heart from its seat. The other stabbed his neck, so that his head separated, and he was dead before he could draw breath to scream again.

Oh shit!

Matlal reeled.

Tezcatlipoca shouted in triumph and for a moment, the whole temple seemed to flicker on the verge of passing completely into the spirit world.

My priestess offers me a fitting sacrifice. The god's voice shook the temple stones, and he was *there*, behind me, almost in the physical world.

He snatched the corpse: body, heart and head, as I shut my eyes and willed us away, turning my spirit arms into more dark wings to make a barrier between me and Tezcatlipoca.

Matlal was screaming at me.

"You fool! You'll let him out onto the world."

His relentless assault paused.

So Matlal understood the danger of what he was doing. Did he have some way of using Quetzalcoatl's power while keeping the god from taking him over? Was there something I could use myself to protect me from Tezcatlipoca while feeding off his power?

I couldn't think of that now. Just a thought to spare the Naga pain and it'd transformed into a sacrifice for Tezcatlipoca, and almost let him through. A flicker of a thought while using magic like this could make a connection, because that was what I was good at, connecting and channeling other entity's magic.

Double guessing myself and fighting like this was exhausting, mentally and physically. I'd stood up from the altar and now I was staggering. And yet, at the same time, my Blood was singing. It wanted to use magic again. It wanted the most powerful magic, no matter how dark.

The only good thing was that Matlal seemed to be as tired. I couldn't see him, but the aura around him seemed paler. The substantiation pressing against mine was less hard.

I could see why. He and his whole coven had *flown* after the helicopters carrying my House away, and I got a sense of how much energy that had taken. And then he'd assaulted me recklessly. With anger. He'd put so much into it, he'd had to stop the flying. Dropped the illusion of spanning the sky. He was just a man surrounded by a group of children and lunatics, standing at the foot of my temple.

He's almost at his limit, Nai said. *Attacking takes more energy than defending. Even while channeling Quetzalcoatl.*

That was good to know.

It could be that channeling the Lost God and keeping himself safe from him at the same time is even more tiring. But he can start to use his coven as reserves. That is limited, too, because it will kill them.

Shit.

While I took that on board, the pause gave me an opportunity to learn about my opponent.

Our substantiations were pressed together, so he would be learning more about me at the same time.

I was still a novice in magical fighting, and he had much more experience, but with the Serpents' gift and Nai's insight, I could tell he had little skill. He was a brute force fighter. He relied on overwhelming victims. The Hidden Hand tactic with the spear had been the limit of his finesse and I was getting better at defending with each attack.

He resumed his attacks, and I responded.

Power touched power, darkness and light, high and low, probing like fencers unwilling to commit to a thrust, but with spirit power, needing no point or edge in the spirit world. His strikes flared and when I countered, the meeting of auras threw off sparks that sank and vanished reluctantly into my darkness.

Even at this more measured attack, I could continue to defend and he would drain his batteries more quickly than I would.

Then Theris could take him out.

Or I could, physically. I still had a sword. And a spear. If I didn't collapse first.

I guessed Quetzalcoatl came to the same conclusion when the aura around Matlal's coven changed.

That paleness transformed, like dawn in the desert, but rushing faster and faster.

In a second, it was like looking straight at the sun.

Matlal's attack renewed. Much harder. Forcing me back until I felt the stone altar behind me again. My shield wings still took the blows, but they were *me*. The attack hurt.

Quetzalcoatl raised another aspect of his powers: the wind. A hurricane enveloped us, screaming around the ancient temple, making it impossible to see Matlal and hard to concentrate. I could not hear the chanting of the temple's spirits.

I gritted my teeth. I couldn't let my guard down, but I was tiring very quickly now.

The inevitable end was near.

Tezcatlipoca spoke again. *You must allow me through, my Priestess. You cannot stand against my brother.*

I felt Theris twitch. The Sword of Damocles was ready at my back.

"No," I said aloud. "I won't condemn the world to save myself."

You would condemn the world anyway, if my brother comes through.

"I won't survive if Quetzalcoatl helps Matlal. I won't survive if Quetzalcoatl comes through into the physical world. But I wouldn't survive if I tried to let you through either. Your brother is about to win, and that will condemn you to losing forever."

I felt a flare of his anger then. Not fire-bright like Quetzalcoatl, but a deepening in the utter darkness that waits beyond the light of stars.

"You have a choice, Tezcatlipoca. You deal with your brother, and I'll deal with Matlal."

You are failing. You cannot defeat Matlal alone. You need my power, and if I drag my brother back to the spirit world, I will not have any spare power to give you.

"It's a risk and it's getting greater every second you delay."

The maelstrom of winds around the temple was now full of burning sand. Blows erupted out of it and shook the temple. I held it all at bay with my wings, and yet I could feel that sand scouring my flesh. I could feel fractures in my bones. Bruises in my body. A stuttering in my heart. A spreading numbness. In another few seconds, I was finished.

A deal then, my priestess. I will take my brother away. Take some of my power now from the sacrifice you just made. Without it, you will fail.

It was the truth. I would have to bear the cost.

"Yes! Do it!"

A moment passed. It was the moment between one heartbeat and another. Or hours. I wasn't sure, but both the Lost Gods were gone, and it was like I discovered air again.

Matlal's spear and my katana lay on the ground next to me. In my hands, I held the Naga's bloody, still-beating heart.

Chapter 66

As the wind dropped and let the sand billow away, I saw Matlal standing near the foot of the temple, surrounded by the rings of his coven.

He knew Quetzalcoatl had left and I'd been responsible. He wasted no time in attacking me again.

I didn't attack. Like a heavyweight resting on the ropes, I covered up and just watched for anything that I could use.

It was still painful. His energy blows had enough physical force transmitted through my shields that my body was still shuddering. I was reeling and stumbling in front of the temple's altar, which encouraged him to redouble his efforts.

I had to do something soon.

Use the heart. That was Nai.

"Drop it!" Theris yelled to get my attention. "It's too dangerous."

I ignored both of them to focus on defending a renewed flurry of spirit-energy blows from Matlal.

"Hey!" I shouted out to him. "Nothing like as strong without Quetzalcoatl. And you wanted to warn *me* about letting a Lost God loose."

He was getting angry again. He'd thrown his spear; this time he sent one of the children with a knife. A young girl. Pretty. Delicate. And completely intent on stabbing me.

Smart move. I was too committed to spirit energy defenses, my shield against physical attack was as weak as tissue. The girl barely slowed as she ran through and up the steps toward the altar.

This was bad. I was overextended. It was going to be impossible to defend against Matlal's attacks and stop the girl as well.

I didn't have time to do anything. Mirela and Rita moved in front of me. Mirela punched the girl on the chin and her legs buckled. Rita caught her before she fell back down the steps of the temple and took the knife away.

But I'd underestimated Matlal again. It was another Hidden Hand.

His aura reached through the weakness in the substantiations that the girl's entry had caused. Reached through and snuffed out her life like he was clicking his fingers. Tried to gather her energy and attack me from inside my shield.

I kept Tezcatlipoca's gift in my left hand and raised the right.

Even without the Lost God, with just the echoes of his power and my fading strength, I summoned lightning from a clear sky because he had done it for me, and I had learned. Bolts burst down, shattered and coated Matlal's substantiation in a fractal pattern of electric pulses. And fire. Quetzalcoatl had called fire while we were linked through our battling auras, and I had learned.

Matlal laughed.

"Using fire against the priest of the God of Fire?" His shouted question boomed out, amplified by his powers.

While he laughed, I sheered his access to the dead girl, harvested her energy for myself, making me sick to my stomach, hating what I was doing, offering a prayer to her spirit for all that had been done to her because I had to be part of it to benefit.

I poured her energy into the spirit fire. Made the sphere of fire *much* larger.

Strong as it was, it made no impression on Matlal's defenses.

But while he kept laughing, the ice in the cenote turned into fog.

I'd watched and learned.

This was the spirit world equivalent of a Mandaviran. We were engaged in a duel. I couldn't win against Matlal in exactly the same way I'd won against Chrysos, and yet the Temple's gift scorched in my veins, seared my mind. The struggle was not my perception of the struggle. Where Nai had kissed my forehead became bright ice.

To be aware of everything…
To be whole in purpose…

No time to warn the others. My chest burned where Chrysos' kinirak had struck and pierced my heart.

To move without thought or hesitation…

The fog from the cenote now swirled around Matlal's substantiation. He *could* see out, and he would soon, but for a moment he relied on his human senses, and he *thought* he couldn't see through the fog. In the spirit world, thought is powerful.

I grabbed Onibi and leaped.

All the way down the front of the ancient temple. All the way through the breach in his shields that Matlal had left open to allow the child to come out.

Into his substantiation.

From inside his shields, I merged our substantiations, and my world lurched nauseatingly.

Shit!

Matlal had been caught out, but he'd reacted with the reflexes of a cat. I was cut off from the others. His full shields snapped into place, preventing my connections to Ash and the African gods and the auras of my team. And physically preventing Theris, Mirela and Rita from following me. Tara and Nai were with me, because they were me.

Worse than the loss of support and power, worse than being trapped, I was reeling, unable to focus.

I'd suspected the depravity of the control Matlal enforced with his coven, but I was part of this substantiation. It was *my* control as well, *my* substantiation, as long as I was inside. I was a full part of the dark spider's web of compulsion between Matlal and his coven.

He'd abused them, mentally and physically. Their minds were twisted. The children were as mentally ill as the madmen, but in their eyes, they were the sane ones, and Matlal was their god. What he took from them, what he did to them, it all delighted them. It was their act of worship to him. And because he wanted to do the same to me, they were eager for it. For me to become one of them.

I could not push it away. I could feel the sick lust as the compulsions tried to press into my mind.

After his initial surprise at my tactic, Matlal was more in control. The madmen in the front rank stumbled forward to attack even as the desire to submit pressed down on me.

I could fight one attack off, but not both. And I had no more than a few seconds of resistance left.

Tara: *You have to use Tezcatlipoca's gift.*

Nai: *It's limited. You get one chance. Do everything you have to.*

No pressure.

A swing of Onibi, trailing an unnerving, searing blue light, kept the madmen at bay for a moment.

I clenched my left hand, revulsion making me sick to my stomach. My fingers sank into the spongy flesh. My own heart took the erratic, dying rhythm of the Naga's. The madmen fell further back; not because of Onibi, but now the fist holding the heart began to glow with the same eerie blue. It rushed up my arm. Splinters of lightning hissed from my shoulders and spat from my head.

One chance.

I lifted the heart above my head. It stopped beating. It crackled one last time and turned into darkness which started to flow down my arm.

This *wasn't* just the Naga's power. Tezcatlipoca had hidden much more beneath it. That had fooled me and Matlal, and it was too late for me to do anything else.

I was a dark witch, a Blood witch, come into my power, feeling how right it was. The shadows wreathed my whole body now. I was darkness itself.

I took a part of Matlal's substantiation and sent it questing into the cenote. I found the surviving rabioso coming through now that the channel was dry, and I gathered them. It was like picking up burning coal. Each touch of their corrupted spirits was red and searingly hot and painful. I gathered them all regardless, every single rabioso in the tunnels beneath Xibalbá, and I brought them here, where I tore a bigger hole in Matlal's damaged physical shields to let them through, howling and slavering, their minds aflame with the desire to kill.

Matlal had to try and form a second substantiation within the first. He put all his energy into a physical shield.

I didn't attack him directly. He was still quick and powerful, especially here, and I was too weak without my allies.

But I had him focusing that power on physical defense against the rabioso. My move was the martial art technique of *tsukuri* – to use his own strength against him. While all his spirit-energy momentum moved one way, I took the power of his own substantiation, because it was *our* substantiation at the moment, and went the other way. I reached for a connection in the spirit world.

Matlal's power wanted to reach for Quetzalcoatl.

My loaned power wanted to reach for Tezcatlipoca.

Either of those would end with me being an abused slave, obscenely delighting in my own submission.

But with effort, I could reach for something else, something associated with both Tezcatlipoca and me. That way I wasn't fighting the direction the Lost God's loaned power wanted to go, but I was tricking it, as I'd tricked Matlal.

My old substantiation was barely there. It had been almost completely consumed by the City of Lost Gods, and it was infested with flayed wolves and other denizens of the City.

But it was still there. It was still mine. And it had been created by Tezcatlipoca; it knew my power. It recognized the power that made it. The connection snapped into being.

There was a moment when Matlal realized his mistake. A moment of shock as the entire substantiation, coven and rabioso included, slid down into the spirit world, with Matlal struggling like a fly in a web, caught by his own spirit energy construction.

Into *my* substantiation.

With Nai's help, I changed one rule of that working: the one that made time here run faster than the physical world. I reversed it as I left.

Matlal wouldn't even notice. He'd have his hands full with fighting off the rabioso and the flayed wolves. Even if he was quick, days would pass back in the physical world. My House would be well away from him.

But that wasn't the most important setback. He'd been defeated. The fact it was a trick was irrelevant. They'd all seen it. Either he would have to rebuild a coven from scratch, or there would always be part of it that knew he'd been defeated, and that part would be a weakness.

I'd done it.

And I was dying as a result.

Even with Tezcatlipoca's boost of energy, I'd had to dip into the Athanate reserves that protected my body, and with the cumulative damage from the battle, my human body was giving up. I could barely sense the connection back to the physical world. The one that brought me here was still there, just. It would take me back to the place I deserved to be, because I'd used Tezcatlipoca's power, I'd let him in. With a last effort, I flung myself back down the connection to my pelea, who was also my Sword of Damocles.

It was just going to be a matter of whether Theris would kill me first, or I would simply die from my wounds and save him the trouble.

Chapter 67

Just drifting. Listening to the chanting of the spirits.

Dying was easy.

The night is boundless,
And even stars grow cold.

Remembering my House, Alex, Jen, Bian, my human family, oaths and promises unfulfilled; that was hard.

Mirela wasn't letting me forget any of them. It was the other side of the coin. You weren't truly dead while others held you in their hearts. I couldn't die because my heart was full of others.

And Mirela was swearing at me.

After hearing him during this mission, I knew Theris would have been swearing too, but his fangs were sunk in my throat. David's fangs were in my wrist. Rita was trying to use my eukori to connect with me and drag me back.

But it was Mirela, her aura linked so tightly with mine, who had the best grip on me. And the greatest risk. If I died, I'd probably take her with me. Rita as well.

I couldn't do that, so I turned away from the hypnotic lure and found myself lying on the altar stone.

They'd stopped the bleeding. The bones and bruises would heal. Muscles would re-knit. The organs were working again, even if reluctantly.

Theris and David took their fangs back.

I coughed and had to spit off to the side.

"Lot of effort to bring me back, just to kill me," I muttered.

Theris snorted and shook his head.

I frowned. He wasn't getting it. "I used Tezcatlipoca's power. That's how—"

"You've used it before and still been able to deny him," Theris said. "He tricked you. You used it to save people, and then you came back here. To us. It's not a good direction, but it's not terminal."

He took a small towel and water bottle from his backpack to clean my face. "You are, as the poem says, *bloody but unbowed.*"

The others didn't know about Theris' duty to kill me if I succumbed to Tezcatlipoca. There were puzzled glances, but I didn't have the energy to tell them now.

"What happened?" David asked. "We saw you pulling the rabioso out of the tunnels and then you all disappeared. You went to the City?"

"My substantiation." I coughed, tried to grab Theris' towel and sit up. No chance. Everything hurt and I felt about as strong as cooked spaghetti. "It's still there, even if it's mostly been consumed by the City. I left them there and Nai helped me change the rules about the way time runs. Tezcatlipoca set it up to run quicker than the physical world. Now it's running slower. Matlal can change it, but he's busy fighting. A lot of time will have passed before he gets out."

"That won't stop his remaining troops from searching for us," Mirela said. "We have to go."

Before I could complain that I wasn't going anywhere, Theris scooped me up off the stone.

The others gathered their backpacks and weapons.

Mirela knelt over the dead child that Matlal had sent to try and stab me. Very gently, she picked the body up and laid it on the altar where I'd been. She crossed the girl's arms and placed the knife she'd used on her chest, so she looked like one of those effigies on top of medieval tombs.

Then we left.

Mirela tried to report in on the satellite phone as we took the steps down the temple. Unfortunately, the phone wasn't as robust as the rest of our equipment. We'd have to fall back on cellphones when we got clear.

The second problem was we didn't know which direction to go.

The entire area around the temple, for about eighty yards, had been scoured by Quetzalcoatl's tornado wind. The trees were uprooted; the ground was broken where they had been torn out by the roots, and it was littered with splintered debris.

Rita forced a way out and circled the devastation.

"Here," she called, when she picked up the scent.

Fifteen minutes and a couple of hundred yards further on, we found where the main passageway came out.

There was a bunker.

The Nagas had forced it open and taken one of the two diesel pickup trucks that had been stored there.

They'd drained the fuel in the other.

"Twenty miles, I'm guessing," Rita said shoving the side of the truck and listening to the fuel sloshing around in the bottom of the tank. "At best."

"Twenty miles better off than here," Mirela said.

At least we didn't have to hot-wire the truck like the Nagas had. I still had the keys I'd taken from Peterson.

Chapter 68

The fuel light had been on for five minutes when we came across a village. It was almost exactly twenty miles from where we'd started.

I was still 'away with the fairies', as David jokingly put it. Capable of talking, but not really focusing. Recovering, thanks to my boosted Athanate capabilities.

The village was one of those out-of-the-way, hardscrabble places. Dirt roads. Basic square buildings with walls made with gray cinderblocks and roofs of corrugated iron. Dry stone walls separating one patch of weed-choked yard from the next. Bars on the few windows showing. Battered wooden doors reused from older buildings. Piles of building sand left so long, weeds were growing through them. No cars or trucks. No one in the streets.

"Won't find diesel here," Rita muttered.

"Stop. I'll ask. Over there." Mirela pointed at a building with a splash of primary color over the front advertising itself as a tienda—a small store of some kind. It had faded, peeling posters for cheap beer, soda and the local political party promising heaven on earth.

Mirela came back out moments later.

"Might be in luck. Side street a hundred yards on."

"A garage?" Rita sounded skeptical.

She shook her head. "A hotel. The guy who runs the store was speaking the local dialect, but I think he was saying that's where we need to go."

"A hotel? Here? With diesel?"

Mirela shrugged.

We turned the corner, and found that the hotel was the most impressive building in the village by far. It had a couple of floors and ran half the length of the street. In contrast to others, it was well-built and painted pale blue. It had doors that actually fitted the doorways, and they had metal handles. There were windows with glass. Air-conditioning units promised a relief from the scorching air. They'd even made an effort at a welcome: the front was kept in shade by an old advertising gazebo—the sort you might see put up at a fair. It was too faded to tell what brand it had once promoted. The sign above the hotel's main door said 'Buena Vista', which was a triumph of marketing over reality.

There was a well-used pickup truck parked off to the side, but it was a small-engine gas model. No luck getting fuel from that, but maybe the hotel had a diesel generator.

Mirela went inside. She took longer than she had at the store, and she came back with the news that the owner knew someone 'not far away' who would be willing to drive here with four jerrycans of diesel, for a price.

"How long?" Rita asked.

Even in the thin shade of the gazebo, it was baking hot.

"He's not sure. He had a conversation with his wife which I couldn't follow, but I think at least three or four hours."

Theris turned to me. "Any signs of Matlal?"

I shook my head. "I doubt he's even out of the spirit world yet, and even if he is, it's going to take him a while to put his coven back together."

"But his reaction force will already be at Xibalbá," Rita said. "It won't take long to work out where we went after the temple, and they'll start checking roads for this truck. It won't be as efficient as searching for us with an Adept spell, but they won't be far behind."

Mirela gave a short, unhappy nod. "They won't know we're short of fuel, so they'll be looking further away to start with, and the further they go, the more roads they'll have to check. They'll be spread thinly. But that won't last. We can't stay long."

"How much money have we got?" Theris asked.

Mirela pulled out a wad of US dollars. "Enough to make them hurry. Probably not enough to buy his truck, which would be a better idea."

"We can't just steal the truck," David said. He wasn't asking a question.

Mirela didn't argue, though I knew she'd thought of it.

"Here's what I suggest," she said. "We park our truck over there, in the shade of those trees. Not hiding, but out of sight for a casual look. We take a room in the hotel, and we take the opportunity to shower and change back into civilian clothes. We make an offer of a big bonus if the guy brings the diesel quicker."

Nods all around.

"Can you walk?" David asked me.

I nodded. All of us looked a mess, and I looked the worst, but there was no way around that. There was a cloth in the truck that I could use as a shawl. It would have to do. I'd look better after a shower, and a change into the clothes in my backpack.

"They'll probably be so happy with the business they won't worry about how we look," David said when I mentioned the issue.

I snorted. While they'd been talking, I'd been looking at the building and thinking it through. Where it was. How well it seemed to be doing in comparison with the village and surrounding area.

"We need to be careful," I said. "It's not a hotel. It's a brothel, and I think we blew up their clients this morning."

I was right about the place. It looked and felt like a modern hotel on the inside, in stark contrast to the primitive village outside: cool, scented air, pale colors on smoothly plastered walls, comfortable seats, potted plants, simple dining area, low lights, soft music.

Having spoken to Mirela again, the owner retreated to his office to try and contact the man with the diesel. The owner's wife was left to organize a room for us.

She was slipping between Spanish and the local dialect, which only Mirela had any chance of understanding, so I wasn't focusing on that. I was taking in the aura of the place, and I hated it.

It wasn't purely the aura. Rita and I had better hearing than the others. We knew that somewhere in the hotel a young woman and baby were crying. I inhaled a long breath through my wolfy nose, and I got layers on layers of scents. Unsurprisingly sex, but also blood, disinfectant, disease, all hiding beneath the air fresheners.

Misery.

This place pulled me back into the zone.

Good thing. Whether or not the hotel itself was a dangerous place, we were still in the Yucatán peninsula, and we had a long way to go before we were safe. I couldn't afford any more time away with the fairies.

It took longer than it should have to get the room. Mirela had to argue that we weren't paying for several rooms. We weren't intending to sleep here. She eventually settled for the 'presidential suite'.

It was on the top floor. A room with a large window, with a view of nothing much, but which was big enough, even with the emperor bed that dominated the room. The room came with an assigned 'maid'. When we tried to send her away, she said she'd get into trouble.

Mirela and Rita took her back down to the lobby to explain.

I shivered. She was too young. We had to do something, but our top priority at the moment was getting diesel and escaping.

"Shower and change." David ushered me gently toward the bathroom. "We'll keep watch. I really don't trust the owners."

However much I wanted a long, hot shower, I was too uneasy to relax, and I went through army-style. Three minutes and I was out of the shower. Another two and I was dressed in jeans and a shirt, back in the main room and pointing to David to go next while I dried my hair.

Then five minutes later, Theris went in, and I started to wonder how long it would take for Mirela and Rita to explain things to the owners.

Nothing about the Buena Vista felt right, and I was starting to wonder about just taking the owner's truck. We could wire him the money to buy a brand-new one.

I was just about to discuss that with David when Mirela came back, and she wasn't alone. She had the original maid and an even younger maid with her, *and* her baby. It turned out they were the source of the crying sounds I'd heard.

Mirela's face was a picture of calmness, but her aura told a different story.

"Rita's keeping an eye on the owners," Mirela said. "Playing the dumb American tourist who can't speak any Spanish."

She sat the girls down.

"This is Xareni. This is Colel and her baby boy, Luis," she said, her eyes hard with defiance. "We're not leaving them, or their friends here."

Theris emerged from the bathroom as she spoke.

"How many friends?" he said.

Xareni understood and answered in careful English. "There are five, and the baby. The others are Nicte, Alitzel, and Zyanya."

The truck would be big enough, but David was about to make several sensible points such as *it's more dangerous to be with us* and *where would we take them?*

I held up my hand and stopped him.

I could sense Rita downstairs, and I knew something had gone badly wrong.

Chapter 69

"Problem," I said. I grabbed my pistol and limped down, Theris close behind me. We burst into the lobby.

Rita was standing there with bloodied hands, and splatter across her blank face.

"I killed them," she said.

I went over and put my arms around her. She had fewer of these episodes these days, but every now and then, when she let the cougar's instincts loose inside her, she came back in this disconnected mental state, unsure of the morality of what she'd done.

The owners of the hotel were evil, but evil enough to deserve death?

"He wasn't calling anyone about the diesel," Rita said, speaking clearly but tonelessly. "He recognized the truck. The Nagas use this place. He was calling an emergency number that he'd been given. He was speaking to Matlal's reaction force. They're on their way here."

He would have had to speak in Spanish to Matlal's people, and for all her acting, Rita's Spanish was perfect.

She wasn't finished.

"The wife was laughing with them. She wanted them to take the baby away. She said if they did that, they could have the mother for the evening. Said it would teach her to not snivel."

I hugged her, not caring about the blood. I let my eukori open to her, our hearts falling into sync, breaths becoming smooth and even together.

"You did the right thing," I said.

"You're getting blood all over you." Her voice had regained a little warmth.

"Then we'll both have to clean up, in a hurry." I turned to Theris. "Find the keys to his truck. We're taking it and all the girls who work here. We leave in fifteen."

It took us twenty-five.

A couple of minutes of that was taken with Mirela sending a coded message to the mission's central reporting number, using the dead man's cell. She kept it to the bare minimum: we were okay, we had the drives, we were out and on our way.

We left in the dead man's pickup. David was driving and Theris sitting shotgun in the cab, despite wanting to be next to me. The rest of us, including the five 'maids', were in the back, with shawls hiding our faces.

I sat between Rita and Mirela, trying to comfort both of them.

Nicte, Alitzel and Zyanya were drugged and didn't really understand what was going on. Xareni was holding Rita's hand and speaking in Spanish to her, sensing she was upset and assuring her that the owners of the hotel deserved everything they got. Mirela was trying to soothe Colel and Luis with Athanate pacifics when they needed far more.

"They're ill," Mirela whispered to me. "I know you..." She hesitated before continuing. "I know this House has a constitution, and I think the rules are they're too young to bite."

I nodded. "I set the rules in place to preserve innocence. This poor girl has precious little innocence left, and my senses are telling me she's not going to recover with standard methods. If she agrees, you can bite her. We'll try sourcing medicine for the baby."

How? A visit to a doctor while escaping from Matlal's pursuing troops?

"I think I have a way around that," Mirela said. "If I can get her to allow me to bite, I can probably make her pass the aniatropics on in her milk. The poor girl hasn't even been able to feed the baby yet. She knows something's wrong."

I left her to explain to the traumatized child that her rescuers were actually vampires and needed to bite her to cure the diseases she and her baby had been infected with.

Mirela would manage. She'd changed out of all recognition from the woman who'd run the spying operation for Vega Martine, but she'd lost none of her resourcefulness.

With Rita and Mirela busy, I had my own tasks.

I tentatively reached out with aura, but there was nothing. Matlal trusted no one, so there was no backup coven ready to search for us.

Also, no Tezcatlipoca. No Quetzalcoatl.

Using my aura hurt, as if I'd sprained a muscle in my leg and was trying to run, but it couldn't be helped. I carefully spread my search further, sensing there were Basilikos Athanate and Were and Nagas at the edge of my reach, but they were a long way behind us.

They knew we'd been at the Buena Vista. They'd find out the owner's pickup was missing. They'd have people out looking for us, and we were still a long way from safety.

We couldn't go to Mérida, or anywhere in that vicinity. Cancun to the east would take us too close to Mérida.

South down to Belize was too far, and took us too close to the pursuers.

West was the city of Campeche. In the briefing document Mirela had given us, there were what she'd described as fallback options for escape— Hail Mary options. She'd also warned us that by the time it came to use them, those options might be compromised. I understood her thinking, but if everyone else had gotten away using our primary escape method, basically helicopter and ship, then it was possible the Campeche route was good, despite being a city with a Matlal sub-House.

Campeche was where we would go.

I wasn't sure whether to be more concerned about that, or the continuing silence from Tezcatlipoca.

Was he that sure of me he didn't need to try any more?

Chapter 70

Campeche was pastel colors and cheerful streets and mercifully cooler than the jungle had been.

We'd stopped at a store outside of the main town and we were kitted out in tourist style. Brighter shirts, floppy hats, shorts rather than jeans, sandals, woven bags and sunglasses. We totally looked the part.

We'd also picked up a couple of cellphones.

Closer to the center, we'd left Mirela and David with the girls in a hotel.

Now, Theris and I were walking arm in arm, through the old town, down towards the long promenade, with Rita just in front of us.

I had our pistols in my bag. My fingers were itching to touch them and the hairs on my neck were standing up.

We were being very cautious about using workings to check ahead. Matlal might not have a full backup coven, but there would be other Adepts scattered around and they'd pick up on someone using workings. However unlikely I thought it was, Matlal *could* have made his way out of the spirit world by now. Quetzalcoatl might have helped him. If he was out, no matter how much we'd set him back, he'd be able to do a simple search for us, and I didn't doubt he could have hundreds of troops here very quickly.

Theris and I had recreated the nothing-to-see-here working, and we were depending on our senses to tell us whether there were Basilikos here out looking for us.

Sea walls and palm trees gave us tantalizing glimpses of the Gulf. Somewhere out there, on the horizon, there should be a yacht waiting for us, if Mirela's coded calls had gotten through. All we had to do was get out there.

"It's beautiful," Rita said over her shoulder.

It was. Unfortunately, it was short of the tourist crowds that such an attractive area should have had, and which would have given us better cover. Not exactly empty, but just enough that my senses were prickling. I felt noticed.

We went back into the old town, through a small park in front of their city cathedral, past colonnaded fronts and down whitewashed streets.

"I feel too exposed," I said.

The prearranged procedure was for us to contact the owner of a fishing boat. The man took tourists out to try for tuna and imagine themselves as Hemingway's old man. The owner had said he was happy to arrange a transfer out of sight of land, for a fee. Given the rest of the House had gotten out by the primary exit plan, there shouldn't have been any reason to suspect that this route was compromised. No one else had used it. No one else had even come here to Campeche.

But I did suspect something. Old Ops 4-10 instincts were on alert.

Still, Theris was getting impatient with the wide-ranging tourist stroll, and we agreed to get closer.

Our contact, the man who ran 'Tuna Total', didn't have a shop front. He had a tiny office, a boat, and an agreement with a dozen hotels that allowed him to put up little stands for a few hours at a time.

We got lucky. We found him in the second hotel we tried.

Theris and I had a cold drink at the bar while Rita called David, who left the hotel he was in and jogged away from it for five minutes before he put in the call to Tuna Total.

I was watching the man and his glamorous lady assistant out of the corner of my eye.

He was a good salesman; jovial, a little loud, full of promises about the wonders a day spent on his boat out in the Gulf waters. His cell pinged and he excused himself from the conversation he was having with an elderly American.

I could see the moment David used the coded terms *perseguir un sueño*, *mar altura* and *tesoro*.

The man's voice continued to be hearty, but his head jerked a little and his eyes went across to his companion. They nodded at each other and there was suddenly tension in their bodies. She left the little booth and made a call on her cell.

Sometimes, paranoia just means they *are* out to get you.

Theris made no complaints as I collected him and Rita and took them out a side door.

We headed toward the town center where we caught a cab back to a hotel not far from our hotel.

"The good thing," I said as we walked and I tried to find something positive, "is that they're looking in the wrong place for us now."

"But they *are* looking," Theris argued, "and they're looking in Campeche."

"We'll make a call to some of the other alternatives."

"They'll track the signals. All the calls will come from Campeche."

"Good point. We'll see if Mirela has a way to ask someone else to make those calls."

But it turned out Mirela had something completely different to offer. Or rather, the girls did.

"My great-uncle," Colel said in Spanish. "He is a fisherman, a working man. He has a boat. He and his colleague go out for the tarpon."

Her eyes were wide and scared, but when she turned to Mirela for encouragement to go on, I saw the tiny bumps on her throat, and I could practically feel the bond of trust between them.

I took a quick glance at the others. The three coming down off their drugged state were too calm. They had fang marks as well. Even Xareni, who had been the most composed of them all, was looking at Mirela and unconsciously touching her throat.

We'd been away most of the morning, but still! Quick work.

"He is very poor," Colel's voice had dropped to a murmur.

Xareni took over in her careful English. "It is a very hard life, to chase the tarpon today. Everyone is in the oil, and they are rich, but not gran tío Jandro."

Slowly, it came out what they had been planning. Save the little tips some of the 'nicer' men gave them. Escape from the Buena Vista, by stealing the truck and driving to Campeche. Persuade Jandro to sail them away to the United States where they would be safe and free and happy.

I had to squeeze my eyes tight shut. They'd saved less than a hundred dollars between them. Three of them were addicted to the drugs they'd been fed. They probably couldn't read maps and none of them could drive. But sometimes it was dreams that kept you going through the nightmare.

And sometimes dreams come true, just not quite in the way you expect. With vampires.

Denver Return
Chapter 71

The return of the raid was well organized, from a top-down perspective. Everyone got back to Denver within a couple of days, which was astonishing.

For us on the ground, even once we'd landed in Louisiana, it was a chaos comprised of cabs, confused directions, helicopters and missed flights.

Bian, Alex and Yelena had skipped their flight back to wait for us. They had full comms access to mission HQ and full access to the reports which I'd been dreading.

Strategically, the mission was a complete success. We'd incinerated the virus stockpiles. The Carpathians, without revealing details, had obliterated the remote factory down at the border with Belize. David had a full set of drives from Matlal's servers, and his team had already come up with a preliminary report that the full set of drives would deliver us almost all Matlal's worldwide network of spies and traitors. They held his electronic currency, and access to his banks. We'd stolen only something in the region of ten million dollars of Matlal's precious metal stockpiles, but we'd blown up some of the remainder. We'd destroyed Xibalbá and killed or injured the majority of his Naga troops stationed there, including Peterson, their commander. We'd dealt a massive blow to his coven and set all his plans back.

Matlal would have seen Mirela with me, and we were sure he'd believe Vega Martine had betrayed him and attack her.

The drives didn't deliver the identity of Askrynos, but David was sure we would find him or her from all the clues in the data.

All good. We'd achieved all that with a minimum of our own casualties, but that minimum was not zero.

Four of Alex's werewolf team had died to ensure the escape route from the bank to the airfield was safe for everyone else. Three of Mirela's daredevil motorcycle team that had leaped ahead of us to prevent the bank being sealed had been killed by the guards. Two in Rita's team had been shot and died. The four of the team attacking the south side of Xibalbá had died when they were hit by shrapnel from one of our own explosions.

Ophira was missing. As Matlal's coven had closed on the fleeing helicopters, just before I pulled him back, she'd flown the Hind straight at the flying coven. She'd been out of ammunition. Someone said she'd seen her fall into the sea. Boats were searching.

And Mirela's team had just one fatal casualty.

Leyla had died of her wounds before they'd gotten her to the helicopter.

I couldn't sleep, couldn't talk on the flight to Denver. Alex, Bian, Yelena and Rita sat with me and kept their silence, comforting me by their presence. Everyone else left me alone.

I barely noticed the car journey from the airport back to Haven. It was only when we turned at the gates that I realized something was happening.

The members of my extended House were waiting for me. Everyone. Athanate, Were, Adepts and humans.

Yelena reached across me, popped open the door and shoved me out.

I had no idea what this was. They were all standing silently. Those nearest were the ones who'd been down in Yucatán, and they were the first to move. They were led by Dosia, one of Mirela's senior Athanate. Her red hair was braided, and it shone in the sun. She wore black for mourning, of course. House Tucek had lost half its strength in the short time it had been my sub-House.

For a second, I expected her to hit me in anger.

Instead, she dropped to one knee. Before I could stop her, she took my hand and pressed her lips to the back.

"Kyria," she murmured. "Life for life. Body and Blood."

There was no answer I could make other than to echo her: "Body and Blood."

As she stood, another knelt to kiss my hand and call me Kyria, and then another and another.

I'd held my eukori down tight in my grief for the dead. They burst it open.

As Bian explained later, when I'd called on the spirits in Yucatán, when I'd called on the power of Blood magic and I'd seen my House fleeing in helicopters, pursued by Matlal, they'd seen me too. They knew what I'd done and what I'd risked for them.

We buried Leyla and the others that evening, as the sun went down.

Bian threw one of her parties the next day. We had news that Ophira had survived; she'd been found by one of the search boats. So, in a way, the party was a celebration of life. Or a celebration of all the survivors' lives. Or a wake. I didn't know, and no one tried to explain it.

Bian used up a whole floor of Haven.

In one wing, she had brought in Electric Breath, Denver's hottest rave DJs. In the other, she had an Athanate string quartet playing stately Athanate dances. In the middle she had food and drink, comfortable sofas, even some aimious seats so the Athanate among us could exchange Blood politely.

It was midnight, I was hot, tired and mildly drunk when I sat down to share some snacks with Rita and Annie. Theris was on the other side of the room, leaning on the bar, not looking at me, but very aware, as if he expected something to happen in Haven itself.

I was halfway into explaining to Rita and Annie my ideas about all my House becoming hybrid when the doors to the quartet ballroom opened and Marguerite came through. She collected some food first, but I knew she was heading for me.

So did Rita and Annie.

I'd chosen the pair of them well. Rita was fascinated that, given she'd learned how to shift into a jaguar from me, I believed she could as easily learn how to produce Athanate fangs and Blood channels. Annie was similarly intrigued with the idea she might have inherited, through my infusion, the ability to turn into a cougar.

They saw Marguerite coming, carrying a tray of food and drinks.

They stood.

"We'll do some… research," Annie suggested.

Rita growled quietly and Annie blushed, which I still found sweet.

"House Labastide," they greeted Marguerite with polite and formal Athanate style bows. "Thrice welcome."

After returning their greeting, she sat beside me and watched them walk away.

"You have an attractive House," she said. "I like it."

"My House likes you back."

She laughed abruptly and had to pat her chest to ensure the food didn't go down the wrong channel.

I leaned over to rub her back, and because I was a little drunk, I took a sip from her drink, then held it to her lips.

Oooh.

Her eyes vamped out a little and we were both pumping out *bite me* pheromones.

This was an Athanate party, after all, despite the Were and Adepts present.

I put her drink back down on the coffee table and offered my neck.

"You have the freedom of my House," I murmured.

"Mmm. Well, we'll talk further about those mutual freedoms, dokaria," she responded, slipping arms around me. "In a moment or three."

A kiss, sweetened with the bourbon on our lips.

Another, squarely on the pulse in my throat, lingering, letting our eukori open slowly to each other until the sensation of my heartbeat against her lips became urgent and her fangs slipped into my neck.

I shivered and groaned, both at the rush of pleasure and her barely restrained eagerness. She *pulled*, and my Blood sang in her.

So brief.

Her fangs slipped out and she licked my neck, sealing the wounds.

Then it was my turn to search out that sweet spot on her throat, feeling the slow and steady thudding from her heart against my lips. The soft parting of her flesh to my fangs, the exquisite flow of rich Blood as I *pulled*, and the delicate, delighted shudder of her response.

The wonder of it seemed to grow with every bite I made.

We stayed in each other's arms to allow the pleasure to linger. Shared a kiss. Sipped more of her bourbon.

"That was entirely wonderful," she breathed in my ear.

"The overtone of wolf didn't ruin it?"

She laughed. "I am teaching my ear to listen out for the House Farrell sense of humor. No, if anything, I may have to rethink the whole idea of who fits in my House. And my bed."

"That sounds dramatic."

"The League alphas?" she said thoughtfully. "Felix and Cameron... I mean they *are* currently based in Louisiana."

"A little early for them in their relationship, I'm guessing. But they wouldn't be at all insulted by the offer. On the contrary."

"Interesting. And you, dokaria. You're a little early in your relationships too, aren't you?"

I took another sip of her bourbon and kissed her again.

"Body and Blood," I said.

"Yes, I know you wouldn't deny me, or any of your House. Your Diakon has explained this to me, and it's part of the great good humor of this House. I will wait, as they do."

"You know they have a betting pool going as to how long it will take?"

She laughed again. "Yes, I do. What's the phrase these days? I have skin in that game."

"But on the other hand," I said, spotting members of my House across the room, "what about someone even more unusual in your bed tonight. Or should I say *someones*?"

"Oh?"

"The Athanate saying is never bed a witch, but what about a pair of outlaw shamans?"

"I've not tried that."

"A pair or a shaman?"

"Either, minx, and you know it."

Flint and Kane arrived, summoned by my wave.

"Marguerite. Flint and Kane."

"House Labastide," the Lost Boys murmured in sync, eyes all lively.

Marguerite had sat back up as straight as she usually did, and now she looked them over in that stiff-necked, measuring way to see if they wilted.

My Lost Boys did not wilt.

"I suppose," she drawled, "you come as a pair."

Solemn faces. Not a flicker of laughter at the joke, just a tightening of the skin by their eyes.

"It has been known to happen. But actually, tonight we'd prefer—" Kane started.

"To come as a House," Flint completed and turned his head to indicate.

Amanda Lloyd sat on the sofa the boys had come from, with her arm around her other young kin, Claude.

The poor lad wasn't made of the same stuff as Flint and Kane. He wilted under Marguerite's look.

"A night of different experiences, then," she said, her eyes softening. "Very well. If you'll excuse me, Amber, I believe these young gentlemen have some introductions to make."

Flint and Kane offered their arms.

As she stood, Marguerite inclined her head to make me look to where Jo and Xavier waited for me. Then she turned her full attention to the shamans and began the slow stroll over to Amanda, listening to some low-voiced banter from Flint and Kane with a small smile on her lips.

Jo and Xavier came and sat beside me.

"Marguerite has said we should stay here in Haven—" Jo began.

"If it's okay with you," Xavier put in. "To learn some of the techniques you're teaching the packs."

"Of course it's okay with me." I pulled them into a hug. "And what better way for Marguerite to spy on me."

They twitched and looked uncertain until I laughed.

"Spy all you want. I have no secrets from my dokaria."

I had them turn around to cuddle me and enjoyed the weight and warmth against my body. Our hearts slipped into sync.

"I have to warn you," I said, "there may be things that happen that you don't want to report back to your House."

"Like what?" Xavier said cautiously, though he was aware I was enjoying teasing them.

"Well, the two of you are both part of House Labastide security, and I bet there's a rule for security that you aren't allowed relationships with other members."

Xavier was better at hiding his surprise. Jo's body went quite tense.

"We don't have that rule here," I went on. "As my kin, shared with Marguerite, when you're staying here, you get your own room just down the corridor from mine. Now, enjoy the party, then go to your room and enjoy the rest of the night together. Those are orders."

"Kyria," they murmured, both a little tense now.

Bian turned up as they left, hand in hand. I was willing to bet that enjoying the party would take little time, and they'd spend much more enjoying the night.

"Some more happy people," she murmured, slipping in beside me.

"Mostly." I was looking at a few of House Tucek, surrounded by Were, who were still valiantly trying to seduce them. "I haven't seen Mirela though."

I expected a reaction from Bian at Mirela's name, but not the one I got: she laughed.

"She doesn't think this party is suitable for her young kin, so she's kept them in her room. They made dinner and had their own, much quieter party."

"You're spying on her."

Bian took on the voice of an English aristocrat she told me she'd once met in India, a century ago. "Heavens, no—I have people to do that for me."

I laughed, but I wasn't going to be put off. "There's something else your spies have reported. I can tell."

Bian took a sip of Margurite's abandoned bourbon.

"Yes. Obviously, we've sanctioned her taking those girls as kin, but I was hesitant until my spies reported back to me."

She ate one of my snacks, deliberately making me wait.

"You know the plan you concocted about how to cure the baby without biting him?" she said.

"Mirela's plan. She was going to bite Colel and see if she could make her pass on the aniatropics in her milk to Luis."

I should have checked on them, but someone had reported they weren't in danger, and I'd had other things on my mind.

"Yes, and that worked very well. Both mother and baby are cured of the diseases they contracted. But what convinced me that we were right to let those girls become kin was what happened to Mirela. Her bond with Colel is so strong, she's expressing milk too. Baby Luis now has a choice of four places to get his milk."

I had to laugh, and protest: "It's a little funny but really, it's sweet."

Not something I'd ever thought I'd say about Mirela.

I prodded Bian with a finger. "And what are your spies saying about other people I haven't seen much of tonight. Diana, for one. And Salar, and Solange."

"Diana is initiating them into the sacred mysteries of Athena. Laying a good foundation for a close association of Houses."

I snorted, nearly choking on the bourbon. The sacred mysteries. There would be dancing, and wine involved, slow dancing to start, and then faster and faster. And then the ecstasies of Body and Blood.

"Yes. And now, I think the rest of your House can make their own matches," Bian said, pulling me up with her. "I promised Jen you wouldn't stay up too late."

I followed her out and left my House to their party.

Chapter 72

"Where did Alex go?" I asked as we entered Bian's suite. *Our* suite now, right down to our clothes mixed together in the closets. And my favorite pillow on the Olympic size bed.

I'd danced with Alex at the beginning of the party, then I'd seen him with Bian an hour or so ago, but he'd disappeared after that.

"Errands." Bian waved it off. "Haven has to keep running, even when there's a party."

He'd be back. He'd know where to find me. He'd wake me up and then…

"Shower." Bian gave me a little shove in the right direction.

I knew better than to expect a shower on my own, but Bian was simply helpful, sponging my back and washing my hair. I returned the favor, wondering all the while when she was going to switch back to normal mode. At the very least she'd bite me.

Not when we came out of the shower, though. We had hot towels, then big, soft bathrobes, then hair-drying, brushing and loose braiding. Candles. Soft music. My favorite rum. Chocolates.

And a question I wasn't expecting. "Have you been practicing your Athanate?"

I laughed. "No."

"Hmmm." She went across to her bookshelf of erotic poetry and pulled a volume down, opened it at what was probably a favorite page. She had many.

"This one, I think," she said.

"Really? Translating poetry now?"

"Of course. You promised me you would practice."

"It might make me sleepy."

"It might wake you up."

I closed my eyes before rolling them, so it didn't count. Didn't make any difference either, so we spooned on the sofa with me holding the book and Bian holding me.

Translating any Athanate poetry was difficult, even without the distractions. Erotic poetry was especially difficult, but Bian insisted that it was the best literature to convey subtlety, and there was a lot of it to choose from. Whole wings of any Athanate library would be dedicated to the language of love.

Naturally, Bian didn't just want word for word. She demanded I find a way to convey the meaning and the feelings *and* make it all rhyme.

Her lips brushed my ear.

"I'm not going to be able to concentrate," I pointed out.

"When you're good enough you won't need to. That would be an acceptable level of skill."

I huffed and looked at the one she'd chosen for me. The first line wasn't too hard, which was always a bad sign.

I cleared my throat.

"Sweet as the valleys where the mountain rivers run."

"Oh, that's very good," Bian breathed in my ear. "I like the rhythm you've picked too."

My bathrobe had come undone somehow. What a surprise. One of her hands was cupping my breast, the other made idle circles on my belly.

Not fair!

I had to clear my throat again and force my heart rate back down to a normal canter rather than a wild gallop.

"Welcome as the shade in the midsummer sun."

"It's 'midday'—"

"Wouldn't work with the rhythm," I said. "This is poetry, and I demand artistic leeway."

"Yes, you're right. I'm sorry. Say those lines again. Please, my love."

"Sweet as the valleys where the mountain rivers run, welcome as the shade in the midsummer sun."

"Mmmm." She kissed the side of my neck. "That is so sexy. I love the sound of your voice speaking those lines. Go on."

The next lines blurred and there was no way I was going to be able to force my heart rate back to normal as her hand widened its circle and strayed lower.

"If you keep that up, I'm going to come," I gasped.

"No, that's too much leeway. I mean, I suppose it rhymes, but you've completely lost the rhythm and that's nothing like what's written."

I laughed raggedly. The third line of the poem was something about flowers opening in the morning. And that line wasn't supposed to rhyme, though the fourth one was.

I put the book aside and twisted around.

"I thought we were saving this for when all four of us were together," I said.

"We are."

My wolfy ears caught the sound of voices in the corridor outside and I realized I'd been duped and then distracted.

The door burst open. Alex and Jen came in, laughing their heads off.

"We're late!" Jen said.

"Not really." Bian slipped the bathrobe off my shoulders. "But we're nicely warmed up."

I managed to say "You are all evil" before Jen kissed me and stole my breath. And then she kissed Bian, and Alex kissed me, and they swapped over.

"You made the audit damn near redundant," Jen explained when we paused. "The data they're pulling off Matlal's servers is showing us exactly where to look, so Livia told me I could delegate and come home."

"And Alex picked you up from the airport." So much for Bian's explanation of 'errands'.

Jen knelt by the sofa to kiss me in lieu of an apology. Acceptable.

Then, of course, she had to stretch over me to kiss Bian. By the time she did that, her blouse and bra were gone, thanks to Alex.

I made no complaints. I enjoyed the girls, and they enjoyed me right back.

Alex removed the rest of her clothes, and his, with that swiftness that werewolves learn.

We were moments from a point of no return when Jen pulled back.

"The pair of you are fresh out of the shower, and I've been stuck on a plane. That's no good. We're going to have a wash first." She started pulling Alex in that direction, by his most obvious appendage. "You go right ahead, you two. You know what our husband is like."

"Hmm. Where were we?" Bian asked as the bathroom door closed. "About to go right ahead?"

"Line three of the poem, and you were just about to apologize for teasing me," I said.

I got on top and pinned her wrists above her head.

"I am so sorry," she said. She didn't look sorry at all. "Next line please."

I brushed my lips over hers.

"Flowers unfold their fragrance at dawn," I breathed as I trailed fingertips all the way down her body, opening her robe and enjoying the response that my touch caused.

I traced the edges of her abs. Ran the end of my braid over a nipple.

She sighed "Good, so very good. More."

Our hearts had slipped into sync, slowing down, stretching every blissful moment. A kiss. Familiar, yet richer with promise of a desire that wouldn't be denied this time.

Our eukori merged and then reached to pull in Alex and Jen. Sensations blurred. Hot, slippery, kissing from the shower. We could hear them, too.

I trailed more kisses down Bian's throat, closed my mouth around one tender nipple and sucked.

Her back arched and she groaned. I pushed her thighs apart.

I had to let her hands go and she sank fingers into my hair, her whole body shivering beneath more kisses as I made my patient way down her belly.

"Oh, yes," she whispered.

I didn't hurry.

I let her feel how excited I was, how much I wanted her, how much I wanted to give her pleasure. My arousal excited her in turn, and we were both trembling with need when I paused one final time.

"Flowers unfold their fragrance at dawn," I murmured to begin the final line of the first verse. I kissed and kissed and slipped lower as I completed it. "Unlocking their secrets to the heat of my tongue."

"Oh, yes. Yes! Yesss!"

Epilogue

Dawn is still a whisper in the east.

I rise and look back at the sleeping bodies on the bed. Mine is there too. I smile. It has been a very good night, the pleasures more intense with every passing hour.

Now, where Nai kissed me on the forehead, when I was returning from the Temple of Serpents, it burns with a cold fire, and an eye opens there.

I am spirit. I see with spirit eyes in the dreamworld.

Haven's walls were shadows and transparent veils to me. I could wander through at will, but it would be creepy to spy on my House. I didn't need to anyway. Last night had been a great success for the whole House, not just for me. A lot of... what was David's phrase? Ah yes, 'horizontal integration'. I'd felt it because they were my House, because their auras were entangled with mine.

But I wasn't here to think about that.

Something is calling me.

Outside the shadows of the walls.

Waiting.

It didn't feel threating exactly. It didn't have the ominous atmosphere of the City of Lost Gods. And it wasn't Tezcatlipoca. 'My' Lost God had gone quiet. I was afraid I knew why that was: He didn't need to be whispering in my ear, because the seeds had been planted in me. I'd used that power, and my veins still tingled with the thought of it. Burned with the desire to use it again. With the *need* to use my Blood magic again.

I knew an excuse would come my way soon enough, and when I used my magic, every time I used it, his grip on me would grow stronger.

But right now, I wasn't using my magic.

There was a figure waiting in the next room. Theris had insisted he have the room next to mine, but it wasn't him waiting for me.

I drifted through the walls.

Theris lay in bed, asleep. Tara was sprawled across him. Or more accurately, her physical body was, because her spirit was standing waiting for me.

"Tara!" I pointed at the naked bodies on the bed.

She laughed. "You have to admit, he's the handsomest man in Haven. Except maybe Alex."

"But he's supposed—"

"To kill you if you Tezcatlipoca is going to succeed in forcing his way through you into the physical world. I know. I don't think his resolve to do that will change. And it was you who lit this fuse with that little love bomb on the levee down in Louisiana."

I ignored the teasing and thought about Theris' determination and commitment. My gut said she was right. And of course, he would know it was Tara and not me in his bed. This wouldn't lead to any difficulty working with him.

I hoped.

He *was* handsome.

Distractions aside, what was happening wasn't theoretically possible, at least not as far as my imperfect understanding went. Tara could either be a spirit guide or a physical woman within Kaothos' substantiation. Not both. And thinking about that brought me back to what I was doing here, in spirit form without using magic. Theris and I were entangled on the spirit level. If I were spirit walking, he'd sense it and wake up.

What was this?

"There are deeper levels of the spirit world than Theris is familiar with," Tara said, reading my mind again.

"But you are familiar with them?"

She shrugged. "I sense them. I can't explain or even describe them." She sighed. "I'm sorry, sis, I'm only here to start you off."

"Eh?"

She raised her hand. She was holding the end of a piece of string. Because this was the dreamworld, where the strangest things made sense, I knew it was my piece of string. The string I kept with memory knots in it, one for every person who'd died instead of me. The string that was a foot or two long and somewhere among my belongings in the room behind me. Not this string which Tara held, which was so was long, it snaked out of Haven and into the gardens behind. And unlike my physical piece of string, it started with a knot.

Because I was dreaming, I knew this was Tara's knot.

"You never made me a knot, but you always thought it," Tara said. "You always felt guilty that you lived, and I didn't. But it wasn't a choice either of us made. It's not your fault. Not something you should feel bad about."

She seemed to be fading, and I held out my hands as if I could stop her.

Instead, she gave me the string, and as she did, her knot simply unraveled. She smiled. A small, warm smile of love, and then she was gone as well.

'Roll call' was what I called my string. Making my way through all the knots in the string always became harder every time I added a knot. This string was longer than mine. It threatened to have more knots. I knew I had to walk wherever this dream string took me, and so I began, feeling it run through my fingers.

I felt guilty that I hadn't added the latest deaths. There were too many even to think about.

There was my first knot. Handsome Joe from Nevada. My roll call had always begun with him, even though, as Tara had pointed out, the first knot should have been hers. Joe was smiling, but he was as translucent as Haven's walls, and he faded into nothing as his knot unraveled.

What was this?

I walked on and found them one by one. The rest of my Ops 4-10 comrades, especially my team from the nightmare at Hacha del Diablo. Then later: Valery, who I'd failed to protect because I was afraid of losing my job in the police. Larry, who'd come to seek sanctuary from me in Cheesman Park and sacrificed himself by leading Matlal's hunters away from me. The two pilots of the Apache gunship who'd died rather than fire on me when I rescued Colonel Laine out on the high plains of eastern Colorado. Melissa the forensics specialist who'd deduced the existence of the paranormal and had been murdered by the psychopathic Noble because I was too stupid to see the truth about him. Barbara, the vet who'd been murdered by Noble just because she resembled me. Frank, who'd died because I talked to him in a shop. Felix's sister Martha, and his pack lieutenant, Silas, who'd died in the battle down on the border with New Mexico. Dozens of Denver Were behind them. More from the Cimarron and Cheyenne packs, who died there as well.

More and more and more of them. More than I'd made knots for, because I'd known as it went on that every knot was no more than a token of the people who'd died while I lived.

Every one of them smiled and faded as their knots unraveled.

And then I reached those whose deaths were so recent, I hadn't made knots for them.

A host of them. Vaughn of the White Sands pack, who'd died when we'd crossed into Juárez. Too many to process. One here and there stood out. Suri, from Billie's pack, who'd died when they attacked the Tijuana pack on my orders. And there was Isabel, who'd had to kill herself because I hadn't executed the madman de Socorro, as he deserved.

So *many*.

I tried to walk tall, but the weight of grief and guilt made me stumble and sink to my knees on the lawn behind the house.

And all the while I knelt, they came to me, the dead, in their pale ranks.

They came in silence, with warm smiles and soft touches, and I cried as I wondered why they weren't hitting me and screaming at me. I'd failed them. I'd cost them their lives. I couldn't look at their faces.

But still they came, and their knots unraveled, and their translucent bodies faded into the lightening dawn like mist.

Until the end.

It would be wrong to say the last meant more than others. It was simply a fresher grief. A pain unblunted by the passage of time.

Donatienne knelt in front of me.

She was shining from inside and there was a look of utter joy on her face.

She spoke silently, and I had to read her lips.

Je suis retournée à la mer. Je suis à nouveau entière. Merci, ma Dame. Merci, Kyria.

I have returned to the sea. I am whole again. Thank you, my Lady. Thank you, Kyria.

I closed my eyes and wept. I felt her hands tilt my head and she kissed my eyelids, and then she was gone too.

Leaving Leyla. Who spoke: "Well, she warned me you would overthink it. That's why I agreed to hang around."

"She?" I asked, even though I thought I knew the answer.

It turned out I was right.

"Speaks-to-Wolves. Cool name, hey."

She knelt in front of me where Donatienne had.

"This is a dream," I said. "It won't make sense. I'm not going to get any answers, am I?"

"True answers aren't things you're given, they're things you find."

"You sound like Medusa in the Temple."

"Yeah. That was a surprise to your grandmother, the Temple coming on board, but they may help. She did ask me to warn you that all weapons can turn in your hand, so don't get over-confident."

She sighed.

"Also, she wanted me to warn you against power. It may not be what wins the battle."

"Really? What *would* win the battle?"

"I think she's betting on things like sacrifice and love. I can't tell you exactly because she doesn't know, and if she doesn't, I sure as hell don't. I'm really here to set your head straight on a couple of things. First, all those dead people…" she paused and frowned before continuing. "Me included, I guess, so… all *us* dead people don't want your boneheaded guilt. You've been told this before, so I see I'm going to have to make it real simple for you. You didn't kill any of us, and you taking responsibility for our deaths steals *our* agency, *our* decisions. Stop it. Keep the memories, Kyria, lose the guilt."

I snorted. Now she said it, I could see the symbolism in my dream about the knots unraveling.

Yet so many questions.

I cleared my throat. "A couple of things, you said. What else is there? And while you're at it, what did you mean about hanging around? Where? Are you just in my dream? Why can you speak, and they can't? Where did they go?"

"Whoa, Kyria! Ease up."

She rocked back and frowned in thought.

"Important things first," she said finally. "How did you think Donatienne looked?"

"She looked… good." It felt strange to pick that word, but there wasn't any other way to say it.

"Yeah. *Good*. She looks like that because you gave her your blessing. You helped redeem her. You helped make her soul pure and whole again, like she said."

"That's crazy! I don't have that power! I'm no kind of saint!"

"Well, it seems some of us have a difference of opinion on that. Look at me. *Look*."

I looked. She looked good too. Not quite like Donatienne. *Unburdened* was the word that came to mind for Leyla. Or maybe *freed*.

I shook my head. "This is just a crazy dream. It's not making any sense now, let alone when I wake up."

She sighed.

"The Temple called you a paladin. An anointed warrior. Does that fit easier?"

"Not really. How can I be? I don't deserve it. And I don't know what to do. And how would it work if I don't even believe it myself?"

"No one is competent to decide for themselves what they deserve. Donatienne didn't think she deserved redemption, any more than any of us did. What matters more is that there is someone who believes we deserve it.

You. *We* believe in you. *I* believe. You're allowed to have doubts, but it will help others in the future if you don't show it."

She got to her feet and pulled me up. Poked me in the gut.

"You are sound. Do what you will always be proud of. There is such a power in you, and it grows as we add to it, if you just allow us."

The expectations felt like a weight on my shoulders, trying to pull me down, back to my knees. To make me surrender.

My head fell, and immediately, Leyla's touch on my chin raised it back.

"Unbowed," she whispered.

I knew she was right. *Can't fight looking at your feet* Top had said back in training. I couldn't do what I had to do with my head hanging low. And I couldn't stop now. I had to unmask Askrynos. Then I had to find a way we could deal with Vega Martine, followed by Matlal, Quetzalcoatl and Tezcatlipoca. All while Emergence unfolded around the world.

Dawn was breaking, and I saw there was a building behind her, in the growing light. A curving corridor, set with arched windows, and stretching to infinity.

Familiar. Memories seeped in. Sights and sounds and thoughts.

Walking. Light and dark. Light and dark. Hot and cold. The scrape of my heels on stone.

I am cursed and blessed. I am none of the things they think I am.

Sacrifices. We'd spoken about sacrifices. Speaks-to-Wolves was big on sacrifices. For everything there would be a cost.

A great heart knows what to offer, my daughter. Strength for strength. Measure for measure.

And decisions. We'd had a conversation in whispers about decisions. About accepting that it was important to go on, no matter the pain it caused.

Speaks-to-Wolves' hands in the light had made clever shapes in shadows.

We are where the shapes you have names for, come from.

"Yes, we are there," Leyla said, her voice faltering. "Where it all comes from. Where it simply *is*. It's my time to walk that passage now, and all my words will be lost to me. I will walk, and it will not be far, because you forgave me, and your actions count here, in ways you cannot know, but must believe."

She kissed me twice. Once with longing, and once with regret. "My thanks, my love, and my power to you, Kyria."

Then she stepped away.

"I don't understand…" I started.

You cannot know whispered the wind.

Leyla was inside the corridor already. Walking. And as she passed each arched window, the rising sun caught her. Her body. Her face. Her eyes. Her smile. It was as if she had become incandescent with joy, and I knew there would be no darkness within that corridor that could dim that light.

"But I walked in that corridor," I muttered.

I remembered the light from the windows. The darkness between. And in this place, where I could remember things I forgot when I woke, I knew I hadn't been there just once, but twice.

Thank you for reading book 8, Snake Eyes
There are more books in the series to come.

If you aren't already signed up to my mailing list –
there's a free prequel called Raw Deal!
It covers Amber's brief career in the Denver police.
Sign up here for the free book and more Amber news:
https://downloads.athanate.com/RawdealBM

Amber Farrell – Paranormal PI
URBAN FANTASY THRILLERS
BITE BACK SERIES
Prequel: Raw Deal
1: Sleight of Hand
2: Hidden Trump
3: Wild Card
4: Cool Hand
5: Angel Stakes
5.1 The Biting Cold (associated novella)
5.2 Winter's Kiss (associated novella)
5.3 Change of Regime (associated novella)
6: Inside Straight
7: Queen of Diamonds
8: Snake Eyes

Charles de Lint
in the Magazine of Fantasy & Science Fiction:
"They represent some of the best the field has to offer."

http://mybook.to/Bite_Back_Series

Also from the BITE BACK universe

Characters from these books appear in the main series

BIAN'S TALE

1: The Harvest of Lies

Anticipated 6 books following Bian from her early life in 1890 Vietnam
to the point she becomes Daikon of House Altau, prior to the start of BITE
BACK

https://mybook.to/THoL

BITE BACK: OUTSIDERS

1: The Biting Cold

https://mybook.to/TheBitingCold

2: Winter's Kiss

https://mybook.to/WintersKiss

Outsiders is a short novella series with a PNR flavor
introducing the background of House Lloyd
This miniseries fits between books 5 and 6 of the main BITE BACK series

LONG ISLAND ATHANATE

Change of Regime

https://mybook.to/ChangeOfRegime

Stand-alone novella set between books 5 and 6 of the main
BITE BACK series, providing some insight into House Altau in New York

More books by me...

SCIENCE FICTION

THE LONG WAY HOME
1: The Dark Takes Fools
2: Out of the Dark
3: Born in Fire

Their war has just ended.
Their struggle has just begun.
Their colony will die if they fail.

Finally discharged from the military, Janice and Bjorn are the only two survivors of a group recruited from the remote and isolated colony of Calloway. It's left to them to find a way to get life-saving technology back to their home planet before everyone left in the colony dies.

It's an impossible task, but no one can convince Jan and Bjorn of that.

Betrayed by the Earth's government, never more than a step from disaster, they have to battle against corruption, greed... and pirates... on The Long Way Home.

"I adore the Firefly/Space Western vibe..."

https://mybook.to/TLWH

AMONG THE STARS
1: A Name Among the Stars
2: A Threat Among the Stars

An heiress fleeing for her life. A forbidden and terrifying Artificial Intelligence loose in the galaxy. A telepathic alien race living hidden alongside humanity. A deadly conspiracy silently spreading through human space. The secret sorrow of a whole planet revealed for all to see. A vow that must be broken. A love that cannot be.
Duty and *honor*.

A huge and developing story set in the distant future with a sweep that encompasses the whole of humanity, told mainly from the perspective of Zara Aguirre, daughter, and last of the great Founding Family Aguirre, who abandons her home world to save her life.

A review of Among the Stars by
Charles de Lint
The Magazine of Fantasy & Science Fiction

"It's a delicious mix of the Brontë sisters, murder mystery, sf drama, space opera, and just general romance and derring-do...
I could sense the joy of storytelling on every page.
This one hit the mark on every point."

http://mybook.to/Among_the_Stars

ACKNOWLEDGMENTS

My thanks to all who worked with me
and continue to support me.

And, without which nothing, my wife and family.

Cover images and marketing provided by
https://www.authormarketingsystems.com/
Contact:
support@authormarketingsystems.com

Email Mark@Athanate.com to request
an email alert *only* when a new book is published

or join the newsletter on:
https://downloads.athanate.com/RawdealBM

Reviews, schedules, news & comments on
www.athanate.com
and
www.facebook.com/TheBiteBackSeries